THE ORPHAN GAME

ANN DARBY

THE ORPHAN GAME

A NOVEL

William Morrow and Company, Inc.

New York

It is the policy of William Morrow and Company, Inc., and its imprints
and affiliates, recognizing the importance of preserving what has been written,
to print the books we publish on acid-free paper,
and we exert our best efforts to that end.

Library of Congress Cataloging-in-Publication Data

Darby, Ann.
The orphan game : a novel / Ann Darby. — 1st ed.
p.   cm.
ISBN 0-688-16778-0
I. Title.
PS3554.A6407   1999
813'.54—dc21   98-43778
CIP

Printed in the United States of America

First Edition

1 2 3 4 5 6 7 8 9 10

BOOK DESIGN BY OKSANA KUSHNIR

www.williammorrow.com

For my sisters,
Arlynne and Barbara,
and my brother, Rich

ACKNOWLEDGMENTS

There are many people I wish to thank, beginning with the gifted writers who read the manuscript: Beth Passaro, the reader I turn to first and last; Denise Dailey, who was ever clear-sighted and open-hearted; Renee Bacher; Jackie Keren; Pat McKenzie; James McSherry; Sandy Tyler; and the spirited Nancy Woodruff. I wish to thank Thomas H. Dailey, M.D., for describing the use during the twenties of clysis to feed unconscious patients; Rob Bonfiglio for telling me about his induction into the army; and the Reverend K Almond, who showed me some of the passages she uses from *The Book of Common Prayer* and the *United Methodist Hymnal*. I want to thank Maureen Howard and Richard Locke, each for saying the right thing at the right moment; Carol Herman and Carol Berne for allowing me the time to write; Ron Grant for his encouragement; and Doug Langston for his friendship and intelligent advice. Certain people who don't know they helped deserve thanks: Cynthia Fox, R. C. Ringer, Laure Swearingen, Beulah Thomas, and Helen Baldwin, whom I miss. I am indebted to my remarkable agent, Emma Sweeney, and to my wise and wonderful editor, Meaghan Dowling. The earliest sketches of Maggie and Emmy were written at the Millay Colony for the Arts; the MacDowell Colony provided time when time was almost impossible to come by; and the first draft was completed during a Ucross Foundation residency. I am grateful to these colonies and the staffs that run them. And I am, of course, grateful to my friends and family: my mother, Mary Ann, who made sure I learned to dance, Barbara Cahill, Arlynne Pollard, Richard G. Darby, Stormy Brandenberger, and Marnie Imhoff.

SLOW BURN

ONE

My father thought land would make us wealthy, and wealth was what he wanted. Although when I was growing up we lived all right off my father's business, although we lived as well as our neighbors, my father wanted more. He wanted something better than our one-story, ranch-style home. He wanted a mansion on a hill, with brocade drapes and chandeliers, and long before anyone knew what microwave was, my father wanted an oven he'd heard about that left food hot and plates cold. Like everyone we knew, he wanted his children to go to college and to marry into families better than his. And he wanted land because he thought land, the right piece of it anyway, would make him rich.

My mother had her dreams, too. She wanted a better class of clients and a kitchen with all new appliances. She wanted beautiful weddings for her daughters and, for her son, a daughter-in-law she could trust, and like most people, she wanted the finer life she believed others lived. It's true, I'd heard my mother say she wanted only what was in her reach, what she could put her tape measure around and chalk and mark and alter to her taste. But she said that only when she fought with my father, and she fought with him, I think, because she feared the risks he was willing to take for wealth. Well, that's my guess anyway.

We were living in Temple City then, on a street of vacant lots and pink and green stucco homes. My father had his paving business in town. My mother had her dressmaking business at home, and we owned a house with rooms enough for my brother and sister and me and an acre of citrus—orange trees that had gone black without water. (It didn't pay, my

3

father said, running the drip pipes.) "One of these days," my father said, "I'll clear the land and sell it, and we'll live someplace better."

Every chance my father got, he was out walking the perimeters of some piece of property, calculating the interest rate and the taxes and the resale value and the chances that the next shopping mall or housing development would go up right there. He crisscrossed Los Angeles County and San Bernardino, hunting down lots he thought he could buy cheap and sell dear. He meant, as I understand it now, to buy with borrowed money, make a profit off the sale, and borrow again for the next property, amassing money by degrees. Except expenses were always higher than he expected and profits always lower, and although my father promised my mother the next deal would make us rich, the next deal always seemed to push us deeper into debt.

Of course, I understood none of this then, when I was still sixteen. As far as I knew all families lived from loan to loan, and to me my father was like any father, my mother like every mother. All I really knew of them was that they interfered with what I wanted, and what I wanted was to be free. After all, I was a girl in high school, heady with God knows what and ready to try, in the absence of adults, the privileges adults reserve for themselves: drinking, driving, and sex.

It couldn't have been true, but it seems to me now the only thing I thought about then was this boy I was seeing and what I wanted to do with him in the dark. Maybe that's why I paid no attention to the risks I took or, for that matter, to the risks everyone else in my family was taking. Maybe that's why I was so unprepared for what followed, for what happened the year my father was teaching me to drive.

It was 1965 going on '66, a dry year, and on the radio we kept hearing about brush fires out of control in the foothills of the San Gabriel Mountains. A few times we heard the fires burned so close to yards and houses that the people who lived there had to abandon their homes and wait it out in one church or another. And although the fires seemed far away, they were close. Close enough that in the right wind we could smell brush burning. Close enough that on Saturdays when my father wanted to see how I handled a car, he had me drive him toward Azusa, where we could view the range of charred hills.

It was a Saturday like that my father took me to see a Mrs. Rumsen, a woman I'd heard about but never met before. I understood she was a distant relation, known in our family for her wayward ways. When I met her, she was widowed and lived in a small house on a lot my father hoped someday to turn a profit on. She paid us a little rent and just by living there, my father said, kept vandals off the property.

The day I met Mrs. Rumsen, my father and I had done more than view the burned-up hills. That day, I'd driven my father through neighborhoods where the ashes were still wet, and when we'd had enough of blackened chimneys and exposed plumbing, when we had seen the blue and red remains of children's toys and the pink and yellow tatters of a singed quilt, my father had said, "Move over, sport," and taken the wheel the way he always did. I thought he'd head for home, maybe stop for an Orange Julius, but instead he headed up into the canyon and back a dirt road. He drove so we hit the ditches and bounced in our seats, as if we had a jeep and not an old Pontiac, but maybe that's the way you drive a dirt road.

"We're not going home?"

"I just want to check," he said, "on that place I rented to the Rumsen woman."

That place was another of the lots my father had bought with borrowed money. He asked me if I didn't remember it, and I said, "Maybe." But all I could remember was the smell inside of beer and burned firewood. It smelled like late nights at the beach, with guys and blankets and fires. I remembered that smell and then the look on my mother's face when she saw the rusted Pabst cans and the overturned furniture, the signs that someone had broken in and partied inside our new debt.

"So who's been sleeping in our house?" she had said, wrapping her arms close around her and nudging an empty beer can with the toe of her shoe.

"That's the last thing to worry about, Marian. Cleaned up, this place is going to sell so fast. Everyone'll be wanting land here. You'll see."

The day my father took me to meet Mrs. Rumsen, we'd had the place about a year, but no one had made an offer. "What I think is we've got to fix it up before it will sell," he said, as we turned onto the drive. Cheatweed and knot grass whisked the bottom of the car, and a branch of scrub oak caught on the windshield, its leaves ticking against the glass.

"I want to get the guys out here when we're up on the work," he said, "and put in a good drive. And I thought maybe a deck out front. And paint. Paint is a fast fix, even if buyers have their own ideas."

We passed through the shifting shade of sycamores and live oak and followed the ruts around to a one-story wood frame backed up against the ravine. I remembered it then, the way it was when my father had bought it: the torn screens and the weeds grown up all around. The house was dark green and stood shaded by eucalyptus, and now with the weeds cut back you could see how the ground dropped away from the foundation, so the crawl space grew wider and wider.

My father tapped the horn and shouted out the window as he pulled up alongside a station wagon. "Hey, Mrs. Rum. The rent collector's here."

We climbed from the car, and my father took the wooden steps two at a time. "Ev," he said as he rapped on her screen door. "It's me." He stood there waiting, a tall man in carpenter's pants. A hot breeze blew leaves across the ground, and my father stroked his hair, that kind of blond that goes browner every year.

"Jimmy," I heard someone say through the screen. No one called my father Jimmy. "Glad you're here, Jimmy. You come to fix my window?"

"What window?"

"The one in the back. Someone broke it."

"Not again," he said, "not again."

My father walked right in, but I waited a moment on the steps, gazing through the screen door, before I followed him into the shade of Mrs. Rumsen's place. Something about it reminded me of party favors I used to get as a kid: pink fans with red tassels, woven straw tubes that gripped your fingers and would not let them go, clams that you dropped into a glass of water and watched bloom into fuchsia and turquoise flowers. I smelled something like perfume, maybe incense, and I saw throws and shawls and spreads draped everywhere.

"They damage anything else?" my father was saying.

"Well, they could have damaged me, I guess. But they didn't. I turned on the lights and that seemed to scare them."

"Maybe this setup is no good," my father said.

"Oh, please. I can handle a prowler, especially one just looking for a little privacy."

She was sitting, or maybe it was more like perching, on a bamboo davenport, the cushions propped behind her. Her skin was covered with shadowy freckles, and her short, uncombed hair, an even shade of auburn, fell every which way. She was wrapped in a robe made of something thin, rayon or silk, I couldn't tell. It was parti-colored but mostly black, with rims of scarlet inside her sleeves.

"Well, sure. But I don't know if I want to be responsible for what you might do to the prowler." My father stood in the kitchen by the back door and touched the yellow gingham tacked over the missing window. "You do this, Ev?"

"Well, of course."

"That isn't too safe. Why didn't you call?"

"But I did."

"You leave the message with my no-good-nik kids?"

"I left the message with Marian." Mrs. Rumsen gazed at my father.

"No," my father said and crossed the kitchen to the front room. "She never said."

"Oh?" Mrs. Rumsen reached for a small lacquered box on the low table before her, and the confetti colors on her sleeves rippled.

"Well, I suppose it doesn't matter much, anyway." She took a cigarette from the box. "They don't seem to be *after* anything. I leave a light on, they drive right away."

"You're saying I should hurry up and rewire the porch light?"

"Did I say that?" She smiled out smoke. "Whenever you fix anything is fine, Jim." Then she turned to me, standing between my father and the front door. "Now, this one here is your daughter, yes?"

"This one's my oldest."

"Grown up pretty."

"Some people say so."

My father put his arm across my back, and I tried to feel pretty, but I knew my looks, my nose too long for a girl, my straight hair that rollers dented but never curled. I looked at Mrs. Rumsen looking at me, the red lining of her sleeves appearing and disappearing with every puff on her cigarette, and I wanted to evaporate through the screen door behind me.

"She doesn't believe us, Jim," she said. "Look at her. She thinks we're making it up."

"You know how girls are. They think they aren't movie stars, they must be ugly. Right, Maggie?"

"Dad."

"Don't worry," she said to me. "Someday you'll see. You'll look at pictures of yourself and wish you looked like you do now. You'll wish you could go back to before all your big mistakes. Isn't that so, Jimmy?"

"Oh, I don't know."

"You do too. Don't contradict me. Besides, she's good-looking. She looks a lot like you."

"You think so?" My father took his arm away from me.

She smiled. "Mr. Rum was always right about you."

"Was he?" My father slid his hands into his pockets and studied the floor.

"Sure he was. Always said you were too bashful for your looks."

My father touched the blue tassels of a shawl draped over a standing lamp. "I could reglaze that window right now. I mean, if you want me to."

"You see?" Mrs. Rumsen said to me. "He can't even take a little compliment."

She stood up as she spoke, the crazy colors flamelike in her sleeves. She seemed to me child-sized, delicate, as though her bones would weigh nothing in my hands. To my father, she said, "Do what you want, Jim. I'm fine."

She moved toward us, walking tiptoe in high-heeled sandals, pink satin sandals she wore over black anklets pulled up around her calves. She turned to look at herself in the mirror and flicked at wisps of hair. "Really, Jimmy, whatever you want is fine."

"I try to do right. Really, I do." My father winced a smile. "So I'll go get what I need to do the job," and he pressed himself against the screen as if he too thought he could sci-fi his way through. "Say, Maggie, why don't you keep Mrs. Rumsen company while I pick up a pane of glass?"

Somehow I didn't want to stay with Mrs. Rumsen alone. I didn't want to sit with this small woman who wore pink satin sandals and whose house smelled of patchouli and roses and who spoke to my father as if he were her child. I wanted to go home. I wanted to walk into the plain pastel rooms of our house and hear my mother sewing in the back room. I wanted to shut my door and fall on my bed and listen to the thin sounds of the radio. I wanted to carry the hall phone into my room and call my boyfriend. "Maybe I should go home, Dad."

"Why? I won't be gone a minute, sport." And then he was gone. We heard him take the wooden steps two at a time, heard him gun the engine as if he were a kid my age. And as he drove away, we heard him shout words I couldn't make out above the sound of the engine. I guess Mrs. Rumsen couldn't either because she opened her arms so her sleeves hung like semaphores. "Who knows what's on that man's mind."

"I sure don't. He's my father, is all."

"You'd know his mind better if he were someone else?" She looked at me slantwise. "Yes, you probably would." She leaned forward to flick her ashes into the silver-blue bottom of an abalone shell, and that silence I'd been afraid of, that silence that felt like heat, settled down on us. "You want a drink?"

I looked at her to make sure she wasn't crazy or playing some trick on me. But she seemed perfectly serious, so I said, "Well, I can't really. I mean, Coke, yes. Anything else, no."

It wasn't that I didn't drink. I did, out by the reservoir or down under the bridge over the wash. I drank with my boyfriend and his friends, guys who had graduated and were waiting for the draft, and their girl-friends, girls who were older or who looked it, who had a way with eye-liner and back-combing. It was just that I didn't drink with my father or friends of my father.

"I mean, I'm too young."

"I'm too old, but that doesn't stop me." From under a shawl satin-stitched with roses, Mrs. Rum took two tumblers and in the kitchen poured us ginger ale. She opened a cupboard and pulled out the vodka. "Just a splash?"

"No, I don't think so."

"Come on. It's my party," and she laughed at her joke. "He'll never know."

Before I could say no again, she poured some vodka into our glasses. Leaving mine on the counter, she took hers and moved back to the dav-enport. "You don't have to, of course."

I did take the glass, but I stayed behind, looking at the framed pho-tos on the wall between the two rooms. Most of the pictures were of the same man, dressed differently in each—in a sharply pressed shirt, in riding habit, in a tux. In one, he danced with a younger Mrs. Rumsen. She spun away from him, her skirt plattering out around her, and they both smiled out of the picture. At the bottom of that, in black print, I read: EVELYN NIGHT AND JOHNNY RUN. There were other pictures, too, pictures of people who might have been Hollywood stars before my time, the way they turned their heads to smile at the camera, the way the women wore dark lipstick and the light shone off their hair, and at the bottom of each of these was sprawling black handwriting. I tried to make out the words as I sipped from my glass.

"Pictures of our career," Mrs. Rumsen said. "Our dance routine, or one of them, anyway. Johnny, he was fleet of foot, and I was glamorous as the night. And then his modeling pictures. And our friends and enemies, the De Marcos, the Dowlings, dancers you wouldn't know, I suppose."

No, I didn't know them, I told her.

"Come sit," Mrs. Rumsen said, nodding toward the empty space near her, and not to be rude, I did. "So what do you think?"

"Of what?"

"Of me, of course. What else? Of me and my hodgepodge, of all my nice things dropped down here in this wagon-wheel house your father's nice enough to let me rent."

She waved her hand, as if her cigarette were a wand and with a touch she could change things. She waved at the windows with the cafe curtains, brown with white geese and streaks of orange for clouds, and at the floor with the green wall-to-wall my father must have put in, covered over with straw mats and small rugs she said were Chinese. "Yard sale rugs, but nice."

I told her I thought everything looked nice. "Real nice."

"No, it doesn't," she said, "but it's better now, now that I'm settled in. Besides, beggars and choosers and all that." She sipped from her glass and added, "Not that I'm complaining. I'm happy to have a place all to myself. Especially in my situation."

"I'm sorry about . . ." I was going to say "your husband." But I didn't want to talk to Mrs. Rumsen about death or being a widow. Instead, I said, "I'm sorry about your situation."

"Yes, well, but I landed on my feet, didn't I? I picked up a job or two, so I'm okay."

"What job?" I asked, and then the question seemed childish. "I mean, do you like what you do? My mother says she doesn't always like her job."

Mrs. Rumsen glanced up at me, then stretched her kimono over her knees. "Sure, I like my jobs. As much as you ever do. The one at the theater's fine. And I like the track, too. I have friends at Santa Anita."

"Sounds interesting."

She laughed at that, exhaled her smoke all at once. "Selling tickets?

Working in the betting office? Well, my jobs will do. And then your father letting me live here, that helps. He's really very decent, your father."

"Yeah, I guess."

"Nothing to guess. He sent us money."

I nodded as if I knew, but something must have crossed my face because she said, "When Johnny was sick, you know."

I didn't know, so I had to think about it, about my father, who always said he was small-time smart with money, sending some to this woman and her husband. It made me think of the Red Cross taking care of those people who had to abandon their burned-up homes, and then I thought there was something different about it, something more personal. Uncomfortable with the thought, I sucked my ginger ale and tasted the frost.

"More?" and she stood, ready to take my glass although it was mostly full.

"That's okay," I said. She filled her glass with soda, and when she returned, I said, "How come you know my father so well?"

"I'm family to begin with. And we were all friends, Mr. Rum and me and your father and mother, back when you were a baby." She seemed to wait to see what I'd say. "Mr. Rum and I had a place down at the beach one summer, the summer after you were born. The three of you came down for a week." She sat back into the palm-frond print of her davenport cushions. "Well, of course you don't remember this, but you got your first sunburn down there."

I knew about homes at the beach. My friends had taken me to their places, at Long Beach, Newport, Laguna, and my father had rented cottages for us a couple of summers. I knew about the latticed windows, the ivy, the bougainvillea with its papery red leaves that looked like flowers. I knew how the brick steps down to the beach were slippery with moss and how salt was always in the air. And I knew a little about my parents as a young couple married after the war. I'd seen pictures: my mother smiling, her hair long and curled and pinned with hibiscus, a lei around her neck; my father still in uniform, the hat knocked off his head as he pulled my mother close and kissed her. But I couldn't imagine them with this petite woman in her silk kimono, and I couldn't imagine my father friends with the man I saw on the wall. Evelyn Night, Johnny Run—they seemed so different from the people my parents knew.

"You howled so, I made a bath of tea and soaked you in it." She spread her hands so I could see the weight of an infant in them.

"So why don't I know you the way I know my aunts?"

"You probably should know me the way you know your aunts," she said. "But you know families. Someone always has to be the black sheep, and I guess in your father's family, it's me, the one who always does what no one else approves. But that's life. You go on to what's next."

"Like this?"

"Like this and who knows what else after."

"You mean when my father sells the place."

She nodded.

"He hasn't sold it yet. I mean, I think you won't have to move too soon."

"Oh no?" she said, and I almost believed that I'd told her something she didn't know. "He's big on wishes and promises, your father."

"Yes, he is," I said, although it surprised me to say it, as if my father were just someone I happened to know.

Mrs. Rum and I slid into silence again, a not-so-uncomfortable silence this time. She refilled my glass with ice and ginger ale, saying, "Enough for today, yes?" although I think she knew it wasn't.

We sat with our cold glasses sweating rings on our laps, and I had time to look around without seeming rude. On the low table, there were wooden trivets inset with mother-of-pearl, not that we were using them, and there were small wooden elephants, linked trunk to tail in something like a caravan across the table. And in the center was this white thing that looked to me like ivory. It was a snake at one end and a horse at the other, the horse climbing out of the open jaws of the snake. Mrs. Rumsen must have seen me looking, because she said, "That's scrimshaw, you know," and I said, "Very nice."

Over the stone fireplace a large feather fan was spread against the pine paneling, and on the stone mantel itself were glass boxes, butterflies pinned inside. Against the wall was a lacquered black and red hi-fi, MAGNAVOX in small brass letters against the speaker screen, and standing in the record rack were albums: *South Pacific, Oklahoma!, The King and I, Around the World in Eighty Days,* and others that I couldn't read. I think Mrs. Rumsen was going to ask me if I'd like to hear something, because she was standing and moving toward the hi-fi when she said, "That's your father's car I hear, isn't it?"

I nodded, and she said, "Last chance," and leaned back against the hi-fi, her black-stockinged ankles crossed.

"So after that summer, you and Mr. Rumsen didn't see my father again?"

She raised her hands, a crescent of scarlet flashing on each arm. "That was probably for the best, what with all that family stuff, that no-drink, no-dance religion stuff. Besides, Mr. Rum and I quit teaching ballroom at that beach place and got jobs somewhere else. Johnny got calls to model, and I continued in the chorus. You can see me if you look hard at some of those old movies."

I could hear my father shutting the car door. "And now you've come back? You and my father are friends again?"

"With Johnny dying," she said quietly, as if my father coming up the steps should not hear her, "I needed help, and no one but your father offered."

"Hey, Mrs. Rum-Ta-Dum," my father said, "open the door."

We could see him, standing on the step, glass all but invisible in one hand and his toolbox in the other. Once inside, he worked quickly as he drank the soda Mrs. Rum poured for him. "Mrs. Rum been telling stories on me?" He ran the glass cutter straight down the pane.

"Naw," I said.

"Want me to tell some stories on Mrs. Rum?"

"Ignore him," Mrs. Rumsen said. "He thinks he's funny."

"She tell you how she gave you your name? How she was the first one to call you Maggie instead of Margaret?" He had fitted the glass with brads and was prizing open the can of putty.

"I call myself Maggie."

"Not then you didn't."

Mrs. Rumsen waved a hand through the air, as if she were thinking what I was thinking: A Margaret has to become a Maggie someday. But as I stood at the sink washing glasses and listening to the scrape and suck of my father's putty knife, I felt a small chill, as if someone had shot a BB through our past and a thin stream of cold air were leaking through.

"You don't have to do those, Maggie," Mrs. Rum said.

"Ah, let her," my father said and dropped the knife into his toolbox. "It's a small thing, isn't it?" He pressed his fingers gently into the putty around the pane. "We've got to give it time to dry, but then I can paint. How about I come back in a week? That okay, Mrs. Rum?"

13

She said, "Fine, Jim, fine," and moved close to him for the good-byes. She grabbed his arm and lifted her face with its shadowy freckles and made my father stoop a little so she could kiss his cheek. When she turned to me, I offered my hand. But instead of shaking it, Mrs. Rumsen studied my ring, the class ring the guy I was going with had given me.

"She has a beau," she said to my father.

"I've told her she shouldn't get stuck on one so young," he said.

"I don't know," she said and turned my hand over as if to study my palm. I had wound the back of the ring with string and lacquered that over with clear polish, and the whole thing stood up like a blister.

"We didn't do this when we were young," she said. "No rings unless it was forever." She put her palm over mine for a second. It was so cool; my hand seemed hot and clumsy as an oven mitt in hers. "You don't know your luck," she said and kissed my cheek.

TWO

*T*he guy I was seeing, he was dark-eyed and serious, he was older. He gave me his ring, and I did that trick with the string and polish. I wore it, on my left hand at school, on my right at home, and even then my mother and father didn't like it. "You're too young," they said, my father closing one kitchen door, my mother standing before the other. "These things don't last," they said, the fluorescent tubes buzzing overhead, the stove clock ticking behind me.

His name was Bruce, Bruce Gallagher, and he sat in his car, waiting for me after school. Nearly every day until Homecoming. Then partway through my junior year and a few months after his own graduation, he got tired of waiting and enlisted. They put him through everything, through basic and A.I.T., and then they put him in airborne, the 101st.

He came from a different part of L.A., where the houses were all bunched together, their walls thick like adobe, their driveways what my father called forties drives, concrete strips for the wheels to roll over, a hill of grass in between, and he was new to our town when I met him. He played guitar, that's something I loved, the quiet way he looked concentrating on his guitar, and once he'd enlisted, his tags knocked against its wooden back. He kept a blanket in the trunk of his blue Chevy, a blanket that smelled of oil and exhaust and aftershave and wool, a smell I still remember. He was thin and muscular and looked great in a uniform. He looked great any old time.

I was important for going with him, maybe because he was older, maybe because he was new to town, maybe because I was otherwise so unimportant. I saw it in the looks girls gave me, especially once he'd

15

enlisted. They made room for me, when I moved the ring from my right hand to my left, to my ring finger. They backed up against their lockers, their books pressed to their chests, silent as I walked by, but as soon as I passed, I'd hear their voices, the knit and purl of their gossip, and I'd think, Whatever you're saying, I do worse. I'd pass the music room, the Spanish lab, the math room. I'd see Mr. Yunker wiping the day's equations away, and I'd think, Go ahead, talk trig. Go on about the vascular system of plants, the social contract, the legislative body. Tune to the A and have us sing all the hymns and anthems. Have us stand there in our choir robes, our mouths O's. I'd pass the gym, Miss Arthur with her whistle in her mouth and detention slips in her pocket, and think, Go on, make us stop and kneel and show that our skirts brush the ground. Make us follow the rules. Because when the bell rang and the books and doors and lockers slammed, I was breaking them all: I was walking through the crowded halls, past those girls with books on hips, past the Homecoming Queen and her cheerleader friends, past the Girl of the Month and the Couple of the Year. I was walking across the parking lot behind the school, past all those kids leaning on cars, past all those who were important without trying, past everyone with secrets in their mouths. I was gone across the lot and into his car parked on a street just beyond the school, parked in the California sun, waiting for me because he was home on leave before they shipped him out, and work and school and the day were over.

There in the enclosed shade of the car, he sat like a low rider with his dark cropped hair and sharp profile, though he was never anything other than a skinny tall guy who enlisted too soon, and I was nothing but this angular girl with the too-long nose and the too-straight hair. But inside that car, that private universe we filled, we didn't know that. His slender body seemed weighted with something, desire I guess I'd call it now, and I felt special, as if his looking at me, his wanting me, made up for all the boys who hadn't looked at me, hadn't wanted me. He had a sweet smile I always felt he saved just for me, and dark eyes that made me think of velvet. (Isn't that silly?) He'd give me that sweet smile and touch the back of my neck, saying, "How you doing, sweetheart?"

I'd say, "I'm fine. How was your day, baby?"

"It just got better," he'd say and then, you know, kiss me.

After that, we'd say nothing for a while. We'd sit on the hot vinyl seats and watch the other kids drive or walk away, letting the charge between us grow. Then we'd drive, heading toward the foothills, up to one of the reservoirs or down to the dam, sit there drinking beer and kissing a lit-tle. We were always waiting, to be alone, to finish what our kissing had started. We were waiting for Saturday, and when it was a Saturday night and I had finished my chores and shown my father how little I knew about driving and had curled my hair that would not curl and yelled at my brother and sister and listened to them yell at me, I slipped my shoes with the extra inch of heel into my bag, the deep black purse with a flap and no zipper, and I went out, with a promise: "When you com-ing home?"

"Sometime."

The sky wasn't dark yet, but the streetlights were lit so the palms and pines that lined the roads glowed with a double light, an iridescence. I slid into the car and across the seat. And he said, "How you doing, babe?" He smelled of Old Spice, and his skin was slick as kid. I kicked off my flats, and, barefoot, slipped my leg next to his so we could drive together.

"Driving tandem," he called it, my foot on the gas, his hands on the wheel.

We drove like that into the foothills, dry air pungent with chaparral filling the car. We took the canyon road along the San Gabriel Reservoir and stopped where we saw kids like us standing around a truck or a car. We drank the beer that was going around and offered some of our own, and one of the guys always said, "Say, Bruce, what's it like?" and Bruce always set his feet apart on the ground and told them what the army was like. These were regular guys in blue jeans and T-shirts, guys with bar-bershop haircuts: Mike and Stan and Charlie and Doug. And their girl-friends were plain girls like me—Barbara and Susan and Carol and Joan. We were a little like ghosts in the crowd, not because we were shy or quiet or overpowered by the guys, but because we were all so white, what with peroxide and the way we made our lips light and our eyes dark. Maybe because he was the enlisted man, Bruce and I always left first. We climbed into the car, starting it up tandem, but pulling out slow so the guys could do what they did, Charlie jumping arms spread in front of us, a black X in the headlights, and Mike kicking the rear fender and shouting, "Yeow!" We drove slowly along the edge of the reservoir and out to the main road, the way I imagined newlyweds drove their tin-can-trailing cars.

We wandered, as if we didn't know where we were going, through all the window-lit neighborhoods, but where we wound up was nowhere surprising. Where we wound up was on my street, on Homewood, driving without lights, driving way past my house, to the end of the acre of trees. For no good reason, I put on the shoes with the extra inch of heel, maybe just to make it harder to walk. We took the blanket from the trunk and carried it with us, weeds catching my heels as we walked side by side through the trees. I saw him from an angle, the half-moon whites of his eyes and the V of skin where his shirt was open. We stretched the blanket between us and lowered it to the dry grass, so it seemed to float inches off the ground until our weight pressed it down and we thought we were hidden by the grass and the trees and the dark.

THREE

You don't want me to drive?" I was holding my hand out for the keys.

"No, I want you to watch me," my father said and took the driver's seat. For a second, I worried he knew Mrs. Rum and I'd been drinking. "You might learn something from your old dad." He waved at Mrs. Rumsen, but she had already shut the door. "You drive like *this*," and he pulled out swiftly and drove down to the road, where he rolled to a stop and leaned forward, squinting both ways.

"See how I did that?" he asked. "See how I hardly used the brakes at all?"

My father drove fast out of the foothills, doubling the speed limit away from Mrs. Rumsen's place. "Watch how I flatten the curve," he said and cut first to the inside and then to the outside of the lane.

"Brake into the turns and accelerate out," he said. "And don't ride the brakes. You always ride the brakes."

"Okay," I said. "I won't."

"See how I just let up on the gas to slow down and how I speed up out of the turn?"

We hit a bump as we rounded the curve, and it seemed for a moment we soared. "Yes," I said, "I see."

He worked his hands around the steering wheel. He glanced in his mirrors and grabbed the side view to adjust it, and he whistled tunes from before I could remember. He sat way back, as though deeply relaxed, and showed me a rolling stop at the intersection. "See? No reason to bear down on the brakes."

At the first stoplight, he said, "All you do is just lay back and roll up to it."

He flipped the automatic shift to neutral and idled the engine at something more than an idle.

"It's good for it," he said. "Cleans it out."

As we idled, his whistling became quiet singing. He sang about wisdom and stars in your eyes. He put the car in gear and nosed into the intersection.

"No reason to wait for someone to rear-end you," he said and began singing again, about love making you foolish, and then the green light let him speed ahead.

My father had faith in roads, that's what I believe. He revered freeways. He talked about them all the time, about the details of their construction, about the diamond blades that cut grooves into asphalt so cars wouldn't skid. He liked to show me the way rainwater pooled on an improperly laid road. He would even stop the car in the emergency lane and hop over highway dividers to study the raw open ground of highway construction and the concrete blocks bristling with steel reinforcement. He was a visionary of roadwork. He believed that freeways and high-speed driving would transform our lives, that someday we'd travel from Tijuana to Oregon in just three hours. And he talked about driving as if it were an art, full of moments of private grace. My father wanted me to drive the way some parents want their kids to play piano.

"Drive like you mean it," he'd say. "Drive like you've got someplace to go."

But I was clumsy in the driver's seat and had no idea how large the car was or how far I was from anything. I would stop way behind the white line.

"What are you doing? Pull up to the line."

And I would, slowly.

"Why are you so timid? Do you see any cars coming?"

I would shake my head no.

"Well, then, go on through the intersection."

And he was always right. No car ever broadsided us or sent us spinning into a tree.

By the time we were near home, my father was driving like any other father from the neighborhood. He turned onto our street, and as he approached the intersection at Homewood and Colina, the intersection he always called *blind*, he explained what he meant.

"See that?" he said. "See the oleander all around that corner, and see that wall? See that avocado tree growing out over the wall and the fence running along the Colina side of that house?"

I nodded because I saw it all.

"People like corner lots. But then they want their privacy, so they put up hedges and walls and let the trees go. It's hard to see past any of these things, hard to see what's coming. So you take care at a blind corner. You go slow during the day, maybe tap your horn, give the other guy a warning, but nights aren't so bad because you can see headlights yards ahead of a car."

And then he tapped the horn, perhaps because he saw my sister on her white Schwinn. She turned at the blind intersection, from the steep slope of Colina Drive onto Homewood, coasting fast, her hair flicking behind her, her pink handlebar streamers streaming. (They were pink to match her pink Keds and her pink sweater. She was only ten, and she thought of these things.) Behind her, one of the neighbor boys chased her on an old bike, and across the street, Tommy Dawson straddled his carport roof, a rubber-cupped arrow strung in his bow. As far as I could tell he sighted my sister, not the bull's-eye on his front-yard tree.

Then my father honked his good-father warning honk. Tommy's arrow sailed into a parked car, the neighbor boy swerved onto the grass, and Alison turned to look at us as she coasted past our house. My sister was pretty, pretty in an unexpected way. I've studied prettiness in girls so that I could fake it and act pretty myself. I've noticed that sometimes it's hair, lots of long straight hair or lots of hair in a perfect flip with a sheen you can get from hair spray. Sometimes it's the way a girl crosses her ankles when she sits and twists her body as she speaks so you feel she's always about to turn away. Sometimes, and this is the easiest to copy, it's the eyes, a sweet roundness you can pretend to with eyeliner and mascara. But with my sister, it was a levelness, something perfectly straight in her gaze. Standing on the pedals of her white Schwinn, my sister watched us with those pure eyes. I've looked for this gaze elsewhere, but I've seen it in only a few women, my mother among them, when she's calm and doesn't know anyone is looking, and my own daughter. When I've looked at her, looking for traces of Bruce in her face, I've seen my sister looking back.

Our house was the green stucco after the vacant lot and before the orange trees. We passed the lot with its brown and yellow FOR SALE sign and turned down the wide asphalt drive my father resurfaced every few years. At the back of the yard was the fiberglass carport for "your mother's car" alongside the garage, where my father kept his truck. And in the far corner near the slat fence and my mother's rosebushes, the one orange tree my father had saved grew. As we drove up, my brother Jamie was watering that tree, green hose coiled at his feet.

"Hey, kiddo," my father said. "Don't forget the perimeters."

Although my father didn't want the cost of cutting down and uprooting the acre of dead trees, he thought that they were a fire hazard, so he wanted us to water the first row of dead citrus (the trees themselves, not their roots) and the edge of the weedy lot, as if that would insulate us from fire. My brother, his shoulders bony under his shirt, waved us off, saying, "Yeah, Dad, I know."

The yard was wet and full of the green smell of mud, but I could also smell the drifting smoke from the foothill fire. And I could see how the sky was overcast with ash. We walked back to the house, my father tugging at the weeds of the vacant lot. All the way from the garage we could hear my mother sewing on the converted treadle she had never replaced, sewing in bursts because the machine would not stitch over her pin-basting.

"Long driving lesson," my mother said, glancing up at us as we walked in.

Behind her, hanging from sills and jambs, were whole squadrons of cheerleaders' uniforms, two-tone dresses from rival schools—blue and gold, green and white, black and orange. They hung inside out, but even with the exposed seams of gores and darts, you could see the shapes of the girls who would wear them.

"Sure was," my father said. "Any calls?"

I'm sure he was thinking of Mrs. Rumsen. But my mother nodded toward me, her mouth full of pins. "Ut's his name."

"Bruce," I said. "His name is Bruce," and without thinking, I twisted the ring from my right hand and slid it on my left. "He's not nobody, you know."

"Never said he was anybody I knew," she said, pushing a mouthful of pins into the cushion. "Just wish you knew a few more."

"Would you stop saying that?" I said.

"And quit wearing that ring like you were married."

"Jeez-*us*," I said and pulled the ring off.

"Don't swear," my father said, trading looks with my mother.

"I didn't."

My mother sighed and bowed her head to her work, and the machine rushed forward a few inches before she stopped and pulled out another pin. She looked up and said, "Well, you don't go anywhere unless you finish your work."

"Yeah, I know," I said, leaving the two of them there in the back room and taking the black hall phone with its long cord into my room.

The phone on my stomach, I lay on my bed and listened to my parents. The short bursts of my mother's sewing. The small puff of the cushions as my father settled onto the living room couch. My brother called my room the ear of the house. He said my room was like a shell, holding sound inside. "Even the color," he said, meaning the now faded pink my mother had painted the room when we moved in. "It's this sandy color, like in a shell."

And you could hear everything in my room: a pincushion dropping on the back-room floor, someone setting the comb and brush down on the dresser in my parents' bedroom. So when my brother and I wanted to know what our parents really thought, we would go to my room. We would sit on the floor and lean against the bed, the door ajar. We could hear them pacing in the living room, hear the "What's that?" and the "Oh, you think so?" and my father's voice skidding over my mother's name. We could hear my mother's questions about money and my father's answers. They began, "Debt? Would I get us into debt?" and ended after what seemed like forever with "So, you see, there's nothing to worry about."

As we listened, my brother and I played hangman. We played the game long rather than short, not guessing obvious letters so we could draw the hung man in detail. My brother's touches turned the man into a lizard or shark, with rows of saw teeth and claws instead of fingers. My strokes gave him sideburns and pointy-toed boots, a snake or a heart tattooed on his arm.

That day I lay on the bed, not doing anything I wanted to do, not calling Bruce, not listening to the radio. I was stupid with restlessness until my brother walked in saying, "Where'd you go today?" and I understood I was waiting for the fight I was sure *they* would have about the Rumsen place.

"Nowhere much, driving in circles."

"If you're going to call Bruce, get him to go someplace I can go too, okay?"

"Get lost."

At that, he walked all the way into my room and leaned against the desk.

"So?" I said.

His sneakers were wet, and he'd worn them without socks, so his ankles looked spindly.

"Want to play hangman?"

I heard the radio go on in the back room and from the living room the sound of newspaper pages turning. "I've got to call Bruce."

"Fast game?" my brother said. Idly, he drew ballpoint circles on the cover of a notebook. "I got an easy word."

"So just tell it to me."

"What fun is that?"

"Come on, let me call Bruce."

"This'll be really easy."

Cornered by my brother, I put the phone on the bed and slid to the floor, and Jamie sat near me, drawing dashes on a page he ripped from my notebook.

"That's not short."

There were sixteen dashes.

"I said 'easy,' not short," my brother said.

I guessed Z first and then X, later V and W and U. The unlikely letters. The ones that gave us time to draw holes in the hung man's coat and to give him a beard and a cap. I didn't guess A or E at all, or any other vowel, but after drawing the shoes, the soles flapping away from the leather, I guessed G and then R and saw what my brother was doing: M_RG_R_TG_LL_GH_R.

"That's two words," I said.

"Fooled you," my brother said. "Go on, finish it."

It thrilled and frightened me both, imagining myself married. So I finished the hung man instead, putting a bunch of flowers in his hand, as I listened for sounds from *them*. All I heard was the whir of my mother's machine and the on and off of water in the kitchen. I thought, No fight, and watched my brother to see if he thought the same.

"Go ahead, finish it," he said, and when I wouldn't, he took the pen from me and filled in the A's and E's.

Margaret Gallagher. Inside my notebook at school, I'd written *Bruce*, over and over, carving his name into the cardboard cover with my ball-point pen. And I'd written *Maggie + Bruce*, too, but after I wrote *Maggie Gallagher* the first time, I couldn't write it again. It was the name of a stranger, someone from the telephone book, someone I couldn't imagine myself to be. *Maggie Gallagher* sounded happy and gay. She sounded pretty, with or without eyeliner and mascara, and sprightly. Her hair would curl easily, and she would know how to dance, and men would never look past her to the next girl. She was someone who did not have a thin brother and a startling sister, who didn't live next to an acre of orange trees, whose father didn't pour concrete and asphalt. Someone I couldn't hope to be. "Where'd you get this idea?"

My brother shrugged. "Kids at school," and then that feeling, that feeling of someone behind you, made us both look up.

"What're you doing?" my father said.

He had changed out of his work boots, and his face was a little red, as if he'd just washed it.

"Playing hangman," my brother answered.

My father looked down at the man we'd drawn and at the name that I'd put a few lines through. "You making plans you haven't told us about?"

"It was Jamie's idea," I said.

My father let out a breath, and then he said, "You know, I could stop you seeing that boy anytime I want."

"There's nothing wrong with him," I said.

"Just want you to know," my father said, "it's up to me if you see that boy," and he took the phone from my bed and walked away down the hall, as if that would keep me from calling Bruce. My brother remained, crouched on the floor and sketching a background behind the hung man. I flopped on the bed, and outside one of Tommy Dawson's arrows thwacked the tin target and rattled it against the tree.

"Mom says remember the ironing." It was my sister in the hallway. She had clipped her hair back with pink barrettes and, just like my mother, had tossed a dish towel over her shoulder.

"Okay, I remember the ironing."

"Yeah, but will you remember to do it?"

Ironing I didn't mind that much. It was quiet, and it was a way to please my mother and keep her from grounding me.

"Of course I will, Ali." She hated it if I shortened her name. "In a minute."

She leaned into my room, her hair swinging forward like a lap of fabric off the bolt. "A minute?" she said and smiled. "Okay. I'll tell Mom." Then she pivoted and vanished. That was something else about my sister. She moved almost weightlessly, her movements a kind of sleight of hand.

I watched my brother scribble. He filled a corner of the page with that pyramid eye from the one-dollar bill. He scrawled rough figures, a crowd watching the hung man maybe, and then drew something he must have learned in science, a cross section of the earth beneath the scaffolding, pebbles and rocks and roots, and growing out of that, a tree, its branches lost in leaves that he drew one by one.

"They're going to ground you," he said.

"What for?"

"I don't know. They just are," he said and drew the veins in another leaf. "I can feel it. Something in the air." He lifted his head and sniffed to make me smile, then said, "I'm working on a new trick."

"So?" I said.

I liked my brother's tricks—he was known for them—but they also frightened me, as if he were too reckless, even for a boy. More than once when he was not old enough for school my mother'd had to talk him out of trees he'd climbed too high. He liked walking tightrope on the naked beams of the houses our uncle Chess built, and for a time, when he was maybe ten, he took to crawling into or out of the smallest spaces he could find, climbing out the men's room window at Bob's Big Boy or hiding in the wheel well in my mother's trunk.

That year when he was fourteen, he read a library book on the escape artists, and tried to imitate them, parting his hair dead center and combing it slick with water. He wore a black acetate scarf over his eyes at night (Houdini wore black silk, he'd read) and studied keys and locks (as he said Houdini had done), sketching the bits and wards over and over. At a magic shop, Jamie bought a pair of handcuffs and was forever asking someone in the family to cuff his wrists behind his back and keep the key. The day I cuffed him, I thought for sure he knew the trick of quick release. He must know, I thought, the button or lever or spring that would set him free, but if Jamie knew any such trick, I never saw him use it. Instead, I opened a closet and found him sitting on the floor, his cuffed hands under his thighs and his knees drawn tight to his chin.

"Close the door and let me finish," he commanded, and I did close the door, standing outside and worrying that he would use up the air inside.

"Are you done yet?" I asked, and when he didn't answer, I opened the door to find him standing with his joined hands in front of him, hanging limp from the silver cuffs.

"Well, I've almost got it," he said, his smile denting one side of his face.

"So you want me to tell you what my new trick is, don't you?"

"Okay, tell me."

"I jump over a rope," he said, "on my skateboard."

He walked his fingers in the air to show me how he leaped a rope and landed in motion on the other side.

"It's hard," he said. "And I miss a lot, but I'm better than Tommy."

"Thought you didn't like Tommy Dawson anymore," I said.

"Yeah, well," my brother said and nodded toward the street as if to say geography kept them friends.

"I want to do storm drains next," he said.

"Those corrugated things?"

He nodded. "On my stomach or, you know, crouched down."

"Who are you doing all this *for*?" I asked just to tease him. But when I looked at my brother's smooth face, his greeny brown eyes letting on nothing, I understood that there was someone he did this for and remembered a house we passed in the neighborhood sometimes, a nicer house than ours, with a pool in the backyard, a bamboo fence around it, and a rock garden in the front. I remembered a girl sitting on the front steps of that house, a cat in her lap with its chin lifted for stroking, and I remembered my brother sliding low in his seat as if this girl he could barely see should not see him.

"What do you mean who?" he said.

"You're doing all this for someone, aren't you?" I said. "You're doing it for that girl."

"Am not," he said. "I'm doing this for a what, not a who."

"What what?"

"The greater what," he said.

The house seemed calm, as if the fight my brother and I expected had slipped past us, so I stepped into the hallway and called Bruce, the cold black earpiece tucked under my hair. I sat on the cane chair my mother kept next to the phone table and laced the phone cord through my fingers while I waited for Bruce to answer.

"Sweetheart," his mother said when she heard my voice. "Bruce is out now, but he'll call you just as soon as he gets home. I know he wants to see you."

Just for a moment, I felt weightless, the weightlessness of rejection. (I don't know why I didn't believe his mother. I liked her and the gentle way she always treated Bruce.) I thought maybe he wouldn't call. Maybe he wanted to break up with me and would never call again. An unbearable thought. To put it out of mind, I went to take the damp clothes from the refrigerator and found my sister in the kitchen, about to bake cookies. Like some sort of Betty Crocker, she had draped her pink sweater over a kitchen chair and set all her ingredients on the table. She stood on tiptoe before the sink, measuring water into a cup, and she gave me one of those eerie, beautiful looks of hers, the kind that made me feel she was sixteen years older than me, not six years younger, the sort of look my daughter sometimes gives me.

"You can have one when I'm done," she said.

"Thanks," and I gathered up the clothes and went into the back room, thinking how quiet my mother was, wondering if she was hand-basting or whip-stitching. Not thinking my father was there, I wasn't ready for the midsentence silence as both my parents watched me walk in.

"Hi," I said and put my bundle on the ironing board.

My mother sat at her machine, her bangs clipped back and her skin glistening with sweat. My father leaned against the wall behind the ironing board, arms over his chest. It crossed my mind that if the iron was on, I should worry. I don't know why. All my father did was talk, asking simple questions in a quiet voice. But I knew the hand behind the voice, and it worried me that I could see the red arrow set for silk, not too hot, but hot enough.

"Now, how long have you been going out with this boy?" my father asked, although he knew the answer.

"Since last June."

"And what's he been doing since he graduated?"

He knew the answer to that one too. "Working in his father's machine shop."

"How long's he intend to do that?"

"How would I know?"

"I thought you knew all about him."

That one I didn't answer.

"And who are these people you two go out with?"

"Friends of his."

"What did you say that girl Joan did for a living?"

"You know what she does," I said.

"Well, it must be pretty forgettable," he said, "because I've forgotten. So remind me."

I told him that she worked for JCPenney.

"Fitting-room girl, right? And Carol?"

I reminded him that she washed hair.

"Washes hair," he said, as if considering this fact carefully. "You have any idea how much she makes?"

"Not exactly."

"What would you guess?"

"I wouldn't guess," I said. "It's none of my business."

"Not your business?" he said. "You want to live on a beauty shop salary?"

"Not necessarily."

"Doesn't sound so good to you, does it?"

"I don't know. I haven't thought about it."

"Haven't thought, huh?" he said. "So tell me, what do you and Bruce plan to do if something happens? Have you thought about that?"

I asked him, "What's something?"

"Don't play dumb with your father," my mother said.

"None of my kids are dumb. Except this one might be." He rapped his knuckles hard against my head.

"You know what something is, don't you, Maggie?" he said.

"Maybe."

"You know all about just throwing your life down the toilet, don't you?"

"Dad," I said.

"Well, you do, don't you?" he said. "You know all about living for the joystick."

"Dad," I said again, embarrassed he would say something like that to me.

But he kept on saying things like that, as if he knew a cruel word stung more than a swift hand. Soon he wasn't waiting for the answers, and I wasn't offering them. He was raging on about my wayward youth and empty future, and I was standing by my mother's worktable, opening and closing her pinking shears and turning some scrap of linen into dust and threads.

"Listen to me when I'm talking to you. Put those scissors down."

And I did put the scissors down, but I didn't listen to my father. I thought about the cookies my sister was baking. I could smell them, sugar cookies that she must have pressed into the tin sheet with a buttery sugar-coated glass. I could smell the butter and the sugar. I could smell that the cookies had baked a minute or two too long and were turning brown and black around the edges.

"Tell me," I heard my father say. "Are you giving it to him?"

I glanced at my mother. She was the one my sister took after, but you wouldn't have known it then, the way her eyes shut me out even as she looked at me.

"If you are," he said, "it better not be for free. Whores're smarter than you."

I couldn't answer back, and that bothers me. But I didn't cry either.

"What are you trying to do, anyway?" His voice, rubber on pavement. "Ruin your life?"

"If I want to" is what I should have said. "Excuse me" is what I did say before I let the back door slam behind me.

FOUR

*W*ish it weren't so, but I don't think I'm so different from my father. I've thought about this, and I believe if I had ever seen my daughter choosing the sort of men I've chosen, my hand would have flown up so fast. Even now that she's grown, I'd want to slap her into the middle of next week, the way my father always promised. I wouldn't do it, but I'd want to.

I've known women my age whose parents were completely different from mine, whose mothers took them to the doctor and got them the pill or whatever and yelled only if they guessed their daughters weren't using it. I had a friend whose mother said, "Honey, you come home when you want to do it. I don't want you out in some parked car where who knows what could happen."

Imagine.

But if my daughter brought home the likes of any of the guys I've known, even Bruce, I couldn't do that, not even now that she is grown and I am at last settled. I just couldn't say, "Fine, sweetheart, use my bed."

I made friends once with a woman whose life was like mine, except she had her baby even younger. At sixteen. By the time I met Holly, I had moved east, to find a new life for my daughter and me. Holly was a cabdriver, and she told me her story in the time it took to drive from South Ferry to a restaurant in the east Eighties where I was late for work. Her story was simple, she said. Her mother wouldn't let her out at all. (That's the way she put it: out, like out of a cage.) And the one time she did get out, well, she ended up with her kid.

"You marry the guy?" I asked.

31

She shot me a look in the rearview mirror. "You serious?"

"No, sorry, stupid question."

That's how we learned what we had in common.

After that first ride, she came into the restaurant a few times for coffee, which caught my manager's attention since the place isn't the sort of place you go just for coffee. But she was thoughtful and always dropped in during the evening setup lull, and there wasn't much he could say to that. What he could say, he said to her, and I have always thought he liked her. She would sit there in her wool work shirt, her scraggly hair tied back, and slowly drink her coffee light with extra sugar. The manager would come over and lean across the table, his paisley tie dragging on the cloth.

"You cadging coffee off us?" he'd ask with a glint of a smile.

"You know me," she'd say. "I *pay*," and she'd look up at him with an out-of-the-clouds smile, so you could see her overlapping teeth and her dimples.

The manager would linger, saying, "You know I'm not supposed to" and "Why should I let *you* stay?" But he always did, and he always sat at a nearby table to trade words with her.

She was game, that's what I thought, and I could see why the manager couldn't stop talking to her. I couldn't either.

She liked to go out drinking, and she was always trying to get me to join her, to go with her to these places she liked. Maxwell's was one, I think. And there was this Texan place she talked about. But I never could, never would. Although I hadn't met the man I eventually married, my daughter and I had a semipermanent relationship with a man then, and there simply are limits.

Holly and I talked about getting our daughters together, but before that could happen, she decided to move to Tarrytown, to get her kid away from some bad crowd in the city. After that we kept in touch by postcard. She wrote that T-town was better. The cabs her company owned weren't so good, but she never had an empty car and usually she had more than one fare riding at a time. She said her daughter liked it up there too—more snow, more places to play. But then Holly wrote that she had started to look at the kids her kid was hanging with. Like mother, like daughter, she wrote, and she didn't want a pregnant preteen. So she moved again, this time to Poughkeepsie. Said she'd considered Kingston, but decided it was too close to Woodstock and who knew what Woodstock would lead to?

Last address I had for her was Troy. And in the card she sent from Troy, she wrote that she had her eye on smaller towns farther north: New Russia, Jericho, Swastika. I wrote back that if those were her only choices, I hoped she chose Jericho. Jericho was a place I'd go, I said and, imagining a woodsy vacation, suggested we'd visit sometime. But I never heard from her again.

Though I'd never do what she did, I understood. Anything to save your children from your errors. Of course, sometimes I think about Holly's daughter and wonder if she felt she was being punished for her mother's mistakes. And then I wonder if she had heard she was her mother's big mistake. That's the kind of thing that can slip out of your mouth if you're not careful, the kind of thing you say when your kid is ungrateful, unrecognizing of your sacrifice.

My child was born when I was seventeen. I named her Maria—for Maria in *West Side Story*. I wanted to name her for the girl who feels pretty. And then again, in my family there are lots of Mar-women, my mother Marian, my mother's mother Marie, my father's mother Margaret Ruth, and then me, Margaret. I wrote Grandmother Marie that Maria was named for her, but it wasn't true. I just liked saying Maria. As the song says, I liked saying it loud and soft. But when she started to walk, when I found myself all the time having to tell her no, having to stop her from pulling irons off the ironing board, to get her to stop opening drawers and emptying them, to stop reaching for whatever was just beyond reach, I shortened her name, first to Marie, then to Mar, and finally to M. Just that, M.

One day some guy I dated for about two minutes called her Emmy. And that was it. She was Emmy forever, as if she'd been waiting for that name, as if it fit her the way the glass slipper fit Cinderella. She was little then, not talking or anything yet. Still, she knew it was her name. She would listen to me read *The Wizard of Oz*, and she'd want me to read some parts over and over, turning the pages back herself and making me begin again. She especially liked everything that happened before the cyclone—the aunt, the uncle, the farm in Kansas. What pleased her most, I think, was the name Auntie Em. She'd hear it and grin and point her finger at the book.

"Em," I'd say to please her. "Em," my voice as warm and promising as I could make it. "Auntie *Em*. Just like you, little girl, just like Emmy."

FIVE

This was late summer, when I met Mrs. Rumsen, and we kept hearing predictions on the radio of rain that would drown the fires. But we were close to Halloween before we got any, and that was just a drizzle that only made the brush grow thicker. I know it was October because the back room was full of black-cat and fairy-princess costumes my mother was making. A bolt of blue satinette she left on the windowsill got wet in the short rain, and my mother had to cut around the water spots to make the fluffy skirts other mothers had ordered.

You could tell the season by what my mother sewed. Cheerleader and song-girl dresses all summer. And then in the early spring my mother did long-sleeved formal gowns for the women's-club balls, the doctors' wives and the lawyers'. You knew it was March because of the long sleeves ("They think their arms are flabby right here," my mother said, poking my underarm with a yardstick) and because of the colors the women chose—beige, copper, black, pearl gray. "Grown-up colors," my mother said. Except sometimes among all the dark and muted March gowns there'd be one with ruffles and flounces of pink taffeta and chiffon.

"For a woman who forgot she grew up," my mother said and smiled as much as the pins in her mouth would let her. She said it as if she disapproved, but I'm not sure she really did. "It's all dress-up, isn't it?" she said once. "Dress-up for girls, dress-up for women."

Late spring, prom dresses filled the room, and around Christmas whatever she stitched, blazers for the men's a cappella choir or a dress for the maid of honor, was some shade of red or green. Only the wed-

34

ding gowns didn't give the season away. She was always at work on one, cutting satin and sibonne, ordering organdy. She even did her own beadwork. All hours of the night she'd peer through her black-framed glasses and stitch seed pearls into fields of lace.

It was time-consuming, time-devouring work, and I once heard my father say, "No shotgun weddings for your customers."

"Guess not," my mother replied, as she slipped a pearl onto her bead needle and watched it spin down the thread.

Her work filled the back room with nests of thread and lint. Her pinking shears left dusty half-moons and wedges on the cutting table, and the floor was scattered with pins she paid us to collect. She said her work filled her hands but not her mind, or not the important parts of her mind. I guess I looked surprised when she said that because she glanced toward me and said, "What? You don't think I have a mind?"

She was cutting blue satinette, and I was folding laundry, at home and listening to her because I was grounded again.

"Well, here's a piece of it. You think this love stuff is so exciting now? It gets boring quick. So get yourself married first. And get yourself through school before that."

I watched as she cut quarter-circles of fairy-princess skirt, her pinking shears ripping their zigzag way through the fabric. She pushed the scraps aside, and I said, "I don't think anything is so exciting."

"Oh? That's not how it looks to me."

We talked like that all the time. It seemed like every other week I was grounded for staying out too late or for just not listening. But Bruce and I found ways to see each other. My mother out of the house, I'd call him, just to show I could. I listened to his voice thinned by the phone. Behind him I could hear the din of the shop, the echo of drilling and grinding, and the sound of all the other men talking over the noise around them. I would talk as quietly as I could and hang up quickly when I heard the back door open.

"Who're you talking to, Maggie?" my mother would call out.

I'd move away from the hall phone, try to act like I was just coming out of the bathroom. "No one, Mom," I'd say, leaning out of the door and fake-drying my hands on a towel.

"Oh? Is that right, Alison?" my mother would say to my sister, who was usually dressing her dolls or sitting at the kitchen table and drawing on her sketch pad with colored pencils.

Alison would look up from the doll half-clothed in its latest outfit, a little silver trapeze artist's tutu or a Parisian painter's smock, and give my mom one of her earnest looks. "No one was on the phone, Mommy." And then my sister would look down the hall and cast her pure gaze on me. "No one."

Getting out at night was easy, really. I'd just wait until Dad fell asleep on the couch in front of the television, his head buried in one of the cushions, his hand dangling on the floor, and then I'd go out the door, tiptoeing in my high heels, and walk to the end of the grove, where I'd see Bruce, his profile low in the car. Sometimes I'd tap on the window to wake him; other times I'd open the far door and slide in next to him, hardly rouse him at all, and just sleep there in the car with him.

When things were at their worst with me and my family, I just walked out the front door in plain sight of everyone, my mother and father, of course, but also my sister and brother and all the neighbors, and didn't come home until nearly morning, when my father would yell at me and ground me even longer.

"Looks like we have two kids," Bruce said in my ear.

I took in our reflection in the blue-tinted mirror behind the popcorn. We were out on a date, a real one when I wasn't grounded. It was early November, the night before Homecoming, and I'd been dutiful and for two weeks come home every day on time, just so we could go out this weekend. There was nothing my father could really do except smile and shake Bruce's hand and ask him how he thought the L.A. Rams were doing. So there we were at the movies, my brother and Tommy Dawson and Bruce and me. I looked at the four of us in the mirror behind the machine for popcorn and the fountain for Coke. Framed in red velvet drapes tied back with gold braid, we did seem to be a family. A family in a snapshot, a step picture maybe, with Bruce the tallest, dark eyes and dark hair slick as chrome over his ears, followed by me, my mouth chalky pink and my hair blond streaks, then Jamie, sandy-haired and skinny-necked from growing, and Tommy Dawson, whose family had moved here for his father's job in aerospace.

"Thanks for the non-compliment. I mean, I'm only two years older than these kids."

But the dark of the red drapes and the blue of the mirror did disguise our ages. We did look like a photo some woman might pull from her wallet.

"The future?" Bruce said quietly, and staring into my reflection, he smiled his sweet smile and touched the back of my neck. He was taller than me (have I mentioned that?), and not every boy was. So when he touched my neck and spoke softly, I had to look up, and just doing that, just lifting my face, was like offering myself to him. For a kiss, if for nothing else.

"The future?"

"Don't you think we have one?" he asked.

What is it people say? That before death your entire life passes before your eyes? Right then, my life went fast forward. What passed before my eyes was the station wagon I'd use to cart the boys around and the dog, our collie, in the back, anxious to leap out as soon as I drove up to our house in the country. I don't know why I imagined a house in the country, but I did, a house surrounded by fields. And I had this funny, satisfied feeling, imagining all this, as though I—the problem of me—had been solved. The future? I thought. Does he mean it?

Just then the girl behind the counter asked Bruce to pay for the Milk Duds and Jujubes and large popcorn and the four Cokes, and I did not have to answer him. She had the sort of spit curls I could never get my hair to hold. A white tag on her red uniform said Darlene, and in the hollow of her breastbone a gold cross dangled. Bruce pulled his wallet from his hip pocket and handed her a five curved in the shape of his body.

"Your change, sir." Darlene held out the money until Bruce took it from her hand, and then she smiled right into his eyes, as if I weren't there at all or as if my being there didn't count. I couldn't have felt plainer. So I grabbed Bruce's arm with one hand and passed out Milk Duds, Jujubes, and napkins with the other, the way my mother would have done it.

Inside the theater, we kept it up, sitting like a family with me in the middle handing out food.

"Your Coke, Tommy."

"Thank you, ma'am."

"Straw?"

"Yes, please. Thank you."

Who knows what movie we saw that night. It was never the movie that mattered. It was being out. It was the excuse for later, one of maybe three excuses, football and bowling being the other two. We saw movies with Hayley Mills and Julie Andrews, cartoon movies with spotted dogs and runaway brooms, movies with Tony Curtis, Dick Van Dyke, Jack

Lemmon. Some movies we lied to go to see. We said we were going bowling and went instead to see *The Days of Wine and Roses*. We said we were going to a party at Carol's and went to see that movie about the Englishman, about the illegit son who eats and eats until he is soaked in juice and fat. We even had to lie to see *West Side Story*, and I'm not sure why since I'd seen it with my parents when I was younger. It seemed there were some movies you couldn't watch sitting next to a boy. Watching that one sitting next to Bruce, I thought that he looked like Riff, and then I wondered who I was more like. I don't mean who I looked like. I looked like Anybodys. I mean who I was inside. I wanted to be Maria, but I'm sure I was Anita.

The scrollwork on the walls was painted dull gold, and the seats were made of rough stuff, of upholstery velvet or horsehair or something. On the stage were heavy drapes, deep red or purple, and when they moved their fringe slid across the floor and you could smell the dust, in the drapes and in the seats around you. You could smell it on top of the smell of popcorn and spilled Coke and Dr. Pepper.

I can tell you that at the movies I always wanted to be in the last row, back there with the bad girls. Bruce was politer than that. He liked to sit farther front, where he'd hold my hand or touch my neck under my hair. I liked that, but still I wanted to be near the lovers. I swear you could hear the blouses unbuttoning. You could hear the clatter of a zipper slowly opening. You could hear hair tousling and clothes rumpling, straps sliding off shoulders and hooks being freed from their eyes. If you sat far enough back, you could hear the sound of lipstick sticking, of stockings snagging and runs running. And later, between features, you could stand in the ladies' and watch the girls from the back row paint red polish over the holes in their hose. *I'd* stand in the ladies' and watch those girls tease their hair and spray it thick.

"Hey, gingersnap, what you staring at?"

"Who's staring?" And then I'd tease my own hair, lean across the sink and make my mouth into that little Oh! so I could touch up my lips just the way they did.

What it is about teenage sex is you're always waiting to be discovered, by the usher in the aisle, his flashlight swinging up and down the rows, or by headlights sweeping over you in a parked car or by some cop, rapping on the window and shining a nosy light in on you. It was that, it was light. At the movies the screen would brighten to daylight, a shot of an open sky, and suddenly all those couples who had somehow straddled armrests and twined around each other on the horsehair seats, they would fall back into their separate chairs. They would tug at their blouses or shirts and wipe at their smeared faces until the screen darkened again.

Whatever movie we saw that night, we didn't sit in the rear. We sat somewhere in the middle, for the sake of Tommy and my brother. And whatever was playing, we stayed for both features, because it was late by the time we dropped my brother and Tommy back home. Through the front window we could see my parents, my mother sitting by the lamp, her sewing on her lap, and my father leaning elbows into knees, toward the glow of the television.

"Thank you very much for taking us to the movies," Tommy said.

"Why, hey," Bruce said. "My pleasure."

"You're not coming in, Mag?" Jamie asked.

I ignored my brother and dug in my purse for the high-heeled shoes.

"Don't you know I've got to feed your sister?" Bruce said.

"She eat a lot?"

"Tons and tons," I said.

"Better watch your plate, Bruce," my brother said.

"Hey, I already let the biggest appetite out of the car," Bruce said, but by that time Jamie was halfway down the drive and disappearing in the dark.

We did stop somewhere, but not to eat. There was this bar off Azusa Road where Bruce could get a drink and me a Coke and where no one minded if we drank from each other's glass. We sat there with nothing much to say. Bruce played with the coaster, and under the table I slid my feet between his. He was still wearing his dark green work jacket, *Gallagher* in red script on the pocket, and we talked machine-shop talk, until he said, "I want a job like Tommy's father," resting his arms on the table and studying the cardboard disk. "Just so you know."

"Yeah," I said and thought *future*.

"Something in aerospace," he said and glanced up at me, then down again at the coaster in his hands. "Something with Lockheed."

The way he kept glancing at me and then looking away, I thought he was going to ask me to marry him. I really thought that.

"So I've been thinking about enlisting," he said, and it surprised me not because he hadn't talked about it, but because I was so lost in thinking about myself.

"You're what?"

"Well, yeah, I've decided to go ahead and do it." He pressed the coaster between his palms. "Before, you know, I get a letter that doesn't give me any choice."

"So if you have a choice, you'll do navy, right?"

That's what I'd heard other guys tell him, do the navy.

"Don't think so," he said.

"So what then?"

He shrugged, as if he didn't want to tell me. "Whatever comes up."

"Enlisting doesn't just come up."

"My brother liked it okay." He tried to roll the coaster like a wheel, but it wobbled and fell each time he set it rolling. "Want to go Sunday out to Riverside and watch the cars?"

I took the coaster from his hands, and then I took his beer.

"Okay," he said, "so I think it'll be army."

There was something about all this I was supposed to understand, something about how the army was better than the navy or even the marines. Something about the democracy of it all and the manliness. I'd heard Bruce discuss this with other guys, but I didn't understand. Later, I mean months later, Bruce wrote me from somewhere in Georgia that he would be airborne, and I didn't understand why he'd joined the army to be airborne.

Before we left, I stepped into the gals', where I whitened my lips and fixed my eyeliner and slid off my bra, pulling it through my sleeves and over my elbows and stuffing it into my purse, because that was another thing about sex back then. It was all about straps and buttons, all about getting out of and into clothes. So the fewer, the better. When I returned, Bruce was standing there at the table, waiting for me. He was holding his money in one hand, as if he meant to pocket his change, and he was staring at an aquarium they had there in the bar. Orange and yellow fish, fish with bright stripes, moved like flames in the water. Shadows quivered over Bruce, as if he too were submerged. And then he saw me. "Hey, babe. Ready?"

"Where to?" he said in the car.

"Anywhere."

We headed up toward the San Gabriel Reservoir, taking the streets without lights when we could because they were better somehow, everyday trees and bushes disappearing into one another, gardens and landscaping flattened by the dark. We came from one of those dark roads back to the canyon road, the stretch of it that swings around the foothills before it climbs along the concrete reservoir. Just here a road veered off, past a cinder-block house with lights too bright and yellow, and I thought this was the back way to Mrs. Rumsen's place.

"Turn here," I said.

Bruce looked at me as if to say, "You know what you're doing?"

"Go on."

When the car hit the ruts and the jack rattled in the trunk, he said, "Hey, where're you taking me?"

"You'll see."

Leaves clattered against the car, and a branch snapped. "I better see."

"It's just that property my dad's been talking about. You know."

"You want to look at that now?"

"Come on. The dark is nice."

I don't know what I expected. Maybe that Mrs. Rumsen would be up, waiting for us, that she would be drinking vodka and soda and listening to *The King and I.* But we drove up to a dark house, all the windows blank, the only lights our headlights shining into cinder block and dirt.

"So what's to see?" Bruce asked.

"Mrs. Rumsen. The woman who lives here," and I thought of her and her broken window. I thought she might be lying in bed waiting for kids like us to break another.

"Looks like the woman who lives here is asleep. Or out."

"You got something to write on? I'll leave her a message."

He didn't have any paper. But I found an old Spanish quiz in the bottom of my purse. I wrote: "Very late Saturday. Came by to see you with my boyfriend. Hope we didn't wake you. Maggie." I ran up the steps to slide it under her door, and somehow, touching the wooden frame, slipping the note over the jamb, I felt like a thief. I tried to move quietly to the bottom of the stairs, but my heels kept catching between the boards. And then I saw rectangles of light on the ground and my shadow against the dirt and knew that Mrs. Rum had turned on the lights in the main room.

She did not shout "Who's there?" and did not come to the door. Instead I heard music, not *The King and I,* but *Oklahoma!* "Oak!" I could hear, "la-homa, where the wind . . ." loud enough I could make out the words. With the music, I felt less like a thief, so I tried knocking on Mrs. Rum's door.

"Yes?" I heard.

"It's me, Mrs. Rumsen."

"Me?"

"Me Maggie."

She opened the wooden door and seemed to recognize me through the screen.

"I just didn't want you to worry. Thought you should know it was me, not someone else."

"Are you okay?"

I told her I was. "I was just going to show you Bruce."

She spread her arms, and I could see the scarlet lining of her kimono. "Well, I'm not exactly dressed. Not for strangers."

I smiled and took off the shoe that kept sticking in the boards. "We don't have to come in. You can see him from here."

"That's him?" she asked. "Sitting in the car?"

I told her it was, and she opened the door and watched him sitting alone in his Chevy, staring into the dark sycamores and canyon oaks. Seeming to feel her stare, he looked up, and she waved, wide, like a beauty queen. "I suppose he deserves you," she said. "He's not a runaround guy?"

"I don't know. I don't think so."

She glanced his way again. "No, he looks like a settle-down guy." She pushed her hair back, but it still clung like sleep around her face. "Luck. Didn't I say?"

I felt transparent when she looked at me, as if she could see the bare skin beneath my blouse and slip.

"Nice looking but true." She stepped inside and closed the screen door. "That's what you want, you know. Good enough looks but true." She pressed her hand against the screen. "So say hello and good night for me," and she waited until I'd slid across the seat next to Bruce before she shut the wooden door and switched the lights off.

Bruce left me at the edge of the grove and drove away with his head-lights out. I watched his Chevy disappear, and with my heels stuffed in my purse, I walked barefoot. The grass squished under my feet, my purse swung from my arm, and inside the night-light glowed. And then I heard the voices from the back bedroom, from their room.

My brother was sitting in his pajamas on the front step, the front door ajar behind him. I passed him and walked into the house to check on my sister. Inside, their voices were loud, muted only by their bedroom door. Thinking a light would tell them I was home, I felt my way in the dark down the hall to my sister's room and found her lying on her bed, dressed in a blue fairy costume some mother had ordered but never picked up. The skirt fluffed around her, but in the dark the blue satinette looked silvery as metal.

I sat on the bed. "You okay?"

A door slammed open, and my father said, "We really lose if I quit working on that house now. So why don't you go ahead and put a rope around my throat? You might as well," and my mother cried, "What do you think you're doing to *me*?"

"Leave me alone," my sister said and rolled away from me.

"You want me to stay with you?"

"Go away."

Her arms were wedged under her and her face pressed into her pillow. I pulled a cover over her, but she kicked it off, so I stroked her back before I left and joined my brother on the front step. My brother and I had done this before, vacated the house to make room for our parents' fights.

"Sorry I let Bruce go," I said. "We could have sat in his car."

My brother nodded and tilted his head. We listened to *them* in the living room. "It's all your fault," my mother was crying.

"It's hers," my brother said and hugged his knees into him.

I tried to listen for their exact words. I thought if I could hear them exactly, I could walk in and say the right thing, the quieting words. But as soon as I'd catch something like "Because I owe them, that's why," their voices would tumble all over each other, and I'd have no idea what they were saying.

"It's cold," I said because the damp had worked its way through my clothes. My brother agreed, and without needing to talk about it (we'd done it so often), we stood and walked across to the orange trees, where the weeds were rough on our feet. Jamie climbed a tree and sat in the cleft of the branches. Like all the boys in junior high, even Tommy Dawson, my brother stole cigarettes, from the drugstore or from the parents of friends. Sometimes he even bought packs from vending machines, if no one was looking. That night, he took from his pajama pocket a pack he'd filched somewhere, I don't know where exactly, and tapped out the matches he'd tucked into the cellophane. Just for something to do until *they* were quiet, we smoked in the trees.

Jamie reached for a higher branch. "Look," he said and chinned himself, his cigarette wobbly in his mouth. He hung there, his bare feet swimming in the air until we heard the sound of cracking and he dropped back down to the V of the branches.

"Bruce is going to enlist," I said.

"He's going to go fight somewhere?" my brother asked.

"I guess." I hadn't thought beyond boot camp. "But maybe not. When his brother was in, he went to Germany. That's what Bruce says."

"Think he wants to fight?"

"I don't know. Would you?"

"Maybe," my brother said. "But I bet Bruce would. He's like that."

My brother was right, so I didn't answer. Our parents' voices rose. Words like *goddamn* and *that's what you always say* came through clearly. A light filled a window in the Dawson house across the street.

"You going to marry Bruce?"

I could hear Bruce slip the words "The future?" quietly into my ear and couldn't think what to tell my brother. "Yes." I didn't know I was going to say it. "Yes, I just might."

"Mom says you will," my brother said. "She says you'll have to."

"What does Mom know?" I said, angry she'd say that.

We could hear their voices clearly again, my father asking why she was doing this to him. The cold made me shiver as I listened for her answer. She seemed to have none. All I could hear was the sound of her crying as she moved from the kitchen to the hall to the front room. There was the odor of asphalt in the air. My father had just laid a new surface on the drive, and it seemed like the dark made the smell of tar stronger.

My brother tried the branches hand over hand, testing. He swung himself out, holding by one hand and braced by one foot. "Stubborn disease," he said. "Root rot. That's what she's got."

I nodded because that's what I thought too.

My brother hoisted himself up in the crackling branches and hung from both knees, his pajama top hanging loose around his face. "Look at me," he said, as if proud he could smoke upside down.

"Kid stuff," I said.

My mother's voice cut through my father's. *It's always your family and your business before our family.* I looked around at the lights that had come on in the house beyond the Dawsons' and wished that every-thing—my brother and me, the house, the trees, them inside—I wished that everything would shrink to nothing. Shrink so small you could slap your hand and make it disappear.

SIX

My brother lay on the floor, my bedspread rumpled over him. He had slept the night in my room, and now he was awake, one hand behind his head, the other crushing his almost empty pack of stolen cigarettes.

"Mom sees that . . ." I said quietly.

He slanted his eyes at me, and I shut up. We could hear my mother in the kitchen, hear her running water into some deep container. We could hear my father dropping his boots on the floor by his bed. In the bathroom my sister sang little songs as she brushed her teeth and combed her hair. Between gushes of water, I could hear "Let's do Ali. Ali bali bo pali . . ." My father walked down the hall, and my brother and I waited, sure my father would call out for Jamie, sure he would say, "Where's Jim Two? You coming with me today, Jim Two?"

But he passed my room and stopped at the bathroom instead. "Banana fanana face," he said to Alison, "you going to spend all day in the bathroom?" Then he moved on, whistling "Fe fi mo mali."

We heard the back door open and my father say, "Bye, Marian."

"What?" my mother said, and what I thought was a spoon hit the counter. "Just like that?"

"I have work to do."

"It's just throwaway work," she said. "You might as well stand on a corner and hand out money."

"I'm going, Marian."

"Good. Go."

We heard the first slam and then the second, meaning Mom had followed Dad out of the house, dish towel in hand. We could imagine what she was doing. Walking toward my father's truck, trying to get him to listen. Slapping the dish towel over her shoulder, slapping it against the hood as our father turned his face away and backed the truck down the drive.

My brother sat up and shook the last cigarette from his pack.

"Come on, Jamie," I said. "Not in my room. She'll yell at me, not you."

He seemed to consider what I said before he tore the cigarette in two and shredded the insides into a pile on the floor.

Alison knocked, then said through the door, "Mom says wake up, lazy head, and get dressed."

"Why?" I said.

"Just because, that's why."

"Well, here come my lazy, slumbering teens," Mom said when Jamie and I finally came into the kitchen. She was standing by the sink combing Alison's hair with a comb she kept wetting under the faucet. Alison had dressed in blue and pink, and Mom tied a pink ribbon in her hair. Mom herself had dressed specially, wearing a wool skirt she'd made and a sweater that faintly gave off the mothball odor of unopened drawers. On the counter were the black pumps she must have just polished. She even wore Grandmother Marie's locket, and she'd made herself up, rouge on her cheeks and shadow over her eyes.

"Don't you have anything more presentable than that, Mag?" she asked me. "The print blouse maybe? And give Jimmy's trousers a quick press, would you? The ones hanging on the door."

I didn't question her. I plugged in the iron and changed my blouse while the iron warmed.

"When your sister's done, James, take off those jeans and put on your good trousers, you hear me?"

"Alison, be a good girl and go get Mommy's purse from the bedroom and the car keys from the dresser." Mom kicked off her tennis shoes and slipped on the black pumps.

"Maggie, I think it's time you practiced driving with me and not your father." She took her purse from Alison. "Give the keys to your sister, sweetie." To me, she said, "Go pull the car out. Let's see how well you do that."

When I didn't move, she said, "Go on, Mag."

"Don't you have to be in the car?"

"Not when it's on our property, I don't. Unless you plan to drive into the neighbor's yard. You don't, do you?"

"Sure, Mom, that's exactly what I plan to do," and I shut the door behind me.

It was a bright gray day, the smog sitting high so you could see most of the foothills nubby with chaparral and small stands of trees. The air was cool, but not so cool a sweater wouldn't do. It made me think of finding sycamore leaves at school and pressing them with a warm iron between sheets of wax paper that I would bring home to my mother so that she could pin them to her sewing room wall.

The car felt huge around me, huge and unmanageable. I had no sense how wide or long it was or how much it would turn as I turned the wheel. Without my father there, I almost forgot how to do anything, how to put the keys in the ignition, how to pump the gas twice, how to turn the wheel and back out. I jerked the car back onto the grass.

"Guess you want to ruin my lawn," Mom said as she climbed in the front seat. "Come on. Don't be afraid," she said to Alison and Jamie. "Maggie's not going to kill us, just the grass."

As I pulled the carload of us into the street, I drove over the curb.

"Well," my mother said as the car bumped down. "Grace herself. It's hell on the tires, you know."

"Sorry," I said, and then after a pause I thought showed I felt good and guilty, "Where to?"

"You know the way to that property your father bought in the canyon?"

"Not really," I half lied.

"Haven't you driven up there with your father?"

I glanced at her and saw her mouth was set, her lips carefully made up.

"No," I said, because a whole lie seemed only right.

"Well, most likely I'll remember. Turn left at the end of the street."

She sat back and crossed her legs, but she kept one hand on the dash the whole way. I tried to drive ignorantly, waiting for her to tell me where and when to turn. We even drove up the wrong canyon road, toward freshly leveled land and the skeletons of new houses, and for a moment I hoped my mother would give up and send us home. But she said, "Go back, go back," and soon found the right canyon road. As we neared the turnoff to Mrs. Rum's, I waited for my mother to tell me to turn, but we had passed the drive before she said, "Stop here," and I pulled the car into the shade of a sycamore.

Saying nothing, she climbed out and walked back to Mrs. Rum's turnoff. She paced circles in front of the drive, her heels rapping against the pavement, before she walked toward the house and stood very still, one hand shading her eyes as she stared into the brush. When she returned to the car, she sat silently and looked at her lap.

"Why don't we go home, Mom?" I tried, and she looked at me as if she were threading a needle through my eyes.

"What are we doing here anyway?" Jamie asked.

She turned around and examined him.

"Fix your collar," she said, and when the careless tug he gave his shirt didn't satisfy her, she sat up on her knees, leaned over the seat, and fixed it herself, tugging it this way and that and buttoning the top button of his shirt.

"Look at me, Alison," she said, and my sister put down her doll and looked at my mother. Mom licked her thumb and wiped at a smudge that only she could see on Alison's face. Then she brushed at the fine hair, the wispy hair that always escaped her combing. That done, she settled herself back into her seat and flipped down the visor mirror to judge the faults of her own appearance.

"That drive back there," she said, "that's the drive to that property your father bought, isn't it? The one where that Mrs. Rumsen is staying, no?"

"I don't know for sure, Mom. We only came here that once." I can't say what I thought my lie hid. "With you, before Dad bought it."

She gave me another needling look. "Well, I haven't seen it in a long time, and it's supposed to be all fixed up. So back up and let's go see what's up the drive."

I backed uneasily down the canyon road, dirt under half the car, pavement under the other, and turned onto the drive.

"Good thing he graveled it," I said.

My mother said nothing, so I continued, "It's the cheapest way to do a drive."

"You sound just like your father. And slow down. You're driving like your father too."

"So what do you want?" I said. "For me to act like you?"

"Just drive, Maggie," my mother said. Gravel pinged the bottom of the car, and branches of scrub oak brushed against the sides. "Remember I've lived longer than you have."

My dad's green truck was pulled up near Mrs. Rumsen's black station wagon. Three men, Dad's skeleton crew, worked on the cabin. But my Dad made four, and the house seemed covered with men. One painted the porch white, and two worked on the house itself, painting it gray. My father straddled the shallow-sloped roof and hammered nails into new shingles. And when he saw us, he sat upright and waved the hammer at us.

Alison was first out of the car, crying "Daddy," and he called back, "Hey, Banana Fanana Face."

"Hey James the Second," he called to my brother; then he slid himself backward across the roof and dropped down to the ladder, a tenfooter that didn't quite reach the eaves. He pressed the ladder away from the house, let it totter there on its two legs, while he held his arms wide over his head.

My mother watched him through the windshield, then she got out of the car and shouted, "Jim Harris, what do you think you're doing?" just as my father let the ladder lean back toward the house.

"Saying hello to my kids." He leaped to the ground, then walked over and put an arm around her. "Saying hello to you."

"What kind of hello was that?" She seemed shrunken, as if fear had deflated her.

"I wouldn't hurt myself," he said to her. "Promise."

One of my father's crew, a man named Clifford who stood on a crate and painted the porch railings, said, "Really, Mrs. Harris, he was just a few feet off the ground. He could have jumped from the roof and not broken anything important."

That made the rest of the crew laugh and seemed to calm my mother. She looked around her now, at Alison holding her doll by one leg and Jamie digging his toes into the sandy dirt. She looked at the house, half fresh gray and half peeling green, the porch going from pine to white.

"Think it'll sell now?" my father asked.

She considered the house, the way she considered a dress on a form. "You're painting the trim white? You're putting up shutters?"

"Yes, I guess. I hadn't thought about it."

"Like a beach house. Would you buy a landlocked beach house?"

"If you were selling it," he said, "I sure would."

"Jim," she said and shook her head slowly. "Sometimes I don't know what to do with you."

"Me neither."

"Where's Evelyn?" she asked.

"Somewhere in there," and he nodded toward the house.

My mother looked at us again. "Maggie, get out of the car, and Alison, put that doll away." And then, because she could not climb the still fresh paint of the porch, she walked toward the back of the house. Alison ran after her and grabbed her hand, but when Jamie and I didn't follow, my mother stopped and stared at us. "Coming?"

I don't know what my mother thought she'd see. Maybe she expected the Mrs. Rumsen I'd seen in the photos, the Mrs. Rumsen of Hollywood, of chiffon and satin skirts. I don't think she could have expected the small woman I had met with her dyed red hair and her rings loose on her fingers. She couldn't have expected the Mrs. Rumsen we saw as we came around the corner of the house. She squatted, dust and dirt on her trousers, and she was scooping a weedy plant into a flowerpot. She glanced up at us and swiped at a trickle of sweat on her face. "I was wondering if I'd ever get a chance to see you."

"Well, I wanted to see what Jim was doing to this place, where he was spending his money." My mother swept at her hair and looked away from Mrs. Rumsen, squinting into the smoggy sun.

"I don't think he's spending much here," Mrs. Rum said, brushing at her hands.

My mother eyed the fresh white of the eaves and the door behind Mrs. Rumsen. The trim around the window my father had reglazed was freshly painted, and working ticklishly through the paint on the beam under the eaves was a spider. At first I thought it would sink, that it would walk through the paint the way I might walk through fresh concrete. But as I watched, I saw that it seemed to glide tracklessly. "Anything is probably too much for this place," my mother said.

"Hey, kiddos," my father called as he came around from out front. "What do you think?"

"I've been here before," Alison said.

"That so?" my father said.

"She just means when you brought us all here that time before, when it wasn't ours and was for sale," Jamie said.

"Still is for sale," my mother said, slashing a look at my father.

"No, I don't mean that time before when it smelled," Alison said. "I mean another time, I've been here."

"You have not," Jamie said. "You don't know what you're talking about."

50

"Yes, I do," she said, quietly and slowly.

The spider drifted downward, its thread invisible in the shadow of the eaves.

"Maybe I brought you here when I had some work to do."

"I came here at night, in my sleep."

"You mean you came here in your dreams, Ali?" my mother said.

"No, I do not," she said, turning her small face toward Mom.

"Maybe this just reminds you of something."

Alison gazed at Mom. "Nothing reminds me of anything," she said, as though she were older than all of us.

"Hey, come here, little Cinderella," my father said.

"What?" She walked right over when he called her any of those fairy tale names.

"You're getting pretty big," he said, "but not so big I can't throw you over my shoulder just like this," and he hoisted her up and let her slide down his back, grabbing her ankles before she could fall. She shrieked like a small bird and grabbed at his shirt. "You want down, Alison?" He let her bounce against his back. "You want down, you better not back-talk your mother."

"I won't," she said. "I won't."

"You promise?"

She grunted yes, and he crouched down so she could slide off him hands first into the dirt. She stood, her dusty hands loose at her sides, and he grabbed her chin. "None of my kids is a smart aleck, are they?"

Alison shook her head no, and we were all quiet.

"So. The whole family is here," Mrs. Rumsen said.

"Looks like it." My mother rested a hand on Jamie's back and put an arm around me, her fingers pressing into that soft place on my neck. "Our kids. Alison, Jamie, Maggie. Maggie you remember maybe. From when she was a baby."

Mrs. Rumsen nodded. "And now she's almost grown. God, am I getting old quick."

Something in my mother seemed to relax. She let go of my neck and knitted her fingers into my hair, but she didn't say any of those things I expected her to. She didn't say, "Oh, but you haven't aged, Evelyn." Except, of course, my mother wasn't calling Mrs. Rum Evelyn; she wasn't calling her anything at all.

"Seem like good kids," Mrs. Rum said. "Must have had a good mother."

The spider had spun itself down, and now it lighted in the flyaway strands of Mrs. Rum's hair. She shook her head and brushed at it, and the spider ascended, weightless.

"Well, of course, they've had a good mother," my father said. Alison still stood within grabbing distance of him, her shirt untucked, the pink ribbon untied and dangling. He corralled her toward Jamie and me. "Yeah, I think they're a pretty good lot."

Mrs. Rum smiled a sad smile, a smile of regret or of thanks, the sort of smile I'd give an old high school friend today if she said to me, "I heard you got married and had four boys you were forever carting around in a station wagon," describing exactly the life I don't have.

"What do you think, Marian?" my father asked. "The place looks good, doesn't it?"

She turned toward him and paused, as if ordering the words she wanted in the back of her mind. "Well . . ." she started to say, her hands lifting in commentary.

"You see?" he said and leaned forward to kiss her mouth. "Didn't I tell you you'd think it was a good idea once I fixed the place up?"

SEVEN

There they are, Joan and Charlie," Bruce said.

It was Homecoming night, and we had driven first to the football field, where the bleachers were already crowded with kids my age or younger, kids Bruce didn't know. So we left and drove to the parks where we thought we might find our friends. The better parks for hanging out were the parks in the better neighborhoods. We tried Arcadia Park and Lacy Park, and at Silver Park, in a neighborhood of winding streets lined with globe lamps, we saw a familiar car in the lot and pulled in next to it.

"Think they're in the playground," Bruce said.

It was getting dark and the grass and trees were fading into black and gray. There was a stretch of lawn and all around thick trees that hid the park from the neighborhood, drooping eucalyptus and big firs poking up like steeples. Lights were just coming on in the houses around the park, and windows glowed through the branches of the evergreens. I looked toward the beach of swings and slides and saw Joan's white teased-up hair. She stood on the carousel, that lazy susan meant for children, and Charlie sat on its edge, pushing them slowly around with his feet. Bruce had brought a six of beer with us, and when we joined them, we offered them some.

Joan drank from her can and said, "Look." We turned and looked back over the park, past our cars in the lot, past the roofs of the neighborhood and the lights shining down on the streets, to the rise of bleachers around the high school football field. It sounded as if the game was just beginning. Those huge kliegs were on, and it looked as if the field were an open box of light.

"The thing is going to lift off," Charlie said. "Like some kind of spaceship."

In the park, globe lights lit a path near the parking lot, but the rest was dark, so everything—the trees and the swings and flagpole—seemed grainy and out of focus.

"We could make our own light," I said. "We could start a fire or something."

"We could," Bruce said.

"Why not?" Charlie said.

Joan said, "I *like* fires."

More of the crowd found us. They arrived in pairs, Stan and Carol, Mike and Susan, the guys pulling their cars in near ours. Trekking across the grass, they looked tiny and complete, not like the unformed person I knew I was but like miniature adults with homes and mortgages, the guys in jeans and button-down shirts, the girls with their teased blond flips and the V-neck cardigans they'd borrowed from their boyfriends. Gradually, we filled up the playground. We sat on the swings and horizontals, perched on the monkey bars and climbed the jungle gym. One of us kept the carousel moving, and we clustered there drinking, enjoying the sweet dizziness, or we broke into pairs as though this were a serious make-out party. One couple moved into the narrow shadow of the slide and kissed, the girl's back pressed against the ladder. Another wandered hand-in-hand across the grass and blended into the shadows of the trees. We could hear cheers coming from the game and the deep sound of bass drums and horns.

"Homecoming," Joan said with so much disgust, she sounded wistful.

Someone, maybe it was Stan, said, "So who's coming home? Anyone we know?"

"Can't come home if you haven't left," Bruce said. He sat on the lip of the slide, turning his beer can in his hands. I sat behind him, my toes under his seat, my knees against his back.

"That's a major thought," Joan said.

"Anyone we know left yet?" Charlie asked.

"Me," Bruce said. "I'm gone."

"He didn't mean anyone drunk yet," Joan said.

A cheer rose from the bleachers before Bruce said, "No, I didn't either."

"You're full of it, Bru," Mike said.

"Yeah, you're right." He leaned back, so my knees pressed into the hollows between his bones. "But, seriously, I am going away."

"Where to?" Joan asked.

"I don't know. Georgia, Germany. One of those places."

"Shit," Stan said. "The guy's enlisting. Is that it?"

"Smart guy," Bruce said.

"What?" Charlie said. "They couldn't draft you soon enough?"

Bruce shrugged. "Why wait?"

"That's cracked," Stan said. "Why enlist?"

"You get more choices," Bruce said.

"Oh, yeah?" Charlie said. "You really think they're going to give you a choice?"

We were all quiet for a while. We listened to the band's fight song. The sounds of the neighborhood—a door shutting, a radio playing, the shout of a child—drifted into the park, and we could smell smoke from a fireplace fire. Across the sloping grass, two gray figures came out of the trees and walked toward us. One of the guys let out a whistle, and Joan said, "Mike and Suz are coming back."

At first, I could scarcely tell one body from the other. But as they neared us, I saw how they folded together and crossed their arms around each other.

"Hey," Bruce called to Mike.

"Hey," Mike answered and brushed at pine needles caught in his hair.

"Come on over," Bruce said. "Party here is good as the one over there."

Mike laughed and pulled Suz closer to him. She was the one who said, "Maggie think so?"

Bruce dropped his head back on my knees, so I knew I should say something. "Yes, I think so."

"See?" Bruce said. "Besides, you got to help me." He stood. "You or Charlie. Time to move."

"Yeah?" Mike said.

"Yeah," Charlie said.

Charlie and Bruce walked across the park to a picnic table under the trees and returned rolling a heavy barrel trash can half full of newspaper and picnic leftovers. The three of them lifted it onto the carousel.

"Needs more stuff," Bruce said, "more kindling."

Charlie regarded Bruce a moment before he said quietly, "Anything you say, sarge."

We split up, the girls going one way, the guys another, and searched in the dark for paper bags, candy wrappers, newsprint. I tagged along after Joan and Carol, but they waited for me, something they'd never done before. They were never rude, but they had ways of reminding me that I was younger. They shared a can of hair spray, puffing clouds of scented mist at their hair. They traded a cigarette, passing it back and forth under the stall in the ladies'. They licked their fingers and wiped flecks of mascara off each other's cheeks.

"So are you and Bruce," Carol said, "are you two engaged now?"

I reached for something that turned out to be newsprint. "Not any more than we were before."

"You're just steadies, right?" Joan said.

"I guess," I said. "That's what his ring means, doesn't it?"

Carol and Joan glanced at each other.

"He's got great eyes, you know," Joan said.

"Yeah, so?" I said.

"You're going to let him go without getting some kind of promise?" Carol asked.

"I don't know. I haven't thought about it."

"I'd get something," Joan said, "an engagement ring or something."

"Me too," said Carol. "You don't want him going after anybody else."

"I don't think he would," I said.

Carol giggled, and Joan turned around and glared at me as if she were angry.

"Maybe you're young," Joan said, "or maybe you're just dumb."

She said *dumb* as if it were a pit and I stood on its edge.

They walked ahead of me, and Carol turned to say, "She just means you can't be naive, you know?" before they moved farther into the trees.

I didn't follow. I groped the ground where I was for leaves and pine needles. Just beyond the park, a woman's voice called "Sam-my" over and over. "Sam-my, Sam-my." From the shadow of the trees, I could hear Joan saying, "I don't believe it. I don't believe we're doing this." Across the park, the guys laughed and shouted. "Hey, Bru," I heard someone say and turned to see Bruce leap up and shake a branch down. "Good God, girl." I heard Joan nearing me again. "I always knew there was a reason I didn't join the Girl Scouts."

"Too much work," Carol said.

"I'll say," Joan said and squinted at me. "You're not crying, are you?"

"Of course not," I lied.

"It's just this," she said. "If you put out, be sure you get something back and be sure you don't get caught."

I asked her how I would do that, and Joan rolled her eyes and put her hands on her hips. "Didn't I say you were dumb?" she said and stalked away.

We dropped our sticks and twigs, our handfuls of newspaper and leaves into the barrel and waited for the others, sand sifting into our shoes. Joan struck a match, the flame whitening her face except for her eyeliner and the streak of green creasing into her lids. She lit up a cigarette, then shook each abandoned beer can until she found one that wasn't empty and was about to knock it back, when she looked at me and asked, "Want some?"

"No, that's okay."

"Carol?"

Carol shook her head, and Joan polished off the can. Suz and a girl they called Markie returned and dropped a few paper sacks into the barrel, and then the guys came running across the grass. They hollered, carrying zigzaggy branches in their hands. Charlie and Bruce broke the branches, stomping on them and cracking them across their knees. They stomped and cracked and filled the barrel until branches crowded over the top and crumpled newspaper clung to the twigs like Christmas ornaments. Charlie pulled out his matches, but Joan stopped him.

"Let me." She took the cigarette from her mouth and held its lit end against the newsprint. The paper burned away in a circle, the cindery edges looking as if they'd never catch, and then Joan blew on them and the flames flew up and everything caught, the way it does with fire running loose over the surface of things.

"Let's go to that game," Bruce said.

We sat in the car, watching the fire burn down, making sure burning paper didn't float off and light the trees. Once it got going, the fire had burned hot and big and the guys had each grabbed a handle on the carousel and run around and around, so the fire orbited in the playground. Across the park we heard someone call, "Fire!" and we all ran to our cars. The others drove off, saying they'd meet in the canyon, but

Bruce refused. Someone's got to see we don't burn down the neighborhood, he said. When I asked if we'd get caught, he said, "If the fire department comes, we'll hear the sirens in good time." So now we watched the low flames curling over the top as the barrel rotated slowly on the carousel.

"You don't want to go up the canyon with Charlie and Joan?"

"Not especially," he said.

I thought about it, about the teachers and the cheerleaders who would be there at the game. I imagined Bruce nodding slightly at the kids I knew, shaking hands with former teachers and telling them what he was doing with his life. I thought about the silent regard of Charlie and Mike. That was something I could see in the firelight, in the way they looked at Bruce when he wasn't looking at them. So I said, "Sure, let's go to the game," and I moved his ring from my right hand to my left.

But once we got there, we didn't climb the bleachers. We slipped through a gap in the chain-link fence and watched from below, except of course we couldn't see much. We could see the cheerleaders, the girls in dresses my mother had made, black corduroy with orange gores and lining that flashed every time the girls kicked their legs or tossed their pom-poms overhead. We could see the mascot with his papier-mâché tiger's head and his striped tail diaper-pinned to his jeans and watch the way he pulled a big yellow handkerchief from his pocket and wiped his papier-mâché eye every time the team lost yards. We could see the backs of the benched football team and the feet of the people above us, but we could hardly see the game.

"A night to remember," Bruce said laughing and took a can of beer from inside his jacket.

Popcorn and streamers drifted down from above, and spilled Coke dripped. We leaned into the cold steel and traded sips from the beer, trying to guess what was going on in the game by the actions of the cheerleaders and the mascot. Once it seemed as if everyone above us stood and stomped their feet hard as they could. The sound rang in the struts, and we had to cover each other's ears. We curled into each other, laughing as the cheerleaders jumped in and out of our slatted view. We stood close, our hands under each other's shirts, my skin prickling to his touch. Bruce slipped his hand up my back and pinched my bra loose, and I waited for Homecoming-night air up my shirt and for what Bruce would do next.

He removed his hand and pulled a pint of vodka from a pocket inside his jacket. I gave him a what're-you-doing look, and he shrugged and poured the vodka into the half-empty beer can. "Hey, I'm allowed," he said. "I'm going in Monday."

"This week?"

He nodded. "My brother says they're escalating and I should count on going in the day I show up."

He had disentangled his arm from me to mix the beer and vodka, but my hand was still under his shirt. I felt foolish, in the disarray of our clothes. His body, his skin, felt to me the way my brother's would feel, childlike and familiar. But pulled up close to him, I smelled the sweat in his clothes, and on the hand I kept on his back, I wore his ring, the bubble of string and nail polish denting his skin. He told me that stuff about enlisting and the army escalating, and I wrapped my arm around his waist and squeezed. I dug the ring into him.

"Hey," he said, "that hurts."

We got in the car and drove, Bruce taking streets I didn't recognize. We drove past houses that looked familiar but weren't, one-story stucco houses like I lived in, small fake adobes like Bruce had lived in. We drove through neighborhoods full of these houses. And then the houses stopped and the apartments began, tall gardenless blocks, one after the other, windows checkering each side.

Sometimes Bruce and I drove to overlooks in the foothills. We'd sit on the edge, our legs hanging down into the air as if into water, and we'd look out at our section of L.A. We'd gaze at the strings of lights marking streets and freeways and spot the wavering blue of backyard pools with underwater lights. We'd find what we guessed was my house and his house, and we'd figure out where our friends' houses had to be. And then, by counting lights, we'd try to count the houses of the people we didn't know, until we couldn't count anymore, because except for the black patch of the cemetery the lights went on and on, the distant ones tumbling out of order and disappearing in a hazy horizon.

Looking at that endless patchwork of houses and neighborhoods, I'd never thought about how many people there were in the world. I had never pictured them all, at home late at night, the shells of their houses suddenly removed. I had never pictured row after row of them lying in their beds. But driving past those apartments with their TV-blue and yellow windows, that's exactly what I did. I pictured all of them, the skeletons of their apartments removed, standing on top of each other's heads. I thought, how can there be so many people? And then I thought, every single one of them is the end of one act of sex, every single one of us is two people doing it in the dark.

"This is where my brother lives," Bruce said, pulling up in front of one of those buildings.

"We're going to see your brother?"

"Not exactly," he said and put his hand on the back of my neck. "We're going to see where my brother lives."

I understood. I understood perfectly, but I said, "Why visit him when he's not home?"

Bruce got out and came around to my side before he answered me. "Tim's got a new stereo he said we can listen to," and he opened the door for me, even offered me his hand. I took it and stepped out over the stream in the gutter. He continued to hold my hand as we walked up the concrete path to the center court of the building. I remembered that I hadn't changed into my heels, that they were making lumps in my purse, but as we crossed the courtyard, I kept thinking that all the tenants, all the products of sex, were standing behind their front-room windows watching us. And I couldn't bring myself to slip on the heels. I wore Keds, soft-soled, quiet-walking Keds, and they brought me silently into that apartment building with Bruce.

He led me to the stairs, and both of us nearly tripped on a tricycle some child had left at the bottom. "Don't you wish you were five again?" Bruce said and pushed the trike aside. "Don't you wish all you had to do all day was play?"

"I'm not sure I do anything else."

"Oh yeah?" He laughed as we watched the tricycle roll away, as if a ghost child rode it. It stopped only when it crashed into the building. Bruce said, "Five would be just fine with me."

Five would never have been fine with me, so I said, "That's too old," and we laughed some more and walked up the stairs. But what I think was on my mind was that at five I already had an inkling of sex. At five I had sat with my girlfriends on the concrete landing of the building where we lived. I had sat there in my cotton jumpsuit, the kind with the ruffles around the tops of the legs, and waited for my best friend to trickle her fingers inside my thighs. At five my girlfriends and I already knew there was more to come.

"Here it is," Bruce said at the top of the stairs.

I hung back while he searched for the lights. Inside, the place smelled of Lysol and dirty socks and leftover tuna casserole. The place smelled like a boy lived there, and when Bruce turned on the light, I saw it looked that way too. There was one lamp that Mrs. Gallagher must have given Bruce's brother, and a beige couch that might have come from their den. A pink chenille spread hung over the curtain rod in the front room. But that was it—no rugs, no pictures, not even posters, just a stereo, an open suitcase affair with speakers hinged to a turntable, sitting on the floor. A jar of purple and orange flowers was balanced on top of the speakers.

"Tim's new stereo?" I asked.

"Yeah," Bruce said from the kitchenette.

The one light he'd turned on was an office lamp, sitting on the counter between the kitchen and the front room. Near it stood another jar of flowers. Bruce came out of the room with a bottle and two glasses.

"I don't think I can drink any more."

"Me neither, or not usually," he said. "But nothing's usual."

"No, it's not."

I should have been thinking about what going into the army might mean. I should have been thinking about boot camp, because even I had heard about boot camp. I should have at least thought about everything he'd told me, about basic training and A.I.T. and fourteen-day leaves. Instead I thought about us in the car, about us under the bleachers and us on the couch where we were sitting right then and how all of that would end.

"Hey, don't cry. It's not as bad as that. Really. Nothing's going to happen."

I hadn't thought anything would happen, not to Bruce, anyway. That I could be so expertly selfish made me cry more.

"Look, if you want me to take you home," he said, "it's okay."

I didn't want him to take me home. We had tucked in our shirts and buttoned our buttons so we could leave that football game, and now I wanted them all undone again. I wanted his hand under my blouse, his hands up my skirt. I just plain wanted, so I said, "No, don't take me home," and I stopped crying, because who wants to kiss a crying girl?

Things were normal for a while. We stayed quiet. Neither of us spoke. Neither of us put a record on that stereo, both of us ignoring our excuse for being there. Finally Bruce twisted the cap off the bottle of sparkling something or other. "Best I could do," he said and filled our glasses. "We're alone."

"Yeah," I admitted and then drank the sparkling whatever because I realized that being alone scared me. It's no secret you can want and not want in one breath, so I won't pretend that I wanted to do back to him the things I had to do. Even today when women tell me, as they sometimes do, that they like men's penises, that they like the taste and feel of them, I don't quite believe them. My friend Holly, for instance, the cabdriver who kept moving north, said to me, "You don't like that? You don't think that's fun? Maybe you need the Holly handbook on how to do it." But I didn't believe it was fun or that her instructions could help. I mean, that thing inside your mouth, that sometimes leaky thing inside your mouth, surrounded by your tongue and the teeth you must remember not to bite with. The stuff we did in the car, I didn't even like reaching in under his elastic waistband, the awkward way you have to slip your hand in. And the way it felt—it was not like the skin on any other part of his body, not like his arm or the back of his knees or the palm of his hand or the soft place under his chin or his thin and kissable mouth. The way it seemed to me was almost rubbery, like something I'd never really want to touch.

Later, when I was trying to raise my daughter on my own and still having a hard time just getting by and paying rent, I took a job dancing in clubs in Jersey. I remember one time a man standing right in front of my nine square feet of stage and yelling at me. He was an ordinary looking man, brown hair going gray, a plaid shirt and brown slacks. He wore a decent enough watch and a wedding band. I mean, he was no derelict. But he stood by the stage and watched me dancing in not too many clothes, the whole time yelling what foul things women are. "Bunch of smelly cunts, all of you," he said. "You're nothing but rotting meat down there. That's right, rotting dog meat."

Everyone in the bar turned to listen to him. But no one stopped him. No one told him to be quiet, none of the men and none of the women. I was embarrassed to the bottom of me. I wanted to swallow myself up and disappear, but I just kept dancing. I was getting paid, and in a way I understood. Still, he didn't stop. Even when I worked up the nerve to bend down and say, "What makes you think your penis is so pretty?" he raved on as if I hadn't said a word. He piped down only when some man he must have known walked into the bar, slapped him on the back, and said, "How you been, Ben?"

So about Bruce, it was hard for me to touch him, and I haven't even gotten to the aftereffects, the what-might-happens. What might happen is your mother might call you a tramp and she wouldn't be lying. Your father might say you're nothing but a whore and he'd probably be right. And you might be sitting there in the kitchen listening to them yell about their embarrassment before family and friends. You might be sitting there growing heavier by the minute, your skin going waxy with zits. You might be expelled from school with nothing to do but sit on a wooden chair and listen to *them* while responsibility bloomed in your lap.

When Bruce and I got as far as real sex, I didn't even like to reach down and touch him and show him where. That was too much, as if doing that meant I was willingly doing these things, and besides I didn't really know where *where* was myself. But I did do it, because of what he did to me, what he made me feel with his mouth on my breasts and his hands anywhere. I did touch him and I did show him where. And one other thing: Maybe I didn't like to touch it, but once we got that far, I did like him in me, and he seemed to like that too, and when he came home on fourteen-day leave, I found I liked it more, him in me, the hairy parts of us crunched together.

"I'm hoping," Bruce said, "you won't see anyone else while I'm gone. I'm hoping we'll go on like we are, being steadies." He took a drink from his glass, and I watched his Annette Funicello eyes look everywhere but at me.

"I'll have more money when I get out, you know." He set his glass down, but he kept his hands to himself. "So then we can, maybe we can, who knows how things will be then. Except you might wait. Maybe."

I watched him and figured he was scared too, scared we were alone where no one could shine a light in the window and tell us to stop. So I moved close to him, slid over and pushed the what-might-happens off the couch and started on his buttons, figuring he would catch up on mine.

"Hey," he said. "Hey, we've got a bed. We've got a bedroom."

He made me stand up and walked me in there, into Tim's room. The sheets on the bed were fresh. On the windowsills, on the dresser, were jars of those purple and orange flowers, and on the nightstand sat one white candle in a glass candlestick holder. I knew Bruce had done all that, made up the bed and put the flowers out. I knew it was Bruce who'd sprayed the place with Lysol. It had to have been him. It's funny what I didn't know then: A guy who makes the bed is a real catch.

"So this doesn't mean I don't respect you," he said.

"I know that," I said, not sure I did but too overwhelmed to say anything more.

I don't remember that either of us had such a great time that night. I mean, it's one thing to come in each other's hands in the backseat of a car. But it's another to really find your way around a body. Sex that night was all thumbs and hands and twisted underwear. Not exactly memorable, not yet. I do remember, though, the popcorn that fell out of our clothes and the flowers in the peanut butter jars and the pictures on Tim's wall, pictures of airplanes, of fighter jets. They were the planes he worked on at Lockheed, I think.

EIGHT

Chess and my father bought a house together when I was nine or ten. It might have been the first time my father tried to be something other than a contractor, I'm not sure. "We're speculating," my father had said when I asked why we were moving into a house that wasn't really ours, that never would be ours. "This is a way for us to make more money," he said, "for me not to have to take so many jobs."

I learned later that Uncle Chess made most of the money off the deal because he had put most of the money in. But then, at that age, I did not know about families and money. I just knew that my father and my uncle had bought a big old house, and my father was going to make repairs and improvements, and we were going to live in it until it sold. Next year, my father and uncle bought another house together, but that one they never sold. That was the house on Homewood, the house where my mother still lives today.

The year we lived in that big old house Chess and my father renovated, my brother and sister and I were allowed to use only a few of its many rooms, the rooms that my father hadn't yet repaired and improved. Mom and Dad slept in what Mom called the guest room, and my brother and sister and I slept in what she called the library. At first the three of us curled up in sleeping bags and blankets on the floor, but later my father bought cots, three cots in a row, like a hospital ward or a dormitory. Dark wooden shelves covered the walls around us, and on the shelves were our clothes and toys. The floor itself was a toy. My father had sanded it, and my mother had covered it with paper runners, and we were not allowed to wear our shoes in the house or to walk on anything but the runners. So when we walked, we slid down the paper in our stocking feet.

One wall of this room was glass, many small panes making one large window, and in the middle of all these panes were double glass doors that opened into a garden. A brick walk curved from the doors to a wrought-iron bench under a tree with tear-shaped leaves and white bark thin as paper. Behind the tree, a stone wall marked the end of the garden, and beyond the wall, the yellow-lit windows of another big house looked down on us. At night we could see the dark shapes of the people who lived in that house, people who belonged in this neighborhood. They passed the window, casting giant shadows on the grass, while Jamie and Alison and I watched from inside the double glass doors. The doors leaked in the rain and were sealed with heavy tape, and we were forbidden to open them. But sometimes we did. Sometimes we sneaked out while my parents were gone and ran around barefoot in our pajamas, playing the game of orphans.

"My parents died in a plane crash," one of us would say.

"My parents left me in a doghouse."

"I am the daughter of the Queen of England, and you are the Prince of the Moon."

We ran around the grass hiding from the wicked people who would send us to reform school and creating homes for ourselves in the corners of the garden. A large stone became a chair, a patch of moss a bed with pretend sheets we pulled up to our chins.

Afterwards, when we really did have to put ourselves to bed, I would stand on a chair, my bare feet still damp, and press the tape against the door and jamb. No curtains covered the windows, and I remember thinking that the people in the house on the other side of the wall could see me stretching up to seal the door, that they could see me in my nightgown, see the X I made against the glass. There was something exciting about that, that they could watch our life of dressing and undressing, of quarreling and running in the garden. They could see the puddling shapes we made as we curled and uncurled in our sleep.

Living in one room, we all had to go to bed at the same time, and being the oldest, I hated that. But if I complained, my father said, "Come on, sport. Do it for me. Do it for a year of mortgage-free living."

Angry, I would lie awake at night, doing nothing but making sure I didn't close my eyes until *they* were asleep. Lying in my cot, watching the crisscross of shadows on the papered floor, I'd think about a boy I liked, or maybe it wasn't that I liked him. Maybe it was just that I had noticed him. The boys at school—to me they were like so many stones in a shoebox, like rocks you might collect on a hike, sandy, dusty, none much different from the other. But one day as I left school, as I looked through the chain-link fence toward the asphalt playing field, I saw a boy I knew, this boy Alex who was a grade ahead of me, pull his shirt over his head so he could change into his league uniform. He had the same bare skin my brother had, the same skin I had, except it was his, his boy's skin, so I stopped to look. I stared, and the other boys, the boys with flecks of mica in their eyes, saw me staring. They laughed and punched Alex in the arm. They pointed their fingers and said, "Hey, she's looking at you." And before this boy Alex buttoned his shirt, he smiled at me, as if he were pleased I had seen him.

So I lay in my cot and wondered. What was it that men and women did with no clothes on? My walk-to-school friend had told me that *he* puts his thing in her thing. I told her *that* was a lie. The most ridiculous thing I'd ever heard, I said, mimicking my mother. I told her to go look in a mirror and she'd see, no way some boy could get his thing into her thing.

So I tried to guess what people really did. I imagined two indistinct people, and I undressed them. I took a ribbon from her hair and slipped a dress off her shoulders. At first it was a shirtwaist, one of the ones I wore to school, then it was a ballerina's tutu, and then a dress my mother wore sometimes, a dress with a layer of black lace over a brown skirt. The man I didn't know how to undress. I knew to untie a tie from his neck and to drop cufflinks from his loosened cuffs into his jacket pockets, but then I got stuck. So I said "poof" and their bodies were bare, and fleshy, and I wondered, what? What do these pink bodies do?

I tried them out in different positions. I imagined them sitting side by side, naked on the wrought-iron bench, the shadowy neighbors looking down into their laps from those yellow windows. But that wasn't enough, wasn't daring or exciting enough, so I sat them both in the upper branches of the tree, their bare bottoms pressing into the papery white bark and the neighbors looking up at their dangling legs, but that too wasn't enough. So then I put them where everyone could see; I put them on the flagpole at school, the two of them up there on that small globe that dotted the staff and everyone at school—the principal, my favorite teacher, the kindergartners—gazing up at them. That seemed embarrassing and exciting and scary, but it also seemed impossible. Did they face each other or face away? Did she stand on his shoulders or cling to his back? And if not, how could four feet fit on that small globe?

So I got rid of the flagpole and I got rid of the crowd, and I imagined the two of them just out there in the air. Flying naked. And that seemed better. That seemed closer to I didn't know what. I imagined they were water-skiers in the sky, harnesses strapped around their bare bodies so they could be pulled through the wake of a plane. The two of them hanging there, side by side, wind rushing and burning their skin red, the miniature world beneath them.

That was to me the most exciting thing two naked people could do, so that is what I settled on. Every night before I fell asleep, I'd strip these two people who weren't exactly me and this boy Alex, but who weren't exactly not me and this boy Alex either. I undressed us and strapped us to the airplane and even had us kiss as we were pulled through the sky, the scratchy wind tugging at our hair, but it still wasn't exciting enough. The drone of the plane, the loud air in your ears and mouth, your eyes streaming salty tears that dried instantly and left your face cool and grainy, the tandem swaying of your bodies as the plane flew giant figure eights over Duarte, Temple City, Monrovia, Arcadia, Azusa, Van Nuys—and then what? What? Unable to think of anything else, I'd roll over and drag my finger along the shadows on the floor, the real sound of my brother shifting in his cot the last thing I heard before falling asleep.

NINE

*H*ey, it happened," Bruce said to me on the phone. "I got papers. They took me."

"That's great," I said and sat on the straight-backed chair near the hall phone. I could hear my father taking his end-of-the-day shower, hear the spray and feel steam filling the narrow corridor.

"I fly out tomorrow," he said. "God*damn*."

"Swell," I said. Outside, kids still played in the street. They called "Ollie ollie oxen free free free" to each other, and their skateboards rattled against the concrete.

"I can't believe it," Bruce said. "They said I was perfect. They said I was A-one."

"That's wonderful," I must have said.

"That's a joke," Bruce said. "You know, One-A, A-one."

"Yes, I know it's a joke. I smiled. You just couldn't see me." But I hadn't smiled at all.

"You wouldn't have believed it, Mag, all the yellow underwear," he said. "Everyone walking around holding their papers."

"No. I wouldn't have believed it."

My father walked out of the bathroom in his shorts, water beading his back.

"Hey, Mag," Bruce said. "Rev up your engines for me. Show some excitement. Okay?"

"I am," I said. "I am."

But I couldn't stand that he was so happy to leave, especially if it meant leaving me. I hated that he had made himself that much more important, and now he was going, just like that. And I suppose I hated that he had someplace to go and I didn't. Besides, I was sitting there in the chair, and sitting in a chair was different now.

That day, that Monday, when I'd come home from school, I'd seen my sister out riding her bike. She coasted down Colina Drive, her streamers whipping her knees. It looked like so much fun, I changed my clothes and took my brother's bike out of the garage. I wanted to pedal through the neighborhood, so I headed past the blackened orange trees first, but I hadn't ridden much more than a block before I had to walk the bike home. It hurt to sit on the seat.

"You don't sound it, Mag," Bruce said. Behind him I could hear music, his record player, I thought, and his sister saying something.

"I am. Honest. I'm happy for you."

"I'll come by late," he said. "My mom's making a big dinner. Baking a cake and all."

"That's great."

"She was sorry you couldn't come."

I was grounded, of course, for staying out so late Saturday.

"I'm sorry too." I loved dinners at their house. It was always a little awkward, me on my best behavior, but Mrs. Gallagher would sit at the table chatting, insisting we eat seconds. She seemed to like talking to us, even though we were just kids, asking us, for instance, what we thought of President Johnson or of the nuns who immolated themselves to protest Premier Ky. I let Bruce or his sister or, if he was there, his brother, Tim, answer because I did not want to repeat what my father said ("Damn crazy people!") and did not yet have a thought that was quite mine. But I liked that she asked at all. Her name was Betty, and Mr. Gallagher called her Betty Boop, though she looked nothing like the cartoon. Her waist was thick and her arms heavy and strong, and she had long dark hair streaked with gray, which she wore in a loose ponytail down her back. Still, Mr. Gallagher would kiss the top of her head and call her his Betty Boop, and she would glow like a lamp. All that on my mind, I said, "I'm really sorry my parents won't let me come."

"Me too," Bruce said.

My father put his head into the hallway. "You're not the only one who wants to use the phone."

"Yeah, Dad, I know."

"Maggie?" Bruce said. "What's wrong?"

"Just my father." I didn't have it in me to talk about the bike or the chair or about how I found myself in the bathroom a billion times a day. I didn't have it in me to tell him about the little prayers I said to myself, the ones that went "Let me bleed, let me bleed, let me bleed."

"So you'll come say good-bye?"

"Yes, of course I will."

And I did. My father asleep on the couch, I slipped out the front door and walked through the orange grove to where I knew Bruce would park. The grass was as dry as the trees and scratched against my legs as I walked. A quick tickle sent a ripple like fear up my back, and I brushed at what I thought was a spider. Then I saw Bruce and his blue Chevy, his head back against the seat. Even in the dark, the car seemed to shine, and I thought that he must have washed and waxed and polished it just for his induction. I tapped on the window and crawled in.

"Hey, babe," he said sleepily. "How you doing? How was your day?"

"Same as usual," I said and snugged myself up close to him.

And then we slept, or, I should say, Bruce slept. He slept an easy sleep, like a child, and as far as I could tell he fell into no pits in his dreams. It was the sleep of an exhausted boy, and I was scared to think that, to think of him as a boy, as a child I was responsible for. I sat wide awake, his head on my shoulder, and watched the way our neighborhood slept. Except for the flicker of television at my house, all the windows were black. The low slanting roofs seemed to suck up the darkness. The sky itself was gray and light, and the antennas stood out like hatch marks against it. I could see so much, and I could see it better, undistracted by color. The sidewalks smooth as pond water. The fence pickets delicately rough, the lampposts alert, as if they had stepped from a black-and-white cartoon and would dance back into it. If someone had asked, I might have told him that the best time to live in a place like Temple City or Duarte or Monrovia was after midnight.

Bruce woke after a while. "What do you think of your brand-new private?"

He touched the back of my neck, and I lifted my face to him the way I always did. I couldn't see him smiling, but I knew he was. If my heart were a hoop, he could have jumped right through it.

"Oh, I think he's just fine," I said, and then, because doing nothing was unbearable, we tried doing stuff right there in the front seat, tried doing the real stuff. We were all undone buttons and open shirts, my skirt bunched around my waist, his belt buckle making a slight sound, a sort of clink as it moved with our movement. We were just getting to the important stuff when we heard a sound in the street. We turned and saw a man approaching us swiftly down the center of the road.

"My *father*," I said.

We pulled apart, and I slid down as low as I could, pulling my clothes together. Bruce let his head drop back as if he were asleep, and we both sat so still we might have been holding our breath, until Bruce said, "Jesus H., what's he doing up at this hour?"

I wiggled up and watched the figure glide by: it was just my brother, out skateboarding in the dark.

SILK KNOTS

TEN

Marian

*E*verything about it was new. I am talking here about our first vacation, a week at the beach. There were other weeks and other vacations, but by then we were already old-timers. We knew our way around the dead-end and half-moon streets that bordered the beach. I could make my way to the Market Basket, and Jim could find the quiet bay at Corona del Mar and the Ferris wheel at Balboa, not to mention that by then I knew all the mothers who spent not just one but several weeks, whole summers even, with their children at the beach.

Later, I knew the trip by heart. I knew the orange groves and euca-lyptus breaks we passed and the canyon road that led to Highway 1. But the first time, it was just the three of us in our new used car with a map, an address, and a few directions the caretaker of the cottage had sent us in the mail.

We must have looked so fortunate, a young couple clearly married just after the war, a budding family on vacation. Jim drove, airplaning his hand out the window. I navigated as best I could, and the baby lay rest-lessly between us. I would have let her stretch out on the backseat, but we needed that space for the cartons we had packed, not that we had packed so much—a suitcase of clothes, diapers, a box of towels, the old chenille spread Jim's mother had handed down to us, and some staples we thought would be cheaper from home.

I did bring some work, a few skirts I would hem for my ladies. I'd been happy when Margaret was born to leave my job doing alterations in the bridal department, but since then I'd put up signs in the dry cleaners and was known at the better dress shops, and when our vaca-

75

tion rolled around, I had more work than I had time. But that didn't matter, as I needed something to do the days Jim wasn't there, because most days he wasn't.

We had two nights together that week. He drove the baby and me down to the cottage on a Sunday and spent that night and the following Saturday with us. In between, he spent the week doing a job his brother had landed. It's a measure of something—how much he wanted to be like every other family man—that Jim insisted we take this trip we could barely afford.

Somewhere I've got a picture of us that day. Jim smiles at the camera and holds up the baby, and she waves. Dressed in some gathered skirt and voile blouse that were fashionable then, I lean into Jim and look up at the two of them with the oddest expression on my face, my lips slightly puckered and my chin and cheeks dimpled all over. Like I've swallowed a moth or something.

It's a before picture, the way all pictures of young marrieds are. I can still see traces of the sputtering fight Jim and I had been trying to put out all morning. It was my fault, it always is. The drive had seemed to take hours, and it was hot, I was thirsty, the baby restless. All I wanted was to stop, find a ladies' room, and change Margaret. But Jim said, "Only way to make good time, Marian, is to keep on going."

He may have been right, but I was sitting with a fretful baby, directions I couldn't make sense of, and a map the wind kept blowing out of my hands. We got lost at least once, if not a dozen times, until Jim slammed his hands against the steering wheel, said Godamnitohell, and told me I was stupid. Why had he married me anyway? he said under his breath.

I didn't answer at first, just stared at the telephone poles stuck along the roadside like pins in an endless hem and at the slack running stitch of wires that seemed to pull us toward an end they never reached. Finally I said, "What did you say?"

"Why the hell did I marry you?"

"How should I know?"

"You can't even read a goddamn map."

"I'm so stupid, *you* read it," I said and tossed the map at him, gave it to the wind, really, which whipped it up and plastered it against the windshield. And there we were, doing at least sixty, neither of us able to see a damn thing on the road in front of us, and Margaret was, of course, crying.

All of which, I have to say, was good in the end, because once Jim ripped the map out of the way, he finally agreed to pull over and actually look at the thing himself, giving me a chance, at last, to change the baby, and as soon as I did, things got easier. Jim figured out where we were, Margaret fell asleep, and the air seemed to cool. Even the scenery changed. For miles, we had driven through a desert, first of endlessly pumping oil wells (those derricks that always made me think, ridiculously, of Paris and the Eiffel Tower) and later of small apartment buildings and empty, weed-grown lots. But after we stopped, the land turned dark, as if the soil were rich or wet, and passing on either side of us were herringbone rows of new green plants. The fields of new plants gave way after a time to orange groves, acres and acres of dark green trees parted by rows of towering eucalyptus, like parades of dappled gray giraffes.

In the photo, we're posed in front of the car, the used Caddie Jim had bought—or was buying—from his brother, a shiny black dome of a thing that, when I look at it now, I think only a mortician would drive. The photograph shows all three of us. Which is unusual, since Jim took most of the pictures back then.

But this time the caretaker—a woman my husband described as his mother's relation—took the photo for us. We had finally found our way to the place on Pearl Drive, and Jim had stopped by the caretaker's cottage to get the key and let her know we had arrived. I climbed out to stretch my legs and held Margaret on my hip. We were parked on a narrow scallop of a street that dipped down from the main road. Small cottages and bungalows painted seashore colors (azure, coral, white) crowded up on the beach side, while a patchwork of vine-covered fences and brick and concrete walls edged the far side of the street. The blue sky seemed to sizzle, and I closed my eyes and tilted my head back to the penetrating sun, my daughter's warm hands playing in my hair.

"Hello-oh," I heard someone almost sing.

Go away, I wanted to say.

"Hello," she said again, and Margaret patted my face. So I opened my eyes and took in this woman—Mrs. Rumsen, Jim had called her in the car; Evelyn, I heard him call her now—walking from the deep shade of her porch and across her small yard, her hand tucked into my husband's arm. She was a petite thing, dressed in crop top and capri pants, sunglasses and bandanna. Jim had told me she was a dancer, and she dressed the way I thought a dancer would, too young for her age.

"What a pleasure," she said and took me and Margaret in her arms, her sunglasses poking me and her lips leaving cool spots on my face. "I leave my lipstick wherever I go," she said, lightly rubbing my cheek. "But there's no trace of a kiss on me, is there?" and of course there wasn't since I saved rouge and lipstick for evening. "You're just a natural beauty, I guess," she said and smiled at Jim.

I touched my face where she had touched it and studied this woman, who, it occurred to me, was not just a distant relation of Jim's but my distant in-law as well. I studied her penciled brows and her hair, too deeply red, too evenly colored to be natural, and remembered what Jim had told me on the drive down: "They're not really married," he'd said. "So she's not really a Mrs."

He had stared hard at the highway, as if the road were suddenly icy or wet. "Oh?" I said and thought, Why? as I too stared at the stretch of highway.

"Of course, they might as well be," Jim had said in the car. "They've been together that long."

Might as well be, I thought as I examined Evelyn Rumsen on the street before her house, apparently examined her too plainly, because she plucked at her blouse and capri pants and said, "What? Is my slip showing?"

Jim laughed and cast me a look, and I'm sure I managed to smile. But what I thought was, Why? Every girl I knew then wanted to marry. At least I'm no caretaker, I thought. I'm a real owner, married, with a license to prove it.

"So where's John?" my husband asked.

"Working," she said. "Rehearsing at DiRoberti's. The Roberts let us use the studio on Sundays when there are no classes."

"Working on a Sunday?" he said.

Jim didn't really object to working on Sundays. He always said churchgoers were hypocrites, and he always said his own family were the most small-minded churchgoers.

"Even my industrious wife doesn't work on Sundays," he said.

"John's not working," Mrs. Rumsen said. "He's just listening to records. And trying not to bore himself by coming up with the same old step over and over."

"Thought that's what work was," Jim said. "Doing the same thing over and over."

"That's why I said he's not," Mrs. Rumsen said. "Working, I mean."

"Too bad I won't get to see him," Jim said.

"That's right." Mrs. Rumsen turned to my husband. "I almost forgot. You're only here tonight."

"I'll probably be back next Friday."

"But we want to see you," Mrs. Rumsen said. "So you'll come to dinner. Tonight."

"That's so nice of you," I said, "but we have to unpack and settle in."

I waited for Jim to agree, but he said, "Marian and I would love to come to dinner."

"What about Margaret?" I said, more to him than to her.

"We'll give her a bottle and put her down on our bed," Mrs. Rumsen said, waving the problem away like so much smoke in the air.

It was then, as I stood there fuming, that Mrs. Rumsen, the so-called Mrs. Rumsen, decided she had to take our picture.

"Hey, good idea," Jim said and leaned into the car to rummage for our camera.

"Oh, please, you don't have to," I said.

"Yes, I do," she said. "You'll regret it if I don't."

She backed away from us, taking a spot behind the white fence that fronted her cottage, and bowed her head over the fold-up viewfinder. "Okay, on three. Say, 'Squeeze the cheese, Louise.'"

Margaret laughed, and Jim said, "Squeeze," squeezing his daughter in his arms. And I began to say something I never quite said.

Our vacation. Our car. Our camera. Our baby.

I want to say we were rich. And we were in a way. Jim had come home safe and married me, and Korea and everything sad or dangerous in our lives was hidden in the future. When I think of it now, after all that's happened, I know that fortune was with us then, and I can scarcely believe the small jealousies and petty hurts that seemed so important. We had no money, of course. We scrimped the way everybody I knew did after the war. I counted my bobby pins each night to make sure I hadn't lost one and bought only the clothes and food I couldn't make cheaper myself. I can't even say we felt rich, although we should have, but I do think we felt that we were on our way. That someday we would be. Rich. I don't know why. Maybe because everyone else seemed to be on his way. Jim's brother, Chess. Jim's father. Even Mrs. Rumsen standing behind her white gate seemed to be on her way. ("Not my white gate," she later corrected me. "We just earn our rent by looking after the owner's property.")

That afternoon I think we felt especially rich. Our cottage had two bedrooms, even if the second was tiny, and a bay window with an ocean view that cataracts of ivy threatened to blind. The furniture was worn, but because it wasn't ours, I thought it distinguished, even historic, not threadbare. Breezes blew through the screens, rippling the leaves of the potted mints that sat on every broad windowsill. We unpacked quickly, and in the slatted afternoon light of our bedroom, Jim and I dressed to swim, then carried the chenille spread and the umbrella that came with the cottage down the long flights of damp steps that led to the beach, Margaret toddling between us until we tired of her bitty steps and Jim hoisted her onto his shoulders, saying, "Hold on to Daddy, sweetheart, just hold on."

We spent the rest of the day running in and out of the surf, lifting Margaret over the smallest incoming waves and waiting as the ruffle of water swished back past our ankles and buried our feet in sand. We warmed ourselves on the chenille spread, ate peaches and grapes, dug for sand crabs, dove through the waves, collected Margaret's first seashells, and by the time we climbed the stairs back to the cottage, we were much too sunburned to have supper with John and Evelyn Rumsen. Even Jim agreed.

"I'll go and tell her we're sorry but we can't make it."

"You don't think it's too late?" I said.

"She's family," he said. "She'll understand."

As I stood to go look in on Margaret, my skin stung in places it never had before. "What kind of mother am I?" I said.

"Good question," my husband said, although he knew the answer: Far better mother than my mother.

"Is not," I said back, but the screen door had already shut behind him.

Margaret was still asleep in the tiny second bedroom. I had put her down in the crib that made the rounds of the cottages Mrs. Rumsen looked after, and since my daughter didn't wake, removed her sandy jumper and left her naked, a diaper under her to protect the mattress.

Now I looked down and was frightened. Her bare bottom was so white, but the rest of her, even the creases behind her knees and the tender place at the back of her neck, was so red. I touched her forehead, warm and damp, and slipped her pacifier back into her mouth, then soaked and wrung a diaper in the sink and stretched it across her back. She shivered slightly, but didn't wake. And that scared me. Shouldn't she cry? Shouldn't she holler? Her sleep seemed heavy, as if I had poisoned her in the sun. Standing there in that shaded room, my daughter's breathing inaudible under the sound of the waves, I regretted what I'd said to my husband. I'd never be a better mother than my own, and that was a sorry admission.

"Sunburn?" I heard someone say and nearly jumped out of my own burnt skin.

"Didn't mean to frighten you," Mrs. Rumsen said. She leaned against the door frame, as if she might have been watching me for some time.

"Yes, sunburn," I said. "I can't believe she's sleeping. It's like she's in a coma."

"Everyone overdoes it the first day," Mrs. Rumsen said. "Be grateful she's sleeping. It's probably the least painful thing she could do."

"I hope so."

"I've seen kids do this," she said.

"You have children?"

"Well, no, I mean other people's children. Other cottage guests." She leaned over the crib and gazed dreamily down on my daughter. "She'll wake up stinging and fretful, you'll see. Then you can give her a bath of tea."

"That's supposed to be good for sunburn, isn't it?"

"Your mother never bathed you in tea?"

"My mother never let me sit in the sun."

"Tea just lifts the sting away," Mrs. Rumsen said and stroked my daughter's back.

The back door shut, and hearing men talking, I glanced over to Mrs. Rumsen, who said, "It's just them. My John and your husband."

"Ah," I said and cupped my hand around the back of Margaret's head, her flossy hair against my palm. Then we left her alone, the door ajar so I could hear her cry, and found Jim and John Rumsen sitting by the bay window, an open bottle of red wine on the table between them.

"Why, there you are, Evelyn," my husband said. "John thought we would find you here."

"I was worried when you and Marian didn't appear," Evelyn said, "so I came down to fetch you."

"They don't want to be fetched." John Rumsen leaned back in his chair, arms folded across his chest. "They say they're too burned to eat."

Evelyn laughed. "Well, I would prefer them raw," and my husband, ignoring the feeble joke, said, "No, really, we're so burned, we can't."

"But they have agreed to help us drink the wine," John Rumsen said.

"We have?" I glanced toward Jim.

"Won't you?" John Rumsen seemed wounded.

"Sure we will," Jim said.

"And look what I found." John Rumsen opened the silverware drawer. He pulled out a carmine box inscribed in gold and spilled the contents on the table, a scatter of black lacquered tiles with intricately carved backs, some overturned to reveal their pristine white dots. "Want to play a game or two?"

"Dominoes?" I laughed at the thought of it.

"Why not?" Jim said.

"Please, ladies, join us," and, seeing there were only three chairs at the table, John Rumsen pulled over the one overstuffed chair for looking out to sea, and I sank into its deep bottom. "I'll sit there, Marian. You won't be comfortable."

"But I like it here." Lost in the depths of the chair, I could not see the table easily, but I could see out the window, the rooftop of the next cottage down and the horizon where the sky burned yellow. And as it grew darker, I could see us and the room around us repeated in the glass, our reflections growing brighter throughout the evening.

Evelyn brought four juice glasses from the cupboard, and we all sat around the table drinking "vino," as she called it, and playing dominoes. We shuffled the black tiles and arranged them like small works of masonry before us, matching dots and winning and losing games as Jim totted up our scores, bending his head to his work like a farm boy.

Evelyn smoked and chatted as she played, ribbing the men and making small jokes, but John Rumsen played quietly. *Poise* is the word I want to use for him. I believe he was older than Evelyn by some fifteen years. Like Evelyn, he was short and trim and reminded me of my father in that regard. Unlike my father, he had an economical face, nothing too beautiful or luscious about it. His eyebrows arched steeply, and he had the tiniest cowlick so that, old as he was, there was something boyish, even clownlike, in his appearance.

"You dance?" he asked me as he added another tile to the pattern we were making on the table.

"Hardly. I've heard you do."

"Yes, we do." Evelyn tapped a cigarette from a stenciled leather case.

"They're quite a team," my husband offered.

"Oh, please," Evelyn said, "we're good enough to get by."

"We're not so bad," John said. "Much better than when we started. In fact, Evelyn couldn't dance at all when I met her."

"That's not true. I was working as a dancer when we met."

"We were extras," John Rumsen said to me. "That's all."

"Maybe we were. But I was dancing."

"They didn't pay you for dancing, did they?"

She sighed smoke and said, "No, they didn't."

"She didn't know her knees from her elbows, so I found her a teacher," John Rumsen said.

"I'd already found myself a teacher," she said.

"But I introduced you to mine. And she was better."

"She was Russian," Evelyn said to Jim and me.

"Exactly. *Better*," John Rumsen said.

"And then, a few months later, John asked me to dance with him, who knows why."

"She had a certain look, a look I could use."

"We had a certain look together."

"We still do," John Rumsen said. "We make a good team, Evelyn Night and Johnny Run. We started out in the old theaters, and now we've had a good run of the clubs. But after so many years we're considering retiring. Retiring to teach."

"That's what we're doing this summer. Trying out retirement."

"Well, we're teaching ballroom at DiRoberti's School of Ballet and Dance Arts. For Alice Roberts."

"That's Alicia DiRoberti to her pupils," Mrs. Rumsen said and blew a stream of smoke past her cheek.

"And it's not bad, teaching. Not a bad way to retire."

"Except John will never retire. He's already found employment on television."

John studied his glass and said, "Evelyn is impressed but I am not."

"Pooh," she said.

He looked up, apparently embarrassed, and said, "I don't *do* anything. I just put on a shirt and stand with one hand in my pocket, a pipe in the other, a satisfied smile on my face, while the camera pans and the host talks about the quality of the shirt."

"Sounds like a good deal to me," Jim said.

"Don't bet on it."

"We do have some club work coming up," Evelyn said. "That should make him happy."

"Here's something to make me happy," and John Rumsen played his last tile, a double blank.

"Chalk one up to Johnny," Evelyn said, and my husband nodded and tallied the dots on our remaining tiles.

"Rumsen," I said, looking at the names written on Jim's score pad. "That's your real name?"

"It is."

"But it's not mine," Evelyn said, pushing her tiles to the center of the table.

"Jim told me," I said.

"He did?" She glanced slantwise at my husband.

"Well, yes. Was that wrong?" I asked.

"Not at all," John Rumsen said. "It's just that people have not always been kind when they know."

"He's talking about my family," Jim said to me.

"Not just the Harrises. My family, too. And hotel clerks, landlords, even some booking agents and theater owners."

"Put down the violin, John," Evelyn said. "It's not so bad."

"Just bad enough she uses my name, but still refuses to marry me."

"I don't believe in marriage."

"Freethinker," he said, inclining his head toward her.

"What difference could it make now, after so long?" I asked her. "When you use his name anyway?"

"In my mind it makes a difference," she said as if daring me to say more.

"Oh" was all I said.

Jim stroked a tile absently and gazed at our reflection in the window, and John Rumsen winked at me, in mirth or complicity I don't know, and swallowed the last of his wine.

"More wine?" John Rumsen said.

"There's more?" I asked, as he refilled all our glasses.

"Jim and I didn't think one would be enough."

I glanced at my husband, catching his guilty grin. "Well, it wouldn't be, Marian. Didn't think two would be enough either."

"Oh, Jim." I tousled his hair as I went to check on Margaret between games. I knelt to turn on the night-light, then stood by the crib, breathing in the baby smell that had already begun to fill the room. The diaper I had stretched across her back was still damp, but no longer cool, so I removed it and hung it over the railing. And then I reached to touch her sweet skin but didn't, just let my hand hover over her body. Although I swear she was warm as an oven, she seemed calm, and I left her to sleep.

"Maggie's okay?" Evelyn asked me.

"Maggie? Yes, Margaret is fine."

We each slid seven more dominoes across the table for the next game and then we played and talked and drank, mindless of how much. (One glass, two. Three bottles. Four games, five, and then six, perhaps even eight.) Slowly our scores drifted higher, and by the time Evelyn's reached one hundred, making her the winner, the new moon had risen, a sparkling hoop embossed on the sky.

"What's my prize?" Evelyn asked.

"A dance with me," John Rumsen said.

"With you? But I dance with you *all* the time."

"Well, he is the best dancer here," Jim said.

"Better than me?" she said.

"Come on, Evelyn. You know what I mean."

"Better than *you*, you mean," she said and laughed.

"Well, heck, yes, better than me. Besides, Marian would love to see you dance."

"Yes," I said, "I would."

"Of course, we don't have any music but a radio," Jim said.

"Oh, music," Evelyn said. "Who needs music? It'd just wake the baby, anyway."

John Rumsen pulled back Evelyn's chair and offered his hand as if it were precious but not half so precious as she. "Shall we?"

"If I must," she said and pulled herself close to him.

My mother tried to teach me to dance. It is one of the many things she began but did not finish. It was important, she said, to know how to do such things. Elegance charmed people, she said, more than they cared to admit, and so she set aside one after-school afternoon a week. I cannot say I liked these lessons. My mother's sweaty palm against the small of my back, her turbulent voice with its emotional crosscurrents whispering needlessly in my ear *one*-two-three, *one*-two-three (who was there to hear her except me, and wasn't I meant to hear?), her soft body too close to me, and her liquor-sweet breath crossing my face as every street sound made her turn expectantly and peer out the window. For that was why she did all this, why she sat at the piano and played a few bars of a waltz or a one-step, why she drank her liquor down, tried to hide her glass behind my father's books, and sucked peppermints as we danced together on the living-room rug, so my father would return from his practice and, seeing us, say, "Why, just look at my two beautiful girls!"

You understand, I did not say, "I do not want to do this, Mother," because no matter how much I hated these lessons, my mother did not. It wasn't that she was happy trying to teach me to dance, but she was urgently bright, wearing her best shoes, her finest blouse, her favorite earrings, large pearls that hung like tears. "Now, isn't your mama pretty?" she would say. When she took my hands and showed me where a young lady places them when dancing, she seemed crazy with wishes, like a girl waiting for her birthday cake. I could not blow out the candle for her, and I feared what she might do if I did. I feared opening the door on a silent house and having to search for my mother room by room, knowing I might find her spilled anywhere, her legs limp and bent haphazard, one heavy-heeled shoe twisting off her foot like the head of a broken doll. Places I had found her? Curled on the braid rug between their two beds. Behind the commode in the bathroom. Slumped against the incinerator, the ash-covered bottle between her feet.

My mother must have taught me a few basics. She tried hard enough, she really did, explaining to me over and over that I was supposed to follow, to feel, in her hand on my back, her intentions.

"But I can't," I said the day she was trying to teach me to tango. "I don't know what you want."

"Yes, you do," she said, pressing her hand too firmly into the hollow of my back and turning against my inclination so that all I could do was fall into the next quick-quick-quick. "Besides, if we didn't turn, we'd have crashed into the bookcase."

And so for the rest of the lesson, I tried not to feel but to guess her intentions. If we don't turn here, we will collide with the wrought-iron lamp stand, fall into a heap on the sofa, or unpot the potted fern. If she didn't swing me around just now, we'd step into the fireplace and vanish up the flue.

My mother was saying, "Like this, Marian, like this," the day my father finally came home early enough to find us dancing. He wore his black hat, a fedora, I believe, and his camphor-scented overcoat over the gray suit my mother had deemed appropriate for a man of medicine, not that everyone agreed my father practiced medicine. His tie was removed and his collar loosened, the California winter not really cold enough for all those clothes.

"Is this what you do when I'm not home, Marie?" he said and hung his hat on the hat tree. "You teach Marian how to dance?"

"She *needs* to know how," my mother said.

"Does she?" he said.

"It is important," my mother said, "if she's to meet someone to marry."

This seemed to give my father pause. Without removing his coat, he sat down in a large chair I called the throne because of its erect back and its clawed wooden arms. He wrapped his hands around the claws and watched my mother urge me through slow, slow, quick-quick-quick.

"Elegance charms people," my mother said.

"Does it, Marie?" He glanced about the room, and I knew he was searching for the glass both my mother and I, each for our own reasons, did not want him to find.

"Yours charmed me," she said.

"Your mother finds me elegant," my father said, giving up his search and smiling at us. "What do you think of that, Marian?"

Well, of course, I thought my father was elegant. His dark hair slicked back, his heavy-lidded eyes that opened and closed slowly, luxuriously, the way velvet drapes ought to open and close. And his gentle hands. My mother called them his curing hands.

"Yes, you are elegant, Papa," I said.

"Well," he said, as though he relished the word. "Then we should teach her right, Marie."

"May I?" he said, and still in his heavy overcoat and his gray suit suitable to a man of medicine, he stood and held his two hands out to me.

And I went to him. I abandoned my mother. I left her standing by the fireplace, her skirt sagging and her good blouse awry so I could see the heavy satin straps of her undergarments cinching her soft shoulder. I took my father's hands, and we began to turn like children playing Pocketful of Posies, slowly, and then slowly faster and faster, the weight of my body securely counterweighted, the wings of his coat spreading behind him.

. . .

It is not my mother's fault that Jim and I can scarcely dance. And we can't. I have seen us, reflected in the plate-glass windows of his brother's home. We seem to bounce against the beat like bobbing dashboard figurines.

Evelyn and John looked nothing like that, of course. Even in that little room, on that uneven wooden floor, they danced as smoothly as water pours. I listened for a whispered count, but all I heard marking the downbeat was a cluck in someone's throat, his or hers, I couldn't tell. They moved together, small steps that took them forward and backward but never very far. And then the steps became more intricate. He swung her side to side, in wider and wider arcs, then pulled her close for a simple walk across the floor. Have I mentioned that he wore a sports shirt and trousers, that she wore pants and cork-heeled sandals, her short hair covered with a scarf knotted on top of her head? There was no dancer's camouflage, no wafting skirt, no shoulder-broadening jacket. Nothing to create illusion.

But what I remember is illusion. That music was playing, for instance, that their steps left a tracery on the floor and in the air around them. Well, that's foolishness, but that's what remains with me. At the end, they spun around each other and around the room, inscribing small circles inside a larger circle. That, at least, was my afterimage. It stunned me so, I didn't even realize they were finished until Jim began to clap, slowly and not too loudly, so he wouldn't wake the baby.

"That sure was something," he said.

"We've been working on that one," John Rumsen said.

"This is what you teach your pupils?" I asked.

"Oh, no," Evelyn said. "We teach them simple ballroom to start."

"Simple ballroom would be complicated enough for us," Jim said.

"Evelyn tells me you're quite proficient," John Rumsen said.

"At dancing?" Jim said. "You mean what we did back home? That wasn't much more than square dancing."

"I thought Evvie gave you basement lessons," John said. "Forbidden lessons, at that."

"Everything was forbidden in that household," Evelyn said. "Couldn't play cards, much less dance."

"Oh, well, she tried to show me how to waltz once or twice," Jim said. "Showed my brother Chess, too. He was the better student, I believe."

"He was *not*," Evelyn said. "He was just . . . older."

"Really," she said to me, "Jim was the most . . ."

I think she was about to say *graceful* or perhaps even *beautiful* but stopped herself because we all knew Jim would refuse to be those things. I might even have refused for him and insisted she meant *debonair* or *handsome*.

"Natural," she said. "The most natural dancer."

"What do *you* know?" Jim said. "You hardly knew a thing then yourself."

"And I still don't," she said. "Do I, John?"

Hands hidden in his pockets, John Rumsen was looking out the window, as if he didn't quite belong there. He turned his simple boy's face slowly back to us and said, "I'd say you know a step or two now, Evelyn. Why don't you teach Jim a few?"

"Well, yes, why don't I?" she said and turned to my husband as John Rumsen offered me his hand.

"I can't," I said.

"Of course you can," he said.

"But I can't, really," I said even as he pulled me from the chair, the wine making the room float and my face flush warmer.

John Rumsen may be the only stranger I have ever danced with. All my other partners I knew somehow—our neighbor Oscar Dawson, who danced a polka with me at their Christmas party, my father, and my husband when he was only my husband-to-be. I knew these men, or thought I did. I had listened to them, talked to them, taken their coats, and danced clumsily when asked. But John Rumsen? I had watched him sip wine and slide domino tiles across the table. If someone had quizzed me, had blindfolded me and asked me right then what I remembered, I would have said, "Less than I remember about the boy who bags my groceries."

All right, his arms. I might have remembered his muscular arms and the way he folded them together on the table between moves. But that is all, really all, I would have remembered. I thought of him as a stranger when he took my hand. When he put his palm on my hip (not my back), I thought he meant to guarantee ample space between us, space appropriate for strangers, and I was glad for that. He guided me through a box step, and though my skirt felt coarse against my burnt legs and my limbs seemed to radiate heat, dancing itself did not hurt. It was even soothing.

There was an awkwardness, of course. The unfamiliar size of his hand (smaller than Jim's), the height at which he held mine (lower than

Jim held it), the matter of knees and toes and will they crash? But the awkwardness was all mine. John Rumsen had every right to be impatient (but he wasn't) and every opportunity to make me feel inadequate to be his partner (but he didn't). Or he could have been cruelly charming, his grace a patina over his disdain. But he wasn't that either. He was lovely and friendly and steered me well, for I don't think I tripped once, or not so badly he couldn't cover for me.

Our steps must have been simple. How else could he have kept me from falling? I know that we did not crash into Jim and Evelyn, although we brushed past them once or twice. Call me a fool, but I understood then what pleasure there is in moving foot to foot in time with another body, in time with the music in your mind. Then John Rumsen did something more complicated. He pushed his hands against mine, so I stepped a step or two back, and then, perhaps because he pulled me lightly or perhaps because it is the natural law of things, I stepped a step or two forward.

"Good," he said quietly.

Good! I thought. He said I was good.

"Let's try *this*," he said.

This was a push away from him, so I released one hand before his pull turned me toward him again. And then he firmed his arm across my back and led me in easy rocking steps around the room. It was funny, how comfortable it felt, swaying gently around the room with John Rumsen. Though I thought I never would, I forgot about the baby. For that matter, I forgot about my husband. And when we stopped, when the silent music ceased and I could take in the room as a whole again—the window now moonless, the constellation of dominoes on the table, the small lamp with its flared shade and the one overstuffed chair for looking out to sea, the braid rug we had rolled and pushed to the side, the bright bare floor and John Rumsen and I standing on it—I could see my husband and Evelyn Rumsen standing just inside the door of my daughter's room. They stood shoulder to shoulder, their features grainy in the darkness, like eroding castles in the sand. Watching them, I found myself thinking of Jim and me undressing in the slatted afternoon light. I thought of a wave that tumbled me over and over against the sand and then of waking after a long sleep on the chenille spread, the umbrella's shade nowhere near me and the sun's heavy heat embracing me from behind. I thought of wedging myself between him and her, but John Rumsen interrupted by taking my hand and lifting it toward him with touching grace.

"Thank you, Marian," he said and bowed. As if I'd been raised to it, I curtsied and returned his thanks.

"How lovely," Evelyn said, and she and my husband applauded loudly, forgetful of the baby behind them.

"Encore?" John Rumsen said. He drew me toward him and swung me quickly around the room until I was dizzy all over again. I heard more applause, and then I felt my feet slide out from under me and my body tilt back. Although it nearly choked me, I let my head hang back, for I thought how dramatic I must look, my hair cascading toward the hard, bright floor. And I thought how delicious it was, this lightness of mind and body. So this is what it feels like. Somehow John Rumsen pulled me upright and, as if it were the next and most natural step, he kissed me quickly and lightly. I knew I should be ashamed and tell him so, but it was such a slight kiss, a mere courtesy. After the embroidery of steps, a final knot worked in silk. And I loved it. I was laughing when he let me go, and I bowed again, this time toward Evelyn and my husband so they would applaud for me once more. If I had been wiser, if my heart had been older, I would have laughed and then forgotten what I saw. But I wasn't wiser, and when I swung around to curtsy for Evelyn and my husband, I found they were kissing too, in the doorway to my daughter's bedroom, kissing as if it were midnight on New Year's Eve and they were, just for good measure, standing under the mistletoe.

CHRISTMAS

ELEVEN

Maggie

The day the Rumsen place burned down, I walked home from school alone because Bruce had left for basic. He was gone ten days, and I had marked those days on the same calendar they had given girls in P.E. to mark their periods, a mimeographed sheet covered with small purple grids, except I'd never bothered to mark mine. That meant the day of the fire I had to guess how far gone I was. Eleven days. That's what I thought as I walked home.

The walk was long, or maybe it just seemed long because I wasn't used to it. I was used to climbing into the car with Bruce and letting him drive me home. And the walk was quiet once I passed the other kids, and I always did pass them, catching the whispers and glances the girls my age slipped my way. Well, what did they know, I thought, what did those childish girls my age know about anything? What could they be but jealous, for didn't they want someone to want them the way Bruce wanted me? Didn't they? So I passed them, proud I knew secrets they didn't, and walked alone, not sure how I'd fill the hours Bruce used to fill.

The walk took me through town, a row of low buildings on Las Tunas. The Baskin-Robbins, the branch library (a trailer that was supposed to become a building someday), the Alpha Beta and Jerry's Liquors, the Minit Clean Dry Cleaners, the Good Guys Hardware where my father had an account, the Hillside Pharmacy and Gift Store where we bought our pens and notebooks and the gifts we gave at birthday parties and where guys in junior high bought St. Christopher medals for their girls.

• • •

The day Mrs. Rumsen's place burned down, I walked into the pharmacy, perhaps because it would fill some time, and headed straight for the jewelry counter, I don't know why. The St. Christophers hung from a rack, just the way I remembered them, silver chain after silver chain, and I gathered all the chains in one hand, the way I used to when every girl I knew had one and I wished some boy would give me one too. They felt like a heavy tassel and made me think of fringe whisking the stage at the movie theater. From each one hung a medallion—bloodred, forest green, midnight blue—colors so rich, I had to look away. That's when I saw, displayed beneath the glass, the rows of clear plastic boxes containing squares of foam and birthstone jewelry. There were gold chains with hearts and rings so small they wouldn't fit my baby finger. Set into each gold heart and ring were tiny pastel stones.

"Lovely, aren't they?" It was Mrs. Hill in her blue smock. She looked down at me over her half-glasses.

I nodded and said, "If someone, if my cousin, were pregnant now, what would her baby's birthstone be?"

"Your cousin?" Mrs. Hill repeated. "If she just got pregnant, I don't suppose she'd know it yet, but if she did, why, her baby'd likely be born," and here she counted on her fingers, "in August."

August. If I were eleven days gone, the baby'd be born in August.

"This," Mrs. Hill said and pointed to a ring with a green stone, "this is the stone for August."

The setting was a rose, the stone in the middle, and as if I wanted a baby, as if I wanted to be a mother before I was seventeen, I wanted to buy the ring. Then I had a foolish and scary thought: If I buy it, I'm gone for sure. So I turned again to the chains.

"Like you said, my cousin doesn't really know yet." I held out my left hand and searched for a medal the same shade of blue as the ring Bruce had given me. "Good match?"

"Very good match, indeed," Mrs. Hill said.

I laid my money on the glass counter and waited as Mrs. Hill wrapped the medal in tissue and put it in a box she sealed with tape. The medal knocked softly in my skirt pocket as I walked slowly through the pharmacy, searching for what I wasn't sure. I saw cough drops and nasal spray and Pertussin, canisters of boric acid, sanitary pads and Modess belts, boxes of Kleenex and cotton balls, sterile gauze, iodine in bottles, Mercurochrome, milk of magnesia. Mr. Hill nodded at me, his eyes cloudy blue and large behind thick glasses, and only half believing he could really see me, I smiled back, scanning the brown glass bottles behind him, examining the rows of small cardboard boxes. Stacked on a shelf were cartons of hot water bottles, the orange bladders pictured on the outside, and near them were plastic packages containing puffy sacks attached to long rubber tubes, whose purpose I was too scared to imagine.

"Help you?" Mr. Hill said from behind the pharmacy.

I breathed the tincture of medicine in the air, wishing I could name one thing that could help me, then shook my head no and left.

A bundle of ironing waited for me in the fridge, but I went to my room to study, or try to. Studying, ironing, spending time alone in my room, these are the things I did now that I could not ride with Bruce through the foothills, the air skimming my skin and electrifying my hair, the weight of wanting gathering in me. I pulled the empty shoebox I kept ready for Bruce's letters from under the bed and put the tiny box containing the medal into it. Then I opened a book from my stack and made myself look at the words *phloem* and *xylem*. The vascular system of plants. I could hear my mother's sewing machine, and behind that, I could hear the radio, the serious voice of a newscaster interrupted by the music of commercials. I studied the diagrams, the lateral cross section of a tree trunk with its columns of cells, the xylem and the phloem. I stared at the black lines, but I thought about Joan with her back-combed hair and her white lipstick. I thought about the way she seemed to know everything, how to light a cigarette, how to start a fire, how to keep your boyfriend, and considered whether I should call her again. The day Bruce left, Joan was the one I called. She was the one I asked what I should do *if*.

"Did you use 7UP?" she asked.

"Did I what?"

"Did you, you know, douche with 7UP?" she said. "You shake the bottle and, you know. Something about the fizz does something to you. But if you didn't do it right away, like that night, I'm not sure it'll do you any good. Probably not."

"You don't think so?"

"Definitely not. But you can try."

I decided to try. We had no 7UP in the refrigerator, but we did have a bottle of ginger ale, which I carried along with a bottle opener into the bathroom. I took my clothes off and crawled into the tub. I set the bottle on one edge, the bottle opener on the other. Then I shook the bottle hard and wondered how much would spray on me, on the tiles and the tub curtain, before I could actually slip the neck in. I'd heard that when you were pregnant, the first thing you noticed was your breasts, your nipples. The brown disks would swell, I'd heard. They'd be tender as when they first grew. They'd spread the way a stain spreads, and the very centers, the nubs, would rise stiffly, tiny flags declaring your body'd been taken. Looking at my body in the tub, I thought my breasts seemed swollen and foreign. So fleshy, so beastly, so unlike the breasts of girls in the locker room. I ran warm water into the tub, and then I squatted and fit my fingers into me, just to be sure I'd know where to put the lip. I wished that I'd uncapped the thing before I shook it, but I hadn't. So I church-keyed the cap and thumbed the bottle closed, ginger ale fizzing down my hand. I thought it would never work and I thought it just had to. And then there was the business of putting glass inside me. The bottle was cold and didn't seem to get any warmer as I held it in the bath water. Probably I deserved this, I thought, and besides I couldn't be a goner. So I tried. I tried to slip my thumb off and fit the bottle in. Soda foamed into the tub, sending bubbles up around me.

What fizzed into me tickled and then stung, deep in, and in time, I had to stop.

I sat in the tub and tried to believe I was not pregnant.

"Maggie, are you taking a bath?" my mother called.

I looked to see that I'd locked the door. "I'm almost done, Mom." I sat until the sweetened bathwater began to cool. Then I showered and sneaked that bottle back to the kitchen trash before my mother had a chance to ask what I was doing with ginger ale in the bathroom.

Phloem and *xylem*. Heartwood and sapwood. I read that a tree can live without its heartwood as long as the sapwood is good. Outside a skateboard rattled and kids shouted in faraway yards. I heard my father's truck pull down the drive. My father unloaded and tramped back past my window, maybe to pick up the evening paper. Our back door snapped shut, and my father passed my room on the way to his, his steps in the hallway and the smell of tar on his work clothes. I tried to remember which cells carried water, which nutrients. The sound of the sewing machine stopped, and my mother called out, "You hear that?"

My father passed my room again, quicker this time. "What?" he said.

They were silent, and I could hear sounds but not words, small blocks of noise from the radio.

"God, Jim," my mother said. "What do we do?"

"Well, it's not bad news yet," he said.

"What we owe but don't own." The machine burst ahead. "Up in smoke."

"You don't know that," my father said.

"Never rains but pours," she said.

Curious, I stood in the kitchen doorway. My father sat on a dinner chair, the black phone on the floor between his feet, and through the sewing-room door, I could see my mother, or her back anyway, curved toward her work, forest green skirts strewn near her on the floor. "No answer," my father said to my mother. "Maybe she's hosing it down."

"Or maybe she's smart and left it to burn."

"You'd stick around?" My father stood and shook the keys in his pocket. "What do you say I go see?"

"Sure, go see what's left." My mother leaned back in her chair so she could give my father a look. She threw the skirt she'd been working on down to the floor.

"I want to go," I said.

They gazed at me with what I thought was surprise, my mother tilting back precariously in her chair, my father looking up quizzically, his hair ferned across his forehead and his hands deep in his pockets.

"This is no trip to the dime store," he said.

"Let her go." My mother grabbed another deep-green skirt. "As far as I'm concerned, you should both go see Evelyn."

"Here we go again," my father said. He tossed his keys up, then snatched them out of the air. "I swear, you'd see ghosts in broad daylight, Marian."

"Go play Lancelot or Galahad or whatever it is you want to play," and she leaned toward her work and was hidden by the door frame.

"What I *want* is to check on my property." He'd already swung the back door open.

"So go check," she said, the machine bursting ahead.

"All right," he said, kicking the screen door, and then to me, "You can come, but you can't drive."

He slid between cars, lane to lane, as if driving were a game of checkers. He stayed close to the fenders ahead of him, close enough you'd think he wanted to see his reflection, and he nosed his way past stop-lights before anyone else noticed red had turned green. We were deep into November by then, the ash in the air adding to the early dark. The streetlights shone down, and we passed in and out of bright and dusky light the way you pass through cold and then colder water in a lake.

"Jesus H.," my father said. "A fire's the last thing we need." He drove silently a while. "Last thing Mrs. Rum needs too."

"What'll happen if, you know," I asked, "the place burns?"

My father swatted the air and shook his head. "Could be it's better this way. I think the land's worth more with no building on it." He was quiet a moment. "I've got other irons in the fire, anyway."

I didn't know it then, but he had just used family money, his broth-er's and his father's, to buy another property.

"But Mrs. Rum," he said, "she's got next to nothing to start over with."

"She had all that stuff in the house."

"That's nothing, sweetheart, nothing."

He took his favorite shortcuts, the side roads toward the canyon, passing the large yards of foothill homes. Through the dark green leaves of an oleander hedge I saw two boys laughing as they swung on a tire hung by chains from a tall live oak. As my father slowed to turn onto another narrow drive, we passed a ranch-style home with a yard fenced like a pasture and a dark honey horse, its neck stretched tendon-tight over the half-door of the stable. I swear the horse stared at me in fury, then closed and opened its eyes, and whinnied and snorted as if in com-plaint.

I watched the ridges ahead and waited to see fire curling up over the edges, turning what was brown black. My skin was prickly, not with fear but the anticipation of fear, and somewhere in my head, I was saying, You are a girl who does it, who does it, who does it. At the canyon road, yellow barricades stopped us, and a fireman in his black rubber coat stooped to look into the open window on my father's side.

"You live up here?" he asked. His face had a sheen, and his hair looked sweat-dried. Welts marked his forehead where his helmet must have pressed.

"I've got a tenant up here," my father said.

"Far up?" the man said. "We're really only letting residents through, and then only so they can evacuate."

"Not far," my father said, lying, "half mile, three-quarters. I just thought I should check on my tenant, see how she is."

"It's a lady?" the man asked.

My father said it was.

"She really ought to clear out," the man said.

"Want to help her do that," my father said.

"Well, don't stay long," and the man waved us through.

My father zigzagged up the road, biting his finger and squinting ahead. The smoke and the smell of burning scrub grew stronger. I let my hand drag in the air, and when I saw it later in the light, it was dusted with ash.

As we pulled up, our headlights swept under the house and then across it. Freshly painted, it looked exactly the way my mother had said it would, like a landlocked beach house. My father had added white shutters, as she had suggested, and planters hung from the porch rafters. There should have been a lounge chair, though the only view would have been scrub oak and chaparral. Beyond the house and the ridge behind it, the sky glowed neon orange, and we could hear in the distance an oddly delicate sound, like tissue paper crinkling.

"Oh, Jesus," my father said and ran toward the house as if he just understood his work might be lost. He took a key from under the porch steps, and we went in.

"Mrs. Rum?" my father called out.

"Her car's not here," I said.

"I know it, sweetie."

The dark made the room seem full of dust and my father far away, but he flipped a switch, and the bare bulb overhead lit up everything bright and untouched. A red sweater sprawled on a chair. The pillows of the davenport were still creased where someone had sat. A half-smoked cigarette, the long ash poised on its end, dipped into the abalone shell. On the kitchen table sat a white cup and a tumbler, juice in the bottom, and when we came closer, we saw ants streaming from under the back door up to the sugar and crumbs on the table.

"Mrs. Rum?" he called again, and I followed him to the bedroom with its marred chest of drawers and the single twin bed. He lifted the duster and searched under the bed and in the closet, punching at the clothes as if Mrs. Rum were hiding behind them. On the upper shelf, he found a suitcase, which he pulled down and opened.

"What'll she need?" he asked. "What'll she need?" and he turned again toward her closet full of once-fashionable chiffon dresses, their skirts bouqueted together like some can-can costume. He glanced toward the dresser, toward the Jergens lotion and the eyelash curler, and said, "You do the drawers, Maggie."

I opened them and caught the odor of lavender and camphor. There were her underclothes: slippery nylon in pale blue and apricot, the white elastic and plain cotton of her dress shields, the muslin pouch for her hosiery. I put those things into her suitcase and gathered up the perfume and the lotion, the tube of glue, the red mascara box, the tin disk of rouge, and the small framed picture of a younger Mr. and Mrs. Rumsen dancing cheek to cheek, EVELYN NIGHT AND JOHNNY RUN in small black print. I put those into the suitcase, and I took that other picture off the wall, the one where Mrs. Rum's skirt spins away from her, and dropped that in too.

Then I cleared out the bath, the Breck and the Ipana and the unopened box of baking soda, the brown bottles of aspirin and aluminum hydrate and three-percent solution, the withered toothbrush and the razor, small hairs stuck to the blade. I cleared out the Vaseline and the ointment for hemorrhoids. I almost left the rusted can of Barbasol that must have been Mr. Rum's, except I thought it might mean something to her. Behind the door, I found the kimono with the scarlet lining. I put it all into the suitcase on top of the dresses my father had cleared from the closet, dresses of sapphire, ruby, emerald.

"We should hose this place," my father said. "Just soak the hell out of it." Then he said, "We're going to lose it, godamnitohell." And then, "What are you standing there for? Go get started. Go out and spray the place. Move."

My eyes unused to the dark, I searched outside until I stumbled onto the hose, a scrawl on the dirt. I uncoiled it and found the spigot, then sprayed at the roof and walls, water cleaning out the gutters and washing down the windows and the new white trim. Water rained off the roof, so my father had to duck as he came out with the suitcase in hand. It wasn't nearly enough, the water from the garden hose, but I kept spraying. I even sprayed the trees, until the eucalyptus turned black and water rilled off the leaves. My father took the hose from my hand, and as if it would do any good, we stayed there, taking turns thumbing the hose.

We watered the place until the sound of paper crumpling became the clear crackling of fire, the snapping of limbs, the whoosh as the flames took a tree and left ash instead. I ran to the car, and my father grabbed a carton of Mrs. Rum's belongings from inside the house and locked them in the trunk. That's when we drove away, when it was completely dark and the fire was just coming over the ridge and lighting the trees like candles.

Next morning, reports on the radio said the fire had turned on itself. Winds from the west had blown it back into the mountains, where it was burning itself out in a canyon between a firebreak and land already charred. We heard whole neighborhoods had been spared. Later, we saw them in the paper, an entire ridge of homes in the foothills, houses with slate walks and pools dug into the mountainside. We heard that the evacuees from the neighborhoods that had been spared were allowed to go home before dawn, but for an hour or two that morning, we didn't know for sure whether the lot my mother called "that damned piece of property" and my father called "the Rumsen place" had burned. We all walked in and out of the kitchen, grabbing coffee cake, drinking orange juice, listening to the radio reports, while my father stared at his cup of coffee.

"You think something happened to Mrs. Rum?" Jamie asked.

"I doubt it, sport," my father answered, "but I'll try to find out."

"She could call us," my mother said.

"Does it mean something bad if she doesn't call us?" Alison asked.

"I expect she's got things on her mind," my father replied.

It was nine before my mother looked at the clock and said, "My God, they're all late for school."

"For once in their lives, it shouldn't matter," my father said. "Half the school will be late anyway. Half the school won't show up at all."

My mother didn't answer that, maybe because we all knew that the kids whose houses might have burned didn't go to our school.

"I'll drive them," my father said. "I'll even write the notes, okay?"

"Of course it's okay," my mother said and tossed the dish towel onto a chair.

"I'll drop them off, and then go check on the property."

"Don't get your hopes up," she said.

"Mine aren't," he said. "But maybe yours are."

She gave him a searing look. "No, I don't want the place to burn," she said and, when my father eyed her but didn't answer, added, "Don't want Evelyn to burn either."

My father must have had his hopes up somewhere, because he took us to the canyon before he took us to school, driving slowly and staring out at the blackened hills. I sat in the front with him, and Jamie and Alison sat in the back, gazing out the windows. Our father again took the short-cuts, passing the oleander-hidden yards and the one-horse stable.

"A pony!" Alison said as my father turned the corner we'd turned the night before. Jamie and I both twisted to see the resin-colored horse nipping at a bale of hay propped outside the stable.

"It's a horse," Jamie said.

"Is not," Alison said. "It's a pony."

"Dad?" Jamie said. "A horse is a grown-up pony, right?"

"It's a pony," Alison repeated.

"Like that horse back there," Jamie said. "That was a horse, wasn't it, Dad?"

Our father didn't answer. He gnawed his forefinger and watched the hills.

"See," Alison said. "I told you it was a pony."

"It was a horse, stupid. Wasn't it, Dad?"

"A pony," Alison said. "Daddy, it was a *pony*."

"Quiet, Alison." He spoke so quietly himself, both Alison and Jamie sat back in their seats. "I'm thinking."

Thinking. I believe he was praying his hope, repeating one thought over and over, just as I was (let me bleed, please, let me bleed). At each turn, he eyed more closely the unburned trees and the homes still standing. He seemed to suspect them of fooling or cheating him. But as we neared the property and the land around us was still uncharred, he began to whistle softly an old tune I'd heard him sing about reveille and getting up in the morning.

And then we saw it, through the trees ahead: black land and charred stubble.

"Would you look at that," my father said and put his hand over mine where it rested on the front seat.

Whistling still, he turned onto the drive he and his crew had never finished with asphalt. The gravel complained under us, and the tailpipe screamed across a boulder.

"God *bless*," he said and pressed my hand harder.

"What, Dad?" Jamie asked and leaned forward to peer over the front seat.

"That," our father said, lifting his chin toward the track of the fire. We could see where the fire had quit and burned back. Trees that were unburned stood only yards from those that were nothing but black stumps.

"So the fire ran into an invisible force field," Jamie said.

"It's called wind," our father said and let the car idle as he studied the border. "Just a few shitty yards past our property line."

On our property, the trees were burned to charcoal and the scrub to cinder. My father shook his head side to side. "It's like it was after us."

"Is this where that woman Mom doesn't like was living?" Alison asked.

"Mrs. Rumsen lived here," my father said. "Yes, she did."

Parts of the house still stood, the charred two-by-fours and the cinder-block foundation. The fridge and the water heater, the stove—all the white appliances were blistered and singed. The metal kitchen table and chairs sat just where we they'd sat the night before, the white cup still there but no longer white and rubble and ash covering everything. The tub and the commode were exposed, the bowl cracked in half and water trickling out of it, and melted shreds still hung from the shower curtain rod. The stone fireplace stood, but all Mrs. Rumsen's belongings were burned or buried in debris. Her butterflies and shawls, her scrimshaw. Her red sweater smoldered, and her collection of LPs was melted into the metal record stand. With the freshly painted walls of the house burned away, we could see all this without leaving the car.

"Crying shame," my father said. "Crying shame."

As our father drove us slowly back down to our schools, he did not take the shortcuts. He drove unlike himself, stopping for every stop sign, signaling for every turn. Even so, I heard things shifting in the trunk and remembered Mrs. Rumsen's suitcase and the carton of her possessions. Everything she had left we now had.

Because Alison's elementary was closest to the fire, my father stopped there first, pulling into the school drive, a semicircle through an island of ice plant. The school was low and flat, with broad orange roofs cantilevered over the walkways kids took to class, but it must have been pretty late because there were no kids on the walkways.

Alison turned to our father and said, "You promised you'd write us notes."

"Right," he said and pulled an estimate pad from the glove compartment. "What do I say?"

"You say, 'Please excuse Alison for being late,'" Jamie said. "'Family matters detained her.'"

And that's what our father wrote, three times over.

"Mine should say 'Jamie,'" Jamie said.

"You have to sign it, Dad," Alison said and handed her note back.

"Right," he said and signed the three notes.

Solemnly, Alison kissed our father and hugged him, patting his back the way our mother might. Then she climbed from the car, and he said, "It was a horse, honey, okay? A horse."

She turned that level gaze of hers on him, her face placid, and then as if something inside her melted, her eyes brimmed over. "Okay, Daddy," she said and walked down the walkway that cut through the ice plant.

He dropped me off last, and as I gathered my books, he squeezed my hand and said, "Don't look so worried, sport. Your dad will take care of it. You'll see. We're going to be just fine, and I'm going to figure out where Mrs. Rumsen is. She knows how to take care of herself, you'll see."

Wanting to say more, I said, "Sure, Dad, I won't worry." But as I stepped from the car and straightened my skirt, I was worried about something else. I was worried because I knew I no longer needed to pray, "Let me bleed, let me bleed, let me bleed." I leaned into the window and asked, "Can you give me some money?"

"How's this?" he said and handed me two dollars and change.

It was the change I wanted. "Thanks," I said and then walked to the nearest girls' room. I put the nickel in the machine and waited for the cardboard box to clunk down, shaking it to make sure the pad came with safety pins before I walked into a stall. Later, I got a pass from the office and went to biology, but I couldn't really listen to Mr. Sagata lecture about the phloem and the xylem. I was thinking about which prayers are answered and which are not.

TWELVE

*A*fter that, my mother and father did not talk about the fire, at least not to us, not in so many words. But the routine of their days changed. For a time, it was as if the entire house had tilted: everything slid toward my mother. She acquired several new clients, ladies of the Junior League, who filled our house, not all at once, but one by one at different hours of the day, each woman arriving shortly after the previous lady had departed and leaving shortly before the next arrived. They came for fittings and personal design sessions with my mother because she was sewing gowns for the Junior League Christmas Ball.

Why so many of the ladies hired my mother, I'm not sure.

"Oh, someone told someone who told someone else," she told me, but I don't think it was so casual. My mother spent hours on the phone talking to these women, persuading them to hire her, and soon they did. The back room filled with yards and yards of fabric in all shades of green and red, and the house was covered with the dust of pinked satin, and my mother was sewing all day long. She was clipping her bangs back first thing every morning and slipping on those wing-shaped glasses and disappearing into the sewing room before anyone had had breakfast. She would strap her small pincushion to her wrist and not take it off, not to cook, not to wash, not for anything.

Although I glimpsed the women only on Saturdays or late afternoons when I came home early from school, I could feel their presence in the house. They left traces of themselves, the odor of their perfume, the coffee cups that piled up in the sink, the cashmere sweater or pearls they would sometimes forget. My mother had to buy a large percolator to satisfy the ladies' thirst, and she began to keep flowers in vases, in the front-room window and on the kitchen table, but especially in the back room where she worked.

While my mother acquired new clients, my father took to coming home late. He'd pour scotch into a juice glass and sit in front of the television or stand before the kitchen counter, the pink and green pages of a Thomas map open before him and, for reference, the real estate listings folded into quarters and marked with red and black ink. Prices triple-scored and circled, names and phone numbers jotted in margins.

Observing my mother sewing late into the evening, my father would say, "Marian, you're going to sew yourself sick."

"I'd probably worry myself sick if I didn't sew," she would say, rolling a fine hem in avocado green chiffon.

"Well, you shouldn't," he'd say after a moment. "We're going to make out just fine."

"We are?" my mother would ask, glancing at him briefly before resuming her sewing.

"Yes, we are."

He seemed not to sleep much, most nights lying restlessly on the couch. He took to saying, "We should have known sooner. We should have known from ash in the air, dust on the counters. Tears in our eyes should have told us." Then he'd turn on the television and pull the afghan over him, settling on the couch for the night.

"Come to bed, Jim," my mother would say.

"Soon," he'd say, "soon."

Late at night, I could hear him kicking the afghan and shifting the cushions. Sometimes I'd wake to the brassy sounds of "The Star-Spangled Banner," only to hear him switch to another channel before I drifted back to sleep and awoke still later to the national anthem all over again. Other times, I'd wake to the sound of them fighting: "It's not that big a loss," my father might try not to shout. "Not *that* big," my mother might cry back.

In the mornings, my brother and I would find my father tumbled like laundry on the couch, his face misshapen from sleep or bad dreams.

"Hey, Dad," Jamie would whisper. "Time to wake up."

"What?" my father would say, blinking. "What? Did I fall asleep here?"

"Got to get up, Dad," Jamie would say. "Time to get up."

· · ·

Although no one spoke openly about the fire, my father did mention Mrs. Rumsen, at least to me. One evening as I was writing Bruce a letter, my father came into my room, pulling the door closed behind him.

"Look, sweetie." He stood in my room, staring at my floor. "I just want you to know I spoke to Mrs. Rumsen, and she's just fine."

"She is?"

"She is. She's trying to get back on her feet, so I've given her some money. It upsets your mother if I talk about it. So just between you and me, you know, sport?" He patted my back gently. "Just wanted you to know she's okay."

My mother, however, must have known something about Mrs. Rumsen, because she didn't complain about the suitcase and carton of goods my father had packed, although both sat behind the living-room couch, giving off the faint odor of smoke.

Once my mother did ask, "How long are we supposed to keep this stuff, Jim?" and my father replied, "As long as she needs."

Mrs. Rum didn't come around for weeks, but when she did, I happened to answer the door. My mother was in the back room fitting an evening gown on Martha Rogers. I could hear my mother using her seamstress voice, the approving and admiring voice she used so her customers wouldn't notice how little they resembled the fashion photos tacked to the wall. ("There's only so much I can do with a needle and thread," she once told me. "Flattering lines, flattering colors, and then it's up to them and nature.") When the bell rang, I knew my mother wouldn't want to be bothered, so it was me who opened the door and found Mrs. Rumsen, a pink scarf over her head, her wispy hair clinging to it.

"Where've you been, Mrs. Rumsen?" I said. "We were worried about you."

"About me?" she said. "You shouldn't have worried. I know how to get by."

She wore peach lipstick and a coolie jacket fastened down one side with pink rayon frogs.

"But we didn't know where you were. I guess my dad knew, but he wouldn't say."

"Well, I knew where I was. That's what matters, isn't it? Didn't want to bother anyone before I was settled. Your father said you had my suitcase?"

"Sure, and a box of your stuff," and I pointed to them behind the couch.

"I guess I should take them off your hands," she said, and together we carried her suitcase and the carton of belongings to her black station wagon and set them on the backseat.

"Where'd you go?" I asked. "Where've you been?"

"Nowhere. Washed my face and brushed my teeth at work. Slept in the car. I never liked sleeping in church. Except during the sermon." She laughed at her joke, then stopped herself and studied me, laying a hand on my face. "Are you taking care, Maggie dear?"

It bothered me, this gypsy move of hers, so I looked past her, toward Tommy Dawson's house. One suction-cup arrow stuck to the target and others lay in the grass.

"Something's wrong," she said and took my hands, turned them up as if my palms could tell her. "That boy leave you?"

"No," I said and pulled my hands away. "I mean, he's gone, but he didn't leave me."

I heard the back door open and saw my mother walking down the driveway, Martha Rogers at her side. My mother waved when she saw Mrs. Rumsen, and even Mrs. Rogers, walking rather regally in her pleated skirt and stack heels, smiled.

"I'm so glad you came to get your things," my mother said when she and Mrs. Rogers reached us. "How are you doing? Settling in to your new place?"

"You know me. I land on my feet." Mrs. Rumsen retreated from my mother and climbed into her station wagon. "You ought to come visit. Bring the kids."

"Bring them?" my mother said. "I'd bring them and leave them forever."

"What do you want in exchange?" Mrs. Rum turned the key, and her car rumbled.

"I don't really know. What do you normally get for your firstborn? Plus your second and third? Three wishes? A roomful of gold?"

"That's a little out of my reach," Mrs. Rumsen said. "But if I tried hard, I might manage a room of straw."

"Straw?" My mother stepped back and regarded me, her eyes catching on my flyaway hair, my blunt fingers and shapeless pullover. "No, I don't think that's quite enough."

"No, it isn't. Not for children like yours, Marian." Mrs. Rumsen looked levelly at my mother. "I'll see if I can come up with a better offer."

As if Mrs. Rum had waved a big white flag, my mother relaxed and smiled. I could almost see her unfurl, as if she understood there was nothing Mrs. Rum could take from her. "Yes, they're pretty good kids, aren't they? All except this one. She likes to give me a hard time."

I wanted to protest, but Mrs. Rum spoke first. "Count your blessings, Marian." Then she gunned her engine. "Well, got to run. I'm late for work."

As if she'd thought of something else, my mother leaned into the passenger window. "Where did you say you were living?"

"Don't worry, Marian. I'll send you a postcard."

Mrs. Rumsen drove off, her twine-tied fender rattling as she hit the bumps.

"Isn't she a character?" Martha Rogers said. "What does she do? Work at a carnival?"

THIRTEEN

What do you know about how much money we made or lost?" my father said.

We sat in the car outside the lawyer's office, where my father had just closed on the property, where we had, my mother said, just lost more money than she knew how to think about. "I know it's more than I care to imagine."

"You're damn right you can't imagine it," he said.

We were all there in the car, my brother and sister and me, because it was a Saturday and we were on our way to a family gathering at Aunt Coral's. The lawyer had insisted today was the day, or that's what I figured from the things I'd heard Mom and Dad saying. Mom kept asking couldn't it wait? And Dad kept saying that it couldn't, not if he knew what a good buyer was, and Mom kept saying, "But we'll be late to Coral's," and Dad kept saying, "Aren't we always late to Coral's?"

"Well, maybe I *should* be able to imagine it," my mother said.

"What are you trying to do? Ruin the day?"

We were dressed up for Aunt Coral, my brother in his first real tie and my sister with red and green ribbons in her hair. Maybe because the ride to Coral's is long, my brother had brought a spiral pad and a ball-point pen and was tracing the outline of his magic-shop key and hand-cuffs. Alison had brought her doll in its pink plastic carrying case, and as she sat there with the case in her lap, she gazed out the car window and snapped the latch open and shut, open and shut. I had brought a copy of *Seventeen*, but I didn't really read it. I used it as a garter weight because my garters kept popping up and making a tent of my skirt. I tried crossing my legs and uncrossing them, but it didn't matter. The garters still popped up and my skirt still made a tent, so I gave up and crossed my legs anyway, folded them close together, practicing a look I'd seen in *Vogue* and risking my mother's anger.

My mother did not approve of crossed legs, as she frequently reminded me. Sitting next to me in church one holiday (she didn't go except for holidays), she had whispered during the doxology, "Only adult ladies cross their legs at the knees. Young ladies cross their ankles."

So I uncrossed my legs, but first chance I got, I crossed them and continued to cross them whenever I could. I continued to try everything my mother said only grown women did. I went to the lingerie department at JCPenney and tried on girdles with crisscross tummy panels and bras with wires underneath. I dropped a glass on the kitchen floor and said, "Goddamn it all," just the way my mother said it. I said "Sheit" the way one of my father's men did, and when Joan called me to complain that Charlie hadn't taken her out on Friday and hadn't called her either, I said for the first time, "Well, fuck him," and then because I liked saying the word, "Just *fuck* him."

She said, "Not if he doesn't call, I won't."

More than anything, I looked at people and saw things I hadn't seen before, the curve of muscle under trousers, the way a breast gave shape to a blouse or a neck disappeared into a shirt collar. For me, these were all secret signs of sex. I'd sit listening to Mr. Sagata in biology and watch the boy in front of me. I'd study the twist of hair at the base of his neck, the fur on his arm, the pink lobes of his ears. I'd watch his foot jiggle in and out of his loafer when the teacher called on him. And I'd think, You're a girl who does it, who does it, who does it.

"I'm just asking that we be practical," my mother said. Around us, cars pulled in and out, but we sat there in the green and white Pontiac as if we were inside our own home and no one could see us through our rolled-up windows. "We can't keep buying property we can't afford, much less insure."

"And didn't I ask you not to talk about that?" My father hit the steering wheel, and the horn sounded. Across the parking lot, a woman dropped her Smart Shoppe shopping bags and glared at us over the hoods and roofs.

"Why shouldn't I talk?" my mother asked.

"Because you know I'm right," my father said. "Because you know insurance is nothing but businessman's theft."

"Some would have been better than none."

"You wanted it, why didn't you buy it?"

"Don't I buy enough for the house?"

"Yeah, you do," he said. "You spend money like a house on fire."

My brother nudged me and handed me his pad and pen. Beneath a crest of traced keys, he'd sketched the bare scaffolding for a game of hangman and underneath drawn nineteen dashes for the word he wanted me to guess.

"Spending it on the house is better than losing it on speculation."

"Spending is just spending," he said. "It's money down the drain. Investing in property is business. It's opportunity."

I took Jamie's pen and wrote "Title?" and he nodded yes in answer.

"At least when I do a dress," she said, "I know what I'll earn. But these projects of yours. You never seem to know what they'll cost."

"That penny-ante business of yours?" he said. "You think it matters you know what a yard of silk costs?"

My mother was silent, and my father started the car. "We're talking about money here."

"But look how much money we just lost," she said.

"That's small time," my father said. "That's nothing."

"Nothing?"

"I didn't want that old canyon place anyway. More trouble than it's worth, and this guy gives me a big down payment right now, and I've got ready cash so I can move with this new property."

My father backed the car out and pulled into the street. Above us, a tinsel festoon scalloped from lamppost to lamppost, and the foil bells swayed in the breeze.

"I thought you told me you weren't going to."

"Well, I haven't yet, but it's such a great deal." He hit the steering wheel again. "We'd be fools to let someone else get hold of it."

Outside the car, palms and pines serrated the sky, and the yards and lives of other people passed us like frames in a nickelodeon. A woman perched on a second-floor sill and washed her windows with a large yellow sponge. A man in a sun hat clipped his hedge, and on a wide corner lawn, two guys tossed a football back and forth over the head of a Styrofoam snowman. Inside the car, Alison snapped the clasp of her doll case open and shut, open and shut, and for all the useless XYZ's I guessed, Jamie added new details to the hung man, torn sleeves and dripping blood.

"The place's half finished, so it needs a little work. But when I'm through it's going to make so much money."

"Be realistic," my mother said.

"Realistic? You call realistic turning your head away from a steal? I'm telling you we'll make so much, we'll have a beach house and a mountain house and I'll get you a house like that one Chess and I worked on a few years back, with the library and the dining room and those sweeping stairs, and each house will have its own sewing room, Goddamn it, each one'll have its own piano and the kids'll take lessons, and I'll expand and let the guys take over the business, so I can spend my time developing property, and this will all happen if you quit worrying about the little losses and start looking at the big picture. That's all. Have a little faith."

My mother laid aside the map she had been studying, took her glasses off, and unclipped her earrings from her ears, putting them in her lap, where they rattled softly. She looked away, toward a woman hanging a wreath on her door. "I'm too simple for all this."

"I told you you didn't know the first thing about it, didn't I?"

Jamie jabbed me with the pen and pad. By then, I had guessed S (there were two S's) and T (there were two of those too) and R and N and G and H, so the game looked like this: STR_NG_RS_NTH_N_GHT. I grabbed the pen and scribbled, "You like Sinatra?!?!?!" and my brother laughed.

"What are you laughing at?" My mother turned her head sharply and examined us.

"Nothing, Mom," Jamie said. "Just a game of hangman."

"You're laughing at a game of hangman?" She glanced at his pad of paper on my lap and then at my *Seventeen* and, under that, my tented skirt and crossed legs. She surveyed Jamie, glimpsing the handcuffs in his pocket. "I thought I told you not to bring those." Then she turned to Alison, who was now unlatching, opening, closing, and latching her doll case again and again. "And I don't like you excluding your little sister, you hear me?"

We stopped the game, and I watched the homes float by as we drove down a street of houses with wrought-iron fences and lawns like fairways. Tall houses with curtained windows and waxed doors. Behind one, I glimpsed a tennis court, a crisscross of white lines against dark orange, but I saw no flying balls. I saw no one at any of these houses, except a man in navy trousers and blue shirt pushing a lawn mower

115

across the grass. My father turned once and once again, and we were on the freeway, the car making that whipping sound every time it passed another car, and we could hear that throb you hear on the freeway, the sound of the engine bouncing off the concrete barriers.

"I've got a game we can all play," my father said. "If we could build our own house and it could be anything you wanted, what would you want? Alison?"

"I'd want a room with trees," Alison said, "and animals."

"What kind of animals?" my father asked.

"I don't know." She shifted the case on her lap. "Ponies, maybe, and zebras, giraffes."

"That'll take a tall room," my father said. "What about you, Jamie?"

"If Alison gets a zoo, I want an indoor pond, a big saltwater pond with my own dolphin. And I want an outdoor pool, too, for us to swim in. And I wouldn't mind a track for skateboarding."

Mom wouldn't play this game right away. "Don't we have enough already, Jim?"

"Come on, Marian, dream a little."

"Well, how about a separate wing for the children and a kitchen that cleans itself? Like those self-cleaning ovens and self-defrosting refrigerators," she said. "I want a self-scrubbing sink and a self-washing floor."

"And how's this?" she added. "A silent room where nothing that's said can be heard."

When my turn came, I said, "An empty attic with a big window in the roof." I didn't mention that I imagined a luxury of space, voluptuous, palatial space. I didn't mention that I pictured Bruce and me in this room, sleeping under the window.

"That's it?"

I told my father there was a trunk in this attic, and in it were things from the past. Gramma Truth's wedding dress, Great-aunt Mary Louise's first corsage, piles and piles of handmade antimacassars, a buttonhook and buttoned boots, and everything good as new. "That enough?"

"What about a fireplace?" my father said. "Doesn't anyone want a fireplace?"

He suggested one for each bedroom and large windows with velvet drapes. "Come on, doesn't anyone want a ballroom? With a chandelier? And a room full of books that none of us will ever read? How about air conditioning?"

When we couldn't think anymore, he'd ask us specific questions. "What color is that room? What kind of banister do you want on that stair? What do you see when you open those curtains?"

"I see the beach," my mother said, "I see it late at night when all the campfires are burning down, and the red tide makes the water glow."

"And the windows are open and the air is damp and smells of salt," my father said and leaned over to kiss my mother, grabbing her chin and turning her face to him.

Jamie and I never finished our game of hangman, although Jamie had a good time drawing the hung man anyway. He drew bloody stumps where he should have drawn an arm and a leg. The two of us played around some with the title, replacing letters until we had a list: Strangers at the Fights, Hangers in a Fright, Dangers in the Light. By the last one he wrote, "Love song for moths?" and we were both silly enough we had to stifle our laughs.

FOURTEEN

Chess and Coral's house was all redwood and glass on the outside, all vaulted roof and floating stairs inside. We were standing on their brick porch, the double doors open, and inside we could see the family, people who came from all over, the local ones from Torrance and Claremont and Tujunga and the ones from out of state, from Eugene and Reno and Kansas. There seemed to be so many people who were Harrises or married to Harrises or descended from Harrises.

"Damn the young," Uncle Chess said to my father. "I told them not to drive on the grass." Behind us, cars filled the drive, fender to fender, some pulled onto the grass and under the twisted live oak, Christmas lights threaded through its branches. "But what are you going to do? Take them to court? And look at yours." He chucked Alison under the chin. "I remember when you couldn't keep your thumb out of your mouth, Ali." She looked at him with that green gaze of hers. "Growing up like a sprout, isn't she? And what a beauty," Chess said to my father. "And how's my Maggie?" He hugged me against him, my face rubbed into the wool of his jacket. "How's my favorite Maggie? Am I still your favorite uncle? And you, Jamie boy, you staying out of trouble?"

I said yes, he was, and my brother said yes, he was, and as we moved on into the house, I heard Uncle Chess say to my father, "Hey, I'm sorry about your loss on that property."

"It was no big loss, Chester. Take my word for it."

Inside, gas jets in the grate sent brilliant blues and greens from the newspaper logs, and over the stereo, a voice that made me think of pomade sang about building a snowman and pretending he was Parson Brown.

"Howie's outside," Uncle Chess said to Jamie and Alison. To my father, he said, "Let me get you some grandfather punch," as he steered him toward the large crystal bowl and the dark pink punch.

Chess called it grandfather punch because it *was* just punch, just juice and soda, and it was *just* punch because Grampa Whit was there, and Grampa Whit did not believe in drinking or smoking or dancing. That's the kind of Methodist he was. That was not the kind of Methodist my father was; he drank and smoked and danced and read the *Playboy* he hid behind the bottles in the pantry. And I would guess that was not the kind of Methodist my uncle was either, but then Grampa Whit was their father, and he was the oldest person there we were all related to one way or another.

I suppose I should say that Grampa Whit was the sort of Methodist who believes that sin begets sin, that, as he would say, we deserve the travails of this life. When his sister's grandson, Willy Nash, went to Berkeley and studied Mario Savio rather than the Roots of Western Civilization, Grampa Whit said to every member of the family, "My sister Mary Louise brought her woe upon herself. It's what comes of living in a city like San Francisco." And later when the what-might-happen did happen and it got out in the family that I was "in a family way," my mother said to me, "You know what Grampa Whit said to your father, don't you? He said, 'That's what you get for smoking and keeping liquor in your house.'"

"But, God, all Dad smokes is a pipe."

"How many times do I have to tell you?" my mother said. "Swearing's not ladylike."

Grampa Whit also wrote me out of the will, but that was all later. And it was, as everyone in the family said, a worthless gesture since Harrises have a habit of dying in debt. I suppose I should also say that I never did agree with my grandfather. I would never blame anything I did on my father or the liquor he kept in the house, the pipe he sometimes smoked, or the *Playboy* he hid in the cupboard.

What Chess and Coral called the living room rose two stories undisturbed, so their Christmas tree was twice as tall as most, its branches heavy with snow and gold bows and red Christmas globes. It was a

119

flocked tree, I knew, but standing next to it I felt a chill from its branches.

"One of Coral's designer trees," my mother said under her breath.

My mother carried a casserole dish covered with tinfoil, although Aunt Coral had insisted that no one bring food. She was saying right then, "Oh, Mare, I made enough for an army!" as she led my mother into her kitchen. And I heard my mother say, "Please don't say that word too loud. You'll have Maggie in a fit," before the door swung closed behind her.

My father and Uncle Chess had settled in a wing chair and a love seat and were talking quietly near the fire, and Alison and Jamie had slid through the sliding glass doors and gone outside, where Howie, one of our second cousins, I believe, sat in his blue blazer with its gold and red patch and floated a three-masted boat near the edge of the pool.

I stayed where I was, by the cooling tree, the gift boxes piled up beneath it. That slippery voice sang about conspiring by the fire and facing plans unafraid, and that made me think of Bruce. We'd made no plans, of course, except that he was supposed to be home in time for Christmas. That he wasn't home yet was a relief, really. My parents found fewer reasons to yell, and they hadn't grounded me once in the last six weeks. Besides, there were enough things to worry about, what with my father's property burning up, without their having to worry about me. I even think Jamie and Alison were thankful Bruce was gone. It was as if the house were suddenly larger and we moved through it without danger, without snagging ourselves on the rough edges of resentment or anger. Of course, Bruce left me with time on my hands: afternoons after school, Friday evenings and Saturday nights, Sunday midnights when I used to sneak out to his car, hours after supper when I would sit in the unlit hall and listen to his voice, or just his breathing, over the phone. I felt cushioned by the hours, by all that time suddenly empty and nothing rushing in to fill the vacuum. Oh, I wrote letters and reread the ones Bruce wrote me. Still, there were quiet, vacant hours, hours I spent thinking about him, his mouth (the exact shape of it), his hands (the feel of them), his skin touching me, and I remember being glad for housework, glad to dust and iron and do the dishes. I even did piecework for my mother, sewing all the side seams for the high school choir robes. I almost felt innocent.

Across the room, Grampa Whit stood between the wing chair and love seat where my father and uncle sat, as if presiding over them. He was tall, taller than everyone including my father, and his skin was flushed and pink, especially next to his white crew-cut hair. He complained of arthritis, but to me he seemed strong: He stood more than he sat, and there was nothing bent about him. He was standing, hands clasped behind his straight back as he hovered over my father and uncle, when he looked up and winked at me through his wire-rimmed glasses.

"What a pretty dress," a woman I hadn't noticed said to me. She was short and older, soft as a fresh cake and decorated with a wide white collar. "It's not boughten, is it?"

"I'm sorry," I said. "My dress isn't buttoned?"

"Boughten, I said boughten."

When I understood the word, I understood it was my great-aunt Mary Helen speaking to me. My grandmother's sister, Mary Helen, was one of those here from Kansas, or, I should say, lately from Kansas, because if you got right down to it, we were all from Kansas, Grampa Whit and his sister Mary Louise having moved their families here in the thirties when the bad times were supposed to be not so bad in California. Mary Helen lifted my dotted Swiss skirt and turned me gently from side to side.

"No, my mother made it," I said.

"Well, she *is* clever," Mary Helen said and fingered the red velvet ribbon and eyelet lace. "With the cost of clothes these days you have to know how to sew."

"That's what my mother does, Aunt Mary Helen. She sews."

"Now, which one is your mother, dear?"

I pointed to my mother in her dark red sheath with the delicate topstitching, the dress she packed up in mothballs every year after Christmas. My mother stood chatting with Coral and Lillian, the three similar enough to pass for sisters in a fairy tale, one fair-haired, one dark, one auburn.

"You're one of Marian's children," Mary Helen said. "I am so sorry I didn't recognize you. I get out here so rarely, especially now." She meant, I think, since her sister, Gramma Truth, died ten years before. (My grandmother Margaret Ruth was known as Greta to those closest and Greta Ruth to everyone else, and we children, in our impatience, shortened Greta Ruth to Truth. Gramma Truth, we said.) "I used to come out here every other year and now I don't think I've been here since your cousin Debbi's wedding, what? Three years ago? You must be sixteen now."

121

"Sixteen and a half," I said.

She smiled, remembering something sweet. "So you still count the half years," and she reached up and put her hand on my head, as if I were a girl even younger than Alison.

"Well, whom do we have here?" Grampa Whit said. He made a point of pronouncing the *m* in *whom*, some reminder, I believe, of his life as a schoolteacher. "Do I see one of my favorite grandchildren? Do I see Greta's favorite sister?"

Mary Helen said, "Whit, I was not Greta's favorite."

"If you weren't hers, you're mine. I always said you had more smarts than all of them, next to Greta, of course."

Grampa Whit was forever doing that, judging people's smarts. "Smart," my father once said, "may be your grandfather's favorite word." It had something to do, my father said, with the way Grampa Whit came up through the Normal School in Kansas, the way he advanced to superintendent in La Verne. It had something to do with working indoors and not out. Being quick at figures, spelling well, writing a sure and rounded script, knowing the states and capitals by heart— you did those things and one day you owned the farm, but you didn't work it. You did those things and Grampa Whit valued you; he said you were smart, except no one but Gramma Truth was ever smart enough for him. And she died.

"What are you up to in math?" he asked me right there at the Christmas party. It was actually trig that semester, but I said, "Oh, the usual, Grampa," and waited for him to quiz me.

He pointed to a switch on the wall and to a spot on the ceiling and asked, "If a fly were to crawl from there to there, what path would be the shortest?"

Because he had asked me this before, I knew the answer. It had to do with imagining the room flattened and drawing a straight line from point to point, which is what I told him.

"An easy one, Mary Helen, I gave her an easy one. So then what's the volume of this package?" He lifted one of the boxes we had just put under the tree.

"Jamie is better at this stuff than me," I said.

"Come on, I never could sit still for lazy brains."

So I tried to answer his questions about volume. After all, the volume of the package was not so difficult to figure. But then he asked about the volume of the red Christmas globes and the volume of the tree if it were truly a cone and the volume of the cups that made a set with the crystal punch bowl if they were truly parabolic. I knew that pi(r^2) was part of all of those volumes (who can forget pi?), but I didn't know the rest. So I let him answer his questions and imagined him pacing the floors of the schools where he had first taught and then been principal.

When he was through asking me to picture a parabola spinning in space, I said, "I'm no lazy brains. I'm just not that smart."

Grampa snorted at that. "That's what they all say. That's what Greta Ruth said, isn't it, Mary?"

"I'm sure I don't remember."

"Well, I remember, and that's exactly what she said."

I looked through the sliding door for Jamie and hoped he would come save me. Our cousin's toy boat with its three cloth sails had floated to the center of the pool, and Jamie and my cousin were trying to coax it back to the side. With their sleeves rolled up, they lay on the edge of the pool and stroked the water, as if trying to create a current, and by the back fence, Alison stood on tiptoe and lifted a pool skimmer from its hooks. Twice as long as she was tall, it teetered in her hands like a pole for vaulting.

"And Greta Ruth wouldn't like you lying right now, Maggie," my grandfather said. "She'd say own up to your abilities."

My abilities. What abilities could I possibly have? And then I thought, I am a girl who does it. That's my ability. The very words were in my mouth: I'm a girl who fucks and likes it. But what I said was "I tell you, Grampa, I'm just me."

He leaned toward an end table and grabbed a handful of peanuts, then shook them as if he wanted to coat his palm with salt. "No one in my family is *just* anything," he said and walked away.

Out the large window, I saw Alison push the boat with the pool skimmer. She pushed it far enough that Jamie could reach down from the diving board where he lay and lift the boat right out of the water. I could see that for someone her size, the long pole of the skimmer was unwieldy and heavy, but Alison gripped it, leaned back, and focused on the boat. And as she did so, Howie came up behind her and tossed her skirt up over her head.

"My, my," Mary Helen said, surprising me because I had no idea she was watching. "Being pretty is surely no bargain."

"Guess not."

123

"Not that you're not pretty," she quickly said. Her face wore that expression women wear when, in very high heels, they step on someone's foot.

"I understand."

She was quiet a moment. The skimmer fell from Alison's hands and sank slowly into the pool. The water rippled and scattered the reflected Christmas lights into a million colored glimmers, and inside, the pomaded voice on the stereo sang "In heart and soul and voi-oi-oice."

"You mustn't let your grandfather bother you." Mary Helen rested a soft hand on my back. "He's always liked to leave his mark on people."

Red oven mitts still on her hands, Coral pushed her way through the kitchen door, the bell on her Santa Claus apron jingling.

"When we going to eat?" Chess asked.

"Soon," she said. "We'll need you to carve the bird. How're the kids doing?"

"They were fighting," Mary Helen said, "but Katherine's settled it all, I believe."

I looked toward the window and saw the double exposure you see in glass as it grows dark, the colorful and bright reflection of us inside and, through us, the group of them going gray in the evening outside. Howie looked angry, his hands fists and his face red, as his mother Katherine knelt by him and spoke into his ear. Jamie stood nearby, the boat in his hands and the three masts covering most of his face. Just back from Berkeley, Willy stroked back his long hair and stretched out on a lounge chair, basking in the Christmas lights, and Alison stood quietly.

"Looks like Katherine's put the fire out," Coral said, then stroked her mitt through the air and gave me a look I knew meant "Come with me."

I pushed open the swinging door to a kitchen that seemed to swarm with women. Aunt Coral removed her mitts and stirred gravy on the stove top. My mother whipped potatoes at the Kitchenaid Mixmaster. Aunt Lillian sliced dinner rolls and put a pat of butter inside each, and Coral's daughter Debbi, who was many months pregnant with her second child, sat at the kitchen table, paring and slicing carrots and arranging them in a dish with ice, while Casey, the one cousin about my age, dolloped mayonnaise into the center of a Jell-O mold. The women were colorful in their Christmas dresses and the aprons Coral had lent them, Mother's Day and Christmas gifts that she must have saved over the years.

"What can I do to help?" I asked.

"Well, I think I've got everything under control," Aunt Coral said, "but if you really want, you can wash some of these dishes."

I was glad to do the dishes, glad to fill the sink and squirt soap into the streaming water, to let the baking and frying pans and casserole dishes soak on the counter. I was glad to listen but not to speak, so no one could quiz me, not even about *that boy you've been seeing*.

Lillian, the aunt who seemed to me finer than the rest of us, who seemed to belong in a gallery of small polished objects that none of us would understand, came to the sink and dropped the butter knife into the soapy water. "Nice dress," she said.

"Thanks. Mom made it."

"Here," Lillian said, stepping around me to see both sides, "let me take a look."

"Mom," I said across the room. "Lillian likes this dress."

"She does, does she?"

"Beautiful work, Marian."

I could guess what my mother was thinking, I'd heard her say it so often: "They may admire my work, but they look down on us because I work at all." But what she said was "Oh, well, it's just a kid's dress. Simple stuff. Nothing compared to yours."

"This?" Lillian said. "Just a sale dress. Off the rack."

"Really?" My mother eyed the black dress and the elegant fabric it was made of. "On you it looks designer. Anything would."

"Anyone can buy something," Lillian said. "You're the one who does wonders with a needle and thread."

"That's nice of you, but I just wanted Maggie to have something special for the Christmas dance."

Her words to me had been: Now that Bruce is gone, you have the chance to meet some nice boy your own age.

"She looks very pretty in it," Coral said.

"I think so," my mother said. "Turn around, Maggie. Let everyone see."

I turned, holding out the navy blue dotted Swiss, and the women were obliged to admire the empire waist and the red velvet ribbon threaded through the eyelet lace. Even Lillian's daughter Casey got up from the table to take a closer look. "Not bad," she said, except I found it hard to believe her. I believed she thought it frilly and outdated, but I didn't care because the dress made me seem something I wasn't, almost pretty.

"So why don't you help Maggie?" Lillian said. "Grab a towel and dry."

A look passed between mother and daughter, a suppressed "No way!" and a silent "You'd better," before Casey turned to me and asked, "Where should I start?"

"The ones on the bottom are drier," I said, "but the ones on top are most likely to fall."

"Talk about helpful," Casey said.

"Sorry."

Casey was a year behind me at school, but being a December baby, she was right then at that party my age. To me she always seemed older, and one reason was her looks. She was the sort of girl who makes you feel you'll never be good enough at being a girl. I mean that she was really and truly lovely, the sort of girl guys write poems about, hair a cascade, shoulders like ivory, that sort of thing. And the boys would have been right. Her shoulders, for instance, were like a half-used bar of Camay, and by that I mean that they were perfectly square and perfectly rounded and would fit so nicely into your hand, never mind they'd be gentle on your skin.

I lifted two pots off the top of the stack, so she could start with the bottom dishes. "Take your pick."

"Maggie, dear," Coral said to me. "Would you mind doing me two favors? In the dining room in the top drawer of the sideboard, that's where the hot pads are. Would you set them out and then go tell your Uncle Chess we're ready for him in ten minutes?"

"But I just . . ."

"Don't worry. Casey can finish them."

"I think it's a shame," Mary Helen was saying as I entered the dining room. She sat at the table with Clare and Adele, two of my father's cousins, which made them my great-cousins or second cousins or cousins twice removed. I called them aunts.

They were sisters, and spinsters of sorts, although I was not to use that word in their presence. Adele had never wed, and Clare's husband, I heard, had died scarcely a year into their marriage. ("Lucky there was no child," my mother had said.) The two taught in the same school, would retire roughly the same year, had their hair blued at the same beauty shop, and wore clothes that complemented the other, Clare in a lavender knit suit and Adele in a mauve crocheted dress.

"Whit should have asked you," Aunt Clare said. "She is your sister, and it's not as if you visit every year."

"Now when has Whitman ever considered anyone else," Aunt Adele said. "When?"

"He's a thoughtful man," Aunt Clare said. "He just has trouble with Evelyn."

"Thoughtful?" Aunt Mary Helen said. "There I am staying with him in that big fancy house he bought last time he bought up, and no way to get around if he doesn't drive me in that big cushioned car of his, and not once has he offered to take me to see my sister Evelyn. Not once."

"Jim could offer, couldn't he?" Aunt Clare asked.

"You think he would," Aunt Mary Helen said. "Evelyn may be my baby sister, but she was as good as his older sister."

"What?" Aunt Adele said. "Drive you and cross his father? I'd be surprised if Jim even knows where Evelyn's living since the fire."

"That was a shame," Aunt Mary Helen said, "that fire."

I opened the top drawer of the sideboard, a sleek piece that must have been Danish modern, and said, "Evelyn? Evelyn Rumsen?"

Only then did my aunts seem to notice me. Clare and Adele smiled timid, wilted smiles, then turned toward each other, shrinking like suddenly shaded flowers. Mary Helen said, "Yes, my sister Evelyn. You know her?"

"I met her."

"Oh?"

"She was living, you know, in this house my father had." I opened a drawer and, finding silver arrayed against wine-colored felt, I closed it. "She's your sister?"

"You didn't know?" Mary Helen said.

I tried another drawer. "I guess I should have. I thought she was more distant. Twice removed or something."

Mary Helen smiled sweetly, pleating the delicate skin around her eyes, then glanced from Clare to Adele and said, "Maggie, you're being such a dear, helping out the way you are."

"I don't know. How could I not help?"

"Believe me, you are being just a dear." Mary Helen smiled an extrasweet smile, and then my aunts all sat quiet as potted violets until I left the room.

I stood between the dining and living rooms, mistletoe over my head, and watched the group of men gathered around Grampa Whit, his bristly pink head rising above theirs. What quiz had Mrs. Rumsen failed so badly he would not speak to her? And were the men sitting around Grampa now failing an unwritten exam? The men talked among themselves, but what they were saying was difficult to hear. An organ sounded over the stereo, the fast deep sound of a church organist pumping the pedals with both feet, stops open and hands flying, and then the many voices of a choir. I could hear talk of acreage and price per square foot, of taxes and access roads, but I could make out nothing else. I moved slowly to the core of men, to the place before the fire where Grampa Whit and Uncle Chess and my father sat. My grandfather had kept the wing chair and Chess sat in the love seat, while my father sat on the footrest. He leaned into his knees, his back pitched forward, his head nodding, as he said yes, yes, yes. He looked like a man proposing.

"I got too much money tied up in this new house of mine," Grampa Whit was saying. "So if I put my good money into something, I expect to get money out. More money."

I saw the wince in my father's back, the dragonfly arch in his spine.

"Well, Dad," Chess started to say, but stopped when he saw me approach.

"What is it, sweetie?" my father said.

"Nothing," I said. "Just Aunt Coral said Uncle Chess should carve the turkey in a few minutes." I felt oversized, like a swollen eight-year-old. "In ten minutes. She said ten."

I put my hand on my father's shoulder, and he reached up and patted it. His hands are large and softer than I ever remember or expect them to be.

"Thanks for telling us, sweetie."

He squeezed my fingers and then let go, so I knew I was supposed to leave.

"Okay. Ten minutes. Don't forget."

"But, Pop." Uncle Chess was the first to pick up the conversation. "Maybe there's some tax break here you haven't considered."

The organ music surged. The voices sang "Noel, Noel" as fiercely as they might sing the passion music, and all I wanted was to call my boyfriend and listen to him talk. I went to the guest room, the room where we'd put all the coats. I needed my purse and the slip of paper with the number of the pay phone nearest the barracks, and I thought there might be a phone in that room. But in the guest room I found Howie with his mother, Katherine. Howie sobbed, huge tears rolling down his face, and Katherine cooed and clucked. I searched, embarrassed, through the pile of cardigans and fox stoles and wool jackets, the odor of mothballs and perfume wafting up with each garment I moved.

"Why do I have to share?" Howie was saying. "It's *my* boat."

"Who'd you say you want?"

The voice was small and brittle with static, but also full of health and goodwill.

"Gallagher," I said, "Bruce Gallagher."

"You know, miss, this is a public pay phone. Didn't he tell you that?"

"Yeah, he did, he told me that. But he said if you, if someone, checked the last barrack, then maybe he could, if it was an emergency, maybe we could talk."

"Hey, miss, do you have any idea where the last barrack is? Do you? And last from where, from which end is he counting?"

"He said it's forever and a day to the phone."

"Look, I'll be generous. I'll look for him while you hang on, but it's your nickel, lady."

It wasn't, of course. It was Chess and Coral's. "Hey," I said, "thanks," but he was already gone.

I sat in the dark listening to the static and the occasional and distant sounds of men shouting. The room I'd found was the room Chess used as his office at home. I'd shut the door and hadn't switched on the lamp, but I could see by the light from outside, the Christmas lights on the eaves shining green and orange into the room and underwater lights beaming out of the pool. I rubbed my fingers along the gold embossed on the leather ends of the desk blotter.

"Hello? Is someone on this line?"

The voice seemed to strain, so I cupped my hand over the mouthpiece and shouted, "Yes!"

"Are you waiting for someone?"

"Yes!" I shouted as quietly as I could.

"Look, I need to call my girlfriend, so why don't you call back in a few?"

"Please, just wait a little."

"Okay," the voice said, "but I'm counting. One thousand one, one thousand two."

"That's great, thanks."

Outside, my brother, in his jacket and tie and good shoes, bounced on the diving board. He sprang, his head bowed to watch his toes, arms waving like flippers at his side, as the board quavered beneath him.

"One thousand twenty. Lady, I can't keep this up. One thousand thirty, one thousand forty. I can't, lady."

"I understand." I disconnected, and the tone whirred in my ear. Sitting in the dark, surrounded by Chess's records, his file cabinets and his desk cubbies full of receipts and contract carbons, I watched out the window. Willy sat with his corduroys rolled up and his feet in the pool. The three-masted boat floated a few feet away. Every so often it seemed to motor itself back toward Willy, and then I saw the string, barely visible, tied to the bow. Willy tugged, and the boat glided in the turquoise water. Nearby, Alison sat cross-legged, and she and Willy seemed to be talking seriously, while Jamie bounced and bounced on the board. I tried the number again, and then again. Busy. No answer.

The kitchen door swung open, and Casey hipped her way through, a large glass bowl full of tossed salad in her arms. The aunts, Clare, Adele, and Mary Helen, murmured. "Oh, isn't that lovely."

Through the open door I heard my mother saying, "When he's around, she's like a magnet pointed to true north."

Casey left the salad on a quilted pad and pushed her way back to the kitchen. As the door swung open, I heard, "Just flotsam around the house when he's gone."

I knew I was my mother's subject. So I delayed entering the kitchen by looking busy, opening the drawers and removing serving spoons when I found them.

"Don't you think you're needed in the kitchen?" Aunt Mary Helen asked. "You should go help, child."

"Yes, you're right," and I pressed into the door.

My mother was leaning against the counter, her hands spread in midair as if she were displaying a length of fabric. All the women seemed to listen closely, nodding as she spoke. I heard only "What do you do with a big teenage body lollygagging about the house?"

My mother shook her head and dropped her hands, perhaps pleased by the silence, the unnatural clearing in the forest of voices, until she looked at me. She winced just barely, her pupils closing, as if I'd hurt her by walking in the door just then.

It was Debbi who changed the subject. "Goddamn Grampa Whit. I need a cigarette."

"Debbi," Aunt Coral said, "go out to the garage if you have to. Or up to your room. Just be sure to close the door and open the window." To me, Coral said, "You told Chess, dear?"

"I did."

"Good girl."

"Would he really know if I smoked one here?" Debbi asked.

"Debbi, this is your mother speaking. Go up to your room. Go smoke, go lie down, put your feet up. Just stay up there until everyone's served and then come join us."

Debbi pressed herself away from the table. She wore a blue smock and a pink mohair sweater she used to wear in high school. Loose as those sweaters were, it didn't fit now and hung open on either side of her. "All right, Mom," Debbi said, "I'll go rest."

Big lollygagging teenager that I was, I narrowed my focus and walked across the room, picked up the dish towel and started drying the pans that still sat in the dish rack.

I imagine my mother felt some embarrassment. She said, "Coral, this dish is ready to go? I'll take it out."

Whatever looks passed between Coral and anyone else in the kitchen I didn't see, my back being turned. I just stood there drying dishes as people carried food to the sideboard, and the kitchen grew quiet. Someone, I didn't look to see who, walked in and opened a cupboard, closed it and opened another.

"If what I'm about to do upsets you, just say so." It was Lillian, alone with me in the kitchen. She opened one of Aunt Coral's drawers and dug around. She found some kitchen matches, and she found the wooden box full of cigarettes that I believe Coral usually kept on the coffee table. She lifted the lid, and despite the turkey and yams and rolls, I could smell the musk of tobacco. She lit up, her russet hair draping forward and shading her features, and when she lifted her face to exhale, her hair swung back and smoke curled up like scrollwork. "Really, if Grampa Whit walks in, I'll say you had no part in my downfall. How's that?"

I told her whatever she did was fine with me. "If he thinks smoking sends you to hell," I said, "then I've really got worries."

She smiled and crossed an arm under her breasts. "I can't stand letting him tell me what to do. Not at my age."

131

"Well, you're hardly old, Aunt Lillian, not like Mary Helen."

She coughed a laugh. "I'm only two years younger."

Then I did turn, Pyrex dish and towel in my hand, and stared at her hard, at the slim-fitting dress and the glossy panels of hair sliding around her face. Aunt Lillian was the woman my father said Thomas married for money, but it seemed to me Thomas would have had, still did have, many other reasons to marry her.

"You know, Maggie," she said exhaling cirrous wisps, "you should get to know Casey. She's nicer than she looks."

"I never thought she didn't look nice."

"You didn't?"

It took me a moment to understand that she was really asking me a question. "No, I didn't."

"The boys think she's snotty. Makes them absolutely crazy. The phone rings off the hook." She dropped ashes into the sink and turned on the water to wash them down. "I figure she'll get over it when they get over it. But the fact is she's a good kid, and you should get to know her better."

Before Lillian could put out her smoke, Coral returned, shaking her head. "I send Debbi away, and you just light up."

"Oh, Coral," Lillian said. "Whit's not my father. He's not even Thomas's father."

"Near to," Coral said. And then loudly, "Chess! Carving time!" She pulled parsley from the fridge. "Think I ought to wash this? No one's going to eat it, do you think?"

The grown-ups, or maybe I should say the parents, ate in the dining room. Polishing off cups of grandfather punch, they took their seats at the long table, Great-aunt Mary Louise, Grampa Whit, Thomas and Lillian, Clare and Adele and Mary Helen, my mother and father, Katherine and her husband, Debbi and her husband Paul, and Coral and Chess, all of them moving and talking, leaning across the table or tipping back in their chairs to speak to one another. Candles flickered down the center of the table, and angel hair and pine cones, gold beads and evergreens made an island around the candles. I could see all this from where I sat in the kitchen eating with the rest of the kids and Willy, who'd argued that, being draftable, he deserved to dine with the adults but in time took a seat with us.

We were almost done with everything, and Alison and Howie had excused themselves, when Casey said, "My best friend is *so* dumb."

"Then why is she your best friend?" Willy asked. He leaned back in his chair, his arms crossed over his chest.

"Someone can be a friend," Casey said, "and not be perfect."

"So what's your best friend do that's so dumb?" my brother asked.

"Well, just as an experiment," Casey said, "just to see what she'd say, I told her I thought Frenching was the worst thing you could do with a boy. I said I wouldn't French unless I was married. I said I'd fuck before I'd French. And she agreed. Now isn't that dumb?"

"Sounds like you're the dumb one," Willy said.

"Am not," Casey said. "You are such an ass, Willy Nash."

"Well, Cassandra Harris, which would you do first?"

"Please," Casey said. "You think I'd let a guy do either?"

"You wouldn't?" I asked.

"God, no," Casey said.

"Not ever?" I asked and wondered if this was what made her a better, a more expert, girl than me.

"How else are you going to get someone to marry you?"

"I don't know," I said. "I thought maybe people fell in love or something."

"Who ever said marriage had anything to do with love?" Willy asked.

"You just say that because your mother left your father," Casey said.

"Seems to me marriage is just a piece of paper," Willy said. "A contract like any other contract. And so what's the point? If love comes and goes despite some piece of paper, why get the piece of paper to begin with?"

"At least the paper says love began sometime," Casey said.

"Is that what it means?" I asked.

"Well, I know I'm not letting any boy mess with me unless we've got that piece of paper," Casey said.

"But that's sex you're talking about," Willy said. "Sex is just sex." He grew expansive as he spoke now, spreading his arms, as if to show off the embroidered cuffs of his blue work shirt. "Animal instinct, you know?"

"That's easy for you to say," Casey said.

"It's all just one big hormonal itch."

"You really think that?" I asked.

Casey in his sights, Willy swatted my question away and said, "Isn't it, Miss Cassandra?"

"Willy, you are just so dumb," Casey said. "I suppose you're up there at Berkeley with a dozen girlfriends?" Watching her, I couldn't help but think how many boys I knew would want her for their girlfriend. The blond hair, the bar-of-soap shoulders, the heart-shaped locket—a promise of love—hanging from her throat.

"A few, anyway," Willy said.

"And you don't care who they are or what they look like?"

"I'm just saying urges are urges," Willy said.

"But if it's just an itch, any girl ought to do. Any girl walking down the street, fat or skinny. Or anything female, cat or bow-wow. Why would you care?"

"Urges do come in shapes and sizes," Willy said and stretched out, hands behind his head, as if the wood chair were his recliner.

"Good God. What is going on here?" None of us had seen Debbi standing at the kitchen door, both hands spread, as if in protection, over her belly. "This is supposed to be the children's table. Why all this talk of sex?"

"It's Christmas," Willy said. "A time of renewal, of the winter solstice when the days begin again to lengthen, of the word of God announced to men and their sheep."

"Shut up, Willy," Casey said. "Christmas is the one good time."

"Toy time," he said.

"What's wrong with that?" Jamie asked. I saw that all along he'd been drawing, his pad half-hidden in his lap, a manger scene where the Virgin wore a headband much like the velvet ribbon Casey wore in her hair.

"Nothing's wrong with that, sweetheart," Debbi said. "Let a kid be a kid, why don't you, Willy?"

"He's no kid, are you, Jamie?"

"Not after listening to you," Casey said.

"Help me clear the table?" Debbi said, and it was plain she was speaking to Casey and me. So that's what we did, helped clear the table before Coral and my mother came in to brew coffee and whip cream for the pie. As I ran dishes under water, I asked Casey, "Did you mean what you said before?"

"About Frenching and fucking?" she asked, shaking turkey remains into a paper sack. "Sort of. I won't let anyone do the yucky to me, and I sure won't get caught like that girl I know."

"What girl?"

"Didn't you hear my mother talking about her?" she asked. "I mean, I'm sure my mother told someone. About this girl who had a baby and then moved. To San Francisco. With her new boyfriend."

"Just left her baby?"

"Who do you think was going to raise it anyway?" Casey ripped tinfoil from a roll and wrapped it over the turkey carcass. "Her? She's too dumb to be a mother."

"No, no one would do that."

"Don't worry. She'll come back, she told me so. Called me collect. Said she was living with a bunch of people in a house on some street with a weird name."

Casey scraped mashed potatoes from the large serving bowl into a smaller bowl. "You know what she said? She said the boys in the house want to ball all the time and that they say you should do it because it's natural and what's natural is right and you should do what's right. They want to ball. Isn't that gross?"

"Yes," I said and imagined Bruce saying that. No, he'd never, would he? "Does she want to do it all the time?"

"God, no. She said she's always telling them she has her period. That usually stops them, she said. So I guess that's one excuse I'm going to remember," Casey said. "Aren't you?"

The grown-ups had all moved into the living room, sharing the sofa and the wing chairs, the footrests and the love seat, bringing straight-backs in from the dining room when they'd run out of places. They were all sitting and balancing on their knees saucers and cups of coffee Casey and I had brought from the kitchen, and I was bringing the last cup ("This one's for Mary Helen," Coral had said to me as she poured the milk. "She likes her coffee white.") when I heard the children—Howie, Alison, and Jamie—run through the living room. I heard their wild laughter and commotion and a small, almost musical crash, like tiny wind chimes in a storm.

"Children!" my mother said. "Watch yourselves! If you're going to run around, run outside."

"It's not so bad, Marian," Mary Helen said as I handed her the coffee. "It's just Christmas ornaments." Pieces of ornaments were scattered on the wood floor, like crescent peels of some rare fruit, shiny red outside, glassy gold in. My mother got down on her hands and knees, collecting the pieces in the nest of her palm, until Uncle Chess said,

"Enough, enough. The cleaning woman will get it tomorrow." My mother stood up, her hand full of bright shards, and despite her beautiful red dress, she looked something like a maid dismissed. I couldn't help but think it hurt her, knowing Coral hired a woman to do the housework.

"Remember that, Jim?" Grampa Whit said. "I swear, you broke every last one of Greta Ruth's Christmas ornaments. You pitched them at the wall and they shattered all over." Grampa Whit laughed tears into the corners of his eyes. "And Greta Ruth was so angry, she wanted to tan your hide into one-inch strips."

"Don't exaggerate," Mary Helen said. "Most of Greta's ornaments were tin, I'm sure."

Chess laughed and said, "Whatever they were, he was just showing off for Evelyn."

"I bet he was," Grampa Whit said.

"Make up a truth to suit yourself," my father said. "Just remember who my target was."

Chess shook his head side to side. "I remember."

"What I remember," Grampa Whit said, "is walking into the house that morning and seeing that glass shattered all over the floor and Greta Ruth picking splinters out of your feet for hours."

"Well, it must have been the only time I ever got the best of *him*," my father said.

"I think you beat me a time or two more," Chess said.

"If he did," my mother said quietly, as if broaching an unusual design to a client, "that must have been a long time ago."

My father cocked his head and appraised my mother, as if reckoning how far she would go. Coral leaned forward as if to speak, then sat back and stirred her coffee slowly. But Grampa Whit spoke up as if my mother hadn't said a word. "What I'll never forget is that Evelyn hadn't raised a hand to stop you two. When I walked in, she was just sitting there on the steps putting a comb through her hair. And I'd told her to look after you. That woman has never done one thing right."

"Don't blame her," Chess said. "Trouble was our middle name."

My mother hunched forward as she watched Chess and Grampa Whit. She was, I think, bewildered, even ashamed, they could ignore her so easily.

"I thought I had a purchase on how to rear my boys," Grampa Whit said. "Until Evelyn moved in."

"Heavens, no sister of mine was as bad as that," Mary Helen said. "You were just angry you had to take her in."

"I wouldn't have complained if it had been you."

"I was already married and on my own," Mary Helen said.

"You have to admit Greta and Whit were generous," Aunt Clare said.

"Greta was the generous one," Mary Helen said. "She wouldn't do this. Talk her sister Evelyn down and then act as if she weren't alive."

"I don't act as if she weren't alive," Grampa Whit said. "I act as if she weren't family."

We all breathed in unison, or seemed to. Finally Mary Helen said, "Life has not exactly been easy for her."

"Her life is exactly what she made it," Grampa Whit said. "Any Godfearing woman would have married."

"She and John Rumsen were about as married as any two people I've ever seen," my father said.

"Fine," Grampa Whit said. "Let the Rumsens take care of her."

"There is only one word for you, Whitman T. Harris." Mary Helen, little Mary Helen in her wide lace collar, pointed her finger at him and said, "Cheap."

Chess chuckled and said, "Well, I don't know." Almost under her breath, my mother said, "I'll say." My father glanced a warning at her, and Aunt Coral said, "Now, that just isn't true. Whit is," and here she had to pause and choose her word, "careful."

"Waste not, want not," Grampa Whit said as if four words would settle everything.

"After all, no one has money to burn," Aunt Coral said.

"Jim's the only one I know burning his money," Grampa Whit said. "Burning mine too, for that matter."

My father pitched forward and set his coffee cup on the floor.

"But you always get your money back," my mother said, defending my father.

"Marian." My father sat upright again.

"Well, he does, doesn't he?"

"Let's just say I get a very low rate of return on Jim's projects," Grampa Whit said. "My money'd be better off in a bank. Or under the mattress."

"We all try to help each other out, Marian," my father said. "And we all take losses in this business. Chess, Dad, everyone."

"They do?" my mother said and gazed about the room, at the floating stairs and the large bay windows. All the soft triangles of her face—the cleft in her bangs, the slope of her nose, the arch of her lips—seemed sharpened, and the placid gaze she shared with my sister was not placid but rough, snagging on the furnishings that seemed to irritate her: the drapes (opulent), the rugs (Oriental), the china (bone), the upholstery (plush).

"We've never turned Jim down when he asked for help," Coral said.

"He wouldn't need to ask if he'd gotten his fair share on all those projects. The house he renovated or that development you're always talking about."

"*Marian.*" Plainly angry, my father rose abruptly from the footrest where he sat and then with too much courtesy said to the room at large, "It's probably time for us to go."

"Oh, Jim, don't," Mary Helen said. "How often do we get to see you?"

"Too often, apparently," Coral said.

My mother sighed and shifted in her chair, resetting her arms and legs and turning her face pointedly away from everyone in the room, as if she meant to study the titles on the spines of the leather-bound books in towering shelves near the fire.

"Marian didn't mean it," Mary Helen said, appealing to Coral and my father.

"I didn't?" My mother swung her face back toward the Harrises ranged around the room.

"Marian," my father said. "Let's get the children together."

Again my mother reordered herself, her legs angled steeply under her chair, her dark red dress rippling as her body shifted.

"Marian," he said again. She glanced toward him, then looked away, almost imperceptibly shaking her head no. My father swiped a hand through vacant air. "Maggie, you get the kids together."

"Yes, Dad," I said and moved toward the sliding glass doors. I could see, we all could see, Willy and the children outside, sitting in the dark under an umbrella, dessert dishes scattered on the poolside table. Willy tilted back in his chair, talking to Alison, who sat pert across the table from him. Howie had pulled his seat right to the edge of the pool, and as I opened the door enough so I could pass through, he held up a small key for me to see (I had no idea why), then pocketed it, and lightly tugged the nylon cord that guided his boat through the water, while my brother bounced on the end of the diving board, his hands clasped casually behind his back.

Showoff, I was thinking, when Jamie shouted, "Hey, Maggie, watch this. Watch me win the boat from Howie."

And I did watch as Jamie sprang high, oddly not using his arms, and plunged head first into the aqua pool. As he dove, his back arching and his head reaching for the water, I saw what kept his hands useless behind his back. His wrists were manacled in his magic-shop cuffs.

"Oh my God," my mother screamed from the living room, where something, perhaps my brother's shout, had made her lift her head so she too had seen his bound hands.

A chair toppled, a teaspoon fell, a plate broke, cups rattled, and spilled coffee pooled in saucers as the grown-ups followed my mother to the sliding glass doors she slid open so hard they whacked against the frame and made the glass shudder. My mother ran to the edge, and the rest followed, pitching forward over the wavering water, the men pulling off their jackets and ties and shoes, preparing to dive.

Jamie's jacket spread inkily around him as he floated under water, not heavy enough to sink but not buoyant enough to rise in his wet clothes. He curled and tried to slip his hips and legs through the hoop of his arms, but his hands wouldn't reach beyond the belt revealed by his billowing jacket. He jerked his arms down and tried to sit on his wrists, but his body slipped free.

"So give up," Howie shouted through the megaphone of his hands.

Under the water, Jamie wrenched his arms back, as if trying to lengthen their reach. He undulated, pushing his hips back, and at last they caught between his forearms. But he did not move, and coiled in the water, he began to sink. His jacket and tie, his hair, wafted around him as he drifted to the bottom.

"Someone do something," my mother screamed and my father, in undershirt and trousers, leaped into the shallow end while Chess dove off the board. Both plunged toward my brother, but he tumbled, deliberately I think, away from them, until he was way down at the bottom of the pool where the abandoned skimmer lay. My father dove down again, and my uncle followed, but by then Jamie was freeing himself. His head fell to his knees and his hands slipped up behind his thighs. He jackknifed, folding himself in half, and a shoe tumbled away toward the pool's drain as he fought his feet through the gate of his arms. His clothes furling around him, he straightened himself, his wrists still cuffed but his arms free to stretch over his head. My uncle surfaced, and then my father, saying, "You got him? You got him?" while Jamie scissor-kicked to the shallow end of the pool, where he breached and stood gasping.

POSTSCRIPT

Getting in trouble and all, I wasn't exactly welcome at later family gatherings. Casey is the one member of the family proper I have seen since. She found me, in that apartment above the drugstore where I lived with Mrs. Rumsen. Casey brought some of her friends, even the girl Chrissy she said was so dumb and who of course wasn't, and we all celebrated Christmas there in Mrs. Rumsen's front room, each girl holding the baby for a few minutes, that look of surprise and fear passing from face to face as they passed the baby around. Even girls who, like me, had diapered and burped and cared for babies at home, seemed frightened to hold the baby of someone only one year older than they were. It crossed my mind that they were waiting for Mrs. Rum to come from the bedroom and take charge of the baby, the same way I sometimes did. But there was something else too, something in their eyes I couldn't understand until I'd seen it in lots of girls' faces. Curiosity might be the polite name for it. They looked at me as if overnight I'd turned into a different animal, as if the things I did, holding the baby, nursing it, putting my finger into its fist, were as strange to them as a giraffe slowly munching leaves from the top of a tree.

As I stood at the window and watched them drive away, as I watched Casey thrum her fingers on the soft top of her red Mustang, I could imagine what she might be saying to her friends. What a fool I was, how pathetic to be living with a nut-case who'd never bothered to marry either. But I didn't care, they had come, they'd talked to me about boyfriends and all the everyday things girls talk about. They even brought presents. Casey brought a Playtex nurser kit, the kind with collapsible bottles. This girl Laurie gave me a forty-five by Sonny and

Cher, and Chrissy gave me diaper pins with plastic ducks and lambs on the end. I recognized Mrs. Hill's wrapping paper from downstairs and guessed that Chrissy'd bought the pins only minutes before, but that was fine with me. These girls came and sat in the room and told me what went on. Did I know Alison was wearing a training bra? Had I heard about that girl who'd hitchhiked to San Diego and never been heard from again? Did I know Willy had grown his hair even longer and wore wire-rimmed glasses now, not to mention the fiery-colored mandala his girlfriend had embroidered on his jacket?

"Is she pretty?" I asked Casey.

"She looks like she bakes bread all day," Casey said.

"That's what I look like."

FIFTEEN

The houses and trees seemed stenciled against the sky, and the new moon was a hoop of light, streaky clouds blowing. Wind shook the oak trees, and the Christmas lights flickered behind the prickly leaves. My father and brother more or less dry and dressed in borrowed clothes, we trekked down the lawn and climbed into the car, me in front with my mother, since my father had said to me, "You drive," and him in back with Jamie and Alison.

Mary Helen waved to us from the front step, and Coral joined her, but the rest of the family stayed inside, perhaps embarrassed by the spectacle. We could see them through the plate-glass windows. A few seemed to return our glances, but most gathered, small carol books in hand, around the piano Aunt Clare leaned forward to play. In her prim suit, she rocked back and forth on the bench, conducting her family choir. The sounds that reached us were thin as bickering, but the sight of the family through the tall windows, the look of unison and harmony, of lit candles and flashing flashbulbs and a glittering white tree, that was thick and warm as syrup and butter. I thought it might melt the living-room window and glaze the sloping lawn. His boat under his arm, Howie ducked between Mary Helen and Coral and ran halfway down the grass, waving widely at my brother. I waved back a last time and pulled the car from the curb, air slipping in through the windows and vents.

My mother shivered slightly, then turned herself around and reached over the seat back to wrap a blanket more securely around my brother.

"I'm okay," Jamie said and shook her hands away. He wore an over-sized sweatshirt and a pair of worn corduroys, Chess's old clothes

142

("Don't bother returning them," Coral had said), but his hair was still a wet web, and the sharp odor of chlorine spread through the car. "Just wish I could have sprung the lock."

"Whatever gave you such a foolish idea?" my mother asked.

"Wasn't foolish," Jamie said. "I could have done it."

"You're never going to try a stunt like that again, you hear me?" my father said.

"I gave Coral those hand things," my mother said. "So this one doesn't have them anymore."

"Good," my father said. In the rearview mirror, I saw him grip Jamie by the neck and shake him, just hard enough I was glad he wasn't shaking me. Wedged between them, Alison closed her eyes and slid down as if ready to sleep.

"And your father's suit trousers ruined," my mother said.

"He didn't have to jump in," Jamie said. "It wasn't like I couldn't kick my way to the surface."

"That's enough, Jamie," my father said. "We know you didn't drown. But you could have. You scared the living daylights out of us, that's all."

The streets were broad and winding, and each house we passed was, as my mother would have put it, tastefully decorated. A single oak tree laced with white lights or a door with an elaborate wreath. I drove slowly, and my father seemed not to mind.

"Glad I don't have to see them for another six months," my mother said and resettled herself in the front seat.

"I'm glad you don't either," my father said.

"What do you mean by that?" My mother glanced back at my father.

"Turn left up here." He tapped my shoulder and said close to my ear, "And don't slow down yet. Step on the brakes when you *get* to the corner, not half a block ahead, for Christ's sake.

"You know exactly what I mean," he said to my mother. "I asked you not to talk about money, but you just couldn't keep your mouth shut."

"What? I hardly said a thing. They were the ones talking about money. I just agreed."

"I heard you, Marian. You think I didn't? Think my father didn't hear you? Big help you are, insulting my father."

"Make a right at the light," he said to me, "and don't look over your shoulder. How many times do I have to tell you? Use your mirrors."

"That's not what they teach," I started to say.

"I don't give a damn what they teach."

"I don't see why they get to live the life of Riley," my mother said.

"Do we live so badly?" my father said. "I ask you, do we live badly?"

"Look at that house Chess and Coral live in. With a maid!"

"Cleaning woman," my father said.

"Cleaning woman, maid, it's the same thing. And what about that place your father bought? Never mind that Lillian and her natty Thomas and their Howie in private school. And none of them has lost a penny. We lose the money."

"How many times do I have to tell you? You don't know anything about it. You don't know how they've helped us out."

"I suppose that's what your father agreed to do tonight, help you out?"

"So he didn't. You don't know enough to see how it works."

"I know what I see," my mother said, "and I see they aren't worrying about bills."

"Mom," my brother said.

"Mo-om what?" she said.

"You started it."

"I what?"

We drove toward an overpass, and my father said, "Goddamn it all, Maggie. You missed the turn. Pull over."

"You started it," my brother said. "You started the fight."

"What turn?" I pulled onto the shoulder, in the shadow of the freeway over our heads. "You didn't tell me to turn."

"Your father and I are not fighting," my mother said to Jamie. "We're discussing."

"You can't read a goddamn sign?" my father said. "Letters as big as the star of Bethlehem and you can't read them?"

"How was I supposed to know that's the way to go?"

"There's some other way?"

"Side streets."

"So we'll get home the Christmas after next?" my father said. "Just back up, would you?"

"I can't just back up here. I have to go around the block."

"I said, back up. Now. While no one's coming."

"I'm trying to sleep, everyone," Alison said. "So be quiet."

"That's cute," my mother said. "Sleep! She's trying to sleep."

"I can't back up, I cannot put this car into reverse and back across an on-ramp in the middle of traffic."

"You'll do what I tell you."

"You drive, then."

"Goddamn it all, Maggie." He punched the back of the seat, and my mother said, "Do what your father tells you."

"Jesus H. Christ, all right." I jerked into reverse, and a passing car swerved around us.

"Don't swear, Maggie," my mother said.

"Christ almighty." My father thumped the back of my head. "I didn't tell you to back into traffic. Pull up and try again."

"Fuck," I said. The car jerked forward and stalled. "Fuck and piss and shit."

"Don't talk like that," my mother said. "Where'd you learn to talk like that, for Christ's sake?"

"She learned it from you," my father said. "Start the goddamned engine, would you?"

"What do you mean she learned it from me? *You* taught *me* to talk like that."

I turned the key and the engine rolled but didn't start.

"What are you doing now?" my mother said. "Pump the gas, and turn the key. That's easy enough, isn't it?"

"Don't do that, Mag," my father said quietly over my shoulder. "Just give it a minute." To my mother he said, "That's stupid shitting advice, Marian."

I turned the key and felt the satisfying pull of the engine.

"How dare you talk like that?" my mother said. "Just go to hell."

"Would you think about the kids, Marian?" my father said. "Just for once?"

I drove slowly ahead and made a loop in the lot of a 7-Eleven, so I could return to the on-ramp. My father said, "Should have done what I told you."

I moved into the stream of cars, content to follow taillights following taillights, but my father leaned forward and said, "Come on, Mag. Drive like you've got somewhere to go."

"What?" I said. "You want me to pass?"

"What else are you going to do? Poke along here? Get out of this goddamned lane." He sat back and repeated an old joke of his. "I'll make a man of you before your mother."

My brother asked, "Before my mother what?"

145

My father shrugged and said, "Before your mother. That's all."

My mother tugged her sweater tighter around her and snuggled down in her seat. "Before he makes a man of me," she said.

"One thing I'll say about Bruce," my father said, "at least he isn't full of hogwash, like Willy."

"Wasn't he awful?" my mother said. "All those things he said about that Viet place."

"Only reason he enrolled in that school was to avoid the draft," my father said. "That and the girls. He sure doesn't want to avoid them."

"He says he has lots of girlfriends," Alison said.

"I thought you were sleeping," my mother said.

"I bet he says that," my father said.

"Why shouldn't he have lots of girlfriends?" Alison asked.

"Don't count on it," my father said. "Anyway, those girls he's talking about aren't really girls anyway. They're just boys who studied their nuts off."

"Jim."

"At least Bruce isn't shirking his duty," my father said. "Maybe he'll even be worth something when they get done with him."

"He's worth something now," I said.

"A tinker's damn," my father said. And then, "What are you doing with cars on all sides? We get ahead of that car, you slip right and pass this car in front of us. You hear me?"

People say the craziest things about freeways. They talk about them as if they were man-made rivers, the true landscape of the century. People even talk as if freeways were holy, as if driving onto a freeway were like taking communion, or a cure. But crazy as it is, people are right. Freeways do work a kind of cure. A calm, a peacefulness, settles on passengers. Babies fall asleep on the backseat, and children stretch out like lazy dogs under the rear windshield. The friction of the tires against the road works up through your feet and spine and numbs your legs and arms. Your ears fill with wind and the thrum of rubber on pavement and the radio voices of passing cars, not to mention the chant of the engines, the polyphony of your engine and of the Buick or Studebaker out your window.

Our car grew quiet. My mother slept, her purse wedged between her head and the window. My sister slid herself under my father's arm, and in the rearview mirror, I could see my brother sitting very still, his hands limp on his spiral notebook as he stared out the window. Only my father was alert, watching what I did over my shoulder.

The cities passed us, the apartments and motels, with their lone yellow lights near each red door, the supermarkets and shopping centers surrounded by moats of glimmering asphalt, their signs high on top of poles so you could read them miles away: Van de Kamp's and J. J. Biggars, Broadway and JCPenney. We passed the parks and schoolyards and the houses that covered the hills, nonpareil Christmas lights sprinkling the dark. Somewhere to the east was Linda Vista, a development Chess and my father had worked on together. Each time we drove out to my aunt and uncle's, my father would point to this place in the hills, this web of gray streets ending in cul-de-sacs, and he'd remind us that Chess and he had built the houses there. Sometimes he'd tell us how much money they'd made on the deal, except that that would remind him of how much money he had since lost and he'd grow silent. Other times he'd remark on the changes. "Look at the color they painted that house on Live Oak. Do you believe it?"

Linda Vista changed every time we passed. At first it resembled a 3-D map, a grade-school diorama with gray roads, brown lots, and look-alike houses in four basic colors. As people moved in, cars filled the garages, and the lots turned green with grass and wisps of trees here and there. The first few times we passed, the trees looked like weeds, like foxtails you could rip from the ground with one hand. But now the trees had thick trunks and canopies that shadowed the streets and obscured the houses, and in the dark Linda Vista was almost invisible. I wouldn't have known we were passing it, except for the freeway. After a westward bend and a double overpass, I knew the place was in the hills to our right, and I waited for my father to say, "Look at Linda Vista. Chess and I made a mint off that project."

Instead he said, "Mary Helen was wrong. Every one of those ornaments was glass, and I broke all of them."

The radio of a nearby car blasted, "Let's take a trip down Whittier Boulevard," and the Glasspak muffler roared as the car overtook us.

"Take your mother's advice," my father said. "Wear that dress to the Christmas dance."

"Why?"

"Some guy might look at you twice."

"I don't need some other guy to look at me twice."

"What do you know about what you need?" He leaned forward.

147

"What speed are you doing here? Fifty? Pick it up, for God's sakes. You want to get rear-ended?"

Our neighborhood: all the one-story roofs seemed to have lost their slope, to have flattened and drooped, since we'd left for the attorney's office that afternoon. Our street: the familiar bumps, the familiar cars parked in their familiar places on Homewood, the familiar spots of grease and oil beneath them. Our neighbors' houses: the same lights shining the way they shone every night, the dim lamp in the Thompsons' den, the bright yellow light in the Morrises' kitchen, the glimmer of a night light in the Dawsons' living room. Our house: the porch lamp lit, a felt Santa my mother had made smiling at us from the front door. The tinsel on our tree glittered faintly as our headlights hit the front window. Our house: the balding lawn, the leaves scattered across the yard. Our house and the acre of black orange trees scratching the sky.

"God, does this house need a paint job," my mother said.

"Who left the kitchen light on?" my father asked. "That's sheer waste of electricity. Should make you kids pay the electric."

"Is that your skateboard, Jamie?" my mother said.

"If you'd do like I told you," my father said to me, "you wouldn't drive over the grass every time."

"Did you do that?" my mother asked me. "Did you leave the garbage cans open? As if we didn't have enough problems with raccoons."

"What do you expect of your daughter?" my father said.

"My daughter?" she said. "She takes after you more than me."

They went on like that for hours, stopless, even when my father carried my sister from the car into her room, even when my mother took her shower. As if to spite them, I plugged in the lights of our Christmas tree. Then Jamie and I went out the front door and sat on the porch, concrete my father had poured in circles and ovals, to resemble stone. We stopped by Alison's room and tapped her on the shoulder, but she seemed truly asleep, her body lying in a lazy semaphore, so just the two of us sat there on the disk of concrete. We listened to the rise and fall of their voices, the shouts about taxes and debt and family who either owed us or didn't, and watched the snails, drawn out by the chill, wave their tentacles as they crossed the fake stone.

KISSES

SIXTEEN

Our rough start was, I thought, well past us, our lives more or less stable. My daughter and I had gotten through the worst times, the times she nearly left me, and were living in New Jersey with a man who loved us despite my refusal to marry him. Though not yet a teenager (she was maybe twelve), my daughter seemed to have forgotten, or forgiven me for, the early years. She was happy and doing well in school, and I had found better ways to get by, when she asked me, "Maggie, do you remember making me?"

I dropped the clothes I was washing back into the sink and turned to look at her, my hands dripping water on the floor.

"Come on, Maggie," she said. "I want to know."

"What kind of thing is that to ask?"

"I mean, do you remember when, what day?"

"You think that's a better question?" I shook my hands, and drops of water spotted her T-shirt.

"It had to be around New Year's," Emmy said. "I can subtract, you know."

I turned to the sink and said, "The night before Christmas."

"Really?" she said. "Do you mean like I'm holy?"

"Holy? I hardly think so," I said, running rinse water through the clothes. "But, yes, really. The night before Christmas. Would I lie to you?"

She didn't answer.

"Really, I think it was, Emmy. I think it was Christmas Eve."

. . .

And it could have been the night before Christmas, the first night of his fourteen-day leave, the first night I answered the phone on the hall table and heard Bruce's voice again: "Hey, Mag! I told you I'd be back. When can I see you?"

I'd been thinking about seeing him. I'd been thinking about the car and its smell of polish and vinyl and the Old Spice he wore and the way we used to be, drinking beer and driving around the reservoir, but now that I heard his voice wire-thin on the phone, I was frightened. I wanted to see him, but what if it wasn't the same? What if he took a good look and saw me for the plain girl I was?

"I don't know," I said.

"What do you mean? This is me you're talking to, Mag."

"I mean, Dad's made all these plans. He's taking us out to look at the lights and later we're going to the midnight service, so I don't know. Maybe they'd let me see you tomorrow."

"You don't think they'd let me take you to the service or something?"

"My parents? I don't think so."

"Well, let me ask them, okay?"

"Now? On the phone? When have they ever talked to you?"

"So I'll drop by. Think they'll refuse an enlisted man?"

I don't know what other people did (we couldn't see them in their cars), but every Christmas Eve we dressed up in that year's holiday clothes to go look at the lights on other people's houses, my father in a jacket and tie, my mother wearing miniature ornaments on her ears. We had to drive pretty far to join a line of cars creeping through a neighborhood in the foothills that had gone all out, selecting themes and giving prizes. Afterwards, we would drive home and plug in our tree and maybe go to the midnight service or maybe not. My mother was likely to say, "Well, you all can go, but Santa has too much work."

She was saying something like that when we came home from seeing the lights that night.

"You all should go," she was saying, "but Santa's elf simply has . . ." and then she spotted Bruce's car parked in front of our house and shined up the way it was the day Bruce was inducted. "Whose car is that?"

"Can't you tell, Mom?" Jamie said.

"And who's that?" she said, noticing Bruce.

He sat on our front step. In his uniform, in his hat and jacket, he was an unfamiliar shape under the porch light.

152

"You don't recognize the no-good-nik?" my father said.

"It's Bruce, Mom," Alison said.

"That's him?" my mother said and looked again. "Clothes do change a man, don't they?" She glanced at me in the backseat and then looked straight ahead. "You should invite him in, Maggie."

The end-table lamps casting yellow light, Bruce stood opposite our small Christmas tree, his feet spread and his hands behind his back. My mother tried to turn him side to side to admire the pressed folds and trim lines of his dress uniform, but Bruce seemed rooted to the floor. "You're filling in nicely," she said.

"Mom," I said and wondered if that's what it was about Bruce, that he was filling in nicely. He seemed muscley, more than he had been, but thinner too.

"Am I embarrassing you?" my mother said.

"No, it's all right, Mrs. Harris," Bruce said.

My father sat on the sofa, pillows my mother had embroidered tucked behind him, and stretched his arms across the back. Alison sat next to him, trying to fit in that space between his body and arm.

"Let the boy sit, Marian."

My mother gestured toward the overstuffed chair, but Bruce said, "No, you sit there, Mrs. Harris," and he seated himself in the spare chair from the dining alcove. He removed his hat and placed it on the end table, covering a small lacquer dish filled with a tangle of threads from my mother's hand sewing.

"So what do you think of the army?" my father asked.

"You shoot anyone yet?" my brother asked from the doorway where he and I stood.

"Jamie," my mother said.

"No, not yet," Bruce said to my brother. To my father, he said, "I think it's hard, but I think it's good."

"All that physical training," my father said.

Bruce nodded. "Never thought a mile run would kill me," Bruce said, "until I met the drill sergeant."

"I take it they still send you on night marches."

"Sure do," Bruce said. He sat with his back erect and feet flat on the floor, hands on his thighs, and it made a difference. He now seemed respectful of, but also equal to, my father. "Learned to hate a few guys those times. The dimwits and the gripers."

"Yeah, I'll bet you did." My father cocked his head back and nodded. "One thing about the army, they sure do march you. Once I got out I never wanted to walk again. We don't even own a dog because I don't want to walk one. Ever. And who can trust these kids of mine to walk it?"

"Don't even want to walk a dog." Bruce smiled and shook his head. "Seems a little extreme, Mr. Harris."

"What do you mean, extreme? You're in eight weeks, haven't even done one tour yet. What do you know about extreme?" My father raised his arms from the sofa back and leaned forward, elbows to knees. "We were infantry, and we marched until our feet fell off. Jesus, we're the ones that fought the war."

Bruce nodded and said, "Yes, sir. I guess that's so."

Sir. He sounded like Tommy Dawson. I looked to see if he knew that too, to see if he'd show me a thin slice of a smile, but he just nodded at my father, his mouth straight, his eyes downcast, everything about him serious.

"Think you'll see any action while you're in?"

"Well, I hope so. They're training me for airborne."

"Airborne?" my father said, angling his head as if to get a new slant on things. "Airborne? Well, then I guess things're decided already. They don't exactly need airborne in Germany, do they?"

"I'd be surprised if they did, sir."

"Well, it seems likely you'll see some action."

"Could be, but you do what they tell you to do."

"At least you'll have a little up-in-the-air perspective on things, better than the normal grunt."

"You think so?"

"Yes, of course."

Bruce nodded, and my father said again, "Yes, of course."

"Would you like something to eat?" my mother asked. "I have some cake I made yesterday."

"No, thank you, Mrs. Harris. I would like, though, to take Maggie to see Christmas Tree Lane."

"We just got back from looking at the lights in Sierra Madre," my mother said. "And we're all going to, when does midnight service start? To the midnight service that begins at eleven."

"Well, I haven't seen the lights," Bruce said. "And we'd be back in time to get her to church."

My mother looked at my father. My father looked at my mother.

Then he stood and walked Bruce toward the door, and I followed behind. "So bring Maggie back in time for the service. Or better yet, just take her there yourself."

"We shouldn't, you know," Bruce said. He sat on the edge of his brother's bed, reaching for the chair where his hat hung, as if he meant to put the hat on and walk out the door.

I lay on the bed, the dotted Swiss dress rumpled around me. The Christmas lights on the building across the walk shone blue and orange into the room. "I've been thinking so too. We shouldn't."

"We could just . . ." Bruce said.

"We could." Except, of course, his restraint hurt, as if I mattered less, as if he wanted me less.

"I mean, it would be bad if you got, you know." He turned to look at me. He was all unbuttoned and unbuckled.

"Yes, it would be bad if that happened." I rolled away from him. "You know it almost did."

He said nothing, so I thought he hadn't heard me, or hadn't understood.

"What do you mean, almost?"

"I mean almost because last time I did something. I 7UPped. So I wouldn't be."

"You what?"

I told him about the bath and the ginger ale, and he said, "You can't be doing that, Mag. You can't be sticking bottles inside you," and he slapped his hat against his leg.

"Well, we've got to do something."

"We won't do anything at all."

"Nothing?"

He put his hat on the chair again and fell back on the bed, arms across his chest. "Nothing."

We lay still. Sounds from a television upstairs soaked through the floor, the rush of laughter and applause and then the chiming sound of a carol.

"They're sending me to Fort Campbell," Bruce said, putting a hand in my hair.

"Is that good?"

"Think so. Like I told your father, they're teaching me to jump."

"You like that?"

"I do. You proud?"

"Yes," I said because he wanted me to be, and right then I would do anything to please him.

We were quiet a while, and I thought how I couldn't think what was different now. Bruce's hair was short, of course, shorter than I'd ever seen it, so he looked both older, like my grandfather, and younger, like a boy who'd just made junior varsity. And he seemed bigger and skinnier at the same time. Most of all, he listened, not to me especially, but to my father. But there was something else, something I missed and couldn't quite remember or name.

Bruce rolled to his side, and we cupped our bodies together, his back to my chest. His shirt was crisp with starch.

"Put your arm around me," he said.

I wrapped my arm around him and slid my hand inside his shirt as if he'd hidden what I missed under his clothes.

Somewhere in the building people were talking and laughing. Someone struck a few chords on a piano, then stopped, and the laughter rose louder.

"Don't you want to do anything at all?" I said, but he didn't answer.

I'd like to believe that I didn't really mean to do what we did. I'd like to believe I meant to do stuff the way we used to, half dressed in the orange grove. But I was looking for something I couldn't find, something I just had to have, so we did more. We did it half dressed, but we did it, there on Bruce's brother's bed. We did it once, surprised by need, and then again, because we had the luxury of privacy and because we were making small discoveries along the way, where to put our feet and knees, our arms and elbows, our hands. We were just beginning to learn the language, when to move and when to lie still, when to roll, when to trade and turn. When to arch, when to bite, to cry. We were doing it again when the sound of a door slamming and people talking loudly in the hallway outside the apartment made us stop, as if we feared they might hear us.

"The time," Bruce said.

And then we were in the bathroom, washing and dressing. We ran down the stairs and across the courtyard and sat in the car, scanning ourselves in the rearview mirror for traces of guilt as we drove to church.

We were much more than late. The minister who only reads scripture had already read scripture and the minister who only delivers the sermon had delivered his homily, and as we slid into the pew with the rest of my family, the choir was singing an arrangement of carols.

My mother leaned across Alison and Jamie to say quietly, "You're late!"

Jamie said, "Where've you been?" and Alison told him to keep quiet. My father leaned forward and looked at us warily, as if uncertain whether to be angry or glad, and I thought for sure he would see what I'd been doing, he'd see marks on my mouth, all over my skin, where I'd been kissed and kissing. But he must not have, because in the end he smiled and nodded, and soon the whole row of us stood with the congregation and sang with them, as the minister who only read scripture instructed us, the first, second, and fifth verses of "Silent Night."

That was the first day of Bruce's fourteen-day leave, and it seemed like every one of the thirteen days remaining we found an excuse to spend time in his brother's bed. We'd have some story for my mother. We'd say we were going shopping, we were visiting friends, we were going to the beach just to walk in the sand. But we always went somewhere to be alone. We went sometimes to the reservoir, and once we carried the blanket into the orange grove. More often we wanted the four private walls of his brother's apartment. His brother even gave him a key. "Wouldn't do this for just anyone," Tim had said. "So make good use of the place, you two."

Make good use?

"Aw, well, we'll try," Bruce said, without looking at me or his brother.

After that first night, Bruce walked into the Hillside Pharmacy and asked Mr. Hill for the jelly and rubbers Joan had told me about. A guy in uniform, Bruce could do that. I sat in the car with the ignition key cocked, half listening to the music and watching the traffic creep by. I was humming *Rooms to let, fifty cents* when I saw a small woman in a dark skirt and pumps cross the street. I don't know why I watched her. Maybe it was the bag of groceries she carried and that it seemed impossible such a small woman could carry such a large bag. The woman had crossed the street and walked to a door I'd never noticed before, a door between the Hillside Pharmacy and the Good Guys Hardware, when I understood the woman was Mrs. Rumsen. She hugged her sack of groceries, and with her free hand she tried to unlock the door.

"Mrs. Rum," I said and climbed out of the car.

"Well, look who's here," she said, pushing the door open. "I was hoping you'd pay me a visit."

"You never sent us a postcard," I said. "You know, with your address."

"You didn't think I was really going to, did you?"

She smiled, an off-center smile, and her pink lipstick seemed all talked away, except in the tiny creases around her mouth. It looked nice that way, the way Mrs. Rumsen should look, and it crossed my mind the dark skirt and heels did not look like her and were a uniform.

"Well, yes, I did."

"Didn't I say you were lucky?" she said. "You still think people mean what they say."

"No, I don't. Not always."

"Yes, you do," she said, and then, "Want to come up and see the new place?"

Just then, Bruce came out of the Hillside Pharmacy, a white bag in hand, and walked over to me.

"I can't, really," I said. "We have to go."

She eyed Bruce. "And you're the boyfriend I've heard so much about?"

"That's me. Or that's me if it's Bruce she talks about. And you're?" He squinted down the street and back at Mrs. Rum. "We visited you one night, or tried to, right?"

"Yes, I believe you did. I'm Mrs. Rum, long lost family and friend."

He reached to shake her hand but stopped because her arms were full. "Didn't know you all were so close."

"Close enough. Maggie ever tell you I looked after her when she was a baby?"

"I don't believe she ever did."

"Well, I did." Mrs. Rumsen shifted the groceries to her other hip.

"Let me help you with that," Bruce said.

"No, I'm fine. I can do it." She paused and said nothing a moment. "She's a good girl, isn't she?"

"I think so," Bruce said. He tucked his package under his arm and glanced at me.

"You make sure she watches out for herself," Mrs. Rum said as she started up the stairs. "And tell her to come visit me. It's not far at all. Right here on Las Tunas. I could use some youthful company every now and then."

"Sure will, Mrs. Rumsen," Bruce said.

We watched the dark green door close behind her, and then we drove to his brother's place, the white package between us on the car seat. We did the best we could with the stuff Joan had told me about. It's possible I wasn't lying to my daughter. It could have been Christmas Eve we conceived her, except calendars and counting days made me think it was more likely January sixth. After all, I can subtract too.

SEVENTEEN

*B*ruce gone, I went to church before I went to Mrs. Rumsen.

Joan said to me on the phone, "What're you going to church for? That's crazy. Either you love him or you don't. You think the church knows that?"

"Do you," I asked in a voice I hoped my mother wouldn't hear, "love Charlie?"

"Of course I do," she said. "Look how long we've been going steady. If you don't break up for a long time, that's love."

"Is six months a long time?"

That's how long I'd gone with Bruce.

"It's forever. My rule is a month. You're still seeing him after a month, it's love."

My mother had some rules for love. She said you're in love if making curtains sounds like fun. You're in love if ironing his shirts excites you, not that you'd do that unless you were married or engaged. You're in love, naturally, if you think about him all the time. And you're really gone if you want to have his baby.

I couldn't discuss having babies, not even with Joan.

So I went to the church, to the Methodist Youth Group that met Wednesday nights. Usually they had hootenannies and food drives, but the week I went they had a session on "Love and Dating." That's why I went. I'd seen the posters with the red valentines.

The group met in John Wesley Hall, a large pale-green room with a wooden floor. It was one of the halls where evacuees stayed during the fires, and foldout cots and green blankets were stored in a corner of the room. The floor was taped for half-court basketball and a hoop was mounted at one end. At the other were beige Formica tables, cookies and juice set out on one and pencils and pamphlets on the other. In between were several rows of gray folding chairs, which the Methodist Youth, myself included, would be expected to politely fold and stack when we were through.

I didn't know anyone, and didn't mind that I didn't, so I sat in the back row and waited until the minister, not the one who preached but the one who only read scripture, walked to the front of the room and stood behind a table. Without his robe, he seemed unfamiliar but still recognizable. He was dressed something like a California cowboy, and in his plaid shirt and corduroy jeans, he looked like my science teacher. Standing behind the table, he lifted his arms as if he still felt the fullness of the black sleeves he wore on Sundays and asked us to please come forward and take a pamphlet and a pencil, which I did.

The pamphlet was just a mimeographed sheet folded in half. On the outside it said "Questions About Love" and on the inside there were two columns of questions. The right-hand column was labeled "You" and the left, "Your Loved One." The minister spoke to us briefly about dating and its ultimate goal, marriage. He spoke about the overwhelming love we would one day feel for another, a love that would make us want to marry.

"A love that will spill out onto those around you, that will overflow into the Christian community," he said. "We feel all kinds of feelings, but when we are truly in love, when we truly love, we partake of God's love."

He said that in our lives we would be attracted to many people but we would love only one.

"The Youth Ministry," he said, "has prepared these questions to help you decide whether you're truly in love or maybe just attracted to some good-looking guy or girl. Which is fine. It's healthy to be attracted, but you want to remember that there's only one person you'll want to share everything with.

"So the first thing I want you to do is ask yourself a few questions. I'll read them aloud and give you time to think about and write down your answer."

He took a sip of punch and said, "In fact, don't just write down your answer. Think of an example and write it down too."

He asked, Do you care deeply about the welfare of the other person?

Would you put his or her happiness before your own?

Are you willing to deny yourself for his or her sake?

Do you share the same values?

This last question was followed by two commands: Consider the books you read, the music you listen to. Consider your religion, your political party.

A girl in a blue sweater and reversible skirt sat one row and two seats away. After the minister read each question, she bit her pencil and looked around, her dark ponytail swinging in the draw of her spine. Like me, she wrote no answers.

Did I care deeply about Bruce's welfare? Would I put his happiness before my own? Did we share the same values? Did I even have values?

"Whatever you do, don't lie to yourself," the minister interrupted the silence to say.

"What do you think?" I said to the girl in the blue sweater.

"I don't know," she whispered. "Would I deny myself something for him? I guess so, but I don't think I ever have."

"Do you care deeply?" I read. What I cared about deeply was being close to Bruce in the dark, but I said to the girl in the blue sweater, "I think I care. I mean, I think I care about his happiness more than mine. I guess."

"You got an example?" she whispered, her breath minty.

"While he was in boot camp, I didn't date anyone else."

She said, "If you didn't want to, then you didn't sacrifice your happiness for his, and if you did want to, I don't think you're in love. Do you?"

The minister raised his voice. "Let's move on to the next three questions. Think about the person you're dating and ask yourself if he (if you're a girl) or she (if you're a boy) is concerned about your welfare and happiness."

In the silence he left for us to answer that one, I read on:

Does he or she respect your choices?

Does he or she ask you to do things you do not want to do?

(Does she expect you to buy her presents? Does he take kissing and petting too far?)

"That last one," the girl in the blue sweater hissed, "that's about bases, isn't it?"

"Yes, that's about which base you let him get to," I said. "So does he take it too far?"

"That's personal," she whispered and turned away from me.

"I'm sorry," I said and leaned back in my chair.

But then she turned around and said, "I wouldn't be here if he didn't, would you?"

"No," I admitted, except I thought I might be the one taking it too far.

I tried to imagine how Bruce might answer these questions. Is Maggie concerned about your welfare? *In truth, sir, I do not know.* Does she respect your choices? *What choices have I had, sir?* Does she ask you to do things you do not want to do, does she ask for presents, does she take kissing and petting too far? *Well, sir, what's too far, sir? We go as far as we can, sir, and that's always fine with me, sir.*

The minister told us we should hold onto these pamphlets. He said they might be useful to us some day. And he said we should never be afraid to come knock on his door. He talked a little more about dating, how to save yourself from difficult choices.

"Be sure to respect your curfew," he said. "Try to date in couples and groups and remember that you could always come together to the Methodist Youth Group on Wednesday nights."

A guy somewhere in the room laughed at that, but none of the rest of us did. Afterwards, when the girl and I were standing, uncertain what to do next, the minister approached us. It seemed to me he made a point of speaking to us.

"I don't believe I've met either of you before," he said. "Did you find the meeting helpful?"

"Very helpful," I said.

"Extremely," she said.

"It's a big responsibility," I said. "Love."

"It certainly is," he said and looked at me closely, deepening the extra fold under his eyes and the fine wrinkles he'd worn by squinting at scripture.

I believe that if he could have helped, he would have.

"I sure don't want to marry someone I don't truly care about," I said and hoped I sounded more honest than I felt.

The girl in the blue sweater pressed her palms against her reversible skirt and looked everywhere but at the minister, her thin ponytail switching shoulder to shoulder.

"I'm glad you feel that way," the minister said. "You ought to come to one of our meetings again. We'd welcome you."

"Yes, thank you," I said. "We ought to. We'd be happy to be welcomed."

I looked to the girl in the blue sweater for help, but she had inched herself backward and was heading for the door.

"So you'll come again?" the minister who only read scripture asked. His hand snaked toward me, as if he'd been hiding it inside the sleeves of the robe he was not wearing. Then he pressed my hand firmly, and I swear I could feel him leaving finger- and palm prints all over my hand. "We always have room for one more in our Christian family."

"Two more," I said and then, to recover, turned toward where the girl in the reversible skirt had stood.

"Yes, bring your friend too," the minister said and released my hand.

I walked to the door and, out of sight of the minister, ran to the street, but the girl in the blue sweater was gone. Down the block, a light changed and a car pulled slowly through the intersection, and I considered going straight home. But I couldn't. So I walked back into John Wesley Hall. A few kids were drinking juice and eating cookies, and the minister smiled and nodded at them and then looked at the plate of cookies. He reached for the plate and then brought his hand back empty and folded it across his chest. I watched him do this once and once again. The third time he took a cookie, studying it as if he were counting the chips before he ate them. I began folding the chairs around me, as I saw others were doing, and left the minister to his own decisions.

EIGHTEEN

Marian

Something about kids, about my kids at least, is that you can't lock them in. No matter how you try, they have this way of escaping just to spite you. Every night I lock the doors of our house, although we live where the neighbors sometimes never lock theirs. Still, every night I shake our locks in their latches until I convince myself that no one can get in or out. They can, of course. The burglar with a screwdriver can enter our front door, and while I sleep, the children can simply turn the key and walk out the back. And they do. My son skateboards in the dark or wanders through the dying orchard, hanging from branches that somehow never break. And Maggie, my eldest, she slips out and walks spike-heeled through the grass to the car of that damned boyfriend of hers. She walks through the grass and slides in next to him and sits cozy under the dome of his Chevy. And because I do nothing, she thinks I don't know this. She thinks I don't find the clods of mud and grass her shoes claw up or the oil his car drips on the asphalt. She thinks I know nothing of the treachery of being sixteen.

The only one who doesn't leave at night is my youngest. She probably dreams of smoking stolen cigarettes in the branches of the orange trees. But she doesn't. She lies in bed as if she knows someone in this household must be good.

I was thinking about these things, about the way my kids want to escape although they're young enough they still need me. I was thinking about when they'd ever be old enough, to leave of course, but also to help. I was thinking as I sewed, for sewing gives you time to think. I was beading a bodice at the kitchen table, working under the bright light.

My eyes stung a little, the way they do when you're doing fine work for hours, and I thought perhaps I'd call it a day and go to bed. I glanced at the clock, and it was past eleven. How had it gotten so late?

And then I was angry, and worried (I can never sort the two), because my oldest was out late without even a call. I walked to the living room to look out the window for her, and seeing nothing, I pulled the sheers apart and sat in the overstuffed chair to wait, and waiting only made me angrier, the way it always does. I closed my eyes to rest them, who knows for how long, and when I opened them, there was my daughter walking past the vacant lot, that hair of hers tucked behind her ears as if she had just combed it, as if some boy had just dropped her off at the corner and she had fixed her hair and straightened her clothes so I would not suspect. She walked slowly, with her eyes down, not like a girl who needed to get home. She looked comfortable out there where the moon was disappearing behind the houses. She stopped at the end of the drive and just stood, as if she had the luxury never to come home.

That boy Bruce she'd been seeing was in the service now, which was fine by me. I'd always thought he was too old for her. Old enough to need to control himself, but not old enough to do it. I thought with him away she'd have a chance to slow down and meet some boys her own age, but I should have known that once they start, they don't stop, boys and girls together. Now I imagined a new boy, an even older boy, perhaps a man, who had dropped her off at the end of the street. He was sitting in his car just out of view, his lights out and his windows open as he watched my daughter walk away from him. That's what I thought held her in the dark, the undertow of his gaze pulling her back. And then I thought, "Who the H does she think she is?" And that's exactly what I said when she walked in the back door: "Who the H do you think you are? Coming home late and not even calling?"

"I'm sorry, Mom," she said like a child who has innocently forgotten time while playing in the woods. But we have no woods, and that reedy sound in her voice only made me angrier.

"Sorry? Don't you know I've been worried about you?"

"God, Mom, it's only, what?"

"See. You don't even know what time it is."

"I was only at church."

"At church?" I can tell you we hardly ever went to church. "And what were you doing at church?"

She didn't answer me right away, so I knew whatever she said would be a lie. Truth, after all, is quick.

"I was praying," she said. "Okay?"

Nothing could have seemed more outlandish than my teenage daughter praying. Staying out with her boyfriend I could imagine. But praying? "Don't lie to me, Maggie."

"I'm not."

She threw up her hands, revealing a piece of paper wadded in her fist. I thought, Another detention? Another warning from her teachers? The teachers always told me the same thing. My daughter seemed bright enough, but she didn't seem to care. And this baffled me because my children had so much more than I'd ever had. Didn't I give them the best home I could?

"What's that in your hand?"

"Nothing," she said and walked toward her room.

"Don't you walk away when I'm talking to you."

She slammed her door.

"And don't you slam your door in my face."

She had dropped her precious piece of paper as she walked into her room, and I saw it lying on the floor, curled tight with secrets. I opened it, unrolling it and unfolding the creases, and saw the words "Your Loved One." Your Loved One? I thought. Now who is she kidding? If I hadn't been so angry, I might have sat down on the floor laughing.

"Open your door, Maggie," I said. "Open your door this minute and talk to me."

"What's going on?" My husband came from our bedroom. He must have been sleeping, for his hair stood out like a shrub gone wild.

"Do you have any idea what time it is?" It is like my husband to sleep when Rome is burning. "She just got home. At this hour."

"Open your door, Maggie," he said loudly. "Do you hear me?"

Maggie swung her door open and said, "I just walked home from church, okay? I just wanted to walk. I didn't do anything."

"It's a school night and you're out until God knows how late?" my husband said.

"It's not that late."

"Who drove you home at this hour anyway?"

"No one drove me," she said. "Didn't you hear? I walked."

It would have taken an hour or maybe two to walk, and I didn't believe my daughter would spend an hour, and surely not two, walking.

"Don't lie to me," my husband said and pulled his hand back to slap her.

"I'm not," she said. "I went to church. I prayed."

"Then what's this?" I asked. "What's praying got to do with love?"

She snatched the paper from my hand and crumpled it in her fist. "This is *mine*," she said, "not yours."

"What're you hiding from us?" my husband said and grabbed her wrist.

I didn't really want the other kids to see this. It was too painful. So I checked to see if they were up. His door ajar, a wedge of light slid from Jamie's room, and I could just see him leaning over a notebook in his lap. Then I glanced down the hall toward Alison's room and was glad to see her light out and her door closed, until I felt a tugging on my hand, and I knew she'd come up on my other side. Sleep wrinkles on her face made her look like she might cry.

Maggie was crying, but she wasn't about to let us see it. She looked at her shoes and let one hand slip up to her face. Then she looked at us, first Jim and then me, and said, "I'm getting married, that's all. I'm thinking about getting married."

"Married?" one of us said.

My own mother drank, and I have always thought that if someone should raise hell in this world, it should be me, not my children. My mother drank every night of her life in her own dining room. She sat at her dining-room table, her glass on the place mat before her. She would sit at that table, pouring her liquor into a juice glass, and in the morning, I used to look at my juice glass and wonder if that was the one she had drunk from the night before. She would pour a glass and drink it down, pour another and drink it too. She did this after she had put my father to bed. After he had taken his evening constitutional, after she had served him his glass of milk and his three cookies, after he had crawled into his high wood-framed bed, my mother would sit at that table and drink until she fell asleep.

I saw her. I watched from my bedroom window, the one that looked across the small patio to the dining room. I watched and learned how she did it. She drank seriously at first, as if she were taking medicine, and that's what I thought when I was very young, that she was taking medicine and that she must be sick. But when I was older and understood better, I feared for what she might do. Already I had found her collapsed on the kitchen floor, her legs and arms bent as if while she drank, gravity had shifted its axis and she were trying to scale the floor. Already I knew what she was capable of. Liquor could uncork her, letting clear and sparkling invective pour out of her. It was best, I knew, to leave my mother alone until the drink put her to sleep, so I locked my door against her, locked it and pushed a chair against it. Fearful, I peered out during the night and observed her progress. Sometimes she'd smile and look down at her lap. Other times she laid her head down on the table, as if her head were the heaviest thing in the world and would tumble to the floor if she did not put it on the table first.

One night after she fought with my father (I must have been about nine), I looked out the window and saw her crying, large slow tears she licked up when they reached the corners of her mouth. Filled with sorrow for her, I moved the chair away from my door and stumbled through the dark rooms (my room, the narrow bathroom, my father's study with the hanging skeleton I tried to avoid). I walked like a lost child into the room where my mother sat drinking, the sconces spilling light against the wall and shadows across her face. "Oh, loveliness," she said when she saw me and tried to smile. She opened her arms to me, and I slipped up onto her lap, the damp warmth of her body enclosing me. "My true heart," she said, "my little Marian," a thin wail escaping her and piercing me. "Papa doesn't love me," she said, and though I was sure he did, just the thought made me feel as if my mother and I were standing on top of a tall building, nothing left to do but leap into the air.

Somehow she always made it to bed by morning. I think my father knew exactly when to rise and fetch her, exactly when she would have slept long enough with her head on the table. All his life he arose at a quarter past six, never earlier, never later, and never with an alarm. So I suspect he woke himself in the middle of the night to help my mother. When I was old enough and my father had grown tired of her nights, I was the one who roused myself at two or three and prodded her awake. "Mama, time for bed. Time to go to bed, Mama." It was me who supported her as we stumbled to her single bed in the room she shared with Papa. But when I was young, I locked my door and waited for morning and the sound of rushing water when my father turned on the shower taps at exactly 6:16.

"Yes, I'm getting married," Maggie said.

Jim slammed his hand against the door, but not against her.

"Is that all this is about, Marian?" Jim said.

"All?" I said and thought it no wonder I felt I was raising my kids alone.

"That is the dumbest thing I've ever heard," he said to Maggie. "You can't do it, you know. We won't let you."

"I don't need your permission."

It must have struck my husband that out of state somewhere she in truth wouldn't need his permission, because he said, "Why on earth would you want to get married?"

"Because I'm in love?"

I could picture my daughter parked with a boy, but in love? I wanted to shake her and put some sense into her.

"Now that's even dumber," my husband said. "What do you know about love?"

"How much do I need to know? As much as you two?"

I'm the one who slapped her. I did it before I knew I wanted to. My hand stung, as if it really did hurt me more than her, but her skin was red where I'd touched her and white where I hadn't. Though I'd shaken her from my free hand, Alison clung to my skirt and began to cry.

"You really want to do this?" Jim asked.

Maggie shook her head from side to side, but she didn't speak. I'm sure I took her breath away.

When my father touched people, he cured them. He moved bones. He was a doctor of chiropractic, and when he hugged me, my vertebrae chattered. He had an office on Melrose, and when I was small, my mother would take me there once a week. Every week before we left, she would sit at the dining-room table, swallow what I still thought was her medicine, and say, "Shall we go see Daddy?"

She pinned her hair in a roll of curls and dusted herself with talc. She dressed herself in her finest dress, turning this way and that before her dressing-table mirror and asking me if the seams of her hose were straight. Then she buttoned my hat under my chin and put on my coat and my gloves, and together we walked to the Fairfax trolley, swinging our pocketbooks to a rhyme she made up.

"Little Mar-i-an was an on-i-on growing in the gard-i-en till I plucked her up. Little Mar-i-an was an on-i-on . . ."

I was always too hot in my hat and coat, and I hated her rhymes, and I hated even more the way she smiled at people passing by. She'd smile at strangers, at women in feathered hats, pushing their grocery carts down the sidewalk, and she'd say, "This is my daughter." They would pause and study our faces, frankly puzzled but too polite to say, "You? Do I know you?" Finally they would nod and say, "Why, yes, how lovely. Well, I must be going now."

"That was an elegant woman," my mother might say. "Too bad she doesn't know how to fix her hair." Or, "Do you think that sweater was cashmere? How in the world could she afford cashmere?"

We stood on Fairfax, waiting for the trolley, and my mother said, "We are, you know, very lucky to live in Hollywood," and swept her hand up toward the hills and down toward the avenue.

I did feel lucky to be standing on Fairfax, blue sky overhead and fat, shiny cars rolling by.

"We're lucky to live where some people still have jobs," she said. She turned her head left and right, and like any child, I mimicked her. Whichever way we looked, up or down the avenue, we saw people patiently standing on curbs, crossing only when the light turned green and stopping when the light turned red. We saw people we thought were going to work.

"Imagine," she said. "Wouldn't it be terrible if your father didn't have a job? If he didn't have a waiting room full of patients?"

She touched her hat and snugged up each glove. "And just imagine who his patients might be. Just think who can still afford to pay their doctors." Now she whispered. "All those glamorous stars. Think of that. Think who could be in your father's office right now. Imagine who could come walking out of that restaurant any minute." She gestured toward the Temptee Diner, silver and slick as a lipstick. I waited to see Helen Broderick or Irene Dunne walk out the door, but then my mother said, "Why, Marian, just think how lucky you are to live where you can pick oranges off the trees." She swung her arm toward the foothills above the avenue, where houses seemed to float, riding the crests of the hills, and she seemed to me the most beautiful woman, heroic and monumental.

A trolley car stopped in the middle of the road, and as we boarded it, my mother, gently lifting her skirt to hike up the stairs, said, "Good morning, Mr. Oliver," reading his name from his badge. "This is my daughter, Marian."

And the conductor, obliging a beautiful woman, said, "Good morning, Marian. Lovely day."

· · ·

171

It was always hot on the trolley, and I always wanted to take off my hat and coat and gloves, but my mother stopped me and said, "We're in public, Marian." She straightened her hat and pulled her shoulders back and said, "This is the way a doctor's wife and her daughter dress in public."

We rode the rest of the way in silence, my mother smiling benevolently out the window, as if we were people of privilege. Once my mother even said, "This is just like a carriage, isn't it? We are royalty and they," and she nodded toward the people in the street, "are pedestrians."

At my father's office, my mother announced to the nurse, "I am Mrs. Lisle, the doctor's wife," although the nurse must have known very well who my mother was.

"Yes, Mrs. Lisle, how are you today?" the nurse said.

"Fine, just fine," and my mother seated herself erectly, with me in my hat and coat and gloves beside her. She read a magazine big as a picture book, turning the pages carefully, as if afraid the ink would dirty her gloves, until the nurse said, "The doctor will see you now, Mrs. Lisle."

My father kissed my mother's forehead and said, "Hello, Marie," then gestured her into a curtained cubicle. She returned wearing a cotton robe and sat on the leather table, crossing her dangling feet as if embarrassed they were naked. When he told her to, she obediently lay down. My father paced around his leather table while he worked. He wore a white coat and walked slowly, touching my mother's back as he went, and I almost thought he had invented what lay on the table. I watched him take my mother's head in both his hands and turn it side to side with great care, as if he were gently mixing what her head contained. When he turned her face toward me, I could see that her eyes were closed and she was smiling slightly. Then he walked around to my side of the table, winking his slow-moving eyes, and with his back facing me so I could not see what he did, he swiftly laid his hands on my mother's spine, his shoulders and elbows jerked violently, and my mother groaned a deep sudden groan that frightened me.

"All better?" he asked before he helped her up.

"Oh, yes, much better," she said and disappeared into the curtained cubicle.

My father did me only once, or maybe twice, because, he said, "You are too young. Your bones are too soft."

Still once, or maybe twice, he let me take off my camel-hair coat and my hat and my gloves. Once or twice he sent me into the curtained cubicle to remove my dress and petticoat. Then he lifted me naked but for my undershirt and underwear and placed me facedown on the table. He took my head between his hands and lifted it, turning it from side to side until I felt dizzy and sad and surprised because I'd never known how heavy a head as small as mine could be. He touched my shoulder, he touched my back, and young as I was, soft as my bones were, I heard a sound down my spine, as if all the snaps in the world had just popped open.

"What did we raise you for?" my husband said. "Just to run off and get popped when you're sixteen?"

"What's popped?" Alison asked.

"He means pregnant," Maggie said. "He means p.g., preggers. He means knocked up and a goner."

"Don't talk to your sister that way," my husband said.

I grabbed Maggie's chin and lifted her face exactly the way I used to when it needed scrubbing. I pulled her close and said what I needed more than anything to say, "Don't tell me you're pregnant."

And she didn't. She said, "No, I'm not pregnant."

Somewhere inside, I must have known it was a lie, but it was exactly the lie I wanted. We weren't the kind of people whose children got pregnant before they left high school. We were better than that. I had been a better mother than that. And that is what makes me laugh like a crow now. What kind of mother was I? To have been so blind, I must have been a far worse mother than my own.

I said, "Thank God," and my husband said, "For Christ's sake," and Alison asked, "What's wrong, Mommy?"

My husband shooed Alison away with one hand. "Take her back to bed, would you?"

Worried about all she'd heard and seen, worried she'd think I might slap her too, I put Alison back to bed, pulled the covers up to her chin, and when I returned, I found Maggie sitting on the edge of my bed and my husband pacing around our room, saying nothing. He had switched on the overhead, the light we never use, so the bed and the bureau cast squat shadows, and Maggie and Jim cast short, fat shadows too. In the light, I could see where our walls had collected soot, and I could see the dim halos where the nails were showing through. I looked at my daughter, my handprint still pink on her face, and thought, Why would she want to get married? Why would she want to leave home?

"You think that boy's going to be able to support you?" my husband asked her. "You think in six months' time you won't be all knocked up knocking on our door?"

"I'm just thinking I'll get married," she said. "It's not the worst thing in the world."

"Not the worst?" I said, remembering my mother. "You don't even know what bad is."

I forget all the things my husband and I said to her. I do remember thinking, Don't we have problems enough without this? And I remember thinking how strange it was, with her in our bedroom. Jim and I didn't fight in front of the children, or at least we tried not to. We always went to our room and closed the door, and now here we were in our room with the door closed, fighting with her rather than each other. It was almost a relief.

"So what're you going to do? Just give yourself away?" my husband asked. "Because I sure as hell am not giving you away."

My father did give me away. He walked down the aisle with me in a dress I'd made myself, the first wedding dress I'd ever made. My father handed me over to my husband and let me change my name from Lisle to Harris. That was the one thing I regretted. I didn't regret losing my mother, but I did regret losing my father and his name. I loved my maiden name. I used to think I would never marry unless I met a man with a name like Lisle.

Sometimes I think I learned to sew because we were named for some town on another continent where, my father told me, women made lace so fine it was transparent. More likely, I learned to sew because of sewing itself. Because I liked the order and quiet of it. I liked being in a roomful of women working at machines. I liked the way we all sat, our heads bent over our handiwork, and the quiet chatter in the room, as we traded the few words we could, words that did not break our concentration. Simple talk about children, marriages, beaux. Then too there was something about the woman who taught me that I liked. She wove straight pins into her dress, and she had a bosom deserving of the word, and in the clothes she wore she betrayed no taste for fashion. She was from an old world I knew nothing about, and I guessed that she dressed the way her mother and, before that, her grandmother had dressed. It was impossible to imagine her drinking all night.

I learned to like the simple concentration of watching a seam appear, of thinking about nothing but the needle going in and out, thinking about nothing but keeping my seams straight and my topstitching even. I learned to like my hands needle-stuck and sore, and I always liked cornering a pocket and binding a buttonhole. I loved stitching the last stitch.

My mother didn't finish things. She sat down at the piano and riffled through her tattered sheet music to find a tune from her youth. She put her glass on a trivet, lifted her hands like Rubinstein, and played "She's Only a Bird in a Gilded Cage," singing along on the chorus. But she stopped before the end and turned toward me, her only audience, and said, "Oh, well, who cares?"

She started a garden, even hoed up the yard, but left it to my father to finish. She started needlepoint pillow covers. She started to wax the floor. She started to have another child. She started shopping, only to return home with an empty cart. She started to kill herself, turning on the oven and crawling on her hands and knees to put her head inside, but she didn't finish that either, because I came home from school and found her.

My father thought a trade was not a good idea for me. He said, "Why, Marian? You could stay home and go to college, prepare to meet a husband."

But I knew the day I walked into the shop and heard the steady sound of machines. I knew the day I finished my first dress that this is what I would do. Even my father understood and gave me a thimble, the words *love* and *friendship* engraved at the bottom. I was lucky and got my first job doing alterations in the bridal shop of a department store on Wilshire Boulevard. I saved my money in an empty jar, rolling the bills tighter and tighter as they filled it. Every time I added a few more dollars, it seemed to me I was constructing something, piecing something together, a tent, maybe, that I would soon hoist to protect myself against the sky.

We talked to our daughter. We pleaded with her, we yelled at her until late into the night. I can't imagine what we had to say except, Why are you doing this? Why are you doing this to us? She never once said what was really wrong. She scarcely said anything, and all I wanted her to say was no. No, I won't get married, Mom, not yet. She cried, and I cried, and my husband broke a hairbrush, beating it against the dresser. Late in the night after we must have said everything that could be said, my daughter sat on the edge of our bed. She moaned as if she had used up her tears.

"Wait," I said to her. "Please wait to start your life."

My husband moved close to her. He put an arm around her shoulders and gently brushed her hair back. "We only want what's best for you," he said. "You know we love you so much," and he kissed her cheek and then her ear. She twisted away, but my husband gripped her shoulder tighter, and she began to shake. Needing to comfort her, I sat down and took one of her hands in mine. I echoed my husband, "We're only doing this because we love you."

She fell back on the bed then and buried her face in a pillow. My husband lay down beside her and stroked her hair. "You're our daughter," he said and kissed her again and again.

I looked up at the soot on the walls and, hating the sight of it, stood up and turned out the lights. I put on my nightgown and lay down beside Maggie. I can't explain why, but I didn't want her to leave that room. Like my husband, I stretched an arm across her back, as if that would restrain her. Lying down, I could feel how tired I was, and drained. My eyes still burned from sewing, and spent as I was, I fell asleep quickly.

Sometime during the night, I got up to drink a glass of water. I lay awake for the longest time after that, listening to my daughter and husband breathe. At times, Maggie tossed herself over and kicked the sheets, but she never woke. It reminded me of those nights in her infancy when she would cry, only to fall asleep as soon as I returned the bottle to her mouth. I lay in the dark, as awake now as I was then. If I could have, I would have cradled her right there, gathered her up in my arms and rocked her, but she rolled away from my lightest touch. There was no comfort in that bed. I looked at the arcs of soot on our walls and closed my eyes wondering why it collected like that, like shadows of a dome, when the sound of something tearing woke me and it was morning. I looked around to see who was tearing what, and when I saw no one, I understood that the sound was in my dream, that in my dream, someone, my old sewing teacher I believe, was tearing silk. She stood with her legs wide and rows and rows of pins sparkling on her chest and unfurled a bolt of silk. She unfurled and tore, unfurled and tore, ruining miles and miles of silk.

My husband lay asleep, his face buried in the crook of his arm, but my daughter was gone. I could feel her absence, the hollow in the bed beside me. It was early morning, and no one but me was up. Yet I could hear the silence Maggie had left behind. The weather in our house has changed, that's what I said to Jim later that day. The weather has changed. I climbed out of bed and checked every room. Jamie sprawled, one arm dangling off the bed. Alison lay curled like a sow bug. But Maggie was not there. Her bed was untouched, the faded pink spread pulled taut, just waiting for a body to leave its imprint. I went to the front door. I knew it would not be locked, and sure enough, it wasn't. It wasn't even closed. I pushed the door open wide and felt the breeze, cool and dry. I stood in the doorway feeling empty as a husk, the way you do when you've done something regrettable, something that can't be undone. My daughter had walked out into the world, onto the dangerous streets, without me. Thinking I'd see a trolley or a woman walking down the sidewalk we do not have in our neighborhood, I took a deep breath and waited for someone to say, "Morning, Marian. Lovely day."

NINETEEN

Maggie

*H*ere's what I remember.

"You went to church?" my father said. "You expect me to believe that?"

"Look, it's serious," I said. "I'm thinking . . ."

That was the first lie I told them that night.

"Bruce?" my mother said. "You're thinking of marrying Bruce?"

"And she's not even out of school," my father said.

They looked at me as if I had asked them to drink from a glass marked "Poison," and I knew I was right not to tell them the truth. They sat me on their bed, the green spread welting under me, and they yelled a long time. They said some things I have forgotten and others I never will, and the things they said they said over and over, repeating themselves and repeating each other. The words felt like blows, and though I cowered inside, I sat upright trying not to listen. My father circled as he spoke, wheeling away and striking back to face me. My mother moved from dresser to bed and bed to dresser. She held a white bodice she must have been beading, the way the needle and thread hung from the lace, and she kept tossing the bodice from hand to hand and swinging it, so the bead needle swung and spun in front of me. To deflect her words, to make them matter less, I remember looking at my mother's china blue walls, and seeing soot, ash from the fires, I guess, that had collected in arcs near the ceiling. It seemed to collect where the studs and beams must have been, I can't imagine why. It looked like the bones of the house showing through.

• • •

"Marry this young?" my father said. "You're wasting your life."

I said little because I knew speaking would make things worse.

"She thinks he loves her," my mother said in explanation, and then to me, "You think he loves you, don't you?"

"Maybe," I tried, and then, "He said so," except he never had.

"Oh, sure," my mother said. "He says he loves you now he's how many thousands of miles away? Think there's anyone else around for him to love?"

"There might be."

"Might be?" my father said. "Well, that should worry you."

"You'll get pregnant just like that." My mother snapped her fingers.

"Pregnant?" my father said. "Hell, she'll drop a litter inside two years."

"And then it won't be so much fun anymore," my mother said. "Then you'll see how quick he loses interest in you."

"How long do you think it will be before some pretty girl turns his head?" my father said, staring through me as if just under my skin he could see the faces of those pretty girls.

"Think he'll still want you then?" my mother said. "While you're sitting there all swollen and expecting?"

"What are you going to do to support yourself?" my father said. "Wait for us to come save you?"

"Well, you better not," my mother said, "because we sure won't."

My father glanced at my mother, then walked across the room to her dresser. He picked up her hairbrush, a brush that had belonged to her mother. It was wooden and had a smooth oval back and bristles soft as grass. You'd pull it through your hair, and the bristles almost wouldn't catch, and then they would; they'd pull gently through. My father picked up this brush and slapped the oval back against his palm. Then he walked toward his closet. He put his hand on the knob, and I could hear his belts rattle and clink with the movement. But he didn't open the door. Instead he turned to me and said, "He just wants her to suck his pud." I winced inside but tried not to show it.

"And she wants to just because he's been handling her all over out there in that damn car of his." He brought the hair brush down hard against the dresser, so the back split and the handle snapped off.

I would have given anything not to be in that room, but I could not leave. Leaving was more dangerous than staying. Besides, what bruises do words leave, anyway? Not that I didn't feel the words. I felt them in my muscles and organs. I felt them land on the very thing that is me. And I was embarrassed. I wondered who could hear him say these things. The walls were thin, the door was thinner. I thought of my brother drawing his hung man with bulging biceps and dragon tattoos. Was he listening? Was my sister? Had my mother, standing right there, heard? And if she had, why hadn't she done something? Hit me. Or hit him. I thought, of course, that everything he said was true. Bruce would leave, he'd find someone prettier, I'd be left with a kid. And, yes, the worst stuff my father said, the stuff about what we did in the car, was all true.

"What will people think?" my mother said, the wadded bodice hanging from her hand. "What will the family think?"

I hadn't thought what the family would think. I hadn't thought what anyone would think of this thing that was much worse than my parents knew. "I don't care what they think."

"You don't care?" my mother said. "Think what you're doing to *us*."

My mother's face shone from sweat, and the red marks her glasses left seemed sore as burns. I wanted to say, "Please help me, Mama," but something about her, something about us sitting angrily in that room, reminded me of a kettle boiled empty on the stove, the sharp smell of hot metal filling the room. So I said, "I'm not doing anything to you."

My father shook his head. "You're sure doing it to yourself. You really think he's going to marry you? Don't you know why he's saying that?"

I said nothing. Bruce had never mentioned marriage. He didn't need to.

"After he's used you," my mother said, "think anyone else's going to want you? Think anyone's going to want a used tire?"

"What makes you think I'd want to marry someone else?" I said, thinking for the first time that I would marry him.

"Oh, please. How long do you think this will last?"

"God, you'd think I done something awful," I said. "You'd think I killed someone or robbed a bank. You'd think I said I was pregnant, for Christ's sake."

"You're not, are you?" my mother said and threw the bodice on the floor. "Don't tell me you're pregnant."

Sometime during the fight, my mother slapped me, and sometime I fell across the bed, as if I could burrow away from them. My father's weight hit the mattress, and then my mother shut off the lights, and I felt her sit on the other side of me. My father put his arms around me and kissed me, large damp kisses. He kept saying, "You know we love you, don't you, baby?"

We were red-faced and bruised, sore and hoarse and salty with tears and sweat, my father on one side, kissing me, my mother on the other. They trapped me there in their bed, that's the way it seemed to me. They lay with their arms crossed heavily over me, and they pulled the covers up snug, so I could scarcely move. Worn by the fight, they fell asleep quickly, but tired as I was, I could not rest between them. Curling one way brought me deep into the cove of my mother's legs and bottom. Stretching the other way pushed me up against my father's chest, into the crook of the arm he slept on, hair escaping the sleeve of his T-shirt. I lay spent and cramped between them. The smell of my father grew during the night, a metallic animal smell that I thought was his, mixed with the odor of tar from his work. My mother's smell was softer, but strong, a smell I think I find on myself, something like sweat and lanolin and menstrual blood.

My face stung, not from my mother's hand as much as from my father's mouth. He had kissed me over and over, telling me how much they loved me, didn't I know they didn't want to hurt me? His kisses were wet, maybe from tears, and I'd wanted to wipe them from my face, except my arms were caught. Besides, it was not something I could do, wipe away my father's kiss. I'd wanted to tell him to stop it, to stop giving me these big, wet kisses. I'd wanted to tell him that I knew what real kisses should feel like and that I felt sorry for my mother that this was the man who kissed her before she went to sleep at night.

In the end, I slept, but sometime before morning I awoke. I'd slept hard, as if I'd been drinking, but I woke fast, the way you do when you just know someone who shouldn't be is in your house and you are afraid. I didn't know what frightened me, so I stilled myself and listened. All I heard was the wheeze my father made as he breathed in and out. He lay with one hand behind his head and seemed almost to smile. He opened and closed his mouth, then rolled to his side, one hand a cushion under his face. He kicked the covers loose, and I thought, *Now*, now is the time to go. I waited, though, to see if my mother were awake. She lay on her stomach, her face turned away from me, her hair bunched in the collar of her nightgown. Her breathing seemed even and slow, so I slid myself on top of the covers and worked my way to the foot of the bed. My mother turned her head and threw an arm over the space I had left empty. My father scratched his shoulder furiously, but he did not open his eyes. Neither of them did, so I slid to the floor and crept on my hands and knees from their room. I crawled through the light and shadows on the carpet and, when I reached the door, turned the knob slowly, listening for the sounds in the room to change. Then I stood myself up and walked out.

That was all I wanted, to get out of their room, but as I closed their door, I felt I wasn't far enough away. I went to my room and shut my door, so there were two wooden doors between us. In relief, I leaned against the door and cried. I saw my bed, made the way I'd left it the morning before, and thought about lying in it. Instead, I evened the spread, stretching it taut, then reached beneath the bed for the shoe-box. It had held my sister's Mary Janes, and for one of my mother's proj-ects, I had covered it over with Christmas wrapping, something forest green on the bottom and red on top. Now the lid was splayed, and the corners were wearing white. In the darkness that's what I could see, the frayed, white corners and the small white angels on the wrapping. Open, the box still smelled of my sister's shoes, the rich plastic smell of patent leather. I lifted the black tissue paper and found the pictures of Bruce and me at his graduation, the letters he had sent me in those watery blue envelopes, and the medal I had bought myself. I put these things into my purse, then chose two pairs of underwear and found the change purse with all the money I'd saved putting side seams into choir robes (I'd earned forty-one dollars and had thirty-eight and change when I left), and I walked out the front door my mother in our fights had always said was open: "You think living by our rules is so hard? Well, the door's always open."

I hadn't planned to leave. If I had, I might have done more, looked in on my brother and sister, for instance. I didn't, and that has always both-ered me. The one thing I did: stoop to pick up a piece of paper on the floor outside my brother's room, thinking it was the game of hangman he had played while my parents and I fought. But it wasn't a hung man at all. It was one of my brother's crazy drawings. I folded it and put it in my purse and walked out the front door, not caring whether it shut behind me.

The night had been clear, and the sky over the foothills was glazed blue. What must have been the morning star had risen over the orange trees, and across the street at the Dawsons' house, I could make out the

182

wooden shafts of Tommy Dawson's arrows scattered crisscross under his bull's-eye. I could even see the small dents the arrows had made.

A light flickered on in their kitchen, and before anyone could stop me, I walked to the end of our drive, turned away from the brittle orange trees, and headed down the road.

I walked, on the curb and in the gutter, for what seemed forever, although it was probably no more than a mile or two, and by then, morning had begun to feel like morning. Hedges of oleander and hibiscus regained their dimensions, clusters of dim pink and dull red petals visible among leaves still black and gray. Here and there a kitchen or bathroom window filled with yellow light. Water rushed in pipes underground, and sprinklers sprayed giant blooms of water over the grass. A door slammed shut, someone revved an engine. A thin man in a brown suit waved as he bent to open the door of his yellow Falcon. Although I smiled to be polite, I did not wave because I did not know this man, which somehow reminded me that I did not know where I was going or what I was doing and that I was still wearing the same clothes I had put on for school the morning before. The thought made me tired, and I sat down on a bench to rest. A bus rolled up (I didn't even hear it coming), and when the door opened, I climbed on, no questions asked, and dropped two nickels in the box before bolting to the rear.

Perhaps I slept. The small, low buildings of Monrovia and Rosemead seemed even smaller and lower, as if I were viewing them not from the height of the bus but from somewhere even higher, a glider floating over the towns. It seemed I could see the dun-colored roofs of the businesses and the dark gray grid of the streets. I could see the layers of air, a dim blue up high, a sandy white somewhat lower, pearl gray still lower, a dusky brown hovering over the buildings and foothills, as if dust were sifting from high altitudes to the bottom of this pool of air. I saw the cars below us pulling in and out of driveways. I even recognized, by her stately waved hair, one of my mother's clients pulling into a Union 76. Mrs. Rogers cranked down her window and smiled out at the attendant, a boy I recognized was one of Bruce's friends. He bent to talk to Mrs. Rogers, and she smiled up at him. I watched her mouth say, "Fill it up," but I did not worry about them seeing me through the broad window of the bus. I felt removed, lifted from ordinary life, as if I might never be part of normal life again. And as I watched—was it Stan?—nozzle Mrs. Rogers's car, as I watched him scrub her windshield and take money from her hand, I thought of my mother waking up in that house where I used to live. I thought of my mother opening the curtains and watering her potted fern, I thought of her running water into the percolator, into the pitcher for juice, I thought of her scooping out the frozen Minute Maid, of her opening Alison's door, and then Jamie's, to say, "Time to get up," of her opening my door and seeing my bed untouched. I thought of her opening the front door, peering out as if she might find me sitting on the front step or hanging from the branch of a tree. I saw her face, not seeing me, fracture, and I felt something begin that has never ended, the heavy mineral of guilt settling in me.

"Your stop," the bus driver said.

"My stop?"

"Well, it had better be. Because this *is* the last stop, unless you're planning to ride the bus all day, which you can't do by sitting yourself down on my bus anyway. You have to get off and pay your fare on the next bus out."

The bus had pulled up behind two others in the huge empty parking lot beside the track at Santa Anita. A few people who must have been passengers were heading away, several jacketed men crossing the expanse of white-striped asphalt toward the grandstand walls on the far side and a few women, wearing sensible shoes and toting handbags full of bottles of cleanser, heading toward the houses planted tidily on the other side of the street. Not knowing where to go, I followed these women past houses with yards full of ivy and dichondra lawns and brick walks curving up to brass-knockered doors painted black or forest green until one of the women, a woman with hair going white and a soft, plump body that made me think of my great-aunt Mary Helen, swung the handbag that had been riding her hip around front and cut her eyes at me over her shoulder. "What're you doing, girl?" she said.

"I just, I just wanted to know the time."

"It's about seven-thirty, I should think," she said without looking at her watch. She stopped and studied me, her eyes gentler now. "Are you lost? Is that your problem."

"Not exactly."

"Then why're you following me? You could make a woman nervous."

"I'm not following you," I started to say, but it wasn't true. I was following her simply because I had nowhere to go and no idea what to do. She reminded me of Mary Helen with those soft arms that I thought would have to smell of talc, and that's why I followed her, because I wanted her to wrap her arms around me the way my aunt would. Well, I couldn't say that. "Didn't mean to frighten you." And I turned back and walked toward streets I thought I recognized.

"Holy shit" was what woke me. "What are you doing in my car?"

I had wandered the streets around the track until I found Joan's house. Though I'd been there only once, I recognized it, a red-shingle ranch house with a slate walk. Bird of paradise grew by the mailbox, I remembered that, and then Joan's car was parked out front. I crawled into the backseat, where I stretched out so no one would see me, and waited. I must have fallen asleep.

"Sleeping?" I said, because I wasn't anymore.

"Sleeping?" She climbed into the front seat. "Don't you have a bedroom for that?"

"I don't want to be there." I sat up, strands of hair clinging to my face.

"That sounds interesting. Why not?"

"I just don't."

"Some sort of secret?" She twisted around in her seat to scrutinize me. Her hair, once teased high, lay softer now, curling against her cheeks.

"No, not really."

"Something wrong?" She almost sounded concerned.

"Nothing worth talking about."

She narrowed her eyes at me, rifle slots in a turret.

"Well, if you're not going to tell me anything . . ." She untwisted herself and turned the key in the ignition. "I've got to get to work. Want me to drop you at school?"

"No, I can't face school." I leaned forward, chin on hands, hands on seat back, so I wouldn't feel like the passenger I was.

"Want me to take you home?"

"No, I don't want you to take me anywhere."

"You going to sit in my car all day?" Joan was driving back the way I'd come, and now another bus and another driver sat in the lot. "What is it? You're not running away, are you?"

She sounded thrilled that I might be.

"Just let me ride to work with you."

"Okay. I guess I can do that."

She drove, swinging up streets toward the foothills and the big lot where JCPenney sat next to Sears. My father would have said Joan drove with confidence. He might have said, "Why can't you drive like that?" But he also would have said, "Don't let confidence become nonchalance. Know where every car is." Aggressively silent and knowing, I suspected, exactly where every car was, Joan flipped on the radio to the boss station, the DJ's voice rattling along about a red Mustang some lucky someone might win if they just called in.

"All right," I said, giving in to Joan's silence. "Maybe I'm leaving."

"Really? You're running away? Where will you go?"

I didn't like *running away*. "I don't know. I've never done this before."

"You going to Bruce's?"

"No," I said, shouting by then to beat the sound of the radio. "Not Bruce's."

"What is wrong with you? Are you pregnant or something?"

I shook my head no but said yes anyway.

"Didn't you guys do any of the things I told you?"

"Yes, of course, we did," I said, still shouting, although the DJ was quiet now and the music was soft. "Things don't always work one hundred percent. You know?"

"I told you everyone does it, but only the stupid get caught."

"Like I needed that, Joan. Just let me out of the car."

"Act your age."

"I don't feel well. Let me out."

She was quiet a moment. The radio made comic-book sounds while some girl who'd called in did not win a chance to compete for the boss red Mustang.

"So I guess your parents know?" Joan said.

I shook my head.

"They don't? If they don't know, why are you leaving?"

"Just because."

"I guess they'd know soon enough, wouldn't they?"

"Look, I said I was thinking about getting married, and they didn't like *that*."

"Are you?"

"What?"

"Going to get married?"

Suddenly I felt as stupid as Joan had ever said I was. "Bruce doesn't know, and you're not telling him."

"Why would I tell him?"

"And you're not telling Charlie so he can tell him."

"Well, I don't know what you're going to do if he doesn't marry you," Joan said, and then after a moment, "Don't worry. I'm sure he will. We'll make him."

"I don't want him to."

"You're out of your mind."

"So I'm crazy," I said, and then I did feel ill. "I don't know what I want."

"Bet if he refused to marry you, you'd want to real fast." She had pulled into the lot behind Sears and parked where employees park. "What are you going to do?"

"Sit here until I figure out what to do next."

Joan twisted the rearview mirror toward her face and examined her eyes. She had replaced her slick green eye shadow with a soft powder, the heavy liner with delicate charcoal tracings, and since her boss had put her in Women's Dresses, she'd begun to wear wool skirts and a slip I could hear rustling against her nylons.

"You going to be okay?"

"I think so."

"Just lock the car if you leave," and she slammed the door.

I sat back and closed my eyes.

"Maggie?" Joan opened the door to say. "You'll be here when my shift's through?"

"I don't think so, Joan."

"It's okay if you are," she said. "I could ask some of the girls I work with if you could stay with them."

"Don't. I'll work it out."

"Sure?"

I leaned toward her and rubbed at a smudge of peach lipstick scribbled outside the lines of her mouth. Then I nodded yes and closed my eyes, and when I woke, the car was full of that hot vinyl smell and the sun dazzled off a field of hoods and windshields.

I felt, I don't know, a mess, a complete mess, but I also felt oddly fresh and new, as if someone had just smashed a bottle of champagne against my bow and pushed me into the open ocean. Perhaps that's why I wandered way across the parking lot from JCPenney to the Dairy Donut, because I felt new and free. I mean, I was hungry, but not very, not enough to go to a doughnut shop. That's where I met him, the man I spent the day with, at the Dairy Donut. He was taller than Bruce, and slender, his blond hair grown down around his ears. I suppose it was his hair I noticed first, so fine and light and wavy. The way it was cut, it reminded me of Buster Brown, Buster Brown grown and gone to heaven. He sat at one of the small, pink Dairy Donut tables with a broad-backed man who greased his hair and wore a flannel shirt and heavy black boots, a man so large, I was sure if he stood up quickly, he'd overturn the Formica table and all the chairs around him.

Joan probably would have said this man I thought of as the angel of Buster Brown was the opposite of Bruce, his very negative. She would have asked me why I was bothering with him. But Joan wasn't here to see this man. I was. I was sitting in the Dairy Donut way across the parking lot from JCPenney. My doughnut lay broken on the plate, little crumbs of it escaping onto the counter. I could barely eat it, so I sipped the glass of milk and stared at the cup of coffee I had ordered just so I'd look like every other customer in the place.

The broad-backed man sat looking out the window, but the angel of Buster Brown sat directly across the shop from me. He gazed at me full-faced, as if he admired me (who would admire me?), and then returned his gaze to the broad-backed man sitting across the table from him. Like that man, the angel wore a flannel shirt and jeans, but on him the clothes looked different. They looked good. And he wore a leather jacket, a brown suede jacket with fringe on the sleeves, and no one I knew then wore a jacket like that. I waited for him to look me over again, because all the time he spent regarding the man across the table from him, I felt I'd failed some test. I'd lost him. He did return his gaze to me, but he must have caught me watching because he smiled, as if I amused him, and I felt the heat of a blush rise up my neck and into my face.

I lifted my cup of coffee and tried to sip from it the way I saw others do, exhaling slightly and rippling the surface before tilting the cup. But blowing on it was useless since it was already cold enough for a baby's bath. So I sipped it, the taste of bark and ashes, and washed it down with milk. I felt my insides sway and hoped I would not lose what I'd eaten. Glancing again at the angel of Buster Brown to see if he was watching me, I told myself I was glad he wasn't. But he wasn't watching the broad-backed man across from him either. So I looked where he looked and saw a woman, a girl, really, not much older than me, sitting at the far end of the counter. She returned his gaze, a whispered smile on her face. She ringed her hands around her coffee cup as though it were precious, sipped, and turned away from him, seeming to sit straighter, or longer, so you could see the double curves of her neck and her hair hanging in an S down her back.

It was a contest I had failed. She was worth looking at, and I was not. Like a child, I wanted to cry. I pushed a chunk of doughnut across my plate but still could not stomach it. I thought of my sister eating pieces of a doughnut our mother had cut for us. My brother and I glommed the chunks into our mouths, sugar spilling into our laps. But Alison lifted each piece delicately, as if her fingers were tongs, and shook it lightly, letting the powdered sugar fall before she placed the piece in her mouth. Sugar coated the plate when Alison was through, and my brother, whose shirt was dusted with powder, zigged his finger through it.

I opened my purse to pay the waitress and found the crumpled pamphlet from the church and the picture my brother had drawn. The picture I unfolded, smoothing it out on the counter so pencil lead silvered my fingers. Jamie'd drawn our orange trees, sketching in every leaf that never grew and every fresh orange we never harvested, and then he'd drawn one of those underground cross sections, with the roots of the trees, the soil, and every pebble and grain of sand sketched in. Emerging from the roots and stones was a hollow, a cave. And in that cave he'd drawn a house with tiles on its roof and shutters on its windows, a house with a brook running by and sun and stars shining down on it. In the dark, I had made out only the darkest lines. But now I noticed the small things my brother had drawn, the fish in the stream and the way the windows reflected light. My stupid brother with all his dumb tricks, it seemed he was sitting right there with me in the Dairy Donut. I skimmed my fingers over the picture and could hear him breathe.

I counted out money and subtracted the sum from my thirty-eight and change, then looked toward the waitress. (Should I say, "Miss?") She poured coffee for an elderly man sitting at the counter, and studying her, I could not guess her age. Eighteen, twenty-one, twenty-five? How old did you have to be to wait tables? What tests must you pass? I was thinking this when I felt the too-nearness of someone standing close behind me. All right, already. I'm leaving, you can have my seat, I thought.

"I'll pay for that." The voice was quiet and gentle, somehow comforting. The angel of Buster Brown leaned into the counter and slid a five-dollar bill to the waitress. I turned to look for the broad-backed man and saw him walking heavily out of the shop.

"You shouldn't do that," I said.

"Why not?" The angel of Buster Brown smiled and took a step back, so I had to turn toward him slightly. "I want to, and I usually do what I want."

"But you don't know me." I put my own dollar on the counter.

He slid his five closer to the waitress's hand, and she took it, casting me a don't-be-a-fool look. "No, I don't know you. But if you'll talk to me, maybe I'll get to know you." He sat down on the stool next to mine and swiveled toward me, the fringe on his jacket rustling. "I'd like that. To get to know you."

This pleased me, more than I wanted it to. I asked him who he was, and he said, "My name's Billy Hyde."

"What're you hiding from?"

"That's a Y, H-Y-D-E. But I am hiding. You've got good instincts. Good thing to have, good instincts."

"So what? What're you hiding from?"

"Maybe I'll tell you later. Tell me about you first. Who're you?"

I couldn't begin to answer him. I had a lot of answers that used to be true: I am the daughter of Marian Lisle and Jim Harris; I am the girlfriend of Bruce Gallagher; I attend Rosemead High; I have a brother and a sister and a whole bunch of aunts and uncles, first, second, and twice removed; I live, or used to, in a one-story stucco house with a thinning lawn and an acre of dead orange trees. I am Margaret Lynn Harris, a girl who just walked out of her parents' home.

"My name's Margaret Lynn," I said, keeping something for myself.

He smiled as if he knew what I was doing. "You're a pretty good secret-keeper, aren't you?"

"What secret?"

"Doesn't matter," he said. "I don't need to know your real name. Not yet."

"I told you my real name."

"Right." He asked for the waitress for a cup of coffee. "So what do you do?"

"I work."

Billy Hyde smiled at that lie too. "Yeah, so do I."

"What do you do?"

The waitress put his coffee down. "A favor here, a favor there."

"You get paid for favors?"

"Can't really do anything else." He poured spoons of sugar into his cup. I asked him why not, and he said, "Here's my secret: I'm AWOL."

"What's A-wall?"

He suppressed a laugh and said, "I'm A-W-O-L. Away without leave."

"From what?" I asked, and again turning a laugh to a smile, he said, "From the army."

"So you're in trouble?" It seemed to me it had to be big trouble. From what Bruce had said, you couldn't brush your teeth without permission in the army.

"Not yet. Though I could be soon."

"How long have you been AWOL?"

"Just look at my hair," he said. "That should tell you."

I said it must have been a long time, and he said, "Not long enough. I should have been a C.O., you know?" He added for my benefit, "I should have shown that I conscientiously object to government-approved killing."

"Do you?"

"Sure do. Especially now." As if I wouldn't understand, he added, "Now that they've taught me how to kill."

Bruce never said they were teaching him to kill. He said he was being trained to fight.

"What are you going to do?"

"Try to get home to Boston before I get caught. See if my friends can help me get out or change my status."

"My boyfriend just enlisted." It surprised me I was proud of this.

"There's a secret you didn't keep. You have a boyfriend."

"He's in advanced training, for airborne."

"I guess he's no C.O. then."

"No, you're different from him."

"That's okay. Lots of people see things differently. Imagine I'd even like your boyfriend if I met him." Billy Hyde drew a finger across my cheek and pushed my hair behind my ear, and though I felt pins of alarm all down my spine, I leaned toward his touch. "Not that I ever would meet him." He put both hands around his cup of coffee. "So, look, I've got the day to myself. I've got the use of my friend's truck. And I was just wondering if a pretty girl like you would like to spend some time with me?"

A wiser girl, a truly pretty girl, would never have fallen for it. That girl with the long neck and the secret smile? She left the Dairy Donut before this man had a chance to talk to her, and I knew she never would have fallen for something as easy as *pretty*. But I did. That's all it took, *pretty*, not that I didn't make Billy Hyde wait. "Where'd you want to spend the day?"

"There's this place I heard about. Perfect for a day like this, a kind of park. Doesn't cost much," he said, as if he already knew I had little money. "Anyway, I've got some bread today, so I can pay."

"You've got your friend's truck?"

"Yeah, he left it with me, that guy I was sitting with."

"Where'd he go?"

"This other friend of his picked him up. They have some business to take care of. A little deal to square away."

He finished his coffee, then pulled out his wallet again, a leather bill-fold that had gone dark around the edges, and left another dollar for the waitress. "So what do you say?"

I didn't answer at first. I had no plans, of course, but I didn't know this man.

"Look, I'm just looking for a way to spend the afternoon. So if you want to brush me off, we can just say 'nice meeting you.'"

"I wasn't brushing you off," I said.

"You weren't?" he said. "You're sure?"

"Sure, I'm sure." Maybe I didn't know Billy Hyde, but I didn't want him to leave me alone.

We left the Dairy Donut together, his hand in the hollow of my back, and crossed the lot to a battered pickup. Billy's key fit the lock, which somehow surprised me, and while he held the door open for me, I climbed into the cab of a complete stranger's truck. I climbed in imagining everything my parents might say and ignoring it all.

"There's some Mary Jane in there," Billy said, pointing to the glove compartment. "But I bet you don't want any."

No one I knew then owned up to that kind of smoking. "No, thanks, not now."

He smiled again. "No, I didn't think so. But that's okay. In fact, that's just fine." He reached across me, the fringe of his jacket brushing my legs, and popped open the glove compartment. "You don't mind if I do, do you?"

· · ·

"Look at that," Billy Hyde said.

"What?"

I didn't understand what he was so excited about. He was just look-ing at the peacocks and peahens that roam the lawn outside the Arboretum, a kind of zoo for trees of every sort on a few rolling acres.

"This is where we're going?" I asked.

"Yeah, this is where we're going."

I had been to the Arboretum many times before, on field trips and with my family, such a safe place to go. And I had seen the peacocks many times, picking their feet out of the grass and dragging their greeny-blue tails behind them. I wanted to tell Billy to take me someplace different, someplace I'd never been before, but just then one of the peacocks stopped, raised his rump, and spread his great tail.

"Whoa," Billy said.

The bird swiveled its head, as if allowing those side-set eyes to take in, one at a time, a white peahen picking seeds from the grass. Even with its glistening teal feathers spread, even with its head in profile, one jet eye fixed on the peahen, the bird did not seem proud. Vain, maybe, or suspicious, but not proud. As if stepping over an invisible stile, the bird lifted one foot and then the other, gingerly approaching the peahen.

"Well, that's impressive," Billy Hyde said. "But the poor lady birds. They look naked."

"Peahens. They're called peahens," I said, proud I knew something Billy Hyde didn't.

"They look kind of sad, don't they?"

They weren't much to look at, these yellowish-white birds with their thin tails.

"They clip their wings, I bet," Billy said.

"I don't know. Sometimes they get away, but never far. Someone always brings them back."

When I think about it now, I guess I see why he was so pleased. Everything grew at the Arboretum. Just walking to the gate, we passed roses and tulips, marigolds and bougainvillea, even a flamboyant. All of them growing as if they naturally grew side by side. Billy bought our tickets and in the entry gazebo purchased a guidebook, and as we walked he read me all the stories I had heard before: how many movies had been made there, how they had shot scenes from *Gone With the Wind* in that house under the willows. And that swampy place where the tall reeds grew? Some movie about Iwo Jima was shot there. And here was the herb garden, here the English, here the greenhouse of the tropics, here the chaparral, the savanna, and there once again was the open lawn where they let the cocks and hens range free.

I knew this already, but Billy did not, and he seemed to like it all. We walked along the gravel paths, boughs dipping and bending over us, and he gave each of these things—the willow house, the Iwo Jima swamp, the white and naked-looking peahens—his full attention. He would turn the beam of his gaze away from me, so I felt a little lost, a little empty, and so I felt happy every time he brought his face around and looked at me again. I found myself liking the way he talked to me, as if everything I said was important, and the way he smelled. He smelled of leather and something else, something musty and sweet.

We came to a stretch of grass that rose up from the swamp—the pond and the reeds and the tall trees with their huge roots exposed in the water. Although there was a sign asking people to please keep off the grass, Billy Hyde crouched down and spread his jacket on the lawn, and I followed him, spreading my sweater. A few visitors walking the asphalt path looked at us disapprovingly, but no one asked us to please leave.

"So what's this place like?" Billy asked.

I couldn't imagine what he meant. This place is like what it's like.

"I mean this place, California, what's it like?"

"Can't you tell? You're living here."

"I'm just passing through," Billy Hyde said. "A favor here, a favor there. I keep moving."

Vancouver, Seattle, San Francisco, Fresno. These were the places he said he'd been. "Several months in B.C.," he said, "but no more than a week anywhere else. Have to travel light."

"But you want to go back to Boston?"

"Sure, I want to go home," he said. "Don't you?"

I said yes and didn't ask how he knew I couldn't go home.

"Boston," he said. "Boston's not like this, the houses so small, the buildings so new." In Boston, Billy Hyde told me, the buildings were older, the houses were taller, the winters were cold, really cold, with snow and ice and biting winds. In Boston, you wouldn't be sitting out on the grass at the end of February. And nowhere did every sort of tree grow, not like this.

"And the people who have money there," he said, "they've had money forever."

. . .

194

He put on his jacket, and we walked up a hill to a grove of fruit trees—apple, plum, apricot, lemon—each tree marked with its Latin and its real name. At the far end of the orchard, where the hill sloped down again, I saw a family, or what I took to be a family: a man, a woman, a boy, a girl. They walked away from us, growing smaller and smaller, until they disappeared over the crest of the hill. An imaginary me walked with them over the hill to an imaginary house on a pond, while the real me, weighted with real family, sat soldered to a bench Billy had found.

"What's your real name, Margaret?"

Down the hill below us a group of children followed a teacher as she led them to the swamp and the greenhouse of the tropics, and we could hear their voices, the paragraphs of the teacher's voice, the children's short, high-pitched questions, the shouting of straggling boys. "You doo-doo head," I heard someone cry.

"Maggie. Maggie Harris."

"Maggie Harris," he said, and then, "Margaret Lynn Harris."

I was about to tell him people didn't call me Margaret, when he put his arm around me a certain way, and I thought, Oh, this, and was surprised because why would anyone want to do *this* with a girl like me?

"What's his name?" he asked and didn't have to explain his question.

"His name's Bruce."

"Bruce," he repeated. "Lucky guy, Bruce."

He rubbed my shoulder, and I turned toward him because this is exactly what I had wanted him to do. I wanted Billy Hyde to want me, I don't know why. I almost said, "You know I already have a boyfriend," but Billy didn't want to be my *boy*friend, even I knew that.

He said, "There is nothing to regret."

The first kiss was the surprise. It made me think of blue flowers painted on porcelain. (It still makes me think that.) And then things were more familiar, we were more familiar, and what we were doing was more familiar. We were sitting on a bench, half-climbing on each other and kissing, and though I knew it was crazy to kiss a stranger, it was exactly what I wanted to do. So we kissed, and I kept thinking about his collars, his shirt collar and his jacket collar, and the warm spaces in between.

I've seen some kisses. I've seen women on their go-go stages kiss men from the bar as if they were playing some trick the men would never get. I've seen the captain of the basketball team kiss his girlfriend under the bleachers after a lost game. I've seen women wearing the lipstick off each other's faces and a man kissing the parts of another man, in a car on a street in the not-so-early morning. I once saw a man and a woman kiss and kiss and kiss, in the lobby of a midtown office building. They rolled and undulated as if there were a mattress under them, but there wasn't even a wall behind them. They had forgotten us, the people walking by. They weren't proud of being watched. They simply didn't know.

I suppose I shouldn't have looked at any of these people, even those who wanted or expected me to look, but I did. I watched in curiosity and admiration and jealousy. I looked for that moment of forgetfulness, so I could remember what it was like.

Billy Hyde and I, we kissed like that, forgetfully.

After a while, I remembered something.

"Hey, poop head," one of the children shouted, and I remembered what we were doing and wondered what we would possibly do next and thought whatever it was, I couldn't do it. Billy must have thought something similar because he stopped what he was doing and sat back against the bench, his arms spread across the slats and his legs wide, breathing as if he'd just finished a long hike. I tugged at my clothes and brushed my hair behind my ears. The breeze stirred the leaves, and then I heard a louder sound, as if branches were breaking, and saw two boys climbing a tree and trying to shake the fruit down.

Billy buttoned his shirt and settled his jacket. "I should take you back."

"You don't have to."

"I want to," he said, "and I always do what I want."

So I let him drive me, not to the Dairy Donut but to Mrs. Rumsen's. Somewhere on the gravel paths, between the tropical greenhouse and the savanna, I had decided I would go to Mrs. Rumsen's place over the drugstore, a place that was after all not so far from what used to be my home. So that's where I told him to take me. But before he drove me to her door and kissed me a last time, before I climbed the stairs to Mrs. Rumsen's, thinking with each step, What kind of girl are you?, before all that, Billy stopped and bought me a vanilla ice cream, bought himself one too, and all the way to Mrs. Rumsen's place some bit of a song my mother used to sing kept passing through my mind: Who's kissing her now?

TWENTY

My face raw and candied with kisses, I stood at Mrs. Rumsen's door, sure she would open it, knocking softly and then harder and harder. There was plenty of time to study the welt where the number 7 used to be. (The door, now a sticky-looking brown, had been every shade of green and, once, an orange so bright it should have been primary.) Plenty of time to ask myself how I could be so dumb. What did I think? That Mrs. Rum would take me in and not let on? That she would have room? That she would even be home?

I knocked again, and again no one answered. So I climbed to the top landing (where else could I go?) and sat down to wait, my back pressed against the roof door, my knees close to my chest.

The skylight over my head grew darker. Someone in the rear parking lot shouted, "Goodnight, Matty," and farther away a horn sounded twice. I could hear, one flight below, the heavy slap of shoes on the stairs, the tumble of a lock releasing, tossed keys clattering on a table-top. Billy Hyde had said, "Got you back before nightfall." He'd said that, nightfall, and now here it was. It made me think of a blanket settling over everything, one of the ones Bruce kept in his trunk, full of the garage smells of exhaust and oil, one of the ones that left us smelling like the inside of a toolbox.

Cold, I pulled on the sweater I'd spread on the ground to save my clothes from grass stains. Now the dried grass made me itch, and I was thirsty. I sucked a button and found myself thinking of kissing, kissing my boyfriend in his brother's bed, kissing a stranger on a bench, splinters pricking my thighs. Kissing, that cherubic thing that turns to sex.

Oh, god, sex. Some afternoons I'd climb into the mock privacy of Bruce's car and think, What's wrong? He'd look pinched all over, squeezed into a space too small. It took me the longest time to understand that it was just the thought of sex, cramping him there in the hot car, while kids from school walked by.

Did the thought cramp him now, on the other side of the world, where he slept surrounded by men? He wrote so little, I wouldn't know. He did write that when the transport plane crossed the international date line, someone cracked the expected joke (Does that mean we get international dates?) and half the guys cheered, for no reason Bruce could figure. *Wasn't that funny*, he wrote. *Probably shouldn't say this, sure shouldn't write it, but I think the cheer was fear (hey, the poit doesn't knowit). Hell, we're living on enemy time.*

I put my hand between my legs (this is what I want, Joan), but stopped myself because who knew who could hear me? I thought of the Iwo Jima swamp and the cedar chips under the trees, of Bruce and Billy and the world spinning, peacocks and peahens clutching the grass with the tines of their feet so they wouldn't fall away, and woke hours later to voices I thought I dreamed. From one of the many rooms of my dream, a woman said: "You wouldn't dare."

Before I could answer, a man said, "Why not?"

"Because I asked you not to and you like me," the woman said.

My face couched on my purse, I saw unclearly the banister and the green walls. Voices below me echoed in the hallway. I wiped a bit of drool away with my sticky hands, then focused on the voices and heard the man say, "You're sure of that?"

"Yes, I'm sure." It was Mrs. Rumsen's voice. "Let me open the door first."

"Oh, all right, you win. Again."

The door opened and shut, and from inside the apartment came sounds I could only guess at. A closet door opening? Laughter? A bumped table and furniture skreaking across the floor? Music, I'm sure I heard music, and dancing, I could have heard dancing.

CANNONBALL

TWENTY-ONE

Today when I am working in the restaurant my husband owns, I some-times offer customers candy in a basket. Unwrapped, a certain European mint smells of eucalyptus, reminding me, always, of Mrs. Rumsen. Sage will make me think of her because she kept herbs in pots at my father's house in the canyon. Hot milk, too. Foam rising for the cappuccino I have learned to make so well in the many restaurants where I have worked will remind me of the milk she heated on the stove for me every night I lived with her. Anything dry makes me think of her—cactus gardens, the snakes and lizards at the herpetarium, the sand that used to spill from Emmy's shoes when she came home from school. Anything parched, and party favors.

In the morning, I perched myself one flight below the top landing and one flight above Mrs. Rumsen's, waiting for her to appear outside her door. I wanted a flight's distance between me and her so I could approach her carefully, so I could change my mind and flee if I thought, for instance, my father had called her.

Hungry and thirsty but not especially sick (I wanted a Coke and a hamburger), I listened for sounds from her place, and hearing nothing, I looked at the brass numbers 2 and 3 stuck to the door in front of me.

"Only two places in this building," I later said, "and he numbers them seven and twenty-three?"

"The owner, you know, Mr. Hill," Mrs. Rumsen said, "he said he didn't want to number them one and two or A and B. So he gave them lucky numbers. He called them prime, prime numbers, prime apartments. He said every lucky number is prime. I told him that was fine by me, only prime I knew was rib. Probably he just had those numbers, didn't want to buy anything new."

She talked like that. Carelessly. As if talk were play.

"We should be careless," she said. "Some things just aren't important."

I asked her, what's important? and she said, "That is the question, isn't it?"

She left me feeling giddy, off balance. ("Your father says the air around me is thin," she said.) Most of the time I didn't believe what she said, and I don't think that she believed it either. But she talked this way, seeming to sketch something in the air between us: You know all the old ways of thinking; now try something new.

"Well, look who's here," she said after I finally walked down the stairs and knocked on her door that morning. "Little Miss Long Lost who never comes to visit. I've been expecting you."

"Why were you expecting me?" I asked, sure my father had called.

"I've been expecting you for months. When was it? Christmas? I told you you should come visit me? But you never did, and now here you are. Just like that." She snapped her fingers and flour puffed from them.

I watched for signs of my father's presence. A too-knowing glint in Mrs. Rumsen's eyes, for instance. But she seemed comfortable, inviting, and besides, there was the breath of her place. It smelled of cinnamon and shortening, or maybe lard. Anyway, it smelled of home and food, and I was so hungry.

"What are you standing there for?" She propped the door open with her foot and brushed her hands on a man's oxford shirt she'd tied around her waist as an apron. "Or what? Your mother won't let you visit me? I'm baking, by God. I don't get much more normal than this."

Still, I didn't enter. Deep inside her place, I thought I heard a man speak and imagined my father sitting in a chair and running the corner of a matchbook under his thumbnail.

"Make me invite you again, and I'm taking it as an insult."

She wiped her palms and took my sticky hands to draw me into her place. Her skin was cool, the way I remembered, cool and smooth, like orchids from the fridge.

"So make yourself at home." She looked about as if she weren't sure where she should ask me to sit. "I really am baking. I'm in one of my pie moods. You know, making lots of them."

She turned toward a sound somewhere in the apartment. Again, I thought of my father, handling the things on Mrs. Rumsen's dresser, while he waited for his chance to rail at me.

"It's like being a kid," she said. "Baking. It's like playing with flour and water."

I heard the gush of a toilet and the sound of someone heavy walking and was ready to run down the stairs when a tall white-haired man walked into the room, securing his belt and sliding the loose end through his loops. "I think those crusts are going to burn, Evvie."

"You see?" Mrs. Rum said to me. "I really am baking."

Seeing me, the man said, "I'm sorry," red flush creeping up from under his collar. "I didn't mean to barge in, didn't know you had a guest, Evelyn." He stepped back, putting a little air between us and him, then buttoned his blue jacket, as if there were something indecent about an unbuttoned jacket.

"This is my niece, my great-niece, Maggie," Mrs. Rum said. "I think I've told you about her."

The man nodded and after a moment stuck his hand toward me and said, "Cole," in a way that made me think it was his title, not his name. "Pleased to meet you, Maggie."

"Look, Ev," he said freeing his hand, "I've got to go." He took a hat from her closet and waved a kiss toward her. When he caught me watching, he shoved the hat on his head and said, "Bye Ev." And he was gone, swiftly out the door, leaving Mrs. Rum standing on the threshold and waving after him.

"Faster than a speeding bullet," Mrs. Rum said as she shut her door. "You mustn't mind him. He's not rude, just bashful."

The too-crisp smell of flour and fat going black spread through the room.

"They are burning," she said and ran to her kitchen.

It surprises me now, when I think of all the things Mrs. Rumsen didn't do. She didn't offer me food. She didn't ask after my family. She didn't even ask why I wasn't in school. (I guess she'd never been a mother.) She just went to the kitchen and worried over her crusts, and I followed her.

"What do you think?" she asked, removing her pie tins from the oven. "Overdone?"

She placed the shells on the counter, none of them black, but all too brown, the white darkened out of them.

"Should I dump them and start over?"

"Don't waste them." I don't know what I thought she would lose if she did, but the aroma made me so hungry.

"Just flour and Crisco. What's to waste?"

Mrs. Rumsen dumped the darkest, then turned and stirred something in a pot on the stove, something that smelled sweet and spicy, like winter holidays. As she bent to shut off the flame under the pot, I looked past her, out the window with its view of the small parking lot behind the Hillside Pharmacy. The Dumpster at the back of the lot was half-filled with brown sacks of trash. A few cars were nosed between the white hatch marks, and trees that had outgrown a neighboring yard spread past the fence and dropped leaves on the bright hoods.

"I don't know. It just doesn't seem right," I said.

Right. How little in this kitchen seemed right, how little it seemed like Mrs. Rumsen. A yellow clock framed in a wrought-iron star hung over the door, and on the dinette wall was a picture of a clown with a large tear rolling down his face. The clown wore orange, and I thought whoever put the picture up put it up to match the vinyl chairs, something Mrs. Rum would never have done. Only the kitchen curtains (a skirt that must have come from Olivero Street was tacked across the window) and the abalone ashtray she must have saved from the burned house seemed truly to belong to Mrs. Rum.

"Furnished apartment," she said. "Couldn't be helped."

"I'm sorry."

"Sorry about what?"

About the burned house, I wanted to say, about the melted records, the broken porcelain, the charred butterflies. "Sorry about the accident" is what I did say.

"Accident?" Mrs. Rum said and laughed. "I've lived my whole life by accident. This is nothing new."

"But what about what you lost?"

"What about it? I've lost lots of things along the way," she said and took rolls of dough wrapped in wax paper from the fridge. "At least three times, I've packed everything into one suitcase and lost it. Now, your father, he lost something. But I? A few clothes, a few records."

"But your nice things, your shawls, your pictures. You know."

"Here, sit," she said and pulled out a chair at the dinette table. "You smoke?" She pinched a cigarette from a pack on the table. "You don't? Doesn't hurt, you know, to lose a few things. It's not so bad to have your hands free every now and again." She sat back and looked at me levelly. "So, little Miss No Come Visit Me, are you still seeing that same boy?"

"Yes, but he's gone now. You know, over there, Asia," and I waved toward the parking lot and the houses beyond.

"He's writing you?"

"Not so often now."

"Think you'll see him when he comes home?"

"Why shouldn't I?"

"I didn't say you shouldn't. But, he takes care of you?" She touched things as she spoke, smoothing her makeshift apron and sliding her abalone ashtray in arcs across the table.

"I guess. It's not like he has money to burn."

"No, I didn't mean does he buy you things. I mean, he takes care of you? He wouldn't leave you in any kind of mess, would he?"

I studied the phony wood grain in the vinyl wall covering before I answered, "Not if he could help it."

She quietly kneaded strands of her hair, flour turning to paste in her hands and crusting the tufts around her temples and forehead. "Well, some things can't be helped," she said after a time, "even if they do say God helps those, and you know the rest."

I was afraid she'd ask which was true of me: Had I helped myself? Or couldn't I be helped?

"Besides, seems to me those who help themselves help them*selves*. To a second serving, for instance. And if God had anything to do with it, He'd slap their selfish little hands." She slapped her pack of cigarettes against the dinette table. "And I guess I sound crazy as a loon, don't I?"

I said she didn't. "You're saying people aren't generous, aren't you? And that, that thing you said, that saying, it gives them an excuse."

"Did I say that?" She winked and pressed out a smile. "I'm sure the old Greek who said it first had something more practical in mind, but your Grampa Whit, he loved that adage. It let him walk by the helpless while he helped himself. And he claimed to be so religious, the whole family did. They didn't dance, didn't drink, except water and weak tea, didn't even play cards because who knew what cards would lead to? It's your dad's family I'm talking about."

I nodded and said I knew.

"We weren't, you know. Your grandmother Greta Ruth and the rest of us weren't that kind of religious at all."

Religion. What did I know of religion? All I could think of was the minister who only read scripture sneaking a cookie in John Wesley Hall.

"Well, I guess people your age don't think about the church."

"No, not much."

"It's funny." Mrs. Rum lit another cigarette. "The things that stick with you and the things that don't. Funny the things you still have when you think you've left everything behind."

"Yes," I said, because I didn't know what else to say.

"You never know what will mark you." She stirred the ashes in her abalone shell.

"Like what, Mrs. Rum?" I asked. "I mean, who's marked?"

"Like Coral," she said. "I don't think your aunt Coral will ever know why she doesn't swim. I heard she's never even been in her own pool. She says she never had lessons, but who did in her day? They threw you in the water and meant it when they said sink or swim. I believe she can't swim because her parents couldn't conceive until they moved inland."

"You think Aunt Coral remembers that?"

"Do I think Coral remembers living on the shore and waiting to be born? Of course not," she said, smoke escaping the side of her mouth. "Doesn't mean it didn't mark her. You have a better idea?"

I had to agree I didn't.

"And your mother, now she's easy. She can fit a dress to a body the way she does because she spent so much time looking at bones and flesh when she was young, she just had an eye by the time she was old enough."

This did not sound odd to me. Even I could remember the charts of bones and muscles and the life-size skeleton my mother's father kept in his home.

"So what about you, Mrs. Rum?"

"Myself I can't really see. Or I can, but I go cross-eyed looking."

"But you have all these ideas about *other* people."

"So I'm obliged to have some about myself? All right. I do remember a picture, an advertisement, a bill, I guess it was, of two people dancing. It belonged to my sister, your grandmother, Greta Ruth. The two people, they were the Castles, Irene and Vernon. Imagine being named Castle." She gently spun her abalone shell, and the colors kaleidoscoped. "Like you were royal from the start, you know? Sometimes I think that was it, the thing that changed me." She stubbed her smoke out in the shell.

"That was it, Mrs. Rum?"

"Sure, that was it. Dancers. What else could it have been? How else do you think Mr. Rum and I ended up teaching cotillion, cotillion of all things?"

"But it was just a picture."

"Why couldn't it have been just some picture?" She lifted one of her balls of dough and tossed it hand to hand. "Plus a few memories of July Fourth parties back in Enterprise, parties with the rug rolled up in someone's parlor and everyone happy and dancing, but no one in *your* family, your father's family I'm talking about, not one of them." She slid her pack of cigarettes toward me and then again back to herself. "Too bad you don't smoke. Talking's much more fun if you smoke." She tapped a cigarette from her pack and lit it. "But just because they didn't dance, don't think I lived my life for spite. I didn't."

Of course I hadn't thought that.

"No, I know," Mrs. Rumsen said. "What do you know about spite? Here's something else I think made a difference. Leaving Whit's house when I did. Having to leave it when I did." She walked to the window and opened the curtain-skirt. "And having to leave as young as I was. I was your age more or less. They took me in when times got bad, when my father couldn't afford to keep me anymore, and Whit tossed me out in a year, because I riled him somehow," and then before I could ask more, "I love the view from this window."

I was quiet a moment thinking about Mrs. Rum and my grandfather. It was hard to imagine her—or any of them—really young. But it seemed clear to me, I don't know why, that everything about her—her small bones and her red hair, her smoking and her restlessness—would have enraged Grampa Whit. Thinking my silence was rude, I said, "You like looking out at the parking lot?"

"The parking lot I ignore, but even that's not so bad. I like seeing all these backyards, or as much of them as I can see. I like that big old fir and that laurel making a mess on the cars. I like seeing the backs of people's lives. If I lived in an ordinary house on an ordinary street, all I'd see is the fronts."

"Not always." When Mrs. Dawson sunbathed in her backyard, we could, from my window anyway, see her clearly in her black and yellow swimsuit.

"But almost always," Mrs. Rum said. "Shouldn't contradict when you know I'm right. Contrary, like your father, aren't you?" Again, she seemed to measure me. "You know what I saw from this window last week? The sweet chubby lady who lives over there . . ."

Although I felt weak, I walked to the window and followed Mrs. Rum's gaze toward a small stucco house meant to resemble, I think, a Tudor home.

"She started a barbecue last weekend, and within minutes, the rain broke, and in no time, it was pouring. So she brought an umbrella out and held it over her grill, stood there barbecuing in the rain. After a while her husband joined her and held another umbrella over the two of them. Every so often he'd go in and return with the steak sauce, or the ground pepper, or the fork to turn the steaks. And while he was gone, she held two umbrellas, one over her head and one over the barbecue. I don't think one drop of water fell on those steaks.

"It's a great window," she said.

As she spoke, I looked out at the shingled roofs and the shade pooling on the grass under the trees. I wasn't listening as much as I was thinking about the night before with my parents, about my father's T-shirt sticking to his damp chest and the way the bed deepened in the space between them, when Mrs. Rum's voice grew tiny in my ears, the window seemed to narrow, and everything grew dark, as if sucked into the shade of the laurel tree.

"Maggie?"

I pressed my hands against the table and sat myself down. "Mrs. Rum," I said, "I think I'm hungry."

"You mean you haven't eaten? My God, how long has it been?" She lifted my chin with one hand and waited for me to answer, but I couldn't tell her I hadn't really had a meal since before I walked away from my parents' home. "Well, Miss Plays Her Cards Close to Her Chest, never mind nosy me. I have nothing sensible or balanced in the house, but I bet this will do," and she took the lightest of her overdone shells and broke it into pieces she filled with pumpkin filling she had been mixing on the stove. She poured me a glass of milk with just a drop of coffee, and she poured herself a cup of coffee with just a drop of milk, and then she sat down and ate with me. The pumpkin was warm and sweet, the crust fragile and salty. That's all I thought about for a long time. And then, when I was starting to feel full, I thought about my father. I imagined him striding into Mrs. Rumsen's place and swallowing each pie whole, and I asked, "Have you spoken to him?"

"Who?"

"Have you spoken to my father?"

"Oh, him. No, not in a long time. Now that I'm not caretaking that place he doesn't call much."

Oh, him? To her he was just an *Oh, him.* "Maybe he'll ask you to look after another?"

"I don't think so. He's a little out on a limb with those unfinished buildings. Last I heard, he couldn't borrow any more, and he can't improve them if he can't borrow, can't sell them if he doesn't improve them, can't do anything but take a loss if he sells them now. Last I heard, what he earns, he's using on interest."

"Who told you all this?"

She seemed to know so much more than I did.

"Well, I guess your father said something last time we spoke."

"But you said you hadn't talked to him."

"I haven't. Not in a while. But he mentioned something then, and I'm friends with some of his crew. You know, the ones I met when they were fixing up the canyon place, we talk sometimes."

"You think my mother knows this?"

"Oh, your mother knows," Mrs. Rum said, making a sound almost like laughter. "Believe me, your mother knows. The last few months, the only money she has to run the house comes from her work. Or so I'm told."

"My father," I said and stopped. He was so many things—a metallic smell, a cracking hairbrush, a whistled tune in the car—that I couldn't say one simple thing about him.

"Your father, now, he's a study. Your father I can read like this," and she opened the book of her hands. "From Whit, he inherited land-lust, and from Greta Ruth, faith. Not religious faith. Faith in his prospects, do you know?" She looked at me slantwise. "No, probably you don't. He's a hopeful man, your father."

"For what, Mrs. Rum?"

"I don't know. For everything. For the roads that will take us from Mexico to Canada in a matter of hours. For the land he'll sell for a fortune. For buying your mother a new sewing machine. He's hopeful."

I must have said nothing. What did hope have to do with my parents' midnight fights? *Hope*, did it have anything to do with my father insomniac on the sofa, the test pattern flickering in his eyes? In my silence, Mrs. Rum said, "He's always got three wishes, your father, and he always thinks one of them will come true. What about you?"

The minute she said it I knew. One: I wished I could beat my fists on my stomach or tumble over bicycle handlebars or be thrown against a dashboard and stop whatever was going on inside me. Two: I wished for a healthy baby. Three: I wished I could be alone in a room with Bruce, his fingers playing the freckle game, moving from dot to dot.

"Any wish I have wouldn't count."

"Too young?" she said.

"Maybe. What would I wish for? Peace on earth?"

"Were you wishing for a good meal?" She nodded toward the bowl of pumpkin filling I had wiped clean with my finger.

"I guess."

I looked out Mrs. Rum's window. A flurry of leaves fell from the tree and dropped on a woman putting packages in her trunk.

"You're not going to tell me why your mother hasn't fed you?"

What can I tell her? Tell her that I did it? That I liked to doing it, that my father understood this, and that what happens to every girl who does these things had happened to me?

"There's nothing to tell. I just haven't been home."

"For how long?"

Who cares? "I don't know," I said, and that was true.

In the distance, a bell for morning recess rang.

"Parlor games," Mrs. Rum said. "Don't you hate them?"

"You mean like Spin the Bottle?"

"No," and she choked back a laugh. "I mean like the game you're playing with me now. But never mind. I've got to finish the pies."

"Can I help?" I asked like a seven-year-old.

"Sure," she said, and together we finished five pies. She baked three new crusts, plus the two overdone ones we had not eaten. Two we filled with pumpkin and one with chocolate, and into the last two we sliced peaches and poured sugar. One pie she froze, one she set aside for Cole, and three she gave away.

"Didn't I say I was in one of my pie moods?"

The phone rang while we were baking, a long jangling ring. Mrs. Rum answered it, and I stood by her counter, pressing the tines of a fork into an unbaked crust ("So air underneath doesn't bubble it," she had told me) as I listened for anything Mrs. Rum might say that would mean, "Yes, your daughter's here."

Even when she said, "Oh, *you*. Don't you know me better than that?"

and laughed lightly, I still thought she could be talking to my father. And when she said, "Yes, she's right here," I found myself walking into the other room to pick up my purse and sweater and head out the front door. I had just begun to do that when I heard her say, "Sure, I'll tell her that. Maggie. Maggie?" She walked into the front room. "Oh, there you are. Cole says to tell you he's sorry he left in a hurry. He says it really is a pleasure to meet such a lovely girl and he hopes he gets to see you again."

"Same here," I said, trying to hide my purse and sweater.

"'Same here,' she said," Mrs. Rum said to the phone. To me she said, "Same here? What sort of reply is that?"

I told her I didn't know, and she said, "Well, think a little about what you mean before you speak. It matters, what you say. And what you do." She nodded toward the purse and sweater I had just dropped on the chair, before she turned away and gave Cole all her attention.

When we were through baking, the kitchen was fragrant with pumpkin and chocolate, and we were sticky with sugar and flour. Mrs. Rum wrapped the pies in wax paper and tinfoil, and I stood by her window, looking out. It must have been lunchtime, because I could hear children, lots of children, playing. I could hear the heavy thump of a kickball, the kids' voices bouncing around the asphalt playground, a boy's shout rising over the other's like a pop fly. I watched a woman walk out of the pharmacy, a baby nestled into her shoulder, and felt tears running down my face.

Mrs. Rumsen handed me a paper napkin. "It's okay, you know."

"I'm tired," I said, as if that explained something.

"Yes, I bet you are. Come," and she helped me up, the way she might have helped an invalid, the way she later helped me walk after the birth, and she took me to her room and put me to bed, her coverlet plumping around me, soft as peaches past their prime. I fell asleep fast, before I could really see the touches that were plainly Mrs. Rum's: the curtains made of scarves and bandannas, the plastic combs with tiny silk flowers glued to their ribs ("No, I can't use them, but they're pretty to look at, don't you think?"), and the pictures of dancers on the walls. They were ballroom dancers, as I later saw, men and women standing arm to arm and leg to leg, like shadows of each other.

Red and blue light filtered through the bandannas, casting tinted shadows on the wall. The room was filled with an afternoon silence, the kind of quiet that comes when the younger children are napping and the older children are in school, when the dads are at work and the shops are empty because the lunch rush is over and the end-of-the-day rush has not begun. It was the time of day my mother liked most, the time when, she said, the fabric slid lightly under her fingers, and the seams she sewed were straightest. I could remember being six or seven and home from school, sitting in my nightgown on the floor of her sewing room and sucking a cough drop while I watched her lay gathering threads in yards of white sateen.

That afternoon at Mrs. Rum's, the wrought-iron clock ticked loudly in the kitchen and made the quiet quieter. Even the sound of an occasional car rolling slowly down the street outside Mrs. Rum's place seemed muffled and distant.

"Mrs. Rum?" I called out to no answer.

I walked barefoot around her room, afraid that if I made a sound, God and my father would find me. That's when I saw the pictures of dancers. Some were pinned naked to the wall, others framed in cardboard or tinfoil. A few were signed, "To Howard" or "To Rose Marie," but none said, "To Evelyn." Secondhand pictures bought to replace the irreplaceable ("Oh, please, who needs to be reminded?"), none really belonged to Mrs. Rum, except one, the picture I had packed away, and it still told the same story: Johnny Run was young as a newsboy while Evelyn Night's skirt spun away from her like a Tilt-A-Whirl. Together they were caught in a moment of unconscious grace, a harmony of arms and legs, fingers and torsos, each line and curve a reply to another.

And then, on her dresser, I spotted a photo of Cole framed in pinched tinfoil and understood that I could not make myself a guest. I pulled out the telephone book, hidden on her night table under copies of *Variety*, and thumbed the yellow pages. Not knowing where to begin I tried the craziest places first: *Unwed, Pregnant, Teenage, Wayward*. I found nothing, of course, except as I flipped through the W's, I saw *Wedding Dresses* in boldface and paused at my mother's name in small black print: *Harris, Marian Lisle, SY6-2841*. I must have known she was listed, but it was as if I hadn't. *Expert seamstress, handmade wedding dresses*. I flipped quickly to *Homes* and found *Home for the Blind, Home for Veterans of Foreign Wars*, and even *Home for Old Men and Aged Couples*, but no Home for Wayward Girls.

• • •

"Oh, good, you saw my note," Mrs. Rum said as she walked into the kitchen, a sack of groceries in her arms.

I had seen her note: "You'll be hungry, so help yourself to what's in the fridge. I'll be home sometime not too late. Yr friend, Mrs. Rum." In the refrigerator, I'd found a chicken sandwich cut into four small triangles and dressed on a plate with tomato slices and thin curls of sweet pickles. ("The waitress in me just never dies," she said later. "Can't serve anything without a garnish.") I ate it all, pickle and tomato slices too, then opened her cupboards and found, among jars of Spanish olives and cocktail onions and cans of tuna and clams, a jar of peanut butter. At first, I ate peanut butter straight from the jar, licking it off the knife, then digging in my fingers and sucking the peanut butter away. *Behave.* I forced myself to be civilized, to find her bread in the bread box and make a sandwich, but when Mrs. Rum walked in, I pushed the plate and what was left of the bread across the table and hid the jar of peanut butter in my lap.

"Don't stop because of us," she said. "Now I can feed you properly."

Cole followed, two more sacks of groceries in his arms. He glanced at me through celery greens. "She's still here, Ev," he said. "Didn't I tell you she would be?" To me, he said, "I told her you were too polite to run off without a word."

"Oh" was all I said.

"Want an apple?" Mrs. Rumsen asked as she took one from deep inside the sack she'd put on the counter. "No?"

She kept it for herself and walked toward her bedroom, shedding sweater and purse on the way. I stumbled past Cole to stuff the jar of peanut butter into the cupboard, then followed Mrs. Rum and found her standing before her mirror, the apple on her dresser.

"Mrs. Rumsen."

"Yes?" she said, nudging her hair with her fingers.

"Thank you for the food and everything." (I was so clumsy, that's what I said.) "Thank you for letting me stay here today."

"No need to thank me."

"Well, yes, there is. Because I'm leaving."

"Going home?" she asked, this time snagging my eyes in our reflection.

"Not going home?" she said when I didn't answer.

"No," I said.

"Well, then, where to?"

"I'm staying over at a friend's house. It's okay. I called my mom."

"Need someone to drive you there?"

I told her I could walk, and she said, "So if your father calls, I should say you've gone to whose house?"

"Why should my father call?"

"Because I feel it." She squeezed the air between her hands. "And you know how I am about my feelings."

"If he calls, you can't tell him anything, Mrs. Rum."

"Why?"

"You just can't."

"If you'd give me one good reason, maybe I could help."

She turned toward me, apple in hand as if she might pitch it at me.

"Here's a reason," I said. "Because Whit kicked you out when you were my age."

"Because he was a spiteful man, because he couldn't sort out his feelings," she said and surprised me with her anger. "Not because I was a girl in trouble."

Catching the look that crossed my face, shame I think it was, she turned away, and we were calm a moment, the two of us silent about what we both knew but hadn't said: She had never been a girl in trouble, but I most certainly was. Mrs. Rum turned away and pulled the chain on her dresser lamp, rebalancing the light in the room so the scarves now looked like nothing more than scarves and you could see the dresser's dust, the apple's bruise.

"Trouble?" I said. "It's okay to throw a girl out if she's in trouble?"

"No," she said, sad eyes hugging me. "No, it isn't."

"Because if it is, I can make it easy for you. Already made it easy for them."

"Did you?"

Just then I saw Cole. Behind our reflection, the doorway filled most of the mirror, and his reflected form filled most of the doorway. I wanted to tell him to leave us alone, but even then, I knew he didn't deserve the anger.

"I'm sorry, Ev. I didn't mean to interrupt," he said, "but Jim Harris is on the phone."

She ahhed softly. "Well, then. I'm to tell him nothing, hmm?" She kissed two fingers and pressed them to my forehead as she passed by. I sat on the bed and waited.

"Why, Jim, good to hear from you." Mrs. Rum spoke loudly enough I thought she wanted me to hear. "No, I haven't. Not hide nor hair."

"No, not here, Jim," she said and then, "Yes, if you need to. Come by any time. Just give me a call so you'll know I haven't gone to sleep yet."

"You can stay in my room," she said. "He'll be none the wiser, I promise you. And that's *if* he comes over, and who says he will? All he asked was had I seen you, and you heard me say no." She stood backlit in the doorway, waving her smoking hand. "Or if that doesn't put you at ease, you could take a drive with Cole. He wouldn't mind, would you, Cole?"

I told her I should go.

"You're safer here."

I couldn't ask her to lie to my father again. "I can't ask . . ."

"You haven't asked me for anything. And you haven't told me anything. Remember that."

I nodded and sat down on her bed. For no reason at all, I felt sleepy, tired the way grown-ups always said they were. Bone tired. I wanted to be abandoned to sleep, as if sleep were an island far away. I imagined people passing me, like those ships pass the shipwrecked, blind to the smoke sent up. But before I could risk sleep, I had to be sure Mrs. Rum understood.

"My father, my mother, they don't know, Mrs. Rum."

"If they don't know, why're you running?"

"I told them I wanted to get married. That was bad enough."

"And you want to?"

"No, I don't. But you can see it'd be worse if I really told them, can't you?"

She didn't answer me, and I guessed she didn't see. But somehow I believed she would keep my secret. Some people you tell your secrets because you know they will tell everyone what you can't. Others you tell because you know they won't. Mrs. Rum was like that.

As if we had settled something, Mrs. Rum left me alone in her room. I pulled the chain on her dresser lamp and fell on her bed, and though I wanted to swim away in sleep, instead I lay awake watching the scarves in the window growing dark and mottled.

The phone never did ring, or I never heard it. But long after the streetlights lit, I did hear my father's car, or I should say I heard his driving. The quick acceleration from the corner light, the squeal of rubber as he pulled his vehicle tight to the curb, and then the way he gunned the engine before he shut it off. I knew it was him before I pushed back the scarves and peered at the green roof of the Pontiac and my father closing the car door as he gazed down the block at something I could not see. He circled the car and leaned into the rear window. I thought perhaps he was talking to my mother, until his gestures said something final (I imagined him promising ice cream or candy or maybe an Orange Julius) and Alison leaned out to kiss her daddy's face. He unzipped his jacket, tugged at his cuffs, and headed toward the building. I should have grabbed my things and run right then, but I paused to watch my sister climb from the car. She wore her pink sweater and her pink Keds, and, leaning back as if she owned the car, she shook a box of Good & Plenty, one pink piece slipping into the palm of her hand. Tilting her head back, she popped it into her mouth and gazed up, directly at me. I stepped away from the window and opened the bedroom door, ready to run up the stairs and hide on the top landing. But my father was already knocking, and Mrs. Rum was stuffing my sweater and purse into her front closet when she frowned me back into her bedroom. Shutting the door, I heard her say, "Why, Jim, how good to see you."

TWENTY-TWO

I sat, my ear pressed to the crack between the door and jamb.

"How's business?" Mrs. Rumsen asked, perhaps searching for a safe topic.

"How's business?" my father scoffed. His voice was small, almost boyish. It made me think of Bruce. "Just fine. Just hunky-dory. Ask me if I can meet payroll."

"Can you?"

"I could if I could just close on one of these properties."

"Is that likely?"

"Of course it is," he said, sounding more like himself. "These sites're worth double what I'm asking."

"But by Friday?"

"There's tax I can put off. There's an interested investor."

Mrs. Rum was silent a moment and then said, "You can repay someone who puts money in?"

"Don't see why not."

"Oh," she said and "Well," and "There could be lots of reasons." After a moment, she added, "But what do I know?"

"Sure, it'll take time, but there's money to be made. Look at Chess, look at the world. Lots of people with less smarts than you or me're making money."

"You're right, I'm sure."

"Of course I'm right. I've planned it carefully, every property I've managed to buy. It's just they're selling slower than I thought."

"You know, I have a little something to give you, Jimmy."

217

"Aw, Mrs. Rum."

"You understand, I'm just trying to pay you back."

"Mr. Rum would never forgive me for taking this from you. Johnny wouldn't like it."

"So, Mr. Rum's not around to see. Besides, I can afford it. Cole picks up the rent and the groceries now and again. So take the money. It's not much anyway."

He took his time answering. I imagine that though he waved the money away, she pushed the bills persistently toward him across the yellow Formica.

"I appreciate it," he said at last. "Boy, do I appreciate it. I get to feeling I'm carrying the load all alone."

"Why're you all alone?"

"Marian never forgets, and she never forgives. As you know." He then added quietly, as if he was ashamed to say it, "And my daughter."

"What's that?"

"My daughter. Maggie. She's gone. She abandoned us," my father said. "I mean, we can't find her."

I could hear him tapping something, perhaps his billfold, against the dinette table.

"What do you mean?"

"You know how kids her age are, sure they know how to live. We got up the other morning, and she was gone like Sunday on Monday."

"Maybe she had a reason."

"Aw, hell, Mrs. Rum, what reasons?" The two of them were silent a moment. "Because I gave her some good advice she'd be smart to take?"

"At her age, I don't think I would have taken anyone's advice. And I know how you give advice, Jim."

"You're saying I said things I shouldn't?"

"You had a fight? Then it wouldn't surprise me."

They were quiet again, and for no good reason, I thought of Mrs. Rumsen sitting on the stairs in the house where my father grew up. I pictured her wearing an old flannel gown and my father sitting two steps higher, studying the flickering red tinsel of her hair as she brushed it. A young Uncle Chess hung ornaments on the tree, while Gramma Truth scrambled eggs in the kitchen and Whit, upstairs in his room, pulled garters up around the tops of his fine Sunday socks as he dressed for church.

"We called everyone we could think of," my father said. "We didn't exactly ask if Maggie had gone to their house. We didn't want them all to know. But we did call all her friends' parents, and we called that boy's mother. She said she hadn't seen Maggie since before Bruce left, then thanked me for calling, said it would be nice if we got to know each other. And why is that, I'd like to know? Does she think I'm letting my daughter marry her boy?"

"Is that the worst that could happen?"

"Hell, no, the worst is if the business goes under," he said. I heard my father rise and cross the room.

"The worst is if they die," he said quietly. He sounded tired, as if he might have waited up for me all night, and I was standing to open the door and show him I was not dead when the front door clicked open and he said, "Oh," and Mrs. Rum said, "Why, sweetheart," and right outside the bedroom door my sister said, "I have to go." Then Alison opened the door and looked at me, not with surprise exactly but with some question in her eyes. I waited for her to open the door wider and say, "Daddy!" but Mrs. Rum said, "The bathroom's on the right, sweetheart." Alison said, "Uh-huh," and leaving the door half open, walked on in.

Where I stood, I couldn't see my father and he couldn't see me, although I'm sure Mrs. Rum could see me plainly in the streetlight. I fixed on those sad eyes of hers and thought, *Please don't tell him, please don't.* Mrs. Rum watched me a moment, her arms crossed in front of her, and then searched a drawer until she found a cigarette. She wore that black kimono she wore the day I first met her, and as she moved, the confetti colors of the lining appeared and disappeared. She lit the cigarette and fixed me again with her eyes, the damp odor of burning tobacco reaching me slowly.

"Ali*son*," my father said.

Mrs. Rum said, "I'll go get her."

"I'm coming," Alison called.

Water ran in the pipes and splashed in the sink, and when Alison left the bathroom, her hair was wet with comb tracks and the bow she wore was freshly tied. I hate to admit I pleaded with my sister silently, but I did. I even closed my hands together the way I'd seen widowed women close their hands in prayer and understood then that they did not clasp their hands in virtue. They clasped their hands together because they could not clasp what they wanted to clasp, just as I gripped mine because I could not grip Alison. Blinking back tears, she shook her head and walked over to touch me, just touch me (I could have been made of wax). Then she reached up, her lips rolled together as if she meant to swallow them, and put her arms around my neck, pulling me toward her. She pressed her face into my hair and whispered, "Please come home." Then she walked out, shutting the door behind her, and I heard my father say, "Well, kiddo, all set?"

TWENTY-THREE

Mrs. Rumsen

Ought you to have done it?" Cole asked.

I thought he was asleep, so his voice startled me.

"I don't know," I said, because I didn't. "It's a hard thing to lie to a friend."

But it is not always difficult to lie to family. It is just possible that some memory of the bitter root of kinship allowed me to lie to Jim.

Our kinship was simple. I was his aunt and he was my nephew. But our kinship was also complicated because we were somehow closer than nephew and aunt. My sister's family was small, but she and I were born into a large family, a farm family, ten children, eleven if you count the one that didn't make it. Jim's mother—Margaret Ruth—or Greta Ruth or Gramma Truth as the grandchildren called her—was the eldest, and I was the youngest. She was eighteen and already married when I was born, and I was three when Chess was born, six when Jim was christened, and seven when she slept through the end of her third pregnancy and awoke birthing a girl who would never breathe. She practiced her mothering on me and my brother, so I have always felt that my sister was more like a mother to me, and Jim more like a brother. That's how I lied to him, the way you lie to a brother. What else are families for?

And then, there was Maggie to consider. If she didn't want to talk to her father, maybe she had good reason.

"If I were you," Cole said, "I wouldn't have done it." He rolled to his back and nested his hands under his head. "I would have told her to speak to him."

"You've never been a girl. And you've never been in trouble."

"Never could be and never will be. But I've had other troubles, and I know what's right."

"Do you? You know what's right for her?"

He rolled toward me and said, "I know what's right, period."

"Well, you don't know her father."

I knew him the way you know a younger brother, both as graceful boy and pesky troublemaker, as handsome and bewildered young man, baffled by the girls he courted. I knew his temper and his troubles, because it was at our table, John Rumsen's and mine, that he discussed them. He told us about his plans and about the risks he took, and unlike his wife, we did not judge him. It is, I think, what angered Marian most about me, that I listened when she could not.

"What are you going to do, then?" Cole asked. "Keep her nine more months?"

Maggie lay in the other room. I had thrown a sheet over the sofa and plumped a pillow, pulled a blanket from the closet. I did not believe she would stay on that sofa for nine months. I believed that in time she would sort things out, if someone would give her time. I thought of her as a plant that needed water, that needed to sit on a wide sill and soak in the sun.

"You're not jealous, are you?" I asked.

He laughed quietly. "If I were, I'd put up with it." After a moment he added, "For your sake."

Space in a bed changes so quickly. The same six inches of cotton sheet can widen and narrow in a moment. He rolled toward me, and I thought how sweet it all would be. Then he rolled away and stepped from the bed, and I thought, Aw, Maggie will be the end of us. Cole wore pajamas, in shyness, I think, and he stood there gesturing in the dark, the pajamas making him seem awkward and boyish, until I understood I was to follow him to the makeshift bed he was preparing for us on the floor. Cole was a divorced man, with two grown children, and he often behaved as if his children might be watching. He'd lift his head and scan a restaurant, as if Jean or Tom might be spying from some hidden table, before pressing his hand to my back and escorting me to ours. At home of a sudden, he'd notice our disheveled clothes in the TV light and button and tug at his shirt. He'd even brush my hair with his fingers, until I'd say, "It's okay, C. They don't know you're here."

It had been difficult enough to convince him to visit with Maggie staying over. He kept saying it wasn't proper, until I said no doubt Maggie's sense of propriety was different from his. So I believe it was out of consideration to those children, who were not so much older than Maggie, and perhaps to the wife he had lived with for so many years, and as a courtesy to me as well, and, of course, to Maggie, that he spread the blanket on the floor. Whatever we did should be quieter there.

Unlike Cole, I didn't worry much about our sounds. I was grateful for sex. I still am, of course, and if I had known I should have been grateful when I was younger, I would have been then, too. Not grateful for any old rub-a-dub, but grateful for sex with a beginning, middle, and end, sex I did not want to forget and that did not render me forgettable. Grateful, in short, for the sort of sex that is difficult to find. Even in a life as unconventional as mine, how rarely I've really wanted to let this one or that one inside me, and I don't think I've been stingy or treated myself preciously. There just haven't been many I've really wanted to touch. I was grateful for a reasonable man.

I was grateful, too, because wisdom had it that at my age, I was only good for companionship, and I was better off without that if the companion was male. If your husband died and you were beyond a certain age, you were expected to grieve a time, perhaps a year, perhaps two. But then you were to hang your dark clothes at the back of your camphor-dense closet. You were to teach Sunday school and organize socials and potlucks, to go to the beauty parlor once a week, to keep a clean house, to cover all your appliances with tatted or crocheted cozies. Surely my family thought the death of John Rumsen would be the end of my life of sin. But how could I allow that?

Among all the people who came to the theater every two weeks to see the new double feature, Cole was the lone man I remembered. I noted that he always wore a hat and that when he greeted me behind my grille, he always tipped it. I saw the careful way he folded his money and wondered if he was stingy or just cautious with what was his. I saw him yield his place in line to others, to the women I was meant to become, women who walked with canes and who kept their money in white teller's envelopes wrapped tight with rubber bands. I saw that he recognized me the third time he came to the theater during my shift. He smiled and took a longer look, and the fourth time he appeared at the grille, I asked him what he thought of *The Guns of Navarone*.

"I liked it. But I like almost anything."

"So do I," I said, which was not true. A professional in the theater, even a small-time dancer such as I was, always has too many opinions to like almost anything.

The fifth time, I admitted him for the price of a child. He hesitated and pushed the money back under the grille. "You've made a mistake . . ."

"Mistake?"

He smiled and kept his change, bowing his head to hide the flush, and, as he later told me, returned to thank me after the show only to find I was gone. It was the next time he said he owed me a cup of coffee.

The sound of a chair scraping the floor made us both pause in our rocking and glance toward the door. We remained still a moment, and I thought how the next day my wrists would be sore and my knees bruised. I wanted to say, "We're going to feel this in our bones," except of course I couldn't because we were listening for sounds of Maggie. I heard nothing except our hoarse breathing and the small sticking sounds of flesh on flesh. I closed my eyes and listened for the creaking of floorboards moving under linoleum, the rasp of a closet door opening, of Maggie's tread on the braided rug. Then a part of Cole that did not care if his children were watching moved; it stretched inside me, and soon I forgot about the wakeful.

Afterwards, he slept and I smoked, this was the rule. He slept then, sprawled on the floor. I covered him but knew that, for at least a few hours, I could not wake him enough to walk him to the bed. So I stood by the window in the old kimono Mr. Rum had given me years before and smoked and thought, as I always did at night, how odd it was that life had brought me here.

And then I saw Maggie across the street. I don't know why I didn't notice her sooner. A bus pulled to the curb, its lights flooding her, and that's when I saw her, climbing onto that well-lit bus and looking lost, like the only shopper in an empty supermarket. I stuck my feet into a pair of slippers I had once knit for Mr. Rum and dug in Cole's pockets for his keys. I kissed his forehead (he looked like such a child on the floor with the blanket hooked over one arm and his feet kicked free of the covers), then I ran down the stairs in my silly old kimono and found Cole's car in the lot behind the Hillside Pharmacy. I figured the car would move faster than the bus, and it did. Pulling up behind the bus idling at a stoplight, I spotted Maggie among the few passengers, her head bowed and her hair falling forward, and I followed her, followed the clouds of exhaust and the small sign on the back that said BARBARA ANN BREAD.

The day I left home, such as it was, Whit stood at the door of his small clapboard house on Crenshaw and said, "I'm sorry, Evvie."

He wore spectacles, and I thought his blue eyes glinted through them like dimes.

"We've kept you to your majority, and that's all anyone can ask us to do."

"I understand, Whit," I said, surveying him and taking my satisfaction in small defects: his frayed cuff and the strands of hair that had escaped his comb, the curling paint of the porch ceiling that threatened to fall on him like dirty snow. "I'm old enough I can care for myself," I said. In a way, I was able to care for myself. I had saved a small amount of money sweeping out a store regularly and cooking in a hospital kitchen. Well, it was cooking if peeling potatoes and slicing onions was cooking. Even paying Whit and Greta some rent, I had managed to save. As I stood on that porch saying good-bye, I thought of the dollars rolled up in a sock in the small bag I carried. "I'll be fine, you'll see," I said and thought that he truly would see, for I imagined a future fame for me that would shame him.

"Sure you will, Ev."

"So good-bye, then, Whit."

He didn't answer, just stepped behind the screen door and lifted his hand. I walked down his porch steps and the concrete path to the sidewalk and waited a breath or two after I heard the bolt set before I slipped down his driveway to find Greta Ruth sitting on the back stoop, a basket of wet laundry next to her.

"Bye, Greta."

"Bye, sweetie."

The stillborn had taken most of the words from her, and she no longer had the kind of smarts Whit admired. But no one believed she had nothing to say, not even Whit, who, I think, feared her.

"Going for good?" she said.

"Guess so."

"Well, time for falling stars," she said and stood herself up.

"Yes, it is." But it wasn't the time for falling stars at all, it being

October, well past August and two weeks past my eighteenth birthday, two weeks past my majority, Whit would say, and time for me to assume responsibility for myself.

"Go find some," she said and lifted the basket. I started to help her, because helping her around the house was one of the things I did to justify my keep, but she said, "Boys home soon."

"Yes, they will be home soon, Greta." I imagined the boys rounding the corner just as I left, Chess with his hair slicked back and his books banging his thigh and Jim still a slender boy full of the unwitting grace children have and he has never lost.

"Hey, where're you going?" Chess would have asked.

"I'll never tell," I might have answered.

"Good-bye," I said to Greta. I held out one hand for her to shake. She glanced at me and at the windows of her bedroom. "Bye, Ev." She squeezed my hand so hard it tingled for half a block.

As the bus and its Barbara Ann Bread sign turned east toward Whittier instead of west toward Los Angeles, I wondered just what sort of plans Maggie had, if any. Leaving Whit and Greta's, I knew exactly where I was going. Down the block to the trolley and directly to Graumann's Chinese, where I intended to sit in a velvet seat and watch Fred twirl Ginger in *Top Hat*. Whit considered it a sin that I loved movies. Leaving his house, I considered it high time for this kind of sin. It was after the show I had to figure out where to go, and, of course, then I had no idea.

"Maggie!" I leaned my head out the window to call after her as she walked up the steps of a low building with arches and columns meant to suggest Spanish architecture. Maggie looked back with some mixture of surprise and annoyance on her face. I could hardly blame her. She had already left one mother and hadn't bargained, I'm sure, on a second. "Where do you think you're going?"

She ran up the steps and disappeared into the shadows of the would-be Spanish building. I parked in a no-parking and ran after her, pulling my sash tighter, not against the cold, but against wind. I was, after all, not wearing much of anything and thought myself a little old to be arrested for nudity in Whittier.

"Maggie," I called across the open courtyard. She sat on the edge of a silent fountain and eyed me as I approached. "Don't follow me," she said, "please."

"I'm not following you, but I can't just leave you here."

She dipped her hand into the still water. Even in the dark, the water seemed green and her hand aquatic. "Why can't you?"

"Because I worry about you."

"Why worry?"

"Because I know. It's a lot of work, taking care of yourself."

"I've got plans where to go."

"Where?"

"To one of those homes." She splashed a handful of water out of the fountain.

"Oh," I said. "Of course. What was I thinking?" The sky above us was clear, and the stars brittle. "What home?"

"I don't want to tell you," she said, her face losing its angles in the dark.

"I can't stop you from going. No one can."

"No one? Not even my father?"

"I don't know. But who's going to tell him?"

"I guess you won't," she said and then added in a small child's voice, "will you?"

"You know I won't. That's up to you, sweetheart."

"Everything is up to me now."

Something darker than darkness, a cat perhaps, moved in the shadow of the colonnade. Maggie swung her hair back and shivered.

"Yes, it is cold." I was grabbing for something to say, but I was in fact chilled sitting there in that silky kimono thing. "So you want me to drive you to this home?"

"Drive me?"

"You have a better way to get there?"

"I did have a way," she said and perched herself upright. "It doesn't have to be better as long as it's a way."

"Fair enough."

I was beginning to think I was very glad Mr. Rum and I had never had children. Not knowing what to do next, I stalled: I turned my face up to the stars. "I swear, I give up trying to tell the planets from the stars and the satellites from both of them."

"The satellites move."

"That so? But too slowly for me to spot them."

She gazed up and then looked at me. "Really, I'll be fine, Mrs. Rum. I do have somewhere to go."

She seemed so certain, all I could do was put out my hand. "I've made my offer, all right? Can we call it a truce?"

She looked at me as if I were hopeless. "Okay, Mrs. Rum. I've heard the offer. I just want to do this on my own. That's all."

"Fine with me," I said, wrapping the kimono tighter around me.

"Look," she said pointing at the sky. "That's a satellite."

I followed her hand. "Which one?"

"The one that's moving, silly."

None of the stars seemed to move.

"That one?"

She put her chin on my arm so she could follow my sight line. "No, can't you see it moving, Mrs. Rum?"

This time I tried to fix the stars as I gazed, but as I moved from cluster to cluster and back again, I could not tell if any had shifted. "There. That one's moving. It's even pulsing."

"That's an airplane, Mrs. Rum."

"Aw, unfair."

"Yeah, unfair. Look, I'm sorry I'm so much trouble."

"No, you're no trouble," I said. "I better go home, get some sleep. Cole must be wondering what happened."

"Thanks," she said. "I mean, thanks for following me."

"Oh, well." I waved and walked back through the shadowed colonnade and down the steps to the car. I left her side unlocked and let the car idle so I could at least have some heat and music. Who knew how long it would take? I was willing to give her thirty minutes, maybe even forty-five, but an hour would have been just too much. It happened that I was sitting cross-legged and drifting off, don't ask me how, to the sounds of Benny Goodman when I heard the rap on the glass. I was fool enough to think it was the police come to get me for sleeping half naked in a parked car in Whittier, when Maggie climbed in and said, "I'm trying not to intrude, Mrs. Rum. I'm trying to do this myself."

I had no idea if there were homes such as Maggie wanted in Whittier or LaPuente or any of those towns and cities. Perhaps she hadn't boarded some random bus. Perhaps she knew exactly where she was going. I never asked. In the morning, I said, "Let's go," and took her to the only place I knew, a home in downtown Los Angeles where I had stayed, not to term, because I was not and never have been pregnant, but for a week of three squares and a real bed, the week it took the home to find I wasn't pregnant at all.

That first night away from Greta and Whit, I remained in my red velvet seat as long as I could. The heavy red curtains with their black fringe dragged across the stage, and the lights came up on the great lacquered faces of the Chinese dragons mounted high in every corner of the theater. On the walls around me, sampans floated downriver in murals of craggy landscapes, and on the ceiling, mist streaked into gold stars. An usher in a black silk coolie jacket leaned over my seat and said, "The show is over, miss," and I smiled sweet as I could and pardoned myself for my forgetfulness.

He nodded, the red satin knob on his black coolie's cap wobbling, and turned curtly, his silk trousers whispering. I followed him up the aisle, but at the ladies', I paused as he sauntered ahead, and when he turned to hold the great carved-dragon doors open for me, I smiled an apology and hurried inside the rest room. To buy time, I washed my hands and face and dried them on the coarse paper towels, something I learned to do every chance I got in the days that followed, and when I dared peer out again, I saw the usher rocking foot to foot and gliding swiftly in an arc across the carpet, mimicking the steps we had seen on the screen. Absorbed as he was, it was easy to slip back into the auditorium and crawl under the curtains that skirted the stage. Using my carpetbag for a pillow, I made a bed for myself on a pile of musty canvas, though for a long time I couldn't sleep, fearing rats, fearing discovery, fearing the darkness that was so complete. Once I fell into sleep, I slept fiercely, waking the next day only when the audience laughed. I woke in amazement at where I was, listening to the sound of the movie. There I lay on piles of canvas, eavesdropping on the conversation between the soundtrack and the audience. Of course, I could not move, could not take care of my needs, which was excruciating. But I waited until the movie ended, managing to crawl out unseen and join the exiting crowd.

You would think I would have learned, but I didn't. My days spent wandering the streets, nights I returned to see Fred and Ginger again (have I mentioned how I loved Mr. Astaire, how movement slipped out of him the way ink slips from a good pen, and how I wished I could be as dexterous as he?), and though the usher nodded at me in recognition as he led me to my seat each time, he did not let on that he knew what I was doing.

Other nights I spent hiding in the ladies' of the Southern Pacific downtown station, the ladies' being, for its absence of men, securer than most places. I lived on toast and tea and, once a day, a glass of milk, which I always ordered from a different drugstore soda fountain, and one day, maybe the fifth, while searching for a drugstore, I found myself looking at a gray stone building that bore the inscription over its double front doors: THE LOS ANGELES COUNTY HOME FOR GIRLS.

I looked at that inscription for quite some time, trying to understand what it meant. What was a girl? How old was she? Why did Los Angeles County need a home for her? Finally, I just walked in the door and found myself in a county office room, the kind of room you used to find in police stations and board of education buildings, the kind that were filled with heavy wooden desks and chairs, wire baskets stacked with papers, tall wooden file cabinets with one drawer that wouldn't quite close, a portrait of Mr. Roosevelt, and, always, two flags, the American and the California bear. No one sat at either desk, so I quietly invaded a dark corridor. All the brown wooden doors were shut, light showing dimly through each wired, opaque window, but at the end of the corridor one double door stood open. And beyond it I saw a large yellow room full of long tables and seated young women at various stages of pregnancy. Most of the women did not talk, although I heard giggling from a part of the room I could not see. The women I could see peered down at their plates and ate methodically, as if it was their duty to chew every bite fifty times.

But they were chewing. How nice it would be to chew. And where I stood, I could smell the food. Gravy on mashed potatoes, hot bread, molasses. I watched a very pregnant girl spoon corn into her mouth, her loose brown braids falling forward as she leaned toward her plate, but when she caught me staring, she glared at me and stuck out her tongue, yellow specks clinging to it. I turned and walked back down the corridor.

"May I help you, miss?"

The man who now sat behind one of the desks was thin, sweatered, and spectacled. He wore his glasses low on his nose, and although I have never met or seen a monk, I thought he moved with a monkish deliberateness, as if each motion were ordained.

Never once thinking how small, how thin, how thoroughly unpregnant I looked, thinking only about the hot and surely free meals, I turned to him and said, "I'm in trouble, sir."

I scarcely knew what to expect. The building I remembered could have been torn down, the institution moved to another site or closed forever. And who knew if I could find the place? I had no number or street name. The most I could remember was its vicinity, Western Boulevard. I turned right onto the first street that seemed familiar but found no government buildings.

Maggie looked at me askance. "You sure you remember where this place is?"

"No, I'm not sure at all."

I drove cross-hatch through the neighborhood, Maggie peering out the car window saying, "Maybe that's it" and me glancing over and saying, "No, I'm afraid not."

At a stoplight, I spotted a nickel counter I thought I recognized in what had become a Thrifty's. Impossible to tell if it was the same counter, the same soda fountain, or even if my memory served. I turned right anyway, onto a street that was narrower than the one I remembered, perhaps because cars were parked on both sides. I drove slowly, leaning into the steering wheel to read the signs and fronts of the buildings. Magazines were clothespinned to wire strung across the window of a news and tobacco store. The used cameras and rings, the clarinets and accordions, gold chains and silver cigarette cases arrayed behind the gilt-lettered glass of Joe Tuba's Second Hand Instruments suggested a pawn shop. At the end of the block, I read BAIL BONDS in large black letters and tried to remember if there had been a jail nearby. Between the Bail Bonds and Harry's Discount Men's Wear were the neon-lit windows of Murphy's Liquor and Spirits and Brown's Gun Shop. The car behind me honked as I braked for a man zagging across the street, a brown paper package clamped under his arm. The man out of my way, I had stepped on it when Maggie said, "There it is." Angling my head and looking back over my shoulder, I saw the gray stone front and the concrete steps. "That's it," I said and drove around the block looking for parking.

"It's windows are barred. Is it supposed to be a prison?"

"I think the bars're for safety," I said and drove on, finally pulling into a corner space, the rear of the car hanging into the street.

"Safety? You mean suicide prevention?"

"Yes," I said, not only because it was true but also because I wanted her to reconsider. I wanted her to come home with me.

"Jeez," she said and slid down in her seat. "You think this is the way to do it? I mean, I don't have to apply to some other office first, do I?"

"I didn't. Only way to find out is to ask."

She sat up and ran a comb through her hair. "Trying to look decent. No hope, huh?"

"Oh, go on. Remember, all you're doing is inquiring."

It pained me to see her climb from the car, but I didn't believe anything I said would stop her. So I watched her walk away, weaving past men with bottles and men with briefcases. From where I sat, she looked doll-sized by the time she reached the building far down the block. She tilted her head way back, reading that inscription again, I guess, and then climbed the stairs, pausing at each step as if she were many more months gone than she was. She disappeared into the building, and I felt a small tug inside, as if my own child were leaving me.

For the year I stayed with them, Greta and Whit put me up in the enclosed porch off the back of their house. It was where the boys *lived*, where they played and read and studied, and after I arrived that didn't change. If the boys were making a bug jar, playing dominoes or checkers, or recreating Civil War battlefields, they did it on the enclosed porch.

Evenings, Chess liked to sprawl on the daybed, reading adventure stories, and Jim sat at the card table doing homework. Well after supper, when I'd finished cleaning up the kitchen, I'd go to my supposed room and, no chair free, sit on the door sill, picking up yesterday's paper and reading reviews and bits of gossip, anything I could find about theater or the movies. Sometimes the boys and I would talk, about any old thing: blue-belly lizards, school fights, Jules Verne, late-model automobiles. And it was a little like being home, talking with my brothers again, except my brothers were all older, me being the baby of the family. But seeing me there with his boys, Whit would seat himself in his parlor chair, pulling the chain on his lamp loudly and rattling open his paper.

I don't know what Whit thought I would do. I was just a girl, for God's sake, a girl who knew nothing much but farm animals, and, believe me, I didn't want to do what farm animals did. But Whit must have thought I needed a constant chaperone because he watched me. All the while I stayed with them, I felt the chilly touch of his dime-eyed gaze.

He watched me slice the bread and said, "No wider than your pinkie, girl."

He watched me push the carpet sweeper and said, "You missed a spot."

I climbed the stairs to do the beds and heard him say, "A woman's tread should be so light you don't hear it at all."

He opened wide a door I had left ajar, surprising me before the bathroom mirror, and said, "Have you noticed how Greta does her hair?" I nodded because of course I had noticed that she draped her hair over her ears before twisting and pinning it into a small cushion, a ring pillow, on the back of her head. "That's what you should do with yours," he said and closed the door after him.

Young as I was, part of me knew, part of me understood that I was too free, too close to the music in my mind. Here Whit lived with a wife who had lost half her sense, and I knew what he had lost. I knew what Greta was like when young, like water and light. It was Greta who loved the Castles, Irene and Vernon, Greta who rolled back the rugs in our house so everyone could one-step. She had been freer than he, and that's what he loved. And now she wasn't free at all, moving through the uncertainties of her world. Part of me knew how Whit must see me, a young girl not afraid, a girl waiting to be touched, not by him, but by life. And maybe it was then, during the year I stayed with Greta and Whit, that I decided I would never marry.

Pulling the car up the drive one day, he watched me hanging by my knees in the backyard tree, and knowing him well enough by then, I swung down as soon as I heard his car, my fingers and scalp tingling and the hair I refused to pin into a cushion hanging loose to my elbows.

"Don't you have the least bit of sense?" he said, standing outside his shack of a garage, his hat and coat in hand.

"I have plenty of sense."

"What sensible girl your age hangs like an ape and shows her drawers to the world?"

"I beg your pardon, but my skirt was tucked under my knees."

"Didn't look that way to me."

"Then you can't see straight." Which was the truth. But then I added, "Besides, who'd think my drawers were of interest anyway?"

"Boys might be fool enough to think so. Even my boys."

"If I wanted boys, even your boys, to see my drawers, I'd go down to City Hall and lift my skirts. All I wanted was . . ." (Well, what was it I wanted?) "To climb a tree." And I kicked it rather than kick him.

"Remember whose charity keeps you here."

He pushed his hat on his head and walked into the house, where Greta Ruth waited, peering through the back-door window.

The L.A. sun baked me under the windshield, although it was cool outside. I watched the foot traffic. A man leaving the tobacconist's cupped his hands around his lighter, inhaling deeply, before walking on. A woman with a great honeycomb of teased blond hair left Thrifty's and strolled, stopping to catch her reflection in the window of Harry's Men's Wear. Several men left Bail Bonds and headed for Murphy's Liquor, while another squatted on the sidewalk and unlocked the black gate of the gun shop. A tall bearded man swigged from a small paper-wrapped bottle, then swung his gaze up and down the street, until it lighted on me. He tilted his head and seemed to smile right at me. I had already looked away, composing a retort in case he rapped on my window, when Maggie climbed in and said, "Why were you smiling at that man?"

"I wasn't. Just watching the street. So what happened?"

"Nothing. They aren't taking applications now."

"You need to apply?"

"Guess so. They had a sign up: 'No Applications Accepted.' I asked anyway, just to be sure. The one woman said they had a six-month waiting list. The other said she figured some of the women must have already had their babies, they've been waiting that long."

"There must be other places."

"I guess." She sat with her hands between her knees, her head down.

"Really, we'll see if we can't find another home," I said, as if I thought that was a cheerful or comforting thing to say. "You can stay with me. I'd like you to. You know that, don't you?"

"It's too complicated, with my father and all."

"It's not that complicated."

"Those women, they said I should try the churches. 'Try the denominations,' one of them said." Maggie collapsed into the seat, letting her head hang back in a way that reminded me of her father. "I don't know," she said. "I don't."

TWENTY-FOUR

Mrs. Rumsen

You had to feel sorry for the girls Maggie's age. Or I did anyway. I heard those songs: this man, that man, give it to him any old way. And what was that one? With the music descending like the sun going down with a great splash in the drink, and those boys singing that the love you take was equal to the love you make? If I weren't a pagan, I'd say it was a perversion of Christianity, turning the equation that constitutes love thy neighbor into one more justification for sex. You must make love to take love, indeed.

Who do these boys think they are, anyway?

I remember a young man Maggie dated a year or so after Maria was born. He liked to spring up our stairs two at a time (I could hear him coming) and ring my bell in three short bursts. I'd open the door, and he'd be standing there in his madras sports jacket and jeans, his head turned slightly to one side. Every time, his head turned just so, so that I always noticed the fine line of his nose, with its slight double bump, until one day I understood that he posed that way for our benefit, Maggie's and mine, and I said, "Your profile is not that good, sweetheart."

He looked a little taken aback. "And good evening to you, too, Mrs. Rumsen. Is Maggie ready?"

I wanted to slap the boy. Instead, I said, "Notice whom you're dating. She's worth something."

The puzzlement I saw in his eyes gave me a fit.

"She's worth something," I repeated.

"Yes, Mrs. Rum."

I don't think he ever dated her again.

It's not that I believe in virginity or marriage or even fidelity. If I had believed in any of those things, I actually would have married John Rumsen rather than simply taking his name. But that doesn't mean I think every good boy deserves sex. Certainly, not whenever he wants. Maybe not even a quarter as often, and maybe not ever. Good grief, boys can take care of themselves. What else did God give them hands for?

Besides, hasn't anyone told them the one they love best may be the one they never touch?

And all this ruckus nowadays about abortion. (There was no ruckus in my time or in Maggie's because either you knew how to find a doctor who could help or you didn't.) It's just pointless. With all the medical magic available today, you'd think anyone who seriously wanted to end abortion could. They'd enact a national vasectomy law, let all the young men store their jism in some giant sperm bank, and then, when the boys were good and ready to look after another life, they could. In the meantime: far fewer mistakes. Well, men would object, wouldn't they? They'd say it violates something. What, I'd like to know. Their privacy?

My fortune, sad or good depending on your view, is to have been a small, thin woman with infrequent menses. I have lived years sex-free and years thinking of, and even doing, little else, and I have never conceived. But I know the game of sex is rigged. I know the men work for the house and the house always wins.

Well, some days I think that.

Thinking of Maggie, I couldn't help but think the rules unfair. I worried for her. She was young, but Greta Ruth had been young, only twenty-two or -three, when she fell into that coma-sleep well before her third child was due. After the ambulance took Greta, my mother took me and my other two sisters to the hospital to see her. My sisters were fifteen and twelve, and I was seven. With our mother, we sat in four wooden chairs lined up against the wall and said nothing as we watched Greta Ruth breathe. After a time, I stood on my chair for a better view, and my mother did not stop me. Greta Ruth lay very still under the gray-green blankets, but one of her legs was exposed, a pillow placed beneath her knee, so I almost thought it was her leg, not the vessels of her brain, as my mother had explained it, that ailed her. A thick needle was stuck into her thigh, and clear fluid ran through a glass tube from a bottle, where condensation collected. I remember her awful leg, swollen as if it too were pregnant.

"They're feeding her," my mother said later.

Greta awoke in labor. She awoke to deliver her third, this one a girl. I was too young for anyone to tell me what really happened, but over the years I have gathered they gave her nothing, not even gas, because they didn't know what it would do to her, coma and all. They weren't even sure she would need something for the pain. I imagine it was a shock, waking to her body like that. The child was stillborn, as I'm sure I've mentioned. And given the terrible way they had to feed Greta, I have always thought it starved inside her, but no one else ever seemed to think that was so. Months before, Greta thought it boded well to have a girl's name ready, not that she wouldn't be happy with a third boy. She chose Mary Louise, for her own mother and for Whit's one sister. Fulfilling Greta's wish, our mother wrote Mary Louise Harris on the birth certificate, and the Reverend Porter baptized the baby and buried her, all in one service my mother thought I was too young to attend.

Maggie

Other girls at school got pregnant the year I did, but as far as I know, none of them got an abortion. I don't think we knew how. Mrs. Rumsen knew, of course, or at least she knew who to ask. Although she had called in sick the day the L.A. County Home for Girls wouldn't take me, that same day she called her friends at work and asked what they knew. One woman who worked in the betting office gave Mrs. Rum the number of a friend who would know, and that friend gave me a name and an address in Azusa and coached me on what I should say.

"I want to drive myself," I told Mrs. Rum as she spooned honey into her tea. "I want to drive alone."

"I can't let you. You'll need someone to drive you home."

"Not today. She said he wouldn't do it today."

"Well, I don't have my car today. I have Cole's. He took mine in for repairs."

"I'll be careful, Mrs. Rum. I promise."

She stirred her tea, lifting her spoon to see if the honey had melted away. Finally, she gazed up at me and said, "I believe you will." She said neither yes nor no, and she didn't mention I had no license. She simply placed the keys on the kitchen table, took her cup to the sink, and turned her back on me.

Alison

Mom doesn't wake us anymore. Since Maggie's gone, she forgets to get Jamie and me out of bed. The first morning, she even forgot to feed us. She just sat at the kitchen table, not saying anything, even when I said, "Mom!" She sat at the kitchen table not doing anything, until I climbed up on the counter to pull down the Rice Chex, and then she said, "Alison, you're going to kill yourself!" and got the box down herself.

Mom still lets Jamie and me get ourselves out of bed, but she does remember to feed us, and this morning when I walk into the kitchen in my nightgown, I smell cinnamon and melting sugar and know even though Maggie is still gone, Mom is baking cinnamon buns, my favorite breakfast.

Dad's in the kitchen, too, all dressed for work like he's going to leave any minute. But first he pours coffee from Mom's new pot. He sips from an old red cup that doesn't match the rest of Mom's dishes, and he talks quietly, until I hear Mom say, "I will, Jim. I'll talk to the school counselor," and then she glances at me as if she's worried I heard her. Or maybe she's worried about what comes next, because she says, "And you have to do your part." And Dad says, "Yes, I'll call the police, except I don't think they'll have any news."

I sit in my nightgown at the table, one of my favorite things, sitting in my nightgown. It feels like school holiday even though it's not, and I pull apart my cinnamon roll, thoughts bumping around in my head, like why my parents haven't figured out where my sister is. I'm a kid and I know, so why don't they? Mom and Dad move around the kitchen, like everything they do is important. Like it's their job. Mom runs a dirty plate under hot water, and Dad crosses to the counter to pour another cup from the new plug-in pot. So should I tell them? Is it terrible, me not telling? They're going to be mad, and their madness gets bigger inside them every minute I don't tell. Which is why I don't. Besides, it's sort of like not telling Mom I know Maggie's on the phone with her boyfriend when she shouldn't be. It's like not telling Mom I know Maggie and Jamie go out at night after she's asleep. Except maybe it's worse, maybe it's a lot worse.

"Mom? You know Mrs. Rumsen?"

"You know I know Mrs. Rumsen, Alison." Mom is working on lunch now, laying four slices of bread on the counter to make sandwiches. "What about her?"

Dad breathes across the top of his coffee, which steams in the old red cup. And he glances at me, quickly. It feels like a lasso. It feels like "watch it" or maybe even "shut up," and I guess I better not say Dad took me to Mrs. Rumsen's. I guess I better not say where I saw Maggie.

"Nothing. I was just thinking about her."

Dad looks out the window at Mom's rosebushes as he sips his coffee.

"What were you thinking?" Mom drops the knife on the counter and turns toward me.

I pull off another piece of cinnamon roll, still hot, the icing still dripping, and slide a look at Dad standing so still I know I better not tell the truth. "Just wondering where she's living now."

Jamie

Stuffed with secrets and light as a balloon, I swing into the kitchen, skateboard under my arm. My sister eats at the table, my mother puts wax-paper-wrapped sandwiches into brown bags, and Dad tips his head back to finish his coffee. I can feel their feelings: Mom's sad, Alison's in hiding, and Dad's taut and ready to vault. Hey, me too, I want to say, I'm ready to spring. Because I'm the only one close to happy in this room. Happy and helium filled, filled with a girl's voice, a voice soft but ticklish, like grass under your feet. Last night, I lay on the hall floor, the phone pressed to my ear. I lay and listened, and every *um*, every *maybe*, every *you know* was a promise. A promise the girl I love would talk to me again.

These are my secrets: I'm cutting class, I'm buying her a St. Christopher, I'm flying on my board past her house.

All these secrets mean I ignore Mom and Dad and Alison, the ragged edges around the tear Maggie's made in the family.

I drop my skateboard to the floor and, standing on it, roll slightly side to side. Rocking, I pull a cinnamon bun from the pan. Icing drips from my fingers, and the sweet, soft bun fills my mouth. Then Mom turns from the lunch sacks and says, "What do you think you're doing? You're going to ruin my kitchen floor. Take that thing outside!"

Except angry as she is, tears are rolling down her face. I see them; Alison sees them too and leaving her place at the table wraps her arms around our mother. "Mom, I can find Maggie for you. I can."

"Hush, baby," our mother says. "Mommy will be all right. Mommy will be all right in a minute."

Maggie

I took Cole's keys from the counter and ran down the stairs in Mrs. Rumsen's place and out the back door to the parking lot. Cole's car was a white Buick, the sort of car that made me feel I must drive perfectly. I brushed the laurel leaves off the hood, climbed in, and started it up. Just then, as I was pulling out, I spotted a familiar-looking skateboard outside the back door of the Hillside Pharmacy, and through the broad windows I was sure I could see my brother inside. He was standing next to the jewelry counter where the St. Christopher medals boys gave their girls hung in bunches, like sheaves.

I didn't want my brother to see me, so I drove the wrong way down a one-way alley until I uneasily reached the road. It must have been years before I stopped feeling that the car I was driving was a ship. That's the way Cole's car seemed to me then, an ocean liner. Pulling into traffic, I felt I was steering through a channel. I gave wide berth to other cars, and although my father had always said I braked way too early, I braked early, letting the car glide to the stoplights. The directions were odd, instructing me to cross a little silver bridge and turn left at the lone sugar pine, but the directions worked. The silver bridge turned out to be a freshly painted overpass, and the pine was in fact lone. I found the doctor's office on the ground floor of an apartment building at the end of a dead-end street of one-story stucco homes. Outside, banana bikes leaned against the wall, and next door a girl maybe four years old sat in just her underpants on a thin lawn as a revolving sprinkler twirled water over and across her, over and across.

The waiting room was full of women, and I thought none of them looked pregnant, but what did I know? I gave my name to the nurse and saw, as she added my name to a list, that the doctor seemed to have no appointments. Figuring I might have to wait until the end of the day, I leaned against a wall until a seat became available, and then I sat with a *Reader's Digest* on my lap, leafing through looking for bottom-of-the-page pieces with titles like "Was My Face Red!" and, when I was too distracted to read those, watching the women, some with sick children on their laps, get up to take their turn with the doctor. As the children scratched their stomachs through their shirts or fell heavily asleep in their mothers' arms, I thought of all the illnesses of my childhood: mumps, earache, impetigo, worms—and assigned one to each child.

The office was small, and the nurse, with her desk and file cabinets, sat there in the waiting room with us. I could see behind her an open area filled with medical equipment: a scale, an eye chart, a blood-pressure cuff, a glass-doored cabinet stocked with bandages and dressings and brown bottles of who knows what, and something that resembled an X ray machine, although then I couldn't have told you what an X ray machine should look like.

I remember it especially well because the first time I saw the doctor, he was escorting a thin woman who held a Kleenex to her face and coughed from deep in her chest. He was not much taller than the woman, but he leaned forward slightly as if to diminish his height and held her by the elbow as he walked her to the machine and asked her to stand between two glass panels, indicating she should unbutton her blouse to her breastbone. He then crossed the room and flipped a switch, and the whole machine buzzed like a downed power line, the glass plate lighting up behind her. She stood unblinking, perhaps not breathing. Through the gray glass, I could see the darkness of her open blouse, her collarbone, and the shadow of the cross she wore on a chain. The sound buzzed in my fingertips and teeth and then wound down, the doctor gesturing to the woman that the treatment was finished, a treatment I have never seen any other doctor perform. As she buttoned her blouse, I heard him say, "That should help. Remember to pick up the Pertussin, and sleep, Mrs. Wynne. Get some sleep."

Marian

I spent the morning at the school, talking to people—a guidance counselor, the vice principal, even one teacher. No one had seen Maggie, and no one had any advice.

"Has Maggie been having problems lately?" the guidance counselor asked me. The counselor was a young woman with a sweet face. She rested her chin on her hands and looked at me through glasses that magnified her perfectly round blue eyes.

We have all been having problems lately, I wanted to say. My husband's business is out of control. My son sneaks out every night and does God knows what, and my youngest is too good and that in itself is a problem.

"Sure, her boyfriend left."

"Could she have followed him?"

I looked at those perfect round eyes and the unmade-up face the counselor seemed to offer as proof of her sincerity, and I thought, What could you possibly know about where my daughter is?

"Follow him to Danang?" I said.

The counselor blinked a time or two. "I see. Then, have you called all her friends?"

I nodded yes.

"Perhaps there's a relative she might have gone to visit?"

Who? I thought. Chess and Coral? I didn't think of Evelyn Rumsen. I never thought of her as a relative. I shook my head no.

"Well, let's see," the counselor said and opened a file. "Her grades aren't spectacular, although they're certainly above average. The general assessment is she could do better. She doesn't seem to care. I see she's been detained once. No, twice."

"That's right," I said, although it seemed to me Maggie had done more detention than that.

"You say you filed a report with the police?"

"Yes," I said, the word heavy in my mouth.

She looked at me, as if she felt the weight, then down again and said, "Have you driven through all the downtown areas?"

"Downtown?" It was difficult to call Rosemead Boulevard downtown.

"Downtown Los Angeles, downtown Hollywood. We don't have many runaways at this school, but I would think . . ."

So she was calling my daughter a runaway. Runaway? What sort of children ran away? Children whose parents drank and passed out, children who were never fed, whose clothes were never washed. Runaway was what I should have been, not my children, not Maggie. I imagined the word written in her records. I imagined it in big red letters: RUN-AWAY. I tried to refocus on the counselor, but all the time she sat speaking reasonably to me across the desk, widening her blue eyes behind her glasses, I kept thinking, Say it, say what you think, say I'm a terrible mother. I imagined that written in my daughter's records, too.

"So I think that's what you should do," the counselor said. She stood and opened the door to show me out but took my hand before letting me go, saying, "I really am sorry, Mrs. Harris."

No other words could have made me feel worse.

I left and drove like the devil's own bat to make my first fitting. Sewed like a demon all afternoon just so I wouldn't fall behind schedule. I did drop by the police station, but the man on desk duty told me there was no news.

Jamie

*I*t's coiled in my pocket, the St. Christopher medal I cut class to buy this morning. As I walk down the hall, it beats against my chest, my shirt sags with its weight. I cram my skateboard and the books I don't need into my locker and give it a slam, then look for *her* in the crowd of kids, the girl I want to wear this medal. Her hair's wavy, long, and chlorine bright. At school, she wears it loose. At home, she pulls it back with a thick rubber band. I know because she lives just blocks from us, in a new house with a bamboo fence around the backyard pool. I know because I skateboarded there one hot fall day and walked through the open bamboo gate I'd never walked through before. The girl I want to wear this medal lay on a towel, her thick hair ponied back and her face turned away. I nudged her with my sneaker, and she looked up, saying, "Hey, Jamie!" just like that, just like she'd invited me. Shoes off, jeans rolled, I sat next to her, not talking, not drawing, just circling my feet in the pool and listening to her, to Leann.

Now I look for her hair, wavy, long, and bright. She's near, I know it. Next class, she sits far front and I sit far back, where I can watch her lean over her desk, watch her hair fall forward, watch her copying proofs from the blackboard.

My legs knocking the desktop where I sit in the back of the class, I reach in my pocket and pull the chain out, slowly, like it's my silk hand-kerchief and this is my magic trick, my love for Leann. Three seats up, one row over, Tommy Dawson cranes around and silently laughs "ha ha" at the medal he knows I want to give her. "Ha ha," mouths Tommy Dawson. "Lover boy," he mouths, because he likes her too, the girl who sits in the front row, the girl who lives on Colina Drive, the girl whose house we pass every chance we get. Stupid Tommy Dawson mouths "L-O-V-E love," and now the teacher's eyes follow Tommy's straight to me, the inattentive student. The teacher says, "If angles a and b are con-gruent, what can we say about angles c and d, Jamie?" I hold the medal in my hand, knowing Leann, like all the kids, is twisted around in her seat watching me where I sit in the back of the class. "They're congru-ent too," I say, and surprise etching his forehead, the teacher nods and calls on the next inattentive student: "So can we say these lines are par-allel? Tommy?" And I am free, free to watch Leann, to catch her eye just before she turns toward the blackboard and scoops her wavy hair back behind her ear.

The medal sits in my palm, hidden under the desk so the teacher won't see it. It's cool and pleasing as a handful of wet sand. The chain is silver, the medal a perfect blue, not turquoise but not sky blue either. Except it reminds me of sky, the sky I can see sitting in back, by the wall of windows, sky that is rain-cleaned and smog-free. I think myself into a patch of it. I imagine myself test-pilot high, and imagining myself that high I think myself into another patch of sky equally far, equally clear. Practicing my private geometry, I imagine that the patch of sky that is just as far and just as clear must be bluer than sky blue, must be this shade of blue exactly.

The teacher walks back and forth before the blackboard, proving a theorem I swear we proved yesterday. The girl I love, she leans over her desk and copies the proof. She sits at the front not looking at me, giving no sign that we talked on the phone last night, not letting on that she agreed to see me tonight, to sit in her living room after bedtime and wait for me.

Marian

Denise Olmitz was early for her fitting, and I was late. But she sat quietly on our front steps, her arms wrapped around her knees, a gentle smile warming her face. As I pulled to the curb, not bothering to park in the drive, she waved at me and smiled, apparently unperturbed, even happy, to have had the time to sit on our front steps. Relieved she wasn't angry, I studied her as I walked across the grass to meet her. Isn't it funny? I thought. Love's taught her patience. Isn't it funny? Love's made her happy.

I tried to apologize, but Denise said, "I knew you'd be here soon," and I was grateful for her kindness. "Well, I got tied up in a meeting," I said as I unlocked the front door. "Don't bother explaining," she said. "I was happy for a minute's peace."

She was a tall girl with a high waist and a barrel chest, something I hoped the dress would camouflage, because after all, thin as she was, she was so pretty and unassuming. It was my hope that like a spotlight, the dress would make her shine. With the new percolator plugged in, I waited quietly outside the sewing-room door while Denise stepped out of her clothes and into the bodice of her wedding dress, the sleeves and skirt now pinned to it. Jim had made a screen for a corner of the sewing room, a place for my clients to change. But I thought it showed them more respect if I offered them an added measure of privacy. The smell of coffee beginning to fill the house, I waited outside, restless with thoughts of my daughter (did she have a place to stay, and if not, how would she manage another night?), until Denise called, "Ready!" I pushed the door open slowly (I don't like to slam into my clients) and walked in to find this tall thin girl transformed by the white dress. There she stood, a gift wrapped in tulle and lace and satin. The fullness of the dress softened her shape, and something about the sleeves and the dropped waist evened her proportions. The seed pearls I'd stitched into the lace shone, and it hurt me to see that, I can't explain why.

"Mrs. Harris," Denise said. "Are you all right?"

I was crying, crying at the sight of this girl, this bride-to-be, crying and hugging her, which I had no business doing. "I'm so sorry," I said, deeply embarrassed. "I shouldn't have. I hope I didn't get tears on the dress!"

"Your tears would only make the dress more beautiful," Denise said, and her sweetness made me cry harder.

Wiping my eyes with my hands, I got down to the real business of fitting the garment, snugging the bodice tighter here and there, fluffing the tulle that would underlie the skirt to see if I should add fullness, ruffling the satin to show Denise how the finished skirt would look, fitting the sleeves exactly to her shoulders.

As she stood there before the mirror Jim had fixed to the back of the door, Denise lifted the tulle with both hands, a lighthearted gesture that made me think perhaps she saw her own loveliness, and said, "Wouldn't a layer of lace on top be beautiful, Mrs. Harris?"

I wanted to tell her the dress was beautiful as it was, the lace would make the skirt too heavy, but I saw in her eyes I shouldn't.

"Why, yes," I lied, "a layer of lace would be perfect."

Maggie

*I*t was late, perhaps after six, when the nurse called my name. I was tired by then and frightened. I feared the doctor and what he might do to me, but I feared more what would happen if he didn't do something.

As I entered, the doctor lifted his hand without looking up and asked me to take a seat as he continued to write in a manila file folder.

"Yes?" he said, glancing up and setting aside his pen. He wore around his head one of those bands that doctors used to wear, with a small mirror fixed to the front. It seemed to make his forehead furrow and his eyebrows bristle behind his glasses. "What seems to be the problem?" He lifted a folder with my name on it from a corner of his desk and opened it to a blank page stapled inside. "You've never been to see me before, have you?"

"I'm new here."

"Didn't think I recognized you."

"I just came in from Barstow." Barstow had been Mrs. Rum's suggestion. "And I won't be here long."

"Barstow?" He leaned back in his chair and regarded me. "Don't they have doctors in Barstow?"

"Not any"—I grabbed for what to say—"not any who do what you do. No specialists," I said, grateful I thought of the word.

"So I guess the problem is acne," he said at last. Mrs. Rum's friend's friend had told me he would ask about acne.

"Yes, sir."

He leaned across the desk, obliging me to lean forward, and he touched my cheek, the way you might touch dough to see if it has risen. Though gentle, his hands were hardened, like my father's, as if from yard work. He narrowed his eyes to examine my unscarred cheeks. "Well, acne's usually a problem of diet and hygiene."

"I eat lots of fresh fruit and vegetables, and I scrub my face twice a day." I said exactly what I'd been told to say.

"So you think there's another cause for this acne problem?" He swiveled back and forth in his wooden chair.

"Yes, sir, I do."

"Well, then, let's take a look," and he motioned me into an adjoining examination room.

I have since had many of these exams, so I no longer remember what he did or did not do while I lay on the table. Except this. When he placed his two fingers inside me, his hands were bare. I felt they were bare, and I winced and remembered it afterwards. He poked around and thumped my stomach, and I felt somehow empty.

As he washed his hands, he said, "Six or seven weeks."

"Yes?" I said and propped myself up on the table.

"Yes, and I am a specialist, so I can do something for your acne. Go speak to my nurse. She'll set up the appointment." He put his hand on the door to his office. "You don't have any questions, do you?"

Most of my questions came as I drove home, except for one.

"Will I be," I asked, "you know, out while you do this?"

"Do what?" he asked, and when I didn't answer, he said, "Anesthesia's a little risky, so I don't recommend it. My nurse can answer any questions."

Mrs. Rumsen

*T*he accidents you fear are seldom the ones that befall you. I named myself a fool for letting Maggie take those keys. All afternoon, I visioned cars piling up, Cole's car hit broadside and Maggie crushed into the steering wheel. To calm myself, I baked a pie. I had rolled and pinched the crust, browned it, and was slicing peaches when Jim Harris knocked on my door. It was well after five, and I thought when I heard the knock that it might be Cole, except he had a key and it was the night he dined with his daughter and her two children. So as I walked to the door drying my hands, I thought of everyone—my upstairs neighbor, Maggie, Cole's son, even Marian—except Jim Harris. His hair was pushed back from his face every which way, and although he smiled when he saw me, I knew he had a need to talk. He waved away my offer of coffee and sat on my sofa as if he were a teenage boy, his legs sprawled out, his arms stretched across the back of the sofa.

"Bad news?" I asked.

"You could say that."

I pulled the chair closer, so I was facing him, and said what was on my mind. "You're worried about Maggie?"

"Maggie?" Jim ran a hand back through his hair and said, "She hasn't come home, not since I saw you the other day."

I glanced up quickly and then away, trying to judge whether he had guessed I was letting Maggie stay here. Briefly, I considered telling him, and then I thought of Maggie and how, in all likelihood, I could send her home to him in a few days, everyone's secrets and illusions intact.

"Marian's called all Maggie's friends, and no one has seen her. We went to the police and filed a report, but I don't think anything will come of it. I mean, how much can they do? They suggested she might have run away, and Marian about went nuts. I say Maggie's got some new boyfriend, but you know, I don't know if I really think that. So I've driven all over town, all over everywhere. I don't know what else to do."

I wanted to say, "Don't worry, Jim." I wanted to say, "Look, I'll bring her home to you tonight," but he went on.

"And if that weren't bad enough, my business is going under. The bank's just tying me in knots. They loaned me enough to buy the place, but they won't loan me any to finish it. I swear, they're trying to sink me."

"I'm sorry," I said. "What do you think it will take to finish the place?"

The place was a small shopping center, a few stores, two office buildings zoned for no more than four stories, a plaza with a fountain. He'd bought the property unfinished in a sale to pay off back taxes. Or that's what I'd heard.

"Two hundred," he said, meaning two hundred thousand. Not knowing much about the business but being acquainted with Jim, I figured it would take much more.

"I guess there's a lot of work left to do?"

He shook his head. "Son of a bitch, Evelyn. The bank's got me."

"I'm sorry, Jim."

I thought of my peaches half sliced in a bowl and then forgot them for thinking of Maggie, who would, I hoped, be driving back from the doctor. I excused myself, telling Jim I had to phone Cole, and placed a call to my neighbor. I wanted to ask him to put a sign on my door or to watch for Maggie and to invite her to his place, but I got no answer.

"Cole wasn't there," I said to Jim, but he seemed to be puzzling something out and not to hear me.

"I've been trying to find investors."

"And?"

"And I got peanuts from everyone in the family."

"At least you got something." He had told me that at Christmas, the last time he'd asked anyone for money, they'd all said no. "Maybe they're wary."

"Wary? Wary of what? Really, I don't know what the hell is wrong with them," he said. "I shouldn't carry on, Ev, but I just think they're all holding their dicks."

"If you're trying to impress me, Jim, you're not."

"Aw, Jesus, Evelyn, you know what I mean."

And I did know what he meant. All I had to do was think of Whit standing on that old porch on Crenshaw to know what Jim meant. "So what are you going to do?"

"Keep begging at the bank. Use the peanuts Whit and Chess gave me. Try to find some long-term tenant who'll pay his lease money up front. That sort of thing."

I felt sorry for him. "Must be hard, digging up the money."

"It's keeping me up nights, Ev. I plain old can't sleep. Did I mention the worker I had to fire? He showed up claiming I owe him back salary. And to add fuel to the fire, there's Maggie to worry about."

"What are you going to do?"

"What can I do that I haven't done already? Drive in circles until I find her? Well, it didn't work." He stood to leave. "What I'm going to do is go to the office. See if I can figure this thing out. I just don't get what the bank wants from me. An easy foreclosure?"

"No, I'm sure they don't want that, Jim."

"You don't know what these people are like," he said. "They prey on people like me, the people who do all the work."

Really, I didn't know what to say to all this. I wanted to ask why he had bought a property he couldn't afford to improve in the first place. But I didn't. I offered him what he wanted. "I am so sorry," I said several times. As I walked him to the door, he said, "I'm lousy company, aren't I, Ev?"

Maggie

I followed taillights following taillights following taillights. The distant ones wavered, the way they do from dust and smog. I eased up behind cars at stoplights, leaving a wide space between us. And then at Live Oak and Tyler, I heard a honk and felt the car behind me nudge my fender. I looked in the rearview and saw the driver shrug and lift his hands as if to say, "So sue me." The light changed, and though the other driver drove on, I pulled over, scared I had damaged Cole's car. In the dark, I rubbed my hands over the rear fender again and again, until I was convinced there was no dent. I climbed back in and drove on, feeling both fragile and sheltered, as if my life were an ornament wrapped in tissue paper. I knew what I was going to do, when I was going to do it, where I would do it, and how much I would pay. I knew there would be pain, but I felt protected from it. The cotton-wadded feeling of Novocain I felt all over. Besides, part of me wanted to hurt.

I drove back to Mrs. Rumsen's place and parked Cole's car behind the Hillside Pharmacy. Then I went into the coffee shop across the street and ordered a cup of tea, just to be by myself and think about what I was going to do. I poured in milk and sugar, and looking out the plate-glass window, saw my father leaving Mrs. Rumsen's building. He wore a gray poplin jacket he zipped up as soon as he stepped outside, and he seemed to be whistling that funny way some men do, through the side of his mouth. He looked both ways before he walked around to open his door, but he never looked across at me. It struck me then that Mrs. Rumsen must have told my father where I was. Perhaps she had told him that first night. It chilled me to think that, so I sat a good while longer, until the tea was chilled as well. Then I walked back to Cole's car and drove myself to the trailer my father used as an office, and I sat in the car and watched him in the yellow light as he talked on the phone and waved his arms in the air.

I watched him for a long time. He stretched, he poured a drink, he paced in and out of my sight, shaking his fist and punching the air but apparently talking to no one. He poured another drink. One of the men who worked for my father passed me in the car, sprinted across the street, hiking the few steps to the door before knocking. It took my father some time to open the door, and when he did, he stood in the entrance and leaned his weight into one arm, as if he were blocking the way. He kicked the frame a few times as he talked and then closed the door hard enough I could hear the slam. My father's workman knocked again, but this time my father did not answer. Instead, he turned on a television. It was out of my view, but I could see the light and remembered an old set he had moved from our house to his office. I must have sat in that car a few hours as my father poured another drink and talked again on the phone, as he bent his head over paper-work and stroked his hair back on his head. I'm not sure what I was waiting for, but as I crossed the street to his office, I imagined my father's anger consuming the air in that small yellow-lit room.

For some reason, I didn't knock, and the funny thing was, the door was open. I walked into my father's office, and for the longest time, my father didn't look up. He wrote numbers on a yellow pad, crossed them out and wrote more numbers, but he seemed not to notice me until I said hello. That was all I said, hello.

"Son of a bitch," my father said, turning his chair to face me. "Where have you been?"

I felt him put his arms around me and smelled his familiar smell, sweat and tar and, this night, the whiskey he must have been drinking. I hugged him back, hesitantly. Who knew when his affection would turn to anger?

"We've been so worried. Tell me where you've been." He looked like he'd spent the two nights waiting up for me. The lines in his face, the creases on either side of his chin and the furrows in his forehead, seemed deeper. They defined his face, so he seemed handsomer, and he already was a good-looking guy, or so people told me.

"You know where I've been."

"Oh, so now I'm clairvoyant," he said and dropped down in his chair.

"Well, you do know. You have to."

He shook his head. "Your mother's worried sick, and I've got problems out to here." His outstretched arms almost touched both walls of the office. "And you think I know where you've been?"

I shook my head because I could see that he did not and because I'd been wrong. Mrs. Rum had kept her promise.

"And now you waltz in here. You could have been dead in a ditch for all we knew."

"I had things to think about. I had to figure something out."

"You've been hiding out for three days because you had a problem to figure out?" I told him yes, and he shouted back, "Why didn't you come to me?"

"I am coming to you," I said quietly.

He put his hands behind his head and leaned back against the diamond of his arms. "You want to know about problems, Maggie?" He lifted a handful of papers from his desk and tossed them down again. "I'm about to lose my shirt. My shirt," he repeated, as if I hadn't heard. "I've got a goddamn bank that won't back its own money, and I'm on my knees begging members of my family to back me. And they won't do it."

"They won't?" I asked, beginning to feel sorry for him.

"Well, maybe they will, but they're not supporting this the way they should. I mean, we're talking a good investment here. I'd be doing them a favor, for Christ's sake. A favor. This property's going to make money."

His voice rose louder and higher as he spoke, so it took on a helium sound I had heard in his fights with my mother.

"I mean, look at this, Maggie." He rose and pointed at a map he had tacked to the wall. Near the center of this map, he had drawn a red ink square, which I guessed marked the property he was talking about. "Look where the highways are." I looked and saw the highways that crossed near the red ink square. "And look." And he pointed to a green area on the map that was not cross-hatched with roads. "They'll be building homes all over those hills. And we're in on the ground floor, before anyone else's figured out what this property will be worth, really worth, in a year or two." He sat down in his chair, almost flinging himself into it and splaying his arms and legs, so you might have thought he wanted to look crucified. "No one gets it, Maggie. No one."

"I'm sorry, Dad."

"Your mother, even she doesn't understand."

He poured liquor from a bottle, whiskey I'm pretty sure. He poured himself a glass and, without looking at me, poured a finger into a second glass and pushed it across the desk toward me.

"Dad."

"Think a little drink is going to hurt a girl who stays out all night? You don't want it, don't touch it." He savored a mouthful of liquor before swallowing. "Your mother, she just doesn't get it, but I think you do, Maggie."

"I don't know. Maybe." I sipped my drink because I thought I ought to, and the liquor seemed to vaporize in my throat. "Dad, I have to tell you something. I have to tell you now." Because if I don't, I did not add, I may never tell you.

He turned to me and leaned forward, elbows on knees, and said, "First, tell me that you understand what I'm doing. Tell your dad you understand."

"I understand, Dad. This is a good deal you've found."

"And you know why I know what a deal this is? Because I've been watching development around here. I can see where it's going. And, you know, Maggie, this is just the first step in my plan. I make this go, I can get out of roadwork for good. Somebody's got to build houses in those hills. Why not me?"

"Sure, why not?" I said because his plan didn't seem so far-fetched. After all, Chess had sculpted winding roads through hilly land he'd terraced and built houses on. Why couldn't my father?

He righted himself some and gazed at me hard. "The police said you'd come back when your money ran out."

"My money didn't run out," I said because it hadn't.

"No? So where were you?"

"Does it matter?"

"Yes, it matters." He slammed his drink down on his desk. "If you were letting some boy poke you for two days, I want to know who it was."

"Dad."

"Well, were you?"

"No."

"Then where were you?" He stood now and crossed his arms over his chest, his hands clenched so I could see the fine curves of the muscles up his forearms.

"I spent the night in the park." I couldn't, after all, tell him about Mrs. Rumsen. "It wasn't that cold."

"I don't believe this. First you tell us you went to church, and we all know that had to be a goddamn lie. Then you walk out of my house and say you spent two nights in the park, and you expect me to believe you? Come on, Maggie, this is your father. I've known you since you lied and spent the nickel I gave you on ice cream rather than put it in your bank."

"Look, I didn't lie about church, and I'm trying not to lie to you now," I said. "I stayed with Mrs. Rumsen, that's all. Mrs. Rumsen put me up."

"Evelyn? She took you in."

"Yes," I said, surprised at my father's surprise.

"Evelyn took you in and didn't tell me?"

"I asked her not to."

"She lied to me for you?"

Mrs. Rumsen was, I guess, the one who always listened, who always tacitly took my father's side. I suppose that's what upset my mother, that Mrs. Rum could listen to my father when my mother couldn't, when my mother had to put my father's schemes second and her and the family first.

"I told her I had something to figure out. That's all, okay?"

"You know something, Maggie? You're always going to have something to figure out. That's the way of it. And the way I see you living your life, you'll have more problems than most."

"What way I'm living my life?"

"Running around at all hours, for Christ's sake, doing God knows what. Giving it away, for all I know."

"I don't do that."

"You know, Maggie, I thought underneath all this you had some brains. I thought maybe you were smarter than your mother, but she at least has horse sense. You don't even have that."

This is the moment I always reached with my father, the moment when I had only my silence and my unwillingness to cry.

"It's just such a goddamn waste. You, the bank, your mother. No one knowing their ass from an owl's nest."

He continued like that. We were all a waste, me and Jamie, Mom, his crew, the bank, Chess, Grampa Whit, even Mrs. Rum. But me most of all. I was a waste, a waste of all his hard work and money. I suppose he would have continued his complaint, but for the ringing of the phone that sat on top of the television silently broadcasting snowy pictures of Johnny Carson. My father didn't answer it. Instead, he glanced at his watch and said, "Jesus Christ, Mag, I'm taking you home."

Marian

*T*he house was almost silent. I'd put Alison down at least two hours before and had sent Jamie to bed at ten, but my husband was, I guessed, working late, and Maggie was gone, who knew where? I put on my nightgown and crawled in under the covers, lying straight and still, the way I did when I was a child and thought that if I made no noise, if I stepped on no cracks, if I dirtied no clothes, and if I just lay still enough, my father would rouse himself from his bed and walk in his pajamas to the dining room, where he would cap the bottle for good for my drunken mother.

I was lying there in my half-empty bed listening to the sounds a house will make when I heard the distinct snap of the backdoor latch and knew that Jamie had wandered out into the night. I didn't go after him. I couldn't, not in my nightgown. Besides, he would be far ahead of me, and I would never catch him. And I knew what he was doing. He was picking up the coil of rope that lay in the garage on top of the half-empty bag of fertilizer. He was grabbing his skateboard, stepping on one end so the other would teeter-totter up to meet his hand. Though he wanted nothing more than to glide into the night, he wasn't. I knew he was walking because he feared the gritty rattle of his board on the driveway would wake me. He may even have walked all the way to the top of the long steep hill of Colina Drive where Tommy Dawson was waiting to tie the rope across the street and challenge my son to tricks I'd never let him dare in plain daylight, as if I ever had any say in the stunts Jamie tried. No, I knew where he was going.

So I lay there, abandoned by everyone and worried about everyone, except my youngest. She was in bed, that much I knew. I dialed my husband at his office, but he didn't answer. I considered calling Evelyn Rumsen, but I couldn't do that. So I lay still and made lists in my head of the things I would do the next day: lay the pattern and cut out Mrs. Glad's suit, machine-hem the choir robes for the church, call the rector about getting paid, stitch sleeves and skirt to Olmitz wedding gown (be sure to add layer of lace to skirt), call Gail Tyson about next year's cheerleader costumes, shop (lamb chops, lettuce, macaroni, peanut butter), call Rudy about hair trim (special rate with coupon?), drive downtown and look for Maggie (where?), clean.

Maggie

*W*e should drive home quickly, my father said, but he took the long route, driving up the canyon road and surveying the charred land that was no longer his. He took the long route, but he drove fast, so I could feel the car resisting the curves and sharp turns, and he gnawed the side of his finger as he drove. I sat there thinking about the mess I'd made and worrying what I would do, Cole's car outside my father's office, the keys in my pocket, the appointment with the doctor that probably now I would not keep, and me no closer to telling my father anything. His speed pushed me back in my seat, and I felt fear right where I'd come to think of the baby being, a fear to add to my other fears, fear of trying again to tell my father, fear of telling my mother, fear more than anything of what they'd say and what they'd do once I told them. And what in the world was I going to do, anyway? What?

As my father headed home, I wasn't paying much attention to the roads we took or the way my father drove them. I didn't notice the blur of trees against the black sky or the empty white crosswalks we crossed or the stop sign my father didn't stop for. (No need at this hour, he would have said, when you can see the headlights.) I scarcely noticed any of this, and I sure didn't think about my sister and brother and what they were doing at this hour of the night. I never dreamed my brother would be skating down Colina Drive, practicing small jumps, moving the rope he and Tommy Dawson had stretched between the tree and the SLOW sign higher and higher. I had no idea Jamie was ready to showboat down the street and try his highest jump, a blue St. Christopher pressed against his chest.

My father slowed as he neared our neighborhood, the way he always does. He slowed, but not much, and I didn't think about it. Whatever else he is, my father is sure of his driving. But as he made the turn he always made a few blocks from our home and headed to the blind intersection with Colina Drive, his wheels hit the curb, and the car swerved. I pressed my feet against the floor, gripping the armrest, and said, "Dad!"

"What?" he said sharply.

I said nothing more, but I thought, if he's this angry now, what's he going to be like later? What's my mom going to be like? I pictured both of them yelling at me at the kitchen table and wished my father would drive past our house, where, I was sure, everyone was sleeping, and take me to Mrs. Rumsen's. If he just didn't take me home, maybe I could work things out. Maybe my parents wouldn't have to know. I never imagined that my parents' anger should have been the smallest of my fears, and I couldn't know that my brother had just glanced at Tommy Dawson at the top of the long steep hill of Colina Drive and said, "Go!"

I was turning toward my father, about to ask him to drive me, please, to Mrs. Rumsen's, when I heard him say, in a voice pitched high as if for singing (keening I would call it now), "Jesus, God, no. Jesus Christ, no."

I felt the car slowing, my father braking hard, and looking past my father in the driver's seat, I glimpsed something out the window. It was the rope stretched across the road and Tommy Dawson aborting his leap, swerving away, diving for ground, except that's not what I saw. What I saw was a pillowcase whipped from a clothesline and then a fist coming at us in the dark. That was my brother, my brother in a tuck, but I didn't see him. I would have sworn I saw a fist, and that made perfect sense, that a fist should come down and strike me. And it did. The fist struck, and the windshield shattered. Something bounced against the car, we swerved to a stop, and all that time, my father's voice pierced me. "Jesus, no, God. Please, God, no."

My lip bleeding, I climbed from the stalled car and stood in our street. Only two blocks from our home, I should have recognized every-thing, the corner house surrounded by its oleander hedge, the wall around the house across the street, and the avocado tree reaching over the wall and dropping its slippery fruit on the asphalt. I saw it all, but I scarcely recognized it. It made no sense. Tommy Dawson lay on the soft ground beneath the oleanders, and my brother, who should have been home sleeping, lay in the road, not sleeping at all, his head tipped back as if he meant to catch a peanut he'd tossed in the air. And my *father*. My father was down on all fours, his mouth on my brother's mouth, breathing into Jamie as if breath were all Jamie needed. My father blew in and turned his head aside, waiting for my brother's breath against his cheek. He exhaled and waited, exhaled and waited, until he couldn't wait anymore. Between inspirations, my father lifted his head and cried, "Help us, help us," until a neighbor from a corner house gently coaxed him away and a sound I'd never heard before filled me, the sound of my father's voice breaking inside me, "Oh, God, no-oh," breaking the promise we had all taken for granted, that my brother would live to see fifteen.

Jamie

*T*here is this girl, Leann. She lives down there in the green house, the one with the slate walk and the pool I sneak into when no one is home. Her hair, it is coarse and thick, and she bunches it in a rubber band. I see her at night through the curtains, lace curtains in her room, sheer curtains in the living room. At night, she is blue from TV, she is from Neptune. I have seen her dive for a penny on the bottom of the pool. Her hair spreads behind her. She is an urchin of the sea.

I am the magic child. I know this. I feel it as I glide down the streets. I stand on the moving skateboard, and tall and narrow, I cut the air. I sit on my heels, all of me low and small against the wind, and I am the bullet kid. I am all surface and skin, and I want in every part of me. What it is I want my mouth opens and closes around but I don't know. I feel the air. It is in my mouth like a bubble blown in, not out. In my ears like an itch. On my skin like fine wires slicing me. I vaporize, but magically I reassemble in human form. The stars are sugar I lick off my fingertips. Gravel kicks out from under my wheels, and it feels like sparks, like I am burning up.

I hear Tommy Dawson behind me. He wants too, but not as much as me. That's why he's behind. Tommy and I are doing the rope trick we do at night. We stretch the rope across the road at the end of a long hill, tying one end to a SLOW sign and the other to a tree. We skateboard one-footed to the top, and then we surf down and jump the rope we can barely see in the dark, judge the jump by the tree and by the white post of the SLOW sign. My turn, I pull my knees into a tuck and fly over the rope, and then my feet find the board, and from here on I coast, friction stealing my speed. And every time, as my knees touch my chest, I imagine Leann behind the sheer curtains in her living room or the lace curtains in her bedroom. I imagine her seeing me, the sight of me an arrow through her heart. After all, I am spotlighted by headlights. By a car I had not seen, but see clearly now in my one moment, a car I have always known. And here I am, love's acrobat, my feet still feet above the board that I hear grinding against the asphalt. In the air, I think of my bed, where I could be curled and covered by a clean sheet and blanket. I hear my mother sewing in the back of the house, the steady bursts of her machine. I smell the sugar cookies my sister bakes and the tar of my father's work as he sits in the living room before the television. I think: the family at home. And outside, Maggie climbs the branches of an old orange tree and watches for the headlights of the car that is coming to take her away.

But now I am descending, not toward the board, but toward a car I know too well. I fall and fall, and it feels as if the light is holding me, fixing me, but I know it can't. I look through the glass at the face of my father, one moment before recognition, a moment before everything is clear to him, clear as the windshield he cleaned himself at the gas station only hours ago, clear before I make it unclear when I hit and shatter the glass, webbing it into something beautiful and crystalline that I would love to draw with the pencil I have used over and over and sharpened down to nothing, the pencil that I feel in my pocket and that will leave a thumb-sized bruise on my hip, the smallest of the bruises the coroner will find on my body. I want to draw this now. Me airborne, my father in his car, Tommy Dawson's board flying and Tommy crashing to the grass by the pavement, the ground not soft but taking his fall, accepting his imprint. This is my one good dive. Hey, Leann, you there behind the curtains, watch this cannonball.

TWENTY-FIVE

Mrs. Rumsen

The cattle hadn't yet eaten the leaves off the trees, and they weren't dying from eating the cane we had grown for forage because it wasn't stunted yet, and no one had begun to sell off their milk cows, the year our mother died. It was three years later, when I was seventeen, that things got that bad. Drought hit and relief wasn't anywhere near enough, even with most of the children grown and gone, and I wrote to my eldest sister, Greta Ruth, to ask her if I could come stay with her in California. But the year our mother finally died, I was only fourteen and the cattle still lived, and although things were not good, no one really thought they were going to get worse, or at least not as bad as they got. After all, what could have been worse than the death of our mother?

The beginning was slow, but her end was quick. And I don't believe anyone has ever known what took her. She grew frailer and weaker, until fever overcame her. I'm told sepsis could have caused the fever, but I wouldn't know. My sister Mary Helen used to say the wasting was endless dysentery. I've since thought cancer. But whatever it was, once the fever hit, she didn't last.

I was the only daughter still home, so I saw it, sitting in her bedroom and holding damp cloths to her face, washing her hands and body, and, when necessary, cleaning the soiled bed. I squeezed water into her mouth and saw the flecks of foam that caught in the corners regardless. Always listening first for my own name, I heard the words she uttered as her mind sifted through fifty-one years of life. I heard her call Greta, her first born, and even Greta's husband, Whit, but I never did hear my name. She would recite the names of her first six children but couldn't

259

name the next, the one she lost, nor the rest of us. No matter how often I coached her to say, "Cleveland, Mary Helen, Red, Ray, Evvie," she always asked for Mama. "Oh, Mama, I'm sorry," she'd say. "Oh, Mama, help me." She never once asked for her husband, and I think that hurt my father, who sat quietly in her room whenever he had no farm work to tend to. At the end, her eyes turned marble, her gaze rolled inward, and her grip on the sheet finally loosened. That is the only death I've witnessed, and if I believed in a god, I'd say thanks be to him for that.

I lied a little to Maggie when I told her you never know what will mark you. I mean, it's true that you don't know all the small things that dent and shape you. Who can say why I love turquoise and mother-of-pearl, why I like baking pies, why dancing a step in swing time makes me happy? Except that I believe that it is not random, that there is cause after cause after cause. You enter your oldest sister's house and in her bedroom stare at a framed picture of Irene and Vernon Castle, the dance idols of her youth. The rug thrown back at your house, you hold hands in a circle moving to music and someone lifts you in the air, and afterwards you remember that no one was sad and everyone was laughing. Nights you have nowhere to stay, you spend in a theater watching an agile man spin a quick-footed woman from arm to arm, and somewhere you have heard that the studs and waistcoat buttons on the man's tuxedo are truly diamond and ruby, and although you try hard not to believe that paste is real, you can't help thinking of diamond and ruby studs and the abundance of feathers the woman wore, so many that some drifted off in a lazy descant to the dance on the screen. When a boardinghouse friend tells you about a call for extra girls, you think, Why not? Call after call, you see for yourself how woefully little you know, so you take a class here, take a class there, until you take a class from a woman with a face like a walnut, jeweled arthritic hands, and a cane she raps menacingly against the floor, and you feel you have found your place in the world. You think you could spend every minute of every day listening to this wizened woman explain why the hand must be held just so and watching her demonstrate a step in her character shoes, her black skirt wafting around her. Although you don't know much, you know enough to get a job here, a job there. You meet some people, make some friends, love one or two, and soon you have a whole life.

No, you can't predict the slow drift of small influences.

But lives given and lives taken, unpredictable as they are, you can scarcely avoid the mark they will leave on you. That first afternoon, while I tried to get Maggie to tell me what I already knew (don't ask me how), I also knew that having conceived this child, perhaps bearing this child, would turn her life. How could it not? And when she called me well past midnight that day she drove off by herself, I knew that life had turned her again.

We wired Greta Ruth in California about our mother's death and worried whether the body would keep while we delayed the funeral until she got there, but Greta had boarded the train two days earlier and arrived in Enterprise the morning after our mother died. Whit later said that he was concerned about her traveling alone on the train, but even at fourteen, I knew she wasn't simple, just silent. Greta Ruth stepped off the train and hugged me and my sisters Mary Helen and Alice Geraldine and said before anyone else could speak, "I am so sorry. She just burnt up like tinder, didn't she?" We all looked at each other, Mary Helen, Alice Geraldine, and I, because we understood that Greta Ruth had acquired a gift, and then we waited for her to say more. But she said nothing else her entire time in Enterprise, except something she whispered to me when she left: "Be sure to take some nourishment."

John Rumsen's death I did not witness. The nurses at the hospital had sent me home the night he passed on. Few people came to see him off, but the ones who did mattered. Our former teacher came and, supporting herself with that cane of hers, stood by my side. An actor we had known through the years and our old friend Yukio, who in his youth had been tumbled on stage back and forth in the air between his father's feet and who now owned a restaurant on Highland Avenue, both came. Even Arrow Shirts sent a man, which surprised me because John Rumsen had not worked for them since he had served as the first Arrow Shirt man when television was live.

But that was then, and this was later. To Jamie's funeral I was not invited. I mean, no one expected me to attend, except Maggie, who whispered into the phone so her mother wouldn't hear her asking. I wish it had been a drizzly day, but instead the light was flat and bright, refracted through the smog. And I wish I had arrived last. I left late enough I should have, but even though I got lost and stopped by mistake at two other cemetery chapels, I was the first to pull my car into the small lot outside the chapel assigned to Jamie.

I entered the stone chapel and saw the casket had already been set out. The lid was closed, of course. Like Jamie, who still hadn't come into his growth, the coffin was small, and its size hurt me somehow. This small, dark coffin that the boy, no matter what sort of Houdini he was, would never be able to climb out of. In front of it, someone had displayed Jamie's picture, a school portrait, it must have been. It showed a perfectly ordinary and perfectly gorgeous child. I can't say what it was that made him seem so perfect, the crookedness of his eyes, maybe, the way one looked straight at you and the other a little off, or the way his face creased some on one side when he smiled. Except for his sandy hair, the hair he got from Marian, he resembled his father when he was young and lived with Greta and Whit in that house on Crenshaw. Impossible not to love a boy who looked like that.

Candles had been lit around the coffin, and for some reason they seemed to make the odor of gardenia and cedar stronger. I moved to the rear of the chapel and took a seat, watched the play of dust in the light of the doorway and the high chapel windows. Taped organ music began to play, blaring out of hidden speakers until someone sensibly lowered the volume.

After me, Thomas Harris and his wife Lillian appeared. An usher, who had not yet begun his duties when I arrived, greeted them and guided them to the register that I had not signed. Thomas removed his hat, and the usher held it as Thomas leaned forward to write their name in the book. How like Thomas to wear a hat. Thomas and Lillian turned and faced the chapel as the usher guided them to their pew. I could have sworn the two of them looked directly at me, but I saw no recognition in their faces, no stillness in their gaze. Lillian tightened the dark scarf around her neck and turned to seat herself, smoothing her gray skirt under her. She and Thomas spoke from time to time, inclining their heads toward one another, and I thought it would have been a comfort to me, if a scandal to the family, had Cole come along.

Jamie's father walked in and spoke in a forced whisper to the usher, then hurried out. I was grateful Jim did not see me, because I did not mean to distress anyone. I simply meant to pay my respects, whether the family appreciated my respects or not. Alison wandered in, like a child who had walked into the wrong classroom, and Marian followed, taking Alison by the hand as the usher guided them to their pew. Marian wore white gloves, unlike the rest of us women, and I couldn't help but watch her hands and the way they hung beside her. They made me think of a magician I once performed with and the sad drugged doves who could not fly when he pulled them from his hat. Marian sat down gingerly and remained quite still, like someone who has wretched her neck sleeping all wrong, and when Alison grew restless, the way children do in church, Marian did not twist or bend. She simply placed her white-gloved hand on Alison's shoulder until her daughter grew still.

Maggie slipped out of an alcove where I imagined she had hidden. She spotted me, but she did not nod or smile. Her hair all flyaway, she slid into the pew next to Alison, bowed her head, and kept it bowed over the hymnal the usher had handed her. Marian turned her head stiffly, and regarded Maggie in silence. She stared long enough Maggie should have looked up, but she didn't, not until her mother took her eyes off her.

The chapel was filling quickly now. I recognized Jim's brother, Chess, and his wife, Coral, and their son-in-law, but I did not recognize others who must have been neighbors or members of Jim's crew. I saw families with adolescent children, one a girl with woolly wavy hair and eyes that were blue when you expected them to be brown and another, a boy with his arm in a cast. Friends of Jamie's, I guessed.

And then Whit appeared, tall and backlit in the doorway. My sister Mary Helen came with him, clutching his coat sleeve. I was so happy to see her plump body and her child's face. She is the sort of woman you know will always smell of talc, whose arms will always be soft around you. She seemed to have ignored the conventions of mourning, for although she wore a black hat with a veil, her dress was purple and peacock blue, perhaps the darkest colors she had in her closet. She dressed the way the family might have expected me to dress, and that made me smile. But Whit—at least, he didn't make me frown. I waited to feel bitter, but I didn't. Instead, I felt pity, although I don't know why. He appeared as strong as ever, his face pink and his florid scalp shining through his close-cut white hair. It seemed I could see the farm boy in him again. The sleeves of his navy jacket were a touch short, and he wore a plaid shirt and a hat darkened by sweat or oil, a stain that spread from brim to crown. It occurred to me that Whit had finally grown too old to care how he looked, perhaps too old to do more than find a shirt, no matter what color, and put on any jacket, no matter how ill-fitting. I have to admit that I also wondered if Whit couldn't afford to dress himself properly, perhaps he could no longer afford much of anything. Most likely, I thought, he was too cheap to buy new clothes. But that was Whit.

And his own wife dead eleven years, you had to pity him that, no matter what bad blood there was between you. I don't suppose I saw Greta Ruth more than a handful of times from the year I left their house to the year Greta died. I remember in particular a time not long after the second war when she and Jim came to see our act, John Rumsen's and mine. We called ourselves Evelyn Night and Johnny Run, and we danced wherever people would pay us. We were lucky for a while, getting steady work at a small club in Santa Monica, and that's where Greta and Jim came to see us. Whit wouldn't come, of course, not to a club that served liquor. Jim ordered a Bloody Mary with the vodka on the side. Greta sipped the tomato juice, and Jim downed the shot. I hadn't seen Jim in a long time either. He came to see me in a few revues before the war, even came after he had enlisted. Sharp-looking, sweet-hearted boy, I was always glad to see him in the audience. Sitting next to him in the club in Santa Monica, I felt something waiting and wakeful in him. He smiled and laughed too easily at my poor attempts at jokes, and if I asked a casual question, his blue eyes seemed to cloud while he thought through his answer. I remember that he smelled so clean when he leaned across the table to kiss me hello. Me, I must have had that much-used-costume smell of dust and sweat and cigarettes, and judging from the makeuppy smear I was leaving on the cocktail napkins I pressed to my face, I must have tasted of salt and pancake. I looked secretly at Jim while he downed his vodka and thought what a good boy my silent sister had raised.

"Hey, Ev," he said when I was least expecting it. "Raise your glass to me. I'm getting married," and I raised my glass and asked him all about the lucky girl.

I have to tell you it was sad to see Greta that night. She was happy, happy to be out, I think. But her sentences seemed to have dwindled to a few words. When she spoke, which was as ever infrequently, she uttered phrases such as "good girl," which perhaps made sense, or "pretty light," which perhaps did not. Five years before, she'd spent time in Camarillo State, and it seemed she hadn't much improved. Not knowing what to do, I spoke cheerily about nothing, and when she said, "Bring sweet," I kissed her. Whether that was what she wanted or not, she seemed pleased, so I sat and held her hand as we watched Mr. Rum perform a new solo, improvising the parts he hadn't yet finished. I think Greta liked Johnny's dancing because she said, "Shiver, shiver, shiver," after he was through, and shook her head side to side.

Greta Ruth died maybe ten years later, and Johnny Rumsen and I, seeing the obituary, brought ourselves to the funeral. But Whit would not let us stay. My life began after I left Whit's home, as far as I am concerned. Every decision that made me *me*, including my decision not to marry John Rumsen, I made after I left his care. And when Whit heard from others the things I had done—took up dancing, performed in halls where people drank, lived outside of wedlock—he condemned every decision I made, especially the decision not to marry. When he saw us standing outside the Beverly Methodist Church, John in his good suit and I in my black dress, Whit approached us as if he meant to shake our hands and say how sorry he was. Instead, he stood before us, his fists in his pockets, and said very quietly, "Your presence here insults good churchgoing people, so please leave."

"Mind you don't insult the dead, Whit," John Rumsen said, pulling me close to him, before we left.

Someone made the music fade, and the pastor stood before us. He lifted his arms in his white alb and green stole and said, "Dying, Christ destroyed our death. Rising, Christ restored our life." The pastor gathered us and greeted us and graced us with words from Matthew. "Let the little children come to me," he read, and although I am not a believer, seeing those familiar gestures and hearing those words stung my eyes. It made it difficult to read the prayer. Still, my heart broke as I heard the congregation say, "We have not loved as we ought to love."

Whit rose from his pew after the Old Testament selection and moved slowly to the front of the chapel, the pastor making room for him at the pulpit. His head bowed so his white hair bristled at us, Whit removed his eyeglasses from his pocket, opened the Bible, and read to us from the Book of Psalms. He did not read the Twenty-third, which we all read later. He read, "Like as the hart desireth the water-brooks, so longeth my soul after thee, O God." Those were the very words. His voice was strong and clear. It made me think of Enterprise in the summer, of walking into town, all the tickling, rustling, crackling of heat in my ears. Every third or fourth step I took, a breeze seemed to reach me between the rows of corn. It made me think of the fan at the post office that stirred the air so slowly you could feel the motion and the stillness, motion and stillness. Made me think of holding my hand under the icebox where it dripped and waiting for the next chill drop to fall. I listened to Whit and could imagine why Greta Ruth might have married him.

Reading Second Corinthians, the pastor reminded us not to lose heart. The things which are seen are temporary, he read, and the things which are not seen are eternal. I thought of my unseen life, of Maggie's unseen lives. How nice it would be, I thought, if the parts of our lives that we hid from view, the parts we protected, were eternal. I decided that wasn't what the pastor or the scripture meant, and when I listened again, the pastor was promising that under God's tent, death would be swallowed by life.

When it came time for the Gospel, I frankly considered leaving, no matter how much commotion it would create. Why come to me at the death of a boy, and ask me to vote for Jesus? But then the pastor read from John, about Martha believing in the resurrection of her brother, and I thought that might be some comfort to Maggie and her family. He read again from Matthew, saying we must become as little children to enter the kingdom of heaven. The angels of children, he read, look on the face of the Father all day long.

I wiped my nose and folded my handkerchief into a small square as the pastor left the pulpit for the homily. He stepped down the few steps, touching the black rail of the coffin as he passed it, and said, "To lose a child—no parent ever expects this. Those who suffer this loss, suffer one of the greatest tragedies."

When a plant is ripped from the ground before bearing fruit, he said, we feel the terrible pull of its roots. We feel it clinging to life. Like this plant, we cling to the life that has been torn from us before its time. The expectations we had, the dreams of a bright future for this boy, Jamie Harris, have vanished. No sorrow rends us like this sorrow, he said, and everyone shares this sorrow with the good parents of this child.

"We are all stricken by the mystery of death. The lives we live and the deaths we die," he said, "are so strangely wrought of purpose and chance." When a child is lost, we blame ourselves, no matter what the cause of death. But when an accident occurs, we blame ourselves still more. And that is inescapable, he said, that is human. But when we blame ourselves, we risk forgetting God.

We must remember God, the pastor said, remember that He will have mercy for He does not afflict us willingly. And we must remember that no life created and taken is without meaning.

Let us soothe the pain of our loss, the pastor said, by remembering that God loves the children best for he asks us all to become as children before him. Like children, we who are left must trust in God's wisdom and find solace in God's love. The love that is now breaking our hearts is, after all, only the tiniest fraction of God's love. In prayer, the pastor commended Jamie's soul to God and asked compassion for Jim and Marian, praying that the unseen and the eternal would grow more real for us. He lifted his head, opened his arms, and said, "Let us pray."

Pray. How much I would have liked to believe enough to pray, but how could I believe in a church that included Whit but excluded me? A church, after all, is only people and their beliefs. So how could I pray? To whom? For what? I closed my eyes and thought of whatever it was that was outside this church and far away from these people, and I prayed the Lord's Prayer to that. In the silence left to us, I prayed safe journey for Jamie, although it was too late, and safe harbor for Maggie. Looking around the chapel at righteous Whit and all the other members of the family, I didn't feel forgiving, but I did feel kind.

We left the chapel slowly and walked across the lawn to the grave site. Cubes of grass-fringed earth were stacked nearby and covered with burlap. The coffin had been carried by hearse and was mounted beside the grave when we arrived. The family, or families, moved slowly, pulling together and breaking apart, the green grass appearing and disappearing among the gray skirts and black suits. Mary Helen walked with Whit, as if to be sure he had an elbow or a shoulder to hold on to when he walked. Marian held Alison's hand, and Maggie trailed behind them. Chess and Coral and Thomas and Lillian walked as one group, but Jim Harris walked alone.

And that's the way we stood around the grave, families who could abide each other standing close and those who couldn't standing apart. So I could remind her I was there, I took my place behind Maggie, who stood behind her mother and sister. As if she felt my presence, Alison turned and gazed at me with the force of her ten years of wisdom, but she said nothing to her mother. I still thought it possible I would be unseen in this crowd, until Mary Helen left Whit alone with Chess so she could stand near me and take my hand. I couldn't remember the last time I had stood shoulder-to-shoulder with Mary Helen.

The coffin was lowered, the winches making small, painful noises, like mice caught in traps. The pastor commended Jamie to the Almighty and committed his body to the ground. The usher handed Jim a spade, and Jim took it and dug into the mound of dirt, hefting a shovelful into the grave. He dropped the spade and brushed his hands off, then let them fall to his sides. His arms looked too long for his body, his body just looked thin, and his hair seemed to have coarsened. He pulled a handkerchief from his pocket and wiped his hands, wiped his face. He balled the cloth in one hand and stood staring down. I peered between the shoulders ahead of me and across the grave at Jim, and he stared back. I thought, I am so sorry, and he lowered his gaze again, to the ground or the coffin. With a hand on Maggie's shoulder, I thought, You still have children to care for, Jim. I guess I have none of Greta Ruth's gift because he did not look up.

"Death has been swallowed up in victory," the pastor said and then asked the Lord to bless us and keep us and make His countenance shine upon us and give us peace, amen.

We proceeded across the lawn, haltingly now because people were talking together. I held Maggie's hand and Mary Helen clutched my elbow.

"How good to see you," Mary Helen said. "One blessing to come out of all this."

"Good to see you," I said and kissed her. "How long will you be here this time?"

"Oh, a few more days. Whit needs some help getting things in order. He's moving into a smaller place. Anymore the house is just too much for him."

"It's kind of you to help him, Mary Helen."

"As long as I'm out here, why not? My husband can cook his own meals for a few days." And then she said again, "It's so good to see you," and hugged my waist.

It was so much more than good to see her, but all I could say was "Yes, so good to see you."

As we approached the chapel again, the group stopped, as if no one wanted to climb into their cars just yet. Maggie pulled back, saying, "My mother will be angry."

I held on to her a moment and said, "You can stay with me."

She looked uneasily toward her father, then back to me.

"You know I won't mind."

Maggie nodded and shook her hand free, walked across the grass to join her mother and Alison.

"Is the girl all right?" Mary Helen asked.

"As right as she can be."

"I worry about them so."

"So do I."

Mary Helen then took me by the elbow and led me toward Whit.

"Please don't, Mary Helen," I said.

"I want Whit to see you," she said, and then louder, "Whit, look who's here."

He turned our way, and his eyes still seemed cold as coins. "Evelyn," he said after a moment.

"Hello, Whit."

"What a surprise to see you. I've often wondered how you fared."

"You mean since John Rumsen's death?"

He winced, though I'm sure he tried not to. "Yes, I mean since then."

"I've done just fine, Whit. Really, I have."

"I can't say you don't look well."

"Nice of you to say so. And how are you faring?"

"I'm getting old," he said, "and I hate it."

I laughed and said, "I'm sorry to hear that, Whit. Seems none of us can escape."

"I hear you've got a boyfriend."

"Stop that, Whit," Mary Helen said. "It's none of your business if she does."

"Word certainly does get around."

"At least this one doesn't go prancing about, I hear," Whit said.

"John Rumsen was a dancer. And we didn't 'go prancing about.'"

Whit grunted and said, "Think you'll make it legal this time, Ev?"

"No, I'm not planning on it."

"Well, I should have known."

"Let's not have this argument again."

He was about to speak but stopped himself. After a moment, he said, "No, let's not," and as he turned to leave, "Nice to see you, Evvie."

"I miss Greta Ruth still."

"I've been missing Gramma Truth forty-three years."

I'd never heard him regret Greta's silence before.

"She was the best of us all," I said, thinking of the four sisters.

"Always better than I was, anyway," Whit said.

I took his hand and pressed it. "Take care of yourself, Whit."

"Sure will." He tipped his stained hat.

As we were speaking, people began to climb into their cars, and some drove away. Chess stood by his Buick, apparently waiting for Whit and Mary Helen. Whit walked toward the car, and Mary Helen grabbed my hands and said, "You must call me while I'm here," and I promised her I would. She pulled me to her for a long hug, a soft, talc-scented embrace I hadn't realized I wanted so much, and then she left me standing at the edge of the lot. I looked around for Jim so I could say all the things I hadn't. I wanted to tell him to take good care of Maggie and not to neglect Alison. He was talking to the usher, and it crossed my mind that he might have to tip the man, and that bothered me, such a transaction on such a day. Marian was already in the car, sitting in the passenger seat. Maggie sat in the back, all turned around in her place to look out the rear windshield. Alison walked tightrope on the curb, her arms outstretched and her fingertips wavering in the air. I watched Jim walk toward me, folding his billfold and slipping it into his rear pocket. As he passed, he put a hand on my shoulder, but he did not stop to talk. All I had time to say was "I am so sorry, Jim."

"Me, too, Ev. Me, too," and then he strode to the driver's side of the car and opened the door. "Come on, Alison," he said, but she took her time. She remained, tiptoeing along the curb, her arms tilting side to side, and as she walked she practiced that dip you see tightrope walkers do, one toe scooping way below the wire, as if they were testing the water, when all around them there is only air.

TWENTY-SIX

Marian cursed his relatives, but she didn't curse him. He was driving, after all. It was bad enough he was half drunk. Why risk making him angrier than he was already? Besides, she didn't blame him for his drinking, not really. She blamed the family. They'd suggested the lunch, and once they'd done that, who could ask him not to drink? Not even his father could do that. Not today of all days. And it wasn't as if Jim was—how should she put it?—as if he was like her mother. He wasn't like that at all. He didn't drink alone, and he didn't weep and sigh and arrange himself about the house in pitiful but graceful postures. A few drinks (always with company, always with a meal) and he seemed stronger, surer of himself. He drove with a ferocious concentration, silently targeting and reeling in the cars ahead of him. (He couldn't have been driving this fast *that* night, could he?) So she cursed the family under her breath but said nothing to him, as he drove them *home*.

Home: hard to call it that anymore, wasn't it? The house seemed oddly new and silent, as if they had been away a long time and it had emptied itself of the sounds and smells of family. Marian sniffed as she walked in and thought, What clean, unwrinkled air. But she was the first to muss it, saying, "I'll make coffee," as if she were speaking not to her family but to clients from the Junior League. *They* answered by taking seats in the living room, each seat well apart from the others.

In the kitchen, Marian filled the percolator she'd bought for her ladies. She found a tray she rarely used, a gift Chess and Coral had brought back from their first trip to Honolulu, and arranged three cups and a glass on it: coffee for three and milk for Alison. But they should have something to eat, too, shouldn't they? Marian dragged the cookie jar across the counter and opened it, the sweet smell reminding her of Alison baking *that* afternoon. How could they eat cookies baked while Jamie lived, baked only hours before he died? And hadn't she told him not to eat the dough? And hadn't he given her his best "Who, me?" smile? A gift she'd never get again. Briefly, Marian considered dumping the cookies into the trash, but what was she going to do? Throw out everything she had owned before? Sugar, butter, flour, they were harmless enough, weren't they? She arrayed the cookies on a plate and centered it on the tray, covering the painted palm trees and the map of Oahu.

Her family looked at her dumbly as she set the tray on the low table in the living room. *They* had taken the seats, more or less, Alison in the overstuffed chair and Maggie and Jim on the sofa. Thoughtful of them to save her a seat, wasn't it? She pulled up a straight-backed chair for herself and handed round the coffee and milk, her oldest (oldest?) casting her a sour, teenage glance. "Mom?" What? She didn't want coffee? Well, if she was old enough to stay out all night, she was old enough to drink coffee, wasn't she?

"Mom, I think you made a mistake," Maggie said.

"No mistake," Marian said and nothing more, because when she got right down to it, she should blame her daughter, shouldn't she? A thought that worked on her like a hot iron on a damp shirt.

Jim dunked a cookie into his cup and took a soggy bite. "Good," he said to Alison, and she smiled back doubtfully. Even Maggie shot him a look, an angry look he would have said, angry at her stupid father who never said the right thing. At least he knew it, didn't he? He finished his cookie and reached for another, aware again that his daughters were watching him. Well, the cookies were good. What was wrong with that?

It seemed they were all watching him, waiting for him to say something, the right thing, wish to hell he knew what *that* was. He buries his son, and they expect him to be a father, to comfort them? Well, he can't. He doesn't even know what to say to himself. He is beyond comfort, which is only right as far as he's concerned. A father who did what he did, he gets what he deserves. He woke this morning to the flat bright light, too bright for the thoughts that had kept him up all night. He'd pulled the window shade and thought, isn't that handy? Wish he could pull a shade over what he remembered, especially the sound of it, body against glass. Now some thought was slipping over the edge of his mind, some improbable, sweet thought about horses and corrals, marauders and bandits. He could remember, just barely, exactly the way it had been, the way it'd felt, sitting on the old back porch with Evvie and Chess and his mother. The house had been quiet, the way his own house was quiet now, and you could hear the rain and smell the damp earth. Evvie was brushing his mother's hair, sweeping the mane of it off her face and pinning it back a way his mother never had. They must have been going somewhere special, the movies, maybe. Evelyn rubbed lanolin into his mother's hands and rouge onto her lips, and then, when she was satisfied that he and Chess and his mother were properly dressed, she took them out. To the movies, of course. A western, wasn't it? All on the sly, one afternoon when his father wasn't home. Jim'd been younger than—his son. (That's a shade he'd better pull.) Well, certainly older than Alison. He looked over at her, his pretty little girl, and his eyes burned to look at her.

Avoiding her father's attention (what was he looking at her for?), Alison let the toes of her shoes dance under the overstuffed chair. Of course, with the glass of milk between her knees, she couldn't let her legs swing too much. She didn't want to drink her milk, and she didn't want to eat the cookies she'd baked then. Cookies, one of several things she chalked on her mental blackboard and added to a long sum of reasons why Jamie wouldn't come home, why she wouldn't ever again follow him out the door, asking, please, couldn't she play with him?

Oh, death. She knew about death. How could they all act like she didn't know? Never saying the word in front of her. Hugging her and turning away tight-lipped. *They* were the ones who didn't know, not she. Close to the ground, she knew all sorts of things they didn't. She poured salt on snails and water on ant holes. She saw the husks of insects, the decaying leaves under her feet. Hadn't she found that bird in the yard, its eyes pitted, its body light as ashes? That was death, dry and weightless. Like the orange trees that had gone black and brittle. Or Barry Ryan in her class. He'd died, too. Just like the bird, he'd shrunk inside his skin, retreating from his surface. She knew, better than they. She even knew the reasons they had told her. The bird was prey, the trees were thirsty, Barry was sick (BB guns, drought, leukemia). But she also knew these reasons weren't complete. There were other reasons birds and trees and people died, reasons like who was mean and who lied, who kissed in the dark and who wanted to, who was loved and who loved.

"Try to finish your milk," Alison heard her mother say.

Marian watched her husband dunk another cookie in his coffee. Her oldest (no, her older, she must remember that), her older gripped her cup with both hands, tightly, as if otherwise it would burst apart, and Alison dawdled, not touching her milk. God, this was worse than lunch. Marian looked down at her own empty cup (she'd done her part, hadn't she?) and set it on the tray.

"Let's put an end to this, please," she said.

"To what?" her husband said and reached for another cookie.

"Oh, Jim, to this."

She took Alison's glass and Maggie's cup, enjoying the force it took to break her daughter's grip. Then she snatched away the cookies before her husband could dunk another and carried away everything rattling and spilling onto the tray. And wouldn't you know it, her older girl shadowed her into the kitchen. (Aw, Maggie, why today?) Today her daughter decides to pitch in. (Why today, Maggie?)

"It's okay." Marian tossed a dish towel over her shoulder and turned toward her daughter. "I want to do them."

"But, Mom . . ."

"But, Mom, what?"

"But I want to help."

"Really, Maggie, I'd rather do them myself." Marian turned toward her kitchen window and opened the taps wide until she saw her daughter's dim reflection disappear from the glass. And then, just for a moment, she wanted to say, "Come back, Maggie, and help me," but the moment passed, and she couldn't bring herself to leave the kitchen and call her daughter back. She had nothing to spare today, not for the daughter she couldn't help blaming. Marian commenced the comforting work of washing, sometimes studying the plates and glassware in her hands, sometimes gazing through the reflection of herself and the pots and pans behind her to the plot of rosebushes in the yard and the blackened orange trees beyond.

For the few dishes her family had used, she ran a whole pan of suds. She had other things to wash, didn't she? She opened the fridge and pulled out every plastic bowl and foil-covered dish, removed the open milk carton and the twice-punched can of grapefruit juice. From the freezer, she took the half-eaten half-gallon of ice cream and every other frozen leftover she could find. The milk was the first to go, down the drain, glug glug. (My God, it really did go *glug glug*.)

He had just picked up the bad habit of drinking straight from the carton, must have caught it from his father. *He* drank from this, she thought as she tossed the carton away. Marian poured out the juice next, then dumped the peas and casserole, the rest of the loaf of bread. (Well, she'd had been wrong earlier, hadn't she? Everything from before had to go.) Anything he might have touched or tasted, even smelled, she couldn't bear to keep. The *cookies*. He had walked in, skateboard under his arm ("Can't you keep that in the garage?" she'd had to ask) and grabbed exactly three. She'd snapped the dish towel and said, "Want to ruin your appetite?"

"Sure, why not?" he'd said, as if her cooking were nothing special, nothing to save an appetite for, but she had laughed anyway. Now she upended the jar and listened to the cookies and loose sugar spill into the brown paper trash bag.

Jim opened the living-room cupboard he used as a bar and poured himself a drink.

Maggie fell back on her bed, the pillows exhaling under her.

And Alison slammed her door and waited to be punished for it. After a few minutes, perhaps because her mother did not come from the kitchen swatting her dish towel and scolding her, Alison reopened her door, walked over to Maggie's and slammed that, then walked back to her own room and slammed her door again.

That was Alison, wasn't it? First time Marian could remember her slamming a door, and now she slammed it three times. Playing catch-up, Alison? Marian lifted her bubble-crusted hands from the water and thought about giving her daughter an earful, thought better of it, then rinsed and dried her hands and walked to Alison's room, pulling Jamie's door nearly, but not quite, closed as she passed by. (She couldn't bear to peer into his room, to see the poster of whales on the wall and the black acetate scarf he used in his magic tricks. She couldn't bear seeing the skateboard she had dropped on Jamie's bed after the policeman had rung her bell and handed it to her. "Thought you might want this," he'd said. "We don't need it." But she couldn't bear to shut the door either.)

"Alison?" she said as she tapped on the door. "May I come in, sweetie?" Hearing her daughter say yes, she opened the door to find Alison sitting at the small desk Jim had built for her, coloring over the pictures of one of her Oz books, Marian couldn't tell (and didn't care) which. "Sweetheart, what are you doing?"

"Coloring," Alison answered.

"Are you sure you want to do that to your nice book?"

"Yes."

"You want me to read to you?"

"Mom!" Alison said, as if angry her mother couldn't remember she wasn't a mere baby who didn't know how to read, and Marian settled for kissing her daughter, that brief chance to touch her child's body, before she returned to the kitchen.

The sound of the door slapping him, Jim paused midpour and waited to see what his wife would do. Whatever it was, he'd second it, except she didn't do what he expected, tell her daughter to stop slamming the doors, what did she want to do, knock the house down? Instead, his wife walked quietly past the living room (he kept his face turned from her) and down the short hallway to Alison's room. He supposed he should join his wife and try to calm his daughter, talk to her, that's what this called for, didn't it? Then, of course, he'd have to face Marian, difficult to do even with Alison there between them. He swallowed what was left in his glass and poured some more. And he'd have to face Alison. He pictured himself in her room, surrounded by her girlhood (rag dolls on the bed, plastic ponies on the dresser), pictured himself trying to talk like a father. And how could he do that, given the kind of father he now knew he was? He wouldn't even be able to look at her. He'd look away, and damn if he wouldn't catch his face in the vanity mirror. He'd see thickening skin, dark mole, fan of tiny wrinkles around the eyes. You couldn't look at yourself without looking at your eyes, could you?

Words Alison might have sensed but not thought rose and skimmed a horizon in his mind. *Murderer* was the least of them. But the words were too harsh, even for Jim (who prided himself on the hard truths he could face), so they drifted and sank before he could think them. Hell, he hadn't a ghost of what to say. To her or to Maggie and, God knows, not to Marian.

. . .

Maggie unslammed her door, quietly opening it a crack, the way *he* liked it when they used to sit in her room. She waited to hear the stop-and-go hum of the sewing machine and the low sound of her father talking business on the phone. Instead, her mother's hands plashed, dipping into and rising from the water. Her father, standing at his bar drinking, made no sound Maggie could hear, so she imagined him motionless on the sofa, his hands clasped in his lap, his head bowed. The urgent current of habit had always swept her parents back to routine life. She expected it to sweep them back now, but it didn't.

It was Maggie who was swept, swept by the current of sleep. Anywhere, everywhere, sleep drew her under. She lay down, and the air felt heavy, the way it can feel in summer, except it wasn't summer and it wasn't the air that was heavy. This much Maggie knew, or part of her did. Pinned by the weight (of a loss that was wide and deep and immersed her), she slept nearly motionless and awoke hours later, stiff and still. It was impossible to move.

No, not impossible, because she could sit up. But then she understood: she could not leave, that was impossible. Outside this room were her mother and father, her sister (her little sister), and they knew, or could know (it was all the same to Maggie), what she had done and exactly why she was to blame. For everything. For the dust under her bed, the clothes she'd outgrown, the curfews she'd broken, the back talk she'd talked, the restlessness, the percolating something (*wildness*, her mother would call it, *hormones*, Maggie called it when she saw it her own daughter) that made her itch with wanting, not just sex, but life, real life, outside this house.

Her father had told her over and over she would ruin her life, and hadn't she? Perhaps ruined all their lives. Oh, she was the reason, for everything but especially for Jamie. He was not here, he would never be here, and she was why.

Yes, her mother and father and her sister had known this yesterday and the day before that, but yesterday and the day before that they were occupied and had little to say. Now they were not and could say everything they hadn't but didn't need to. Say it or not, he was gone. He was not where he had been, in her room or his room or any of the rooms of their lives. And she was to blame. And so she could not leave her room.

Marian poured cups of boiling water into her freezer to hasten the defrosting. She had thrown out every frozen thing she had baked or cooked *before* and overturned the ice-cube trays in the sink (they had been filled *before*, and now she worked with hot water and a dinner knife to loosen the thick jacket of ice around the freezer box, old bath towels spread at the base of the fridge to catch the overflow. She wedged the tip of her knife between the gray metal and the white ice but only managed to knock one chip off, then another. Poured a little more hot water, and worked the knife deeper this time, taking care not to force too much, not to break the tubes that wrapped like veins around the box. Wiggled the knife and, with satisfaction, felt the sheet of ice lose its grip. It was white in the center, nearly clear at the edges. It made her think for a moment of polar caps, ice floes, glaciers.

And then she thought he was there, standing behind her. As if her skin were iron filings drawn to *him*, the magnet behind her, she had to stop herself from doing what she most wanted to do: turn and say, "No, Jamie, I don't know why they're called polar caps, and please don't suck the ice." She stopped herself, but just barely, closing her eyes and leaning back. If he were there, she'd feel him, smell him. And she didn't.

Marian let her homemade glacier fall into the sink, breaking unevenly in two. Her hands chilled (she liked the chill), she picked up the smaller chunk of ice and soaped them with it, then ran her tongue along the edge. "Hah!" she said in surprise, causing her husband to look up before returning his attention to his glass. Her son had claimed he liked the frost, said you could taste the air. Air? Well, it wasn't just water she tasted, was it? Smog, she'd say, or metal or, more likely, Freon. She licked the ice again, then poured more hot water into her cup so she could attack the stubborn frost that remained, and as she did so, she let her hands pass over the spout, steam slicing through the chill.

Jim looked up. Hah! his wife had said. She'd discovered something? Something he'd done, more than likely. He'd know soon enough. Now he just wanted to get back to where he'd been, webbed in his thoughts, his world no wider than his glass. Except it was a little like sleep and a lot like a dream, hard to get back to when you're taken from it. So he refilled his glass and took another swallow.

His father would kill him for this, very nearly had that time he caught him drinking. Whipped the daylights out of him. Hadn't today, of course, and that was a surprise. Jim'd ordered a third because if he was going to have to sit through that meal listening to them, not to mention pay for it all, he'd be damned if he didn't drink. Even lifted his fourth in toast to his father. The old man'd had to smile back. Not that Jim didn't know what Whit really thought. They all knew what Whit really thought (God's swift judgment). Just that they had to get through this meal, didn't they? Besides, you had to be too old for a whipping some- day. His own kids were. His own kids had no idea what punishment was. It's true, he'd brought them up by hand, but, except for Alison, they were beyond that now. Well, Maggie was beyond that now. God knew nothing would bring her around. And his son? Oh, God, his son. No point even thinking, so he took another swallow, and hey, his father would whip the living daylights out of him for this, wouldn't he? While his mother stood there, her hair slipping from its knot and her empty hands floating uselessly, the way they always did, a few inches from her body.

Alone in the room she would never leave, Maggie took a pencil and notebook from her desk. She meant to write a letter to her mother and father, telling them what she wasn't sure yet. That she was sorry and she was to blame. That because of her, her brother was gone and always would be. That she would go away (if she could only disappear) and their lives would get better. But when she opened the notebook in her lap, she found she couldn't write any more than she could leave her room. Instead, she drew several dashes at the bottom of the page, play- ing her brother's game, hangman solitaire.

In hangman solitaire, you imagined your opponent, just the way, her brother insisted, you imagined the hung man. You marked the number of spaces your imaginary opponent told you to mark. You guessed a let- ter and put it where your imaginary opponent told you to put it, and then you guessed another. Of course, you could have a word in mind before you began, but that was cheating. If you did that, her brother had said, you weren't playing hangman solitaire.

So Maggie tried to imagine her opponent. She put a hat on his head, and he threw the hat off. She hung a necktie around his neck, and he tied it in a big loose bow outside the unbuttoned collar of his shirt. She asked him not to sit on her bed, but he did, picking up her notebook and scribbling in it. She said, "Quit leaning on my desk," and he laughed and replied, "How else'm I supposed to play hangman?" He wore ten- nis shoes with no socks, the cuffs of his jeans rolled up and his ankles wet from watering the yard. Mud and damp blades of grass clung to his shoes as he rolled a skateboard absently back and forth under his feet.

"Draw me something," Maggie said.

Her opponent said, "I'm here to play hangman."

"I was just about to play by myself," and she showed him the eleven dashes at the bottom of her page.

"Ha! Perfect!"

Perfect? There was nothing perfect about this. Maggie fell back on her bed and squeezed her eyes shut (wake up and *think*, think about what you're going to do!), but that only made her opponent laugh.

"Hey," he said, "this is the game you have to play."

"Who says?"

"*I* say. You owe it to me."

"Go away." Maggie squeezed her eyes tighter and pressed her hands against them.

"All right, I will."

She heard him pick up his skateboard and open the door.

"No, don't!" She sat up and grabbed her notebook and pen. "X, I guess X."

"You sure?" He crossed the room slowly and sat on her bed.

"Yes, X. I'm sure."

"Come on, let's not waste time on the X's, Z's, and Q's. What about that little chapel of a vowel?"

"Cheater. You're supposed to let me guess." Maggie wrote two A's, right where she should, in the second and seventh spaces.

"What's wrong with cheating?"

"What do you mean 'what's wrong'? If cheating were right, it wouldn't be cheating."

"If you're going to be *that* way." He turned the skateboard over in his lap and spun the wheels, tilting his head as if listening for the pitch of the whir. "No more hints. Go ahead. Guess."

"All right. E," she said, and he laughed as she filled in the one E and then the two I's. "J. It starts with J, right?"

"I've made it easy, way too easy," and he swung his head back and forth. "I guess that's a kind of cheating, too?"

Maggie smiled and said again, "Draw me the hung man."

"You draw it."

"But that would be cheating. Draw it the way you used to."

"Don't want to anymore. You do it."

"You know I can't."

Her opponent shrugged and set both pairs of wheels spinning.

Reluctantly, Maggie tried to sketch a muscle-bound man in goatee and mustache, but like all her drawings, it looked like a gingerbread man, a lumpy-armed gingerbread man. It was the best she could do but not good enough to show to him. So she tried again. This time she drew lines across the man's lumpy arms to suggest shirtsleeves, across his middle to suggest a belt. She glanced at her opponent sitting hunched on her bed. When the wheels slowed, he spun them again and slapped the center of the board, rocking to a beat she couldn't catch. He seemed to enjoy this, immensely, for she could see the crease of his one deep dimple. No, she could not show him this drawing either, so she tried again.

Her fingers throbbing, Marian wrung the towels out in the sink and plugged the fridge back in. She supposed she should make dinner, but she couldn't and couldn't say why not. Just the thought of food, the thought of cooking, turned her stomach. What was this? Some sort of evening sickness in the first trimester of mourning? But they would need to eat, so she searched her shelves for unopened boxes and jars and set out saltines, peanut butter, sweet pickles. (Starch, protein, and would pickles pass for vegetables?) She stacked four plates on the table, placed a fan of napkins near them. A knife to spread, a fork to spear. If they needed more, they could get it. A dinner bell, that's what she needed now.

Just inside the living room, Marian leaned against the wall and watched her husband drink. He sat formally, she thought, his feet flat on the floor, his back upright against the sofa. One hand circled the glass poised on his knee as he stared at the washed-out green wall (sea-foam green, she would have said to a client). She meant to tell him dinner (if she could call it that) was ready, but instead she stood and watched, watched long enough he should have noticed her, shouldn't he? But he didn't, or didn't seem to. How long could he ignore her? She'd had a few questions for him, questions she couldn't keep to herself *that* night: How fast were you driving, and why didn't you see him? She had asked him in the early morning as they lay in their bed waiting out the night, Jim still in yesterday's clothes. With everyone but Jamie home and in bed, she had asked Jim those two questions, the voice she heard sounding nothing like her.

"I made that turn, Marian. I never thought children would be out, not at that hour. I never thought."

She had tried to imagine making that turn herself, and she almost could, her son appearing from nowhere. Now she wanted to ask, "You were drinking, weren't you?" But as long as she stood there, her husband appeared not to see her (refused to see her, was that it?), and she couldn't bring herself to speak. Still without turning toward her, her husband set his drink on the table. So Marian slipped off her shoes and walked as quietly as she could to her workroom, where, with a shove, she let the butcher paper unroll itself across her worktable and, despite her aching fingers, prepared to make a pattern.

"You hear that?" Maggie's opponent said.

She nodded yes because even through the closed door she was sure she heard the miniature thunder of paper unfurling in her mother's workroom.

"I always knew it would be this way," Maggie's opponent said.

"You did not. You didn't think of it once."

"Did too."

"You did not."

"Well, maybe only once."

"And if you did know, how could you just go ahead and . . . ?"

"But I didn't go ahead. I didn't do anything."

And she did, didn't she? Maggie closed her eyes and saw a web of fractured glass.

"Listen," her opponent said and lifted his ear toward a whistle of a voice. "That's Ali."

Alison murmured the song she barely remembered she hated, chopping her name into pieces (Ali bali bo pali). She sat and murmured and colored the black and white drawings of a storybook. She colored a cave where a headless lady stood (a princess, probably, just look at her gown), many pretty heads perched before her like hats in a store. In her hands, the princess held the head she had just removed, ready to place it on its stand and select another.

The cave Alison colored black and purple, the princess and her many faces, red and orange and burnt sienna. Pink or blue or sherbet green, the usual princess colors, Alison didn't touch. She would change this picture, a lesson about wanting beauty too much (a suspect lesson, Alison already knew), into something else (just what, she didn't know). She covered each face thick with Crayola.

This was what she had feared today. She had not feared the casket or the funeral or the grave. She'd feared that when they came home, their house would be empty (no furniture, no walls, no floors, no ceiling). She'd been afraid their house would be like Barry's, where no one ever came or went or even furtively pushed the curtains back with one hand. Yet she had seen Mrs. Ryan pushing a shopping cart, Mr. Ryan showing samples at his linoleum store. That was the scary part: they were alive but the house seemed dead, as if at home every night, they died.

Alison imagined that if she opened the Ryans' door, she'd see nothing, not light, not even emptiness, and it would feel cool inside, like a basement. And when her father worked the key in their own back door today, she was sure it would open onto nothing. But it hadn't. Behind the door, everything lay where they'd left it, cups and saucers and cereal bowls. And that was scary too.

The tune bubbling in her mouth, Alison appraised her work. For the finishing touches, she grabbed both the purple and black crayons and ran them over and over the walls of the cave. Then she ripped the page from her book and taped the picture to the wall. Unaware she had been humming, she stopped and in the silence overheard her sister talking. Who was there to talk to, anyway?

Alison opened her sister's door. "Who're you talking to?"

"No one," Maggie said.

"You shouldn't talk to no one."

"Okay, I won't."

Alison walked in and leaned against the wall. "What are you drawing?"

"Nothing. A hung man."

"Playing by yourself?"

"Sort of."

"What do you mean, sort of?" Alison glared about the room.

"Okay. Playing against myself."

"Drawn lots of hung men."

"Yeah."

"Looks more like a woman you're drawing now."

"Guess so."

"Is that supposed to be someone?"

Maggie looked at her drawing, her scribble, really, and saw in the tangle of lines a woman in a sack dress, belly pressing against the skirt. "Me?"

"No," Alison objected. "You're not that ugly."

"But almost, right?" Maggie scribbled over her scribble. "I guess it's no one."

Alison seated herself on the bed. "That girl Leann came today."

"Mmm-hmm."

"Does she like him?"

"I don't know."

"Does he like her?"

Maggie's opponent put his hands over his breast and fell back on her bed in mock heartbreak.

"He likes her."

"Yuck," Alison said. "Really?"

Maggie saw him nod vigorously and said, "Really."

"Yeah, well, he was showing off."

Maggie's opponent pushed himself from her bed and dropped his skateboard on the floor. He stood on it and waved his arms as if he were surfing. Want to see me show off? he seemed to say.

"You think so?" Maggie said.

"Yes," Alison said, the word final and solid.

Maggie glanced up to catch her sister's face. It was one of those moments when she could see the miniature adult within her sister.

"I think she's a reason," Alison said.

"She's the reason?"

"And you're a reason."

"Yes, I am the reason," Maggie said.

And she was, thought Alison. Her stinky sister with her peroxide and hair spray, her box of Kotex hidden behind the stack of bath towels. The words *it's all your fault* tipped into Alison's mind but not into her mouth. She had so many other things in mind, all her reasons butting up against each other: Daddy, car, rope, Mom, Leann, skateboard, Tommy (Tommy Dawson!), her stinky sister, and her stupid copycat brother.

"All he did was copy you. Sneaking out just like you."

"I didn't tell him to do that. He did it all by himself."

"He was a copycat. He copied you. And I hate you."

Alison grabbed a piggy bank from Maggie's desk and threw it at her. It thudded against the wall and fell to the floor, pennies spilling from its cracked body. But that did not satisfy Alison, so she grabbed a trigonometry book and a wooden pencil box, a teddy bear and a whelk, a glass paperweight and a painted Japanese fan and threw them one by

one at her sister, missing each time but the first, the math book hitting
Maggie below the ribs and falling open in her lap. (As if her *sister* ever
studied.)

"What is going on here?"

Their mother stood in the doorway.

Alison didn't even think the things she would usually say (it's her
fault, she started it). She simply looked at her mother, with her bangs
clipped back and her stupid sewing glasses raccooning her face, and
bolted, slamming against her mother as she ran to her room.

"What did you say to her?" Marian asked.

"I didn't say anything."

"Well, you must have said something, or she wouldn't be so upset.
Leave your sister alone, you hear me?" Marian closed Maggie's door
and walked a few steps to Alison's. She rested her forehead against it
and said softly, "You okay, sweetie?"

Her youngest (yes, youngest, she would always have three children,
no one could tell her different) didn't answer.

Marian looked at the doors to her children's rooms, three small
rooms that opened like cells off a narrow hallway. Only Jamie's was
open, but only slightly, the way he liked it when he was in his room. She
could close the door, but that would be too final, opening it too painful.
Leaving it ajar, she could at least pretend he was still inside, drawing or
practicing his magic tricks.

The times her mother went away, it was Marian's habit not to look at
the places her mother had vacated: her bed, her chair, her seat at the
table. And Marian avoided, too, the things that belonged to her mother:
the glass box of hairpins and tin of dusting powder, the piles of sheet
music stored inside the piano bench.

Having seen how casually her own children ransacked her drawers, it
surprised Marian to think that, in her mother's absence, she had not
used her hairpins or worn her hats or drunk from her favorite glasses.
But Marian hadn't, couldn't, and she had been rewarded because every
time her mother went away, she returned some weeks later, so happy to
see her Marian, her little on-i-on.

"See the tears? See the tears in my eyes?" Her mother squatted on
the driveway and hugged Marian, enclosing her in the folds of her skirt
and in the sweet and dusky odor of her good stole. (Who had let her
wear that home? Who had brought it to her in the first place?) "See, you
are my little on-i-on."

Marian nodded as if she understood, but she didn't.

"Your mother needed a rest," her father said. "She needed to get away."

Rest from what? Away from what? From Marian? Marian, who tried so hard never to do anything wrong? She knew, more or less, that her mother got better when she went away, but she never knew why. Only later, much later, did she recognize the words for her mother's time away. She was already married and had a child herself when she heard Evelyn Rumsen say, "Well, they sent him away to dry out. Had to shut down production for two weeks, and who was paying us, I ask you?"

Drying out. That's what her mother had been doing away. Marian pictured her mother pinned to the clothesline behind the garage. Her mother, arms spread wide, every few inches a wooden peg pinching sweater and flesh and binding her to the line. Her mother, waving in the breeze. *Drying out.*

Better than getting drenched, Marian supposed, for her mother had gone away to do that, too. Had disappeared without explanation. And wouldn't that be nice? Not getting drenched, of course, but just disappearing whenever you wanted? And where had her mother gone? To cheap (her mother hated that word) hotels to drink and to expensive (as expensive as her father could afford) rest homes to dry out. Wouldn't it be nice to be confined to a small room holding nothing but a bed and chair, a quiet room somewhere no one knew your name and no one could ask you for anything?

Back in her workroom, Marian slid the blade of her scissors under the butcher paper and resumed cutting as quietly as she could. Hadn't she said something to Jim about that once? That she wanted a room that was a sponge for sound, where nothing said and nothing done could be heard?

Maggie closed her eyes, wishing she knew where her opponent was, and remembered, for the first time that day, that she was pregnant. She didn't feel pregnant, didn't feel sick or heavy or tired, hadn't felt pregnant all day, and it frightened her, almost as much as being p.g. in the first place. She didn't want this baby, wanted to be rid of it, but she didn't want to lose it either.

She spread her hands across her abdomen, still alert from the blow of the book, and pressed her fingers against herself one by one. What did the doctor feel when he worked one hand inside her, rested the other where her hands rested now? Maggie felt nothing, nothing she could call *it*, so how could he say, "About six or seven weeks"? Maybe she never was, never had been.

"Don't be stupid," her opponent said. Blocking what light was left as well as any body, he leaned against her windowsill.

"I'm not, but it's not like he did any test. Isn't there supposed to be a test?"

"Dead rabbit test?"

"They take your blood, they take your pee, they take something." And then she said, "Where'd you hear about dead rabbits?"

"Don't remember. School? Mom? You know, when she thought I wasn't listening." He spun the wheels and slapped the middle of his skateboard. "One-man band, yeah?"

"Oh, yeah, you're the Beatles, all right." She rolled onto her stomach to see her opponent better. Yes, there he was, his favorite blue jeans rolled up, ankles bare, cheek clouded with a Milky Way of freckles. "But there was no test. Maybe I've been wrong all this time."

"Grow *up*."

"Yeah, well, you'd wish things were different if it was your problem."

"My problem is nothing will ever be different."

"Jamie!" Maggie said, tears filling her eyes.

He turned his face to the wall and said, "Say that again and I leave."

"But I want . . ."

"I mean it," he said, and so, as the house grew dark, they sat in silence, Maggie gripping her arms around her knees.

Eventually, Maggie's opponent said, "Mom didn't mention supper, did she?"

"You hungry?"

"No, you?"

"I don't care if I never eat again." But even as she spoke, Maggie felt the first ache of hunger. Perhaps she didn't care, but *it* cared. *It* cared a lot.

"Me neither," her opponent said. "Don't care if I eat in a million years."

"Aren't you funny."

"Shhh," he said. "Listen. Mom's laying out her pattern now."

"You hear that?" Maggie asked.

"Well, *duh*."

"Liar."

"Bounces off me and sticks on you."

"I'm not lying. I just can't tell anyone."

"So what're you going to do?" her opponent asked. "Stay here and wait until they notice?"

"You're not supposed to ask what I'm going to do."

"All right. I won't." He dropped the skateboard to the floor. "What's Bruce going to do?"

"How should I know? What do you think he'll do?"

"Marry you."

She could have kicked him. "That's about the only thing I do know. I can't marry Bruce."

"I want to get married."

"You do? To who? Leann?"

"Think she'll have me?" he said. He looked at Maggie then. He hadn't really looked before. She saw his grin was still simple and sweet, but his eyes were bruised and his face swollen.

"Don't," she said.

"Don't what?"

"Don't go."

Maggie closed her eyes so she would not see the bruises and swelling and saw instead the splintered web and remembered the way the glass gave, almost like a pillow, when Jamie hit it. Afterwards, she was not allowed to see him at the hospital where the ambulance had taken him (as if anyone thought there was anything that could be done for him). Even her mother did not go, just her father, and late that night he sat across the kitchen table from her mother as she yelled, "Tell me, goddamn it all. Tell me how bad it was. I want to know how bad he was hurt." Maggie stood in the dark living room and watched her father through the door. It seemed he could not talk, his hands moving from his face to his arms to his body, until he mumbled, "Stop it, Marian. Stop it."

Maggie kept her eyes shut against the sight of Jamie's swollen face, and when she opened them, she was alone in her room, the distant streetlight making ghosts of her furniture. Around her, the house seemed calm, as if she could walk through each room and leave no ripples, but she did not want to because what she wanted would not be there. Her brother would not be there. Ever. So she sat on the floor and folded herself inward.

· · ·

In bed alone, what a relief. But still Marian did not sleep. Sometimes it seemed to her that she never slept. She stayed awake for her mother and now for her children, for their fevers and flus, their bouts of three-day measles. Sometimes, fearing concussion, she stayed awake to keep *them* awake: when Maggie fell off the neighbor's wall, when Jamie flew over his handlebars. Then there was Maggie's first sunburn, when Marian awoke over and over all night long to stand by the crib and watch her daughter sleep. And what about the time Jamie, who'd just learned to walk, tugged the cord of the hot iron, the heavy thing tumbling down and scorching him? Burns on his back and shoulder, his plump little hands, burns all over her sweet little boy. Marian stayed up all night holding him, sure a mother as careless as she didn't deserve children.

The calamities of childhood, how did anyone live through them? It seemed to her Jamie should be the rule, not the exception. And why was he the exception, goddamn it to hell? Look at Whit, living on and on. Look at them, for Christ's sake. She'd trade years of her life for a few more years of Jamie's. She didn't deserve to live if she couldn't protect her own child, did she? She kicked the sheet and stared at the ceiling, daring someone (all right, God) to remind her she had other children. Did she care? She would have traded both in a heartbeat if she could have held the one she lost. *Fool, you don't mean that.* Didn't she? And then she thought of Alikins, sitting at her desk coloring. *No, I don't mean that, just give me my boy back, that's all.*

New drawings were taped to Alison's wall, drawings of caves and of pretty houses whose doors and windows opened onto caverns of black and purple crayon. As Alison slept, the weight of the paper slowly pulled the tape away from the wall, lifting off tiny flecks of pink paint, and the drawings slid one by one to the floor and woke her. Yes, paper tickling the floor woke her, and awake she lay curled in her bed (like a sow bug, her mother would say) staring at the drawings littering the floor. Stupid drawings, she thought (*her dumb brother could have done better*). Even in the dark, they looked stupid (*her dumb brother's pictures were never stupid*). Alison climbed from bed and collected her dumb drawings, then sat with them in her lap and cried quietly, tears falling from her chin onto the stupid drawings her dumb brother would have done better.

• • •

Her father lay on the sofa, sleeping to the dimmed chatter of the television. From time to time, the rising voices of the actors of his youth made him surface. "In a minute," he said, "I'll come to bed in a minute." And then he slipped under, trying, as he had all day, to return to that sweet memory, any sweet memory, anything but memories of the accident. He drifted down, pulling the voices in his wake until they were tangled in the wrack of sleep, and when the actors' shouts drew him to the surface again, he did not remember diving for dreams and finding instead the silty, frightening bottom. "In a minute," he said to no one. "I'll be there in a minute."

Although she did not hear the choking sound Jim Harris made as his dark dreams dragged him through sleep, Mrs. Dawson across the street awoke abruptly, as if she had. After some restless minutes next to her soundly sleeping husband, she went to her kitchen to make herself a cup of Ovaltine, checking in on Tommy on the way. He lay calmly, his arm in its new white cast a big check mark against his blanket. There'd been a night of worry, a fear of concussion, but next day the doctor'd said Tommy would be just fine. And now he was, almost. Sleeping like a little boy.

Once the milk was warm and mixed with malt, Lois Dawson sat at her kitchen table and watched the street, switching on a small lamp that lit the cup she held and the African violet she had recently repotted. Safe at home, she could not see Marian Harris seat herself in a straight-backed living-room chair to keep an eye on her husband as he slept, nor could she see Maggie Harris, arms wrapped around shins, weeping silently and rocking, rocking on her bedroom floor. Through the window of her kitchen nook, Lois Dawson could see her neighbors' house, or at least the modest silhouette of their ordinary ranch-style stucco home, and was relieved that she could look across the street the way she did, without anger, perhaps because Tommy would soon be right as rain or perhaps because she was simply made that way, a stranger to bitterness.

She did notice the sash of one window slide up and leaned forward to see more clearly which of the children was climbing out the window. It surprised her only slightly to see the pretty little one—Alison—clamber down among the hibiscus and walk across the lawn in her nightgown, slowly, deliberately, as if the air were heavy as water. The girl headed for the acre of trees Mr. Dawson called an acre of firewood, and when Lois saw her climb into a crux of branches, she couldn't help but think of all the times she'd spied Jamie Harris in those trees. He must have thought no one could see him because he stayed for hours, sometimes drawing in that tiny notebook he kept in his pocket, sometimes smoking, pulling cigarettes from a pack he kept, like the hoodlum she knew he wasn't, rolled in his shirtsleeve. It was innocent, innocent enough, Lois Dawson never told anyone what she saw, certainly not his mother, but also not her husband, who would have said, "The boy's going to burn us all down, Lois."

Alison wriggled up in the arms of the tree and leaned back against the branches, one foot stirring the air. A moth, Mrs. Dawson thought, that's what she looks like, a big old moth fresh from its chrysalis, waiting for its wings to dry. Lois sat a while longer, finishing her Ovaltine, then rose and washed her cup. She would look in on Tommy again and return to bed. She reached to switch off her lamp and as she did so, glanced out once more at the girl in the tree. Alison leaned against the shoulder of a branch, her head tilted as if she were listening. Whatever could the girl be listening to at that hour of the morning? Lois Dawson couldn't imagine. A cat howling? A raccoon overturning a garbage pail? Funny thing was, even in a nightgown that girl could make you think of her brother. Something about the shape of her face and the fact that she would do this, climb a tree in the middle of the night. In fact, the more Lois looked, the more she could have sworn she saw Jamie Harris hanging from his knees in the highest branches, his shirttails slipping free. A boy like her own son. It was too much for Lois, who rubbed her eyes to erase her vision, and when she gazed out again, she realized her eyes were simply playing tricks on her, for she plainly saw the girl in her nightgown, piking herself down and landing gently in the grass.

TWENTY-SEVEN

Maggie

*B*efore morning, when I thought the rest of the family was sleeping, I tried again to leave. I had to, because I was the splinter that made the family fester. So I pressed myself up from the floor and, carrying my shoes and purse, walked to the kitchen, taking care not to wake my father.

I think I meant to leave by the back door. I was ready to, had slipped on my shoes and put some provisions into my purse (a jar of peanut butter someone had left on the table), when I found myself facing my mother's workroom. The iron sat upright on the ironing board, the sewing machine huddled in a corner. A pattern lay on fabric spread across the worktable, and on the adjustable dress form was the bodice my mother had been beading the night I left. The seed pearls shone dully among the scallops of lace, and sleeves were now attached to the armholes, a gathered layer of tulle pinned beneath the sculpted waist. It looked like a dress for a pretty girl who certainly hadn't messed things up by getting pregnant first. I knew it would never fit, but that didn't stop me from taking off my blouse and skirt. I removed the dress from the form and stepped into it, pins pricking my waist and armpits.

If there'd been a zipper, it never would have closed, but when I saw myself reflected in the narrow mirror behind my mother's worktable, I saw a bride. The big bell sleeves and the gathered tulle did what my mother said they should, made my waist and neck appear slender in contrast. "To make the bride more delicate than she is," my mother once said. "You know, cherishable."

"What do you think?" she said now.

"You scared me, Mom."

"Sorry," she said and turned on the light. "I wasn't expecting to find you here either."

"I thought you were asleep. I didn't mean to ruin your work."

"I couldn't, and you're not. Not yet anyway, but be careful, please. Last thing I need are your pit stains on the dress."

"Jesus, Mom."

I slid off the prickly sleeves and stepped out of the bodice.

"Well, that sort of thing shows up on white, you know." She took the half-sewn garment from me and redressed the form. "Why on earth do you think I wash my hands so often while I work? My God, when I was in the bridal department, they taught us to wear gloves when we made these dresses. I couldn't bear it, it was so clumsy." My mother leaned forward and fluffed the tulle. "I attached this to see how the skirt would look. Easier to keep tulle clean than satin. This girl wants an overlay of lace. I wanted to tell her it would make the dress heavy, but I couldn't."

"I'm sorry she wouldn't listen, Mom." I turned my back on her before I slipped into my blouse. Even though my mother didn't suspect, or I didn't think she suspected, I was embarrassed to stand pregnant and half-naked under the blunt light while my mother chattered as if I were her client.

"What is it with these young women?"

"I don't know, Mom."

"You wouldn't do that. You'd choose something tasteful."

"Mom, you never like anything I choose," I said and stepped into my skirt.

"I must. Sometimes?" She sat down in her dressmaker's chair and stared out the window toward her rosebushes.

"You don't even like this skirt, do you?"

It was straight and dark green. She'd made clear it did nothing for me. Pleats would have been more becoming, she'd said. Now she didn't answer, just shrugged slightly and continued to gaze through her reflection out the window.

"Mom?"

"No, I guess I don't." She lifted her hands, as if about to say more, then dropped them and shook her head.

"What, Mom?"

"Nothing." She found her wrist cushion on the table and slid it onto her wrist. "I just feel like I should rip everything out and start over again."

"But the dress is going to be beautiful."

"Not the dress, Maggie. This." She opened her hands as if releasing a bird. "This life."

"It wasn't your fault, Mom."

"It wasn't? I keep thinking about all the things I should or shouldn't have done."

"It wouldn't have mattered."

"I wish I thought that."

"Well, what? What could you have done differently?"

I imagined her saying she should have barred the doors or hid his skateboard, she should have let him wear what he wanted, eat what he liked.

"First, I never should have married." She pulled a pin from her cushion and stuck it back in.

"Mom."

"Well, I shouldn't have."

"But, Mom, then we wouldn't be here."

"That's the point, Maggie. I probably shouldn't have had kids either. I'm a terrible mother. Look what I've done."

"You're a great mother, and you didn't do anything. It was an accident."

"And when does an accident begin? I'd like to know."

Me, I wanted to say. This accident began with me.

"Well, what do you think?" My mother pushed another pin all the way into the cushion, and then another. "Did it begin when your father didn't hit the brake? Did it start when Jamie headed down the hill? Or earlier? Maybe it was when your dad decided to work late that night? Or was it when Jamie sneaked out the door behind my back? Or maybe, Maggie, it was when you didn't come home. Maybe that's when it began."

"Mom," I said to hide my tears.

"What?"

I nodded at her hands. She'd done something Jamie used to do, something that had always angered her, pushed all the pins flat against the cushion so they were difficult to pull out again. She removed the cushion and straightened herself in her chair.

"What I really think is it was me," she said. "I let him go. I knew where he was going, and I didn't stop him."

"No, Mom, it wasn't you."

"My mother," she said as if I hadn't spoken, "she must have done everything wrong." She turned to face me. "You have no idea what it was like for me when I was your age."

"Tell me, Mom."

"I can't, Maggie." She erased something in the air. "I'd never say something against my mother. I want you to love her."

"But, Mom."

"She's a fragile woman, sweetheart."

I waited, thinking she must say more, but she turned and smoothed the pattern and the gray gabardine that lay on the table. "I need to work here a while. Alone."

"Please tell me."

She evened the selvages before she faced me and said, "My mother did everything wrong. She drank, and half the time she wasn't even home. But here's what I want you to know: I'm fine. I'm married. I take care of my kids. I keep you spotless, and I make a little extra money. I've turned out fine. But you kids, you have me, trying as hard as I try, and look what's come of you."

"What's come of us?"

"Oh, Maggie. The things you think I don't know." She rose and reached for the yardstick, but I grabbed it so she could not work.

"I should have known. You really think I don't know who's slipping out the front door? Who's slipping out the back?"

"No, I know you know."

"Do you?" Her voice was like copper, it was so full of current. "And even that didn't stop you."

"I did what I did."

"And look at the mess you're in now."

"What mess?"

"My daughter disappears. I have to think why."

She took the stick from my hand and turned to her worktable. "What's more, Maggie, I think you're in trouble, and I don't know what to do about it."

Silent (how could she know? how could she *not*?), I simply watched as she stood there, using her yardstick to lay the pattern straight on the warp. I could see the slight curve of her lower spine and the way her shoulders hung straight as a T square. Her hair curled up slightly and revealed that knob of bone at the base of her neck, vulnerable in spite of everything. I stood in the doorway, my hands loose at my sides, not knowing what to do, with them or with anything else in my life. "Mom?"

She turned to regard me, the yardstick resting in her hands. "Well?"

"You're right."

"I *am*?" She slapped the yardstick on the table. "Goddamn it to hell."

"You said you knew, Mom. I wouldn't have told you, but you said you knew."

"Doesn't mean I want to be right," and she slapped the stick again, as if the sound and force of it pleased her.

"Well, you are, and I can't just snap my fingers and say you're wrong."

"I know. Believe me, I know." She sat down in her chair and put her face in her hands. The fluorescent light in her sewing room always seemed brighter at night, its buzzing louder. That's the way it seemed then—too loud, too bright—showing all the dust and lint in the corners. "First your brother. Now you."

"I'm still here, Mom."

"But you've ruined your life."

I'm sure I couldn't imagine a life that couldn't be repaired. And I'm still not sure I understand why a life that deviates, that twists and turns, is ruined.

"It's my life to ruin," I said, with more faith than I felt.

"No, Maggie, you've up and hurt us all."

The truth of that, or what I took to be the truth, hit me sharply. Tears I did not want my mother to see spilled down my face, but she did see them, and she reached across to touch my hand. "I'm so sorry, Maggie."

"I know, Mom," I said and wrapped my arms around her, chair and all. She held onto me, crying, until we were both drained and exhausted.

After a time, my mother patted my hands and said, "Look, it's getting light out." And it was. Out the window, we could see the garage and trees and bushes separating from the darkness. "Time for us to go to bed," she said and righted herself. She walked to the door and shut the light, and I was waiting for her to leave me where she had found me when she said, "We have to figure out what to do, Maggie."

"I don't know what I want, Mom."

"Are you going to marry him?"

"I don't want to."

"Oh," my mother said and leaned against the jamb. "I suppose that's best. But that's what you said. You wanted to marry him."

"I had to say something. It's not like I could tell you."

My mother sighed and slid down the jamb until she was sitting on the floor. "But what are you going to do instead?"

"I don't think I have many choices."

"You're willing to give the baby up?"

"I don't even know if I'll have it," I said, although by then I must have known I would.

"God, Maggie, I don't know anyone who would do that for you. I don't know anyone who knows anyone who would do that. We're not that kind of people."

"Mrs. Rumsen knows someone who knows someone."

"The so-called Mrs. Rumsen would."

"So now you're telling me you want me to marry him?"

"I don't know what I'm telling you, sweetheart." She looked up at me quickly. "Your father doesn't know, does he?"

"I haven't told him."

She nodded and hugged her knees. "I don't think he should, Maggie. I don't think he could bear it."

I remembered then that I was about to leave. My purse, after all, sat slouched on the kitchen table, that jar of peanut butter wedged into it. "I should leave, Mom. I know I should."

She gazed up from her place on the floor, gazed at me through what I believe was a flood of things she wasn't saying. "Leave?" We both knew *that* was the way it was almost always done. If you didn't marry the boy, you went to a relative's, if a relative lived far enough away, or to a home for girls like you. You disappeared and maintained your respectability and, more important, your family's. All the neighbors would know, of course, having heard it on line at the grocery store or in the halls at school or during fellowship hour at church, but all the neighbors could turn their heads and pretend they didn't. That was the way it was done, my mother knew as well as I did, and we both knew that she could never ask our relatives to help us out. Not our respectable relatives, anyway. "Leave? You mean find a home?"

"I haven't found one that would take me."

"You've been looking?" Her arms were wrapped tight around her legs, her knees sharply bent. She reminded me of a child perched at the top of a slide, fearing the steep descent. "I can't believe you've been looking without me," and she began again to cry.

It would soon be light. Just beyond the rosebushes, the grove was visible, the black branches like so many cracks in the deep gray bowl of the sky. "I'm afraid, Mom. I'm really afraid."

She surprised me then, reaching for the doorknob and pulling herself up. In the gesture, I could see how thin she'd grown, as if for days she had not eaten. The surprise was she had pulled herself up so she could hug me, an awkward almost bony hug that even I knew was full of love. Rocking slightly from foot to foot, she said, "We'll work it out, sweetie, we'll work it out."

"Mrs. Rumsen said she'd take me."

"Shush," my mother said. "Tomorrow, the next day, we'll work it out."

Then she kissed my forehead and left, turning off the lights of the house, first the kitchen overhead, then the hall light, the living-room lamp.

"What, Marian? What?" I heard my father saying.

"It's morning, Jim. Time to get up."

"In a minute," he said. "In a minute."

THE NEW WORLD

TWENTY-EIGHT

Maggie

Some years later, when Bruce had reupped twice, signing on again the way so many of the guys he knew did, and my daughter had gone from Maria to M to Emmy, I decided that I didn't want her to grow up in this town where people thought her illegitimate and me unwed (with every-thing that implied). Because in time that is what everyone knew about me and Emmy, including my father, who despite my mother's fears did not collapse from the news. He even came to celebrate my daughter's first two birthdays, but he came in secret, and though he dandled my baby, he sat in awkward silence with Mrs. Rum and me. I was sad for everyone, especially my father, who I'd heard was losing his business piece by piece and was now losing his friendship with Evelyn Rumsen. But I was angry too.

So to spare my daughter and myself, I looked around for a way to leave and found a ride advertised on the community college bulletin board: ANTIWAR FREE SPIRIT DRIVING EAST IN VW BUS, TAKING THE SEE-AMERICA ROUTE. SEEK RIDERS TO SCHOONER ACROSS THE GREAT PLAINS AND DIP FEET IN THE GRAND CANYON. WANT TO SHARE DRIVING, GAS AND GRASS?

I took that ride, sharing driving and gas but not grass (I was a mother) with four other people and the owner of the van, a guy who called him-self Junior Max sometimes and Maximillian others. I took that ride with my daughter, leaving behind everything familiar, and began my second life.

Until then, I lived with Mrs. Rumsen in her apartment above the Hillside Pharmacy. My stay was meant to be temporary, a stopgap until my mother could find, in another state, a home for unwed mothers. In the days following my brother's service, we sat in my dusky pink room and discussed this question, where exactly I should go. My mother would enter my room, her bangs still clipped back for sewing, pull my door not quite shut behind her, and talk in the hushed voice she used to discuss household finances with my father. At first, she said she didn't want me staying with "that woman."

"She's a friend of your father's," she said. "And she will tell him."

"Not if I tell her not to."

"Wish she'd told him where you were those three days." She shook her head and gazed down, as if handwork were spread across her lap, leaving it to me to pick up the stitches of her thoughts: If any of us had done even one thing differently, perhaps all that happened would not have happened.

In the end, my mother agreed that I could stay with Mrs. Rumsen, but only once she understood how long it would take to find a home for me, particularly a home she could afford. "You could stay with her for a while, I guess. But when the baby comes, it would be so much easier to be in a home, where they know how to handle everything."

"Mom," I said, and she cut her eyes away from me, worry disrupting her face. I understood well enough what my mother wanted: for me to have the baby and give it up. But I didn't know if I would do either, have the baby or give it up.

In those days after the service, I gave in to sleep. We all did. Even Alison did not leave her room. My father spent his days on the sofa, curled up facing the back. Only my mother fought the tide of sleep, making herself keep the household running. When my father's workers called asking what to do, she would say my father could not come to the phone, and then, surprising everyone, she'd instruct his workers. "So begin grading the road," she'd say. "Use three men, that should be enough, don't you think?" Near the end of the first week, even my mother had to slow down. She had to call her clients—all except Denise Olmitz, the girl about to be married—and tell them she would need extra time, given her family circumstances, she hoped they understood.

I think it was the following Monday my mother packed a lunch for my sister and made sure she was out the door on time for school. When calls came in for my father, my mother held the phone in front of him until he spoke, until he grabbed the receiver and walked around the living room, black phone in his arms, asking why his crew couldn't do the simplest job without him. And that same week, she withdrew me from school for the year. "The death of her brother has been difficult," my mother said. "I want her to stay with my folks for a while, until things settle down."

And then on the day we had agreed I should leave, she helped me put my belongings into a small blue suitcase, saying as she did so none of the things I wanted, or feared, for her to say. Instead, she said things like "You want this dress with the belt?" and then answered for me. "No, I suppose you don't, but these Empire-waist dresses might be useful, no?"

We were nearly done, she was folding my blouses expertly into tidy bundles the size of prayer books, when I asked, "What did you tell Dad?"

"I told him you were going to stay with my aunt for a while," she said, eyeing me over her sewing glasses. "I told him it would be best for all of us. We need a rest from each other. And I'm telling your sister the same."

That was her final word, I understood, so I said nothing more as we piled socks and underthings into the suitcase and thought that the task of packing would fill the time until Mrs. Rumsen arrived. Except when we were done packing, we had some minutes left to us. (Perhaps my mother planned it this way, I don't know.) She had set the kitchen timer to let us know that Mrs. Rum would soon be here, but it had not sounded yet. With nothing left to do, we sat together on my bed, cross-legged, not unlike the way Jamie and I used to sit together.

"I always loved the color I painted your room," my mother said. "Too bad it's faded so."

"It still looks good, Mom."

"Yes," she said quietly, passing her hand over the tufts of the bed-spread. It was the sort of thing my brother might do, and it was hard not to think of him as I watched my mother.

"I miss him," I said. "I remember exactly everything he used to do."

"Me, too," she said and took hold of my hand. "I miss him too. Very much." She did something funny then, something unlike my mother. She pressed our hands against her breastbone. "I will miss you, too. I always thought we'd give you up to marriage. I never thought you'd have to take on so much, like this, so young." She hated to say it out loud, that I was pregnant. I'm not sure she ever did say it aloud. "Well, I never thought, Maggie." She squeezed my hand and placed it on the bed between us, laughing unhappily.

"I'll be fine, Mom. Really, I will." Scared as I was, I did know I'd be fine, or at least more comfortable, away from home.

"When I think what lies ahead," my mother said.

I put an arm across her back, and she seemed frail and crushable. The timer in the kitchen went off, letting us know that Mrs. Rumsen would be here any minute, and my mother said, "That's so loud. Like you were in the kitchen. Can you hear everything in here that way?"

Then we heard three short honks.

"Evelyn's here," my mother said. She hugged me firmly again, then touched the damp places around her eyes and carried my suitcase out to Mrs. Rumsen's car. "Keep well, Maggie," she said and pressed a thimble into my hand, the thimble her father had given her, the words *love* and *friendship* inscribed around the edge.

As Mrs. Rumsen drove me away in her old black station wagon, my mother stood on the concrete circle of the front step. Her blue dress rising above the trim of her slip, she lifted her arm and waved as if I were going off to camp, and I waved too, smiling and holding my hand up to the window. I watched the distance between us grow, and as I did, I remembered for no good reason something my mother had told me about learning to sew. Whenever she wanted to make a point about waste and the wise use of time, whenever she wanted to explain why she rarely removed her thimble, why she kept her bangs clipped back, why she wore her cushion on her wrist, her pins on her shirt, why she never stitched with a thread longer than one short pull, she'd say, "The first thing you learn becoming a seamstress is how to sew a hundred stitches a minute. You better believe, you don't waste anything."

The day for my second appointment with the doctor had come and gone while we got through the weeks after Jamie's service, and I let it go. But once at Mrs. Rumsen's, I called again, thinking the doctor might agree to see me some other time, only to find his phone had been disconnected.

From friends at work, Mrs. Rumsen collected a few more numbers. I called one and hung up, called another and got no answer.

"It's okay if you don't want to," Mrs. Rumsen said.

But it wasn't okay. I still did not know what I wanted. Well, maybe I knew I wanted to go home, but I couldn't do that, whether a doctor took care of things or not. As for everything else, there were only questions. I knew I'd be no kind of mother, and I knew I didn't want to marry, even if I should. But I also knew how little I had left. I had Mrs. Rumsen, and I had this pregnancy. Sometimes I think Em knows this, that she was born because she was all I had, though I doubt she knows that when you have very little, you can want what you do have very much.

So I remained with Mrs. Rumsen, living like a convalescent, sleeping even more than before.

"It's to be expected," she said with an authoritative nod. "It will pass."

I wished it would, but it didn't. And somehow it was more embarrassing that I overslept in *her* bed, for she had moved out of her room, clearing out her dresser drawers for me, turning her living-room sofa into her bed, her bookshelf into her dresser, her lamp table into her nightstand. ("Well, you're the one who's pregnant," she'd said. "You'll need good support under that back.") Some days I slept until afternoon, waking puffy-eyed, my lashes crusted, and would have to let the shower water run and run over me. I could remember no dreams, but I seemed to live in their shadow, in the ash of dreams, a feeling or memory just out of reach staying with me all day.

Every morning before work, Mrs. Rum left a note for me under the abalone shell on the kitchen table, suggesting first one chore, later two, then three that I might do in her absence. "Go to Ralph's and pick up whole-wheat bread, lettuce (one head), carrots. And a carton of Lucky's." Or "Please take down that awful clown picture and find someplace to store it." Or "Bake some chocolate chip cookies (see recipe on chip bag)—we'll take them to the County Home." Or "Go to the Salvation Army and see if you can't find a mirror or a nice frame (we'll put something in it later), something to fill that blank space."

And in this way, slowly, I was able to find a way out of my arcade of bad dreams. I could wake earlier and do more. I began to take long slow walks, as if I were recovering from some illness. Staying far away from what used to be my neighborhood, I walked up and down the streets, past all the small houses with their rosebushes and box hedges. Some days, I found myself walking toward the sound of children at the elementary school, although I always turned away before I reached it, maybe because Alison might have been there, playing jump rope or hopscotch or sitting under the eucalyptus. Or maybe because Jamie wouldn't.

Twice I made it as far as the playground but could not find my sister among the other children hitting tether balls and hanging from monkey bars. I stood behind the ivy-grown chain-link fence, watching for the color pink, the color my own daughter likes so well, and saw instead a dark-haired girl in a deep red dress swing herself from ring to ring, arms pumping, first one and then the other, until she missed and swung one-handed before falling to the sand. She got up, brushing her knees and checking her blisters, then jumped up to catch a ring and start again.

After one long walk, I went to the library to find a book on pregnancy and saw Alison, in her pink sweater and pink Keds, sitting in the children's room, her knees knocked together and her feet hooked around the legs of a chair. Although I had promised my mother that she would decide if and when to tell Alison why I no longer lived at home, I wanted so much to talk to my sister. I would have been happy if she had just glanced my way. I watched her for a long time, as she slowly turned the pages of a book. Hoping she might see me, I moved closer, standing behind her in the wide double doorway of the children's room, but she continued to read, lifting her book and balancing it on its spine. I could see over her shoulder it was a book of fairy tales.

I myself left the library bookless because the one book I found on pregnancy was no Dr. Spock. It was a medical text stored among dusty books on metal shelves in the basement. I carried it upstairs to the reading room, a new room with wide, blond tables and large potted plants on the sill, their shadows making lace of every flat surface. When I lay the book on the reading table, the pages fell open on their own to a photo of an episiotomy. Glistening skin spread, the scalpel beginning its cut at a delicate fold. It made me think of paper cuts, of slicing a corner of my mouth to widen my smile. Dizzy, I closed the book and made my way outside, and as I stood, hands on knees, fighting nausea, I spotted Alison's bike in the rack, next to a blue Schwinn. Someone had cut her pink streamers, so they looked like stubby ponytails.

"O holy shit, Maggie."

That's how Bruce began his letters, or many of them anyway. My mother had forwarded some to me, and I had written and given him my new address. His first letter back, he asked why I wasn't living at home, so I wrote him I was pregnant, now nearly three months. I made sure to say it happened around Christmas or New Year's because I didn't want him thinking bad thoughts, about me or anything else. That's why I did not write about Jamie.

Maybe my being pregnant was bad enough because he didn't answer me for a long time. I found myself rereading his old letters, looking for signs of how he might feel. He wrote, "O holy shit, Maggie. My feet are turning to prunes, and if the rains don't stop, I'll have to eat them (my feet, I mean)." In another, he said, "Pisses me off. Looks like we'll never get a chance to jump. Guess there are other things we can do, but, hell (sorry!), I'm trained to do that." In one long letter, he wrote, "Found a girl's body off a trail. She was Viet something. Dead a while. Smell was so bad, it was hard to miss. Think of the worst cheese you ever smelled and multiply by a million. That's about it. She looked like she was melting back into the ground is what I thought. So we buried her. Fast."

I was five or six months gone when he wrote, "O holy shit, Maggie. It's hard to believe. I know it's not impossible, but, Jesus, *me*, a father? Told this guy Stark (as in Stark Raving, no one knows how many tours he's done) and he stole a cigar, said, 'Smoke it now. Who knows about later?' Well, I haven't smoked it yet. It's true, I don't know about later, but I'm still trying to get used to the idea now."

As if in relapse, I slept so late the next day, I woke only an hour before Mrs. Rum was due home. I dressed and threw water on my face and found my chore and three dollars on the kitchen table: "Please get flowers for the living room." I hurried to Ralph's, hoping I would find flowers there, and brought home daisies, a newspaper, and two unspent dollars. While I waited for Mrs. Rum to return, I sat at her table, where she and I sometimes sat together watching the backs of other people's lives, and turned the pages of the paper. I don't believe that I knew at first what I wanted to find, or why. But when I happened upon the want ads, I found myself searching for any job I thought a girl like me could do. Stuffing envelopes, selling subscriptions over the telephone, anything a girl who shouldn't be seen could do. My father had said, "That boy'll leave you once you're preggers," and now I saw he could be right. I'd been so busy thinking that I didn't want to marry Bruce, I hadn't thought that he might not want me, that I might really be in this alone.

"So it's time for a job, is it?" Mrs. Rum asked over dinner.

"It's time for something."

"Mmm-hmm," she said and nodded slightly. "Maybe you should talk to Harold. He said something about a job where he works."

Harold, who lived upstairs in number 23, the other prime apartment in the building, was a kind man with a wide, soft face and a ruffle of hair circling his head. He often dropped by after work, bringing me a caramel and Mrs. Rum some flowers he'd picked or a bread he'd baked. He wore sandals over socks and cardigans over shirts, and it was his job to listen to tapes of radio broadcasts, identifying the music played so the composers and songwriters could collect their royalties. His specialties were gospel and country. "I prefer classical," Harold said. "But I'm not sure those boys receive royalties anymore."

I did speak to Harold, and so began my career, the string of small jobs that have gotten me by. My first was to type the lists of songs, the titles and any other information Harold might know. I was a terrible typist, but I tried, and, anyway, some days Harold just let me print. The best part was that during lunch and coffee breaks Harold would put his big soft headphones on my ears as he played tape after tape. I didn't care what the music was, gospel or classical. I just liked closing my eyes with those soft pads on my ears, a new world of sound in each.

Days I typed, and nights Mrs. Rum wasn't too tired, she taught me to dance all the dances she and Johnny Run used to teach at cotillion: the cha-cha, the fox trot, and my favorite, the waltz. Mrs. Rum would get out the record player, a big maroon leather box with speakers in its sides and a penny permanently taped to the phonograph arm, and Harold would bring down some of his records.

"Bus driver's holiday for you, Harold, isn't it?" she'd say.

"Not really, Ev. Not often I hear dance music."

Most nights Cole showed up, too, and the three of us would stand behind Mrs. Rum, our arms in the air resting on the shoulders of imaginary partners.

"And!" she'd say. "Step together, step, touch. Step together, step, touch."

And there we were, the four of us. Tiny Mrs. Rum, her cigarette held out like a baton between her fingers. Harold in his slippers and cardigan, and Cole, his tie loosened, his jacket off, a red flush creeping up his neck the more he enjoyed the music. And me, learning to step lightly as I grew heavier every day.

TWENTY-NINE

O holy shit, Maggie," Bruce wrote after my daughter was born. "You named her for the girl in that movie? You named her for Natalie Wood?"

Maria, I'd named her, Maria Harris, I wrote him. Say it soft, I wrote, and Bruce knew the rest. I also wrote that on the birth certificate he was listed as the father, just in case he was curious.

He promised to come see me when his tour ended, and I looked forward to seeing him, not just because I missed him (I did and I didn't), but because life after the baby was born was a lot harder than life before. Before, I'd had only me to take care of. After, I could only take care of her. Before, I'd had a job, maybe not much of a job, but I'd had a place to go and people to see. Toward the end, when I was really gone, Harold'd had to let me go and hire someone new, and now I had nowhere to go, no people to see, and no one visited me and the baby. Well, except my cousin, who brought along a few girls I didn't know. My old friend Joan called once, but I didn't really want to talk, and I don't think she did either. The one thing she did want was to know what it was like, giving birth.

"I guess I don't really know," I said. "I wasn't really there."

"They gave you something?"

"Yes, they gave me something."

The truth was Mrs. Rum got me through. In the middle of the night, I had climbed from bed to wake her where she slept on the sofa. "I think it's starting." She timed the contractions, drove me to the hospital, waited outside the delivery room. She kissed me in congratulations, asked Cole to bring me roses, even convinced him to lend me money for the bills.

She may even have called my mother. It's the only way I can imagine my mother knew to call me.

First thing she said was, "I'm sorry your dad can't call. He still doesn't know, you know. I think it would be too much for him. His work's such a strain. And then Jamie, of course."

"I understand, Mom."

"So you're okay?"

"I'm okay." When she said nothing more, I added, "The baby's okay, too. I named her Maria, Mom. Sort of for you, sort of for the grandmas."

"Maria. Yes, I know. Evelyn told me," she said and was silent.

"She's beautiful, Mom."

"So were you." She paused, as if holding her breath. "So were you."

It was near midnight, I think. Anyway, it was way past visiting hours. The lights in the ward were dimmed, and I was drifting in and out of sleep, aware of nurses talking and walking, of gurneys being pushed past my door, when my mother appeared in my room. (Yes, appeared. I don't remember her entering, or leaving, for that matter.)

"Maggie?" she said.

In the low light, she was a form more than a person, but a form that belonged unmistakably to my mother, her chin-length hair recently curled and brushed back behind her ears.

"Mom, what are you doing here?"

"What's it look like I'm doing?" she said.

"It's late."

"It's when I could get away."

Which meant, I understood, that she had come without telling my father. No doubt, he was asleep on the sofa at home, and Alison had gone to bed hours ago.

"I'm glad you came."

"I saw her. I saw Maria. I looked at her before coming in."

"You saw her, Mom?" I thought that was the reason she had come to visit, to see the baby and to hold her, so I said, "If I holler or something, I might get someone to bring her in, even though it's not feeding time."

"I don't think so, Maggie."

"No?"

It took a moment, but I understood. If I'd given the baby up, if I'd made arrangements with an agency, I could have gone home. My mother might even have come to fetch me home that night, if I'd given the baby

up. Since I hadn't, she couldn't do that, and I was making her life difficult by not doing what an unwed mother should do. I should have
been living in another state, not in my hometown. It should have been
months, if not years, before I visited my family, especially if I brought
the baby, and it would have been best if I were married by then, so
everyone could pretend the child was my husband's. That was the way
it almost always worked, my mother and I both understood. But living
with my out-of-wedlock child in my hometown? It wasn't done that way.
So I could see why my mother did not want to hold Maria. Even if I
wasn't giving her up, my mother was.

"You won't reconsider?" she asked.

I smiled at my mother's invitation. And, you know, I'm sure I considered it. I wasn't one of those mothers (and I've met them) who loved my
baby at birth. No instant love for me. It took me time to fall for my
daughter, though I did. So I must have considered going home. How
easy it would be, to be a child again. How much I wanted to see my sister, and even my father. But I had left, and it had taken all of me to
leave.

"Oh, Mom." I told her I was sorry, and I told her I loved her. "But I
won't change my mind, not now."

She kissed me, of course, as any mother would, and tucked fifty dollars into the drawer of the bedside table before she left. After that, from
time to time, she sent me a card with fifty more enclosed, and I gave as
much of the money as I could to Mrs. Rum, slipping ten dollars at a
time into her wallet. "Now where did this come from?" she said once
and cast me a suspicious glance. "I thought I was down to two and
change."

"Maybe you miscounted?"

Yes, Mrs. Rum did everything before the birth, but after Em was born,
there wasn't much Mrs. Rum could do. Evenings I could manage.
Sometimes Harold would invite me upstairs to listen to music. He'd put
the big, soft headphones of his own stereo on my ears, the baby on my
lap or in my arms. A few times, I put the headphones on her. She
squirmed at first and waved her little hands, grabbing anything in reach
but those giant earmuffs themselves, and then she quieted and lay calm.
"Bach," Harold said. "The magic of Bach."

The nights Mrs. Rum taught us dancing, I danced with my daughter.
She seemed to like being held in my arms, or in anyone's arms, as we

step, step, changed, step, step, changed to "Tammy" or the "Tennessee Waltz."

So the nights seemed short, but the days were long and slow. They seemed almost airless, as if I were in a sealed room, water rising slowly around me. They were broken only by the baby's need to feed and the baby's need to be changed and the baby's need to cry until I understood which of several things she might want. Once, I gave up trying to understand. I just let her cry, thinking she would exhaust herself and, besides, who would hear? I locked myself in the bathroom and tried to forget her, except she didn't exhaust herself, didn't even tire herself. And she didn't just cry. She wailed, she screamed, she hollered herself red and breathless, hollered herself into huge quaking hiccups that I feared, when I finally plunged out of the bathroom and picked her up, would never end.

Harold and Mrs. Rum did not hear this, but I believe Mr. Hill in the pharmacy downstairs did. I believe he spoke to Mrs. Rum, for the next day she resumed leaving a chore a day for me to do: "Try this apple cake recipe." "Sort through these old clothes and see if any are worth keeping." "See if you can't use this felt and old pillow to make a Humpty Dumpty to tie to the crib (thank goodness we found one!)."

Mrs. Rum must have run out of chores the day she left me a volume of Reader's Digest condensed books and instructed me to choose the best for her. "You can read them out loud, if you like." That is when I began reading to my daughter, from *Kon Tiki, To Kill a Mockingbird, Two Years Before the Mast.* All day long, I heard my voice, cooing and shushing, rising and sliding in high, unfamiliar pitches that made my daughter turn her face toward me as if she understood every word I read. Who knows why I looked forward to seeing Bruce? Maybe I missed him. Maybe I thought he would make my harder life easier. Or maybe I just wanted company, a little conversation with a grown-up. Maybe I just wanted to hear his sweet low voice talking to me in plain daylight.

My daughter was four months old, and I was sitting on the floor, reading the Sunday funnies to her, when I picked up the phone and heard Bruce say, "I told you I'd be back." Just hearing his voice made me homesick, reminded me how much I missed my brother, and everything else, too.

"A man of his word?" I said, as if his voice meant nothing to me.

"That's me."

"So how are you?"

"Alive and breathing hard."

"Bruce," I said but was glad for the lame joke.

"No one heard me."

"So you want to come visit?" I asked, and he said, "Sure, how about Thursday?"

"Don't you want to see her sooner?"

"Her who?"

"Her who? Maria, your daughter, remember?"

He laughed and made an excuse. "Course I want to see her, Maggie. But I promised my dad I'd help out at the shop."

"Every minute of every day?"

"Maggie."

"Well, it shouldn't take a shoehorn to fit us in."

"So Thursday? Around four?"

"I'll think about it," I said, but even then I knew I'd see him any time he chose.

That Thursday, I bathed the baby and, when the time drew near, changed her and dressed her in a pink, smocked thing my mother had made. (It was my daughter's best dress, her only dress.) I had tried to make sure she'd napped, but she wouldn't go down, which was too bad because I feared she'd fuss, too excited by the presence of a stranger to sleep, too tired to be anything but cranky.

Myself, I tried to make as pretty as I could. I had a mother's body now, a body meant to suit a child's needs, or so Mrs. Rumsen said. I just thought I was fat and, remembering my father's words, didn't think Bruce would see much in me. Which should have been fine but wasn't. I wanted him to want me even if I didn't want him. So I dressed as pretty as I could, in an aqua blouse and a floral skirt Mrs. Rum and I had picked up at the Salvation Army when we went searching for a crib. The blouse looked hardly worn, and I hope I did my mother proud by shortening the skirt myself and using the thimble she had given me. My hair I clipped back because it had grown long, and I put on eyeliner and mascara the way I used to. When I was through, I thought, This will have to do. Me in an aqua blouse and my daughter in a pink smocked dress. We will just have to do.

What I'd imagined was my daughter and I would be ready long before Bruce arrived. We would be the picture of domesticity. In her pretty dress, my daughter would lie in her crib, while I pulled a chair up to the bedroom window and knitted or crocheted or embroidered with a hoop (as if I could do any of those things!), watching the street occasionally for his arrival. But Bruce knocked before I had time to tie my daughter's booties. That's the way it was. I never knew how long anything would take.

"Hi, Mag," he said when I opened the door. He had not come in uniform, which pleased me for some reason. He wore a shirt and blue chinos like any other guy. "Remember me?" He smiled his old Bruce smile and touched my face, his touch a kind of question, as if I did not resemble his memory of me.

I did and did not remember him. His skin seemed stretched taut over his face, although he didn't look thinner. I noticed a small scar on his neck, a welt at the base of his throat, and his left eye seemed to squint harder every few seconds so I thought that something, dust or an eyelash, might make it tear over any minute.

"Yes, I think I do," I said and heard the baby fuss from the crib where I'd left her.

"That must be her."

"It is," I said. "Come meet her?"

I led him into the bedroom. Although the baby and I lived there, to me it was still Mrs. Rum's room, and it was full of her newfound possessions, most from the Salvation Army and secondhand stores. Lace that had been a wide collar on a dress was draped like a doily across her bureau. Flowers wilted in a broken vase she had found at a yard sale and glued back together. A large tortoiseshell comb lay on her bureau next to matching hairpins. I was present when she found them, in a box of pink rollers, plastic combs, and bobby pins, and reminded her that her hair was too short for a comb or hairpins.

"Who cares?" she said. "These are beautiful just to look at. Besides, you could use them. Why not?"

She had even found a few shawls, to replace those lost in the fire, and the room smelled of dust and perfume no one wore anymore, of old things preserved. Of course, when I lifted the baby from her crib, the world smelled of sweet, delicious-smelling baby.

"Want to hold her?"

"I could try."

Bruce lifted her way up in the air, scaring me just a little, and brought her down on his shoulder. Lucky I'd thought to put a diaper there, because she spit up as soon as he had her perched.

"She do this often?" he asked.

"Pretty often."

"You're a real live thing, aren't you?" he said to her.

She had discovered his ear and was pulling on it. Her grip was strong, I knew, for she had tried to pull my earrings off. So I took her and the diaper from him, and we moved into the living room, where we sat for some time, the baby on my shoulder, without saying much of anything.

"So," he said at last.

"So," I said.

"So maybe we could go for a drive? Like old times?"

The baby lying on the seat between us, we drove something like we used to, up to the reservoir and along the zigzaggy roads of the canyon. I say *something like we used to* because with the baby between us, we couldn't drive tandem anymore, our legs touching, each of us aware of the body next to us.

"Hey, remember Mike and the boys?" Bruce said with a laugh.

"Yes, always throwing themselves in front of the car."

"You see Carol and Joan and those guys much?"

"Not now. Not since the baby."

She was quiet, the drive lulling her.

"That so?" he said, glancing at me. "That's too bad."

"I can't really go out, with my daughter and all. Maybe once I get a job. Except getting a job'll be hard, maybe even pointless unless I can figure out who can watch her."

"I guess your mom won't."

"I don't think so," I said and noticed he said nothing about his mom. "My dad doesn't know yet."

"Aw, shit," Bruce said, that squint working his one eye.

"What about your family?"

"Oh, I plan to tell them. Just, we have lots to talk about right now."

"And this wasn't the first thing you told them?"

"One of the first things they told me," he said, "was about Jamie. Wish you'd written me, Mag."

"I didn't think you needed bad news."

"Look," he said and put a hand on my head, as if I were my little sister, "I've seen lots of bad news."

"That's just what I meant." I pushed his hand away. "Besides, I didn't want to write bad news either. Didn't want to go through it again myself." Tears escaped my eyes.

"Hey, I'm sorry," Bruce said and pulled the car to the side of the road. "I'm really sorry."

"Just stop it," I said, angry not at him but at my undisciplined tears.

He let me cry, his fingers brushing my collar now and again. After a time, I folded up the diaper I was using as a hanky and told him I was okay. Bruce nodded curtly, as if responding to an order, and pulled back onto the road. The baby fussed a little as the car rocked onto the pavement, but the steady motion soon calmed her. And I encouraged her to sleep, stroking her back, the sweet arch of it as she lifted her head and gazed at Bruce. I could get lost watching her, the folds in her arms and the dimples behind her knees. Babies bring a sweet amnesia, don't they? When I looked up again, I saw Bruce was taking the familiar roads, passing the mottled brown and green of scrub oak and sage.

"How about we go up this way?" he asked, turning onto the road to what used to be Mrs. Rumsen's place.

"That's fine. But you know my dad lost the place?"

"I remember," he said and took the road anyway. "Never did see this after it was burned. Sure did a number here."

Everything was still charred, but knot grass had begun to grow, slender yellow-green blades scoring the ground near the house. Or what used to be the house. The porch my father had built was burned away, and so were the walls and roof, but most of the floor and foundation remained, jutting like a stage from the hillside. Someone had cleared away the debris of Mrs. Rumsen's things, the half-burned bed and kitchen table, but the fixtures remained. The shower head stood alone like a charmed snake, the plumbing under the kitchen sink was all exposed, and the cracked commode had broken in two. The fireplace was blackened, but the chimney had somehow escaped the flames and was still plain gray stone, flecked with mica and marked the way stone is, with shaded bands of minerals revealing a history I could never interpret. Bruce pulled up behind the charred stones of the fireplace, and as the car's engine stopped, I watched the baby's eyelids flutter as she resisted and then gave in to sleep. She lay on her tummy in her rumpled pink dress, her head near Bruce, her feet resting against me.

Bruce reached over her and took my hand, the way a pastor would. "You're getting by all right?"

"Sure, I'm getting by fine." I hesitated but added, "The money is hard. I can't live off Mrs. Rum forever."

"Well, I'll be sending you money."

"I wasn't asking for money."

"I know you weren't, Maggie. But I'll be sending you some anyway."

"Why are you going to send me money? You going somewhere?"

"Yes, I'm going somewhere. I reupped."

I let that soak in a moment. "Why?" I finally asked.

"I don't know. I mean, all the time I'm gone I couldn't wait to come home. You know. Movies, TV, In-and-Out Burgers. And all the regular things, long showers with good soap, clean sheets and clean socks."

"And me?"

"And you, yeah, and you." He let go of my hand. "But then I get here, and it's home and everything, but, I don't know, it doesn't feel right anymore." He gazed ahead at the black stones of the fireplace. "It doesn't even rain right here, you know?"

"There's another way to rain?"

"It's winter, Maggie. It should be pouring. Or snowing. Or something. Not this every day-after-day sameness."

"It's different over there?"

"It's worse there, but there isn't here."

"So go somewhere else. Get out and go to San Francisco. Or Mexico. Anywhere."

"I can't do that."

"You can't get out?"

"No, Maggie, I can't."

"You mean you won't."

"Damn straight, I won't. It may suck over there. But there makes here a joke."

The baby cried in her sleep, as if our voices had entered her dreams. Though she didn't wake, I picked her up and held her until she was quiet and I was sure she'd sleep. Then I stood on my knees and reached over the seat back, stretching her out in the rear of the car and tucking the blanket around her.

"Besides, it's only a year, Maggie. I promise I'll marry you when I come home, really home for good."

"What do you mean promise?" I said, settling back in the front seat. "You never asked in the first place."

"I didn't? I meant to."

317

"Meant to? You're so sure I'll say yes?"

"I'm not sure of anything. I'm sure not sure of that."

Something in his voice made me look at him hard, at the fine lines around his one eye deepening every few seconds, and in that moment, I was sure he was sure he didn't want to marry me. And somehow, I don't know how, I just knew that he had outgrown me, simply outgrown me, his old high school girl.

I was sad. I was relieved, a little angry. I said, "You don't have to leave to leave me."

He winced at that. "I'm not, Maggie."

It was beginning to get dark out. Through the smog, we could see a dim red sun behind the dusty air. The car itself sat in the shadow of the canyon.

"Let me do what I have to. That's all I'm asking."

This was my old boyfriend talking to me, the boy whose car (this car) had been my second home, the boy whose shirts I'd unbuttoned and belts undone, the boy I'd found sex with. He was asking me to set him free. And just then, I didn't want to.

"Whatever you want is okay," I said.

Bruce sat quite still, hands on thighs, serious as a grandfather. So I moved closer, putting an arm around him and holding one hand.

"Aw, hell," he said and shrugged me off.

"What?"

"Shit, I don't know." He pushed the seat back as if to give himself room to stretch or kick or rear, then hunched forward and hugged the steering wheel, laughing, I think, although it sounded like growling.

I cooed and shushed the way I did with the baby. I talked mama-talk and tried again to put my arms around him, and this time he let me. He sat back and let me straddle his lap. I lay my head on his shoulder, a little girl with her daddy, and even with the steering wheel catching my back, or especially with it against my back, we were sweet together, soft and familiar as old flannel.

And then we weren't. We were rough, or he was. It was bite-hard kisses and him grabbing hunks of me, bra pushed up over breasts, my embarrassing, swollen breasts that he sucked first through my blouse and then sucked naked, my milk dripping on my skin, its smell filling the car. He put an arm under me and lifted me, seeming to like just moving my body, the heft of it and the force it took, and then as if we were kids who'd never really had sex, he dug his hand in me, dug in so

I startled at knuckles and nails. And I kept wondering if he knew his free fingers were touching the scar left by birth.

"Move," he said, "move with me."

But I couldn't, not with the baby in the back. I let him stay, but he moved for me, finding what I wanted, that I wanted at all, coaxing me to slip into a small skiff and ride rapidly downstream, but I said, "No," thinking of my daughter under the blanket on the backseat. I said, "No," and saw Bruce watching me, his head back, the jut in his throat sharp, his black eyes watching me as if I were an insect he wanted to pin and mount. "No," I said and pushed his hand away.

I untangled myself and slid down on the seat, and lying there, I found his zipper and belt. At the touch of my mouth, he arched back, his arms somewhere over his head. I could feel the whole taut stretch of his body, his legs bone-hard under me. I did what you do with your face in someone's lap, thinking as always that I did not know how to do this thing, how to please this determined iron arm and its soft fist. It made me think of my baby, the way her feet were so soft and kissable but her legs were so strong, moving wherever and kicking me if she were unhappy. I hoped, of course, she was still asleep, but there was no way I could look.

He put his hands on my head, and I felt fragile, as if my skull were only the skin of a grape and my hair just so many cobwebs. He held my head but did not direct me, simply resting his hands there, even at the end, when his hands might have said, "This, this, I want this." I wanted it to go on, not because I wanted more but because some part of me understood this was our last time. So I moved slowly until, I guess, his sounds and his body made it clear I couldn't, and all I could do was worry I was doing something wrong, biting or scraping or God knows what, and then with a cry it was over. I could feel him lose his fierceness, and my mouth was filled in warm spurts, first the long ache and then the afterthoughts.

One thing about having a baby, at least I had her extra diapers nearby to clean myself and Bruce. He pulled me to him to kiss my mussed up hair. Then he let go and wiped his hands across his face, wiping back tears that continued to pool in his eyes.

The baby whimpered, then began to fuss and cry, and I knew she would soon be wailing. Reaching over the seat back, I poked a finger under her diaper and was surprised to find it wasn't wet. She was hungry, I guessed, and though I didn't want to, I would have to nurse her, even with Bruce in the car. Since my blouse was soaked, I removed it and spread it out to dry. Then I picked up the baby and settled her up front with me, lowering my disheveled bra to feed her. She seemed not to care at first, looking away from my nipple and continuing to fuss, but then she found me, her gums clamping down hard so I could feel the sharp ridge where her first tooth would break. Her hands opened and closed as she sucked, grasping at whatever was near, catching my loose hair in her strong, little fist.

Bruce watched, and I was embarrassed, for my swollen and utilitarian breasts, for the stomach I now had and he could now see, for my too soft arms, for everything he had touched but could not have seen, not really, during sex. He was silent and watched with an expression I couldn't place for many years. At first, I thought it was his child-at-the-zoo face, the face of a rapt boy with a puppy, and in a way, I was right. It was puppy love, the innocent, first love for his daughter. But there was something else in his expression, something harder to place, something I came to think of as fear of that love, and as he watched his daughter nurse, I saw the twitch return to his eye, tiny but regular. In time, he looked away and put his arm across the back of the seat and touched my shoulder. We sat that way until the baby had nursed her fill. Then we dressed and drove home, the baby falling asleep as soon as the car was moving, her chin nestled against my shoulder, her body warm against my damp blouse.

"They're expecting me at home, you know."

"So say good night," I said.

I held the baby up to him, and he kissed her and called her cinnamon candy apple. "I'll call you."

"I know," I said, though I didn't know at all.

Leaning against the door up to Mrs. Rum's that night, I swayed slightly for the baby's sake. She felt then like a big cat in my arms, purring and working invisible claws into my heart. "When do you go in again?"

"Two weeks."

He was backing away, but he returned to kiss me lightly before he crossed the street and waved as he unlocked the door of his Chevy. I could see a corner of his eye clench, but other than that he almost looked like the old Bruce, and I tried to memorize him that way, waving and smiling over the top of his car, the scar on his neck barely visible from where I stood. I waved and made the baby's hand wave. He smiled again, the old sweet Bruce smile, then turned to duck into the car. Just before he did, he stopped, gazing way down the road at something I couldn't see. And that's really the way I remember him, gazing off, his eyes already settled on something far away, something way beyond me or the baby or this place we came from. He had somewhere to go, and I decided then that someday I would have somewhere to go too.

Upstairs, I could hear the waltz even before I opened the door and found Cole and Mrs. Rum and Harold all holding hands and dancing in a chain, Mrs. Rum quietly murmuring, "Step together step, step together step . . ."

"How was it?" she called after me as I walked into the bedroom.

I had no words for how it was or what I felt, and though out of courtesy I opened my mouth to answer, I couldn't. The baby on my shoulder, I stood in the room that had begun to feel like home, surrounded by Mrs. Rumsen's things: the pictures of dancers she had never known hanging on the wall, the old scarves in the windows, the lace collar on the dresser, the shawls draped over chairs and headboard, carrying in their fringe and in the blooming gardens worked in satin stitch the perfumes and oils of the those who had owned them before, those who were likely gone now. Perhaps it wasn't so, but I believed that all those things had once been precious. The comb and pins had held up the thick hair of a girl who'd had dreams and wishes and a beau who'd made promises he might have kept. The lace collar was the finishing touch on someone's best dress, and the pictures captured the brief and limited stardom of onetime dancers. In Mrs. Rum's possession, these things were precious once again. It was possible to reframe the picture of Evelyn Night and Johnny Run. To gather up bits and pieces of the wrecked past and make something fine of them.

I buried my face in my baby's body, breathing in all her fresh and vivid smells, and called out to Mrs. Rumsen, "Fine, it was fine."

I tossed the talc and Vaseline and fresh diapers onto the bed and spread a towel, where I placed my baby, who was no longer dry. She lay there, her limbs rowing in the air. Sweet baby drool dribbled from her mouth (I wiped it with the corner of the towel), and she looked at me, not as though I absorbed her, but as though there were nothing else to see, the way she looked at the Humpty Dumpty I'd strapped to her crib. I put my forehead on her soft stomach, and her sticky damp fingers caught in my hair. She gurgled, and I kissed her and righted myself to get down to business. I wiped away the movement, that day an odd, gluey yellow. Then I wiped her clean and stroked on the Vaseline. She liked it, I think, growing very still and watching me with deeper attention, before I folded on the dry diaper and pinned it, my free hand inside protecting her the way Mrs. Rum had taught me. Maria—not yet M or Emmy—seemed happy in her clean diaper, so, with the waltz in the air, I put a finger inside each of her palms and let her little hands grip mine.

THE ART ROOM

THIRTY

Alison

Didn't used to be, but the art room's my favorite. Like all the rooms at school, one whole wall is windows, so there's light, and you can see way far when you can see blue sky at all. One day a week, we go to the art room, where the visiting art teacher teaches us. (Other days, it's the music room or the remedial reading room. But our pictures are always there, so we call it the art room. Everybody does.) Today, we are doing collage with tissue and construction paper, blue and pink and green, and string and yarn and pieces of colored foil the teacher has given us. She cuts shapes, and we are supposed to follow her, cutting pink, blue, and green shapes ("Random shapes," teacher says) that we will glue or starch to our sheets of manila paper.

Last week, the teacher taught us three-point perspective, and we all went outside to practice. We were supposed to draw the school buildings or the auditorium. I did the playground, where the two sides of the fence meet in the way far corner. Behind the fence, I drew my sister where I have seen her. It's the behind-the-fence that's hard. I drew my sister first, then drew fence and ivy over her. When the teacher came to look at our work, she spent a long time talking to me about perspective. She leaned over the table and pointed with her big finger at the fence, big up close and small in the way far corner. She said lots of stuff and then, tapping her finger on my picture, she said, "Interesting subject."

"That's my sister."

"Oh? Where?"

I pointed.

"It must have been hard to draw all those wires and all that greenery over your sister."

"No."

"No? Maybe next week we'll do a portrait lesson. Would you like that?"

I said nothing and wondered why she couldn't see my sister and her baby where I saw them.

Today with my blue and green and pink paper I do a tree with no leaves. I cut a big trunk and then skinnier branches and starch them to the paper. I use blue tissue for the sky, and for the smallest branches, for the twigs, I unwind some yarn and glue the skinny thin pieces down. I want glitter for the stars, black glitter, but there is none. So I cut a piece of red foil into the littlest pieces and sprinkle them on. Trees are my favorite, my very best subject. Last time I saw my brother, he was in the trees. Every time I draw trees, he is there, just above them. I leave room for him. Sometimes I draw and then erase him in the sky.

The teacher has lots to say to Marilyn, the girl who shares my table. "Beautiful use of space and color," the teacher says. "This shows real development, Marilyn."

My turn, she says, "I hoped we'd do something other than trees, Alison. Something abstract."

I look at my picture and say, "I like trees."

"Next time, we'll try something different, okay?" the teacher says. "Maybe we'll do that portrait lesson I promised, okay?"

I say okay, but I don't tell her Jamie's there in every picture, even when he's not. I don't tell her I make every tree a portrait.